Icelight

1

Icelight

Aly Monroe

W F HOWES LTD

This large print edition published in 2013 by
W F Howes Ltd
Unit 4, Rearsby Business Park, Gaddesby Lane,
Rearsby, Leicester LE7 4YH

1 3 5 7 9 10 8 6 4 2

First published in the United Kingdom in 2011
by John Murray (Publishers)

A CIP catalogue record for this book is available
from the British Library

ISBN 978 1 47124 703 3

Typeset by Palimpsest Book Production Limited,
Falkirk, Stirlingshire
Printed and bound by
CPI Group (UK) Ltd, Croydon, CR0 4YY

MIX
Paper from
responsible sources
FSC
www.fsc.org   FSC® C013604

To Inés
born 15 September 2010

CHAPTER 1

Three doors down from Peter Cotton's office in London there was no door. Nearly five years before, on 10 May 1941, the last night of the Blitz, in a raid that inflicted considerable damage to many buildings, including the Houses of Parliament and St James's Palace, one bomb dropped from one of 550 German bombers had scored a direct hit on a Georgian town house.

Standing in St James's Street, directly in front of where the house had been, the right-hand wall was bare, blackened brick, revealing only how slapdash Georgian bricklayers were when their work was not on view. About twenty per cent of the back wall retained vestiges of what had been there, and the left-hand wall even had ragged remnants of the floors. Like a house-sized display cabinet marked out by strips where the dividing walls had been, that side exposed a human-scale domestic hopscotch. It had retained some chimney pieces, one decidedly grand in yellow and white marble on the first floor, something plainer and more discreet on the second, and bits of a small, metal

1

fireplace at the very top. There was also a weathering patchwork of paint and ragged wallpaper – a block of stained red flock, something torn, green and leafily Chinese above it, and a thick patch as brown as Windsor soup at the top for the servants.

The most striking thing was an ornate cast iron bath still clinging to what remained of the third floor. It tilted and one foot of the bath was in the air, and on clear days it was possible to see that it was being held up by the battered water pipes, wrenched out of the tiled wall and now resembling twisted copper and lead creepers.

'Another bloody bath!' said Charles Portman. Portman was usually called the Office Manager but much preferred to see himself as akin to a Company Secretary. His tone struck Cotton as remarkably similar to his father's when some carol singers had come round the Christmas before. 'Not more bloody singers!' Cotton didn't know quite what Portman meant – that because so many baths had been exposed by German bombs the sight of baths in distress was getting vulgar or trite? That someone else should have done something about them? But his tone had all the plaintive, put-upon huff of an old-style Whitehall stickler finding himself inconvenienced. At least Cotton's father had had to respond, open the door and put on a smile, before he said 'Well, I hope you're better than the last lot.' Any inconvenience to Portman was entirely assumed. For Cotton, Portman's exasperation was just one more of the

2

dreary, uselessly surreal reactions of 1946. Britain's plumbing had been exposed.

Their office was near the corner with Ryder Street. It was called temporary and consisted of four floors of an Edwardian building above the discreet showroom and London commercial office of a manufacturer of coal- and wood-burning stoves and ranges based in Stirling in Scotland. The Colonial Department of the Intelligence Services had a separate entrance and a staircase too narrow to admit more than one person at a time. Cotton worked on the first available floor. Above him was the Africa floor, the Asia floor and the Rest of the World floor.

For the first five months of 1946 (while Portman attempted, unsuccessfully, to have the range manufacturer evicted as 'unfitting') Cotton was set to quantifying the costs of intelligence work in West Africa. In this he was assisted by a reluctant seconded civil servant called Stiles – 'I am administrative grade, sir, not executive' – and an insistently delicate secretary called Phyllis he had to share. 'Now I don't want to get flustered' was one of her favourite remarks. 'I really don't.'

Cotton was told that this task would amount to 'an incisive insight' into the colonies. By May however, he had learnt quite enough of the workings of Whitehall to report to the Head of Colonial Intelligence, Sir Desmond Brown, that he thought it 'germane' to mention that 'the team' were actually going to produce quantified costs, and that some 'possible anomalies had come to light'.

'What do you mean?'

As an example, Cotton showed him that The Gambia (a very small colony) and Nigeria (a very large one) claimed to have the same intelligence budget, while Sierra Leone (a small colony) had more than either.

'That'll be the damned diamonds,' muttered Sir Desmond. He looked up. 'Have MI5 and MI6 collaborated on these figures?'

'No, sir,' said Cotton. 'They refused to cooperate.'

This meant that the sizeable amounts tracked down represented only one small part of what was actually being spent on Colonial security.

'Well, I don't think we really want to involve the Treasury at this stage,' said Sir Desmond. 'After all, we don't have all the pertinent information, do we?'

'No, sir.'

Sir Desmond congratulated Cotton on his progress, took over the files – 'These are *all* of them?' he asked – and Cotton was sent on a month-long course to a sizeable, extraordinarily gloomy Victorian country house in Buckinghamshire. There he had to dress for dinner served by uniformed maids but eat food reminiscent of school, though accompanied by wine and, for those who wished, supplemented by port and Stilton. During the day he attended classes, might listen, for example, to a military historian on classical strategies in the morning and, after lunch, to

4

an unidentified person with a handle-bar moustache on counter-insurgency techniques. He also took part in what were called 'exercises'. These varied from possible choices in situations called hypothetical but often based on real life operations, to debates on what were called 'issues of the day'.

When considering what university to go to, Cotton had been told that he was a Cambridge man, not an Oxford one. He had never properly understood why until listening to the man who was running the course, an Oxford don. In a peculiarly unctuous voice, the don explained to them, as if they were undergraduates, that the British Government had embarked on a disastrous over-commitment: it was spending heavily to maintain the country as a world military power and had also insisted on an expensive policy of nationalizations and the establishment of a welfare state, all while ignoring the creation of wealth that made such policies practicable. Luckily Britain had a bulwark against politicians. It was called the Civil Service.

Cotton was now getting restless, and mentioned this to his father when he visited him in Peaslake after the course ended at the end of June.

'If you've made a mistake you'll just have to stick to it you know. You've only been there for six months.'

Cotton grunted. 'The old "keep calm and carry on" has become "keep quiet, and do please try to look complacent"!'

5

His father frowned at him. 'It was all right to be spoiling for a fight during the war, of course it was. But things are going to take time to get back to normal.'

'I'm not sure we are going to get back and I'm not sure that "normal" has not moved on. All we've got now is more rationing – that's less of everything. I've just done a month surrounded by people whose shirts are fraying, but with maids bobbing at us. We get time off work to queue for two ounces of cheese. I can't get my shoes repaired. The clothes ration is notional and never quite becomes material enough to wear.'

James Cotton looked pained. 'Well, I've dug out some things.'

'What do you mean?'

'I had a lot of shirts made in Mexico. Some I haven't even worn. They might help.'

Though slightly short in the sleeves and tight at the collar, the six shirts had been cut on an ample width for a hot climate. They felt odd in London, too delicate, too light and slippery under Cotton's two heavy suits. But they felt new.

At the beginning of July, Cotton returned to St James's Street to find a group of German POWs had removed what he thought of as Portman's bath from the bombed house. He stopped and pointed upwards. Despite the summer, the POWs were all wearing greatcoats, and the corporal who spoke to Cotton had a rag tied round his right boot to keep upper and sole together.

'The bath,' said Cotton. 'How did you get it down?'

The corporal smiled and got one of his companions to hold up a length of scaffolding. The scaffolding was hollow and at one end they had jammed a half-moon edging tool, the kind of thing used to cut turf.

'Cut pipe,' said the corporal making a jabbing movement. He made a face. 'Mostly poke. Then crash!'

The POWs had no guard or supervision as they sorted through the rubble. They did have two carts and two huge dray horses. In one cart Cotton saw the bath, the door of a cooking range, bits of a flattened galvanized water tank, a bell-pull, and what was left of a chandelier – it had lost its crystal decoration and looked like some stripped winter vegetable. The other was for wood, from the looks of what was left of a charred solid mahogany table and more obvious examples of firewood.

'Suffolk horses,' said the corporal.

Cotton nodded and pointed to where the grand fireplace had been. The corporal shrugged.

'Onteek,' he said – and it took Cotton a moment to understand he was saying 'antique' and, given his subsequent shrug, that 'dealer' came after it.

The POWs had started a fire to burn off what could not be salvaged and to cook some potatoes in a pot. The corporal indicated the space the house had occupied.

'Rich woman,' he said. 'Lady-in-waiting.'

Cotton nodded. 'Where are you stationed?'

'Hendon,' he said. 'Usually? We walk. Six miles here. Six miles there. Bigger problem is brewery. They want horses back. So they don't give us mash any more. We scrounge.'

'The antique dealer?'

'Naturally,' said the corporal mildly. 'Turnips, one big sack. Oats, four bags. Some carrots.' He smiled and shrugged. 'Too cheap. But no shit, no roses.'

The corporal showed him a hand-drawn map of the area, with the bombsites they had already cleared and those they still had to do. They had forty-three bombsites altogether and had cleared thirty-eight. The corporal explained they had a keen interest in the different types of bomb. From their point of view incendiary bombs had been best.

'They cleared everything for us.'

Their main fear was the risk of unexploded bombs. He pointed at the almost demure heap of rubble, some of it now sprouting weeds.

'Clink,' said the corporal. 'It's hard to avoid clinks. If ever you see us running, you run too.'

Cotton turned and looked around him. A uniformed maid was pushing a baggage trolley with three cases of wine up the hill. As Cotton watched, the poor girl suffered what was usually called 'an elastic incident' – the waist of her knickers parted. Immediately she snatched at them in a twisting motion by her right hip. The trolley started to tip. Expressionless as a tango dancer, she swung her hips back and lifted one leg from the knee to secure the cases of Château d'Yquem, and then tied a knot in her uniform. Her exposed shoe had a wooden sole, a poor substitute for leather.

The German corporal grunted, a noise that made approval sound like desire. 'Now she,' he said, 'is a good worker.'

At his office building, Cotton saw that the stove and range manufacturers had applied some paint to their showroom. It was undeniably grey, quite near battleship grey, but it had become the brightest, freshest thing in the street. Apart from that and the Germans, the only observable activity was that the bomb-damaged Bunch of Grapes pub in Jermyn Street was repaired and open for business again.

By November, when mist and soot mingled in the cold, Cotton was taking comfort that he was due for a review early in the New Year. One of his considered options was resignation. He was now working on the Sterling Area. While the British Government emphasized the beneficent effects of civilization that Empire had brought, it had to place this against the need to limit expenditure and grab as much as it could in dollar earnings from the colonies and dominions. Someone had worked out that 'nationalist groups' in colonies might notice this.

At a large, very bad tempered meeting in Whitehall in the second week of December, Cotton heard an officer ask why 'the teeth of the British working class should be more valued than the welfare of my black charges.'

More impressively, an elderly gentleman from the Indian Civil Service wearing a winged collar and striped trousers described the Treasury's behavior as 'equal measures of incompetence and arrogance'. He went on at some length, and during his clear and probably entirely accurate portrayal of Treasury dishonesty, a man turned to Cotton and whispered.

'No gong now.'

Cotton did not quite hear. The man expanded.

'The old buffer is burning his boats! After years of service he has decided to ruin his retirement for the sake of what he wants to believe are his principles.'

There was a break for refreshments. Cotton saw the old man was shaking from fatigue and indignation. He felt some sympathy, but he didn't want to be like that.

That evening he began writing a letter to his sister. Joan lived in New York, was married to a banker called Todd Buchanan and had three children. The year before, they had encouraged him to think of making his life in the US.

'The future is here,' Todd had said. 'Great Britain is over. Give yourself a chance, Peter. Make your life in Manhattan. Here we have possibilities that are not limited and not reduced.'

On Friday, 13 December, Peter Cotton went into work to learn from Portman that a senior Colonial Intelligence agent called Leonard Lloyd had suffered a serious heart attack and was now in Charing Cross Hospital. Lloyd handled the desk for Malaya, Singapore and the Straits Settlements.

When Charles Portman asked him to take over 'for the time being', Cotton surprised himself. His first reaction was pure Whitehall: not me. He softened it when he spoke.

'You do know I know next to nothing about Malaya.'

'You wrote that paper on dollar earnings,' said Portman.

'But that was about dollars. I wrote about Malaya because it's such a high dollar earner, and we need to get rubber and tin production up. I don't really know anything about the place.'

'The desk has to be manned,' said Portman. 'In any case, all you'll really be doing is listening and taking notes. You have a meeting in King Charles Street at eleven this morning.'

'Christ! Can't we cancel?'

'Sir Desmond says we don't cancel.'

Cotton groaned and accepted a very large file. As he flicked through it he did find enough material for a brisk vicarious holiday – words like 'batik' and 'sarongs', and a fruit called 'rambutan'.

Around ten o'clock he was interrupted. Charles Portman put his head round the door.

'Bad news, I'm afraid. I've just heard Lloyd died about nine this morning. They did everything they could, of course. The funeral will be private but doubtless there will be a memorial service later. I'll keep you informed.'

'I'm sorry to hear that,' said Cotton. 'How old was he?'

'I'm not entirely sure,' said Portman. 'Early forties?'

'Wife? Children?'

'Certainly a wife. One, perhaps two children? Lived in Epsom, I think. Sad business,' said Portman, and left.

Cotton closed the file, then reopened it and flicked to the political part.

At eleven o'clock, Cotton was in an empty office at the Whitehall end of King Charles Street. There was an oil painting of a muddy hunting scene above an unlit fire, a round table and four chairs.

The door opened and a secretary came in.

'Is there somebody here called Colonel Cotton?'

Cotton nodded and she gave him an envelope.

He opened it. Inside was a small, whitish bit of paper, more scrap than sheet, and a stiff card suitable for invitations.

The small note told him that a car was waiting

for him downstairs and that he should make his excuses for the rest of the day.

The card was about the size of a wedding invitation. It showed his old rank, initials and surname, medal and degree. Below their typed names, the heads of MI6 and MI5, Sir Stewart Menzies and Sir Percy Sillitoe, had affixed their initials. From bottom left to upper right was a red 'Top Priority' stamp.

Two civil servants came in, apologizing for being late.

Cotton bowed out of the meeting, made a telephone call to Charles Portman at his office to tell them he was not coming back that day, put on his coat and went down the marble steps and through the revolving door. A Triumph 1800 was waiting at the kerb. Government departments had acquired a few of this new model. The car was called the 'razor' – from the side it resembled a Bentley that had been given a shave.

The driver opened the back door for him and Cotton got in. The car smelt of new leather and Senior Service cigarettes.

'Why aren't you in St James's Street?' asked Ayrtoun.

'Someone had a heart attack. I was filling in.'

A fraction before Ayrtoun spoke, Cotton remembered Ayrtoun's laugh included a loud snort.

'Christ, you haven't been reduced to waiting for the man in front of you to drop dead, have you? Driver!'

The Triumph 1800 started up. At the end of King Charles Street they turned right towards the River Thames. It was a dull day and the Houses of Parliament looked more like a sooty silhouette than a real building against the grey sky.

Ayrtoun yawned. 'Do you know Croydon?' he asked.

'No,' said Cotton.

The car rolled on to Westminster Bridge.

'Then you won't know of the Greyhound Hotel. Well, it's a pub but quite a suburban meeting place. The Freemasons gather there in the functions room, the public bar reeks of beer and tobacco. But if you pause a little in the saloon bar you'll find men with rather long eyelashes and dab hands at Brylcreem.'

CHAPTER 2

Cotton said nothing. Instead he licked his teeth and cleaned his mouth. He had last seen Ayrtoun almost exactly a year before in Washington DC. He glanced sideways. As always, Ayrtoun was dressed in a blue, double-breasted suit and Wykehamist tie. He had a tartan rug over his knees and was holding a tin of fifty Senior Service cigarettes in his lap. Judging by the fug of smoke in the car, his strict ten-a-day habit had been abandoned.

'Being away one forgets just how many pubs there are in London,' Ayrtoun drawled. 'They really are crawling distance apart.'

Cotton had been entirely happy to hear nothing from or of Geoffrey Ayrtoun since December 1945.

'I want to depress you as much as I can,' said Ayrtoun.

Cotton nodded. That was Ayrtoun. Ayrtoun smiled.

'Did your father ever give you advice for life?'

'Apart from a few things about money, he told me never to be impressed.'

15

'Anything else?'

'There was his definition of intelligence.'

'What was that?'

'The ability to appreciate something without having experienced it.'

Ayrtoun grunted. 'That's not bad.' He lifted and gently shook his tin of cigarettes as if trying to gauge from the rattle how many were left. 'I'm here because of American pressure,' he said.

Cotton nodded.

'The Yanks are squeezing us,' said Ayrtoun. 'They're worried about security. MI5 and MI6 have reacted by putting me in a painful pinch. It appears I *am* our cooperation. I am responsible for soothing American anxieties.'

'I'm sorry to hear it.'

Ayrtoun laughed. 'You're going to help me handle a couple of minor problems I can't ignore. But I assure you, your problems will be a sight less than mine.'

'If I have a choice, I'll say no then.'

Ayrtoun smiled, almost affectionately. 'Do you know the head of MI5?'

'I know of him, of course,' said Cotton. 'Sir Percy Sillitoe?'

'Right. A poor boy, you know.'

'I don't understand.'

'He hasn't made it to the inner circle. He was a colonial policeman in South Africa and Rhodesia. When he married in 1920, he and his wife were posted to Tanganyika. His wife hated it.'

16

Cotton looked round.

'He returned to the UK in 1922 and applied for jobs as a Chief Constable.' Ayrtoun shook his head. 'It took time but he did get Chesterfield and proved to be so brisk and effective that he was given Sheffield in 1926. Sheffield had a gang problem. He went through them like a dose of salts, introduced plain-clothes police and a concept of "reasonable force" that the politicians were able to overlook because he was effective.'

Cotton glanced at Ayrtoun.

Ayrtoun smiled. 'Politicians always have problems with the deserving and the undeserving poor but usually don't mind at all seeing thugs given a taste of their own medicine by someone, in political terms, discreet.'

Cotton nodded.

'Sillitoe was on his way,' said Ayrtoun.' He was rewarded, given an absolute plum – Glasgow in 1931. Do you know Glasgow at all?'

'I've only passed through it,' said Cotton.

'Dirty, bloody place, at that time plagued by razor gangs,' said Ayrtoun. 'It took a decade, but Sillitoe broke them too. He had to sack a few hundred policemen, but he got non-Glaswegians in, introduced wireless radios, civilian informers and showed a ruthlessly creative use of the law.' Ayrtoun smiled. 'He arrested Billy Fullerton of the gang called the Billy Boys for being drunk in charge of an infant – Billy got ten months for that. Then he rounded up Billy's lieutenants. He didn't put them in jail, he put them in mental institutions. They were told they'd be committed without trial if they didn't cooperate. It worked. Apparently there's something about being kept in a straitjacket and having a male nurse wave a large syringe that convinces even the hardest of thugs.

'In 1942 he was knighted and given the job of coordinating policing in the whole of Kent so as to facilitate the invasion of Europe. After that he retired and bought a sweet shop in Eastbourne.'

'Having been a chief constable?'

'Yes. That didn't last of course.' Ayrtoun was looking out of the window. 'Some of these pubs have quite exotic names,' he said. 'Well, strange. The Crown and Gooseberry? What would that refer to?'

'I've no idea,' said Cotton.

Ayrtoun smiled. 'Now,' he said. 'You've heard of Guy Liddell?'

'I have,' said Cotton. 'He's the Soviet expert in MI5.'

'And he remains so. But everybody expected him to take over as the new head of MI5 last May. Clever, experienced and all up to date as it were, ready for the new Soviet threat.'

Ayrtoun pointed out another pub. It was called the Lamb and Flag. 'I know that one,' he said. 'That means Christ and the Crusades.'

'So why was Sillitoe given the job instead of Liddell?' said Cotton.

Ayrtoun smiled and held up the three middle

18

fingers of his right hand. 'In baseball, you get three strikes before you're out. Strike one. Miss Ellen Wilkinson, who has served under Herbert Morrison in several ways, sometimes I hope with a degree of physical pleasure, told Morrison that our disreputable old friend, "sources in Europe", had expressed reservations about Guy Liddell. Someone in a bar somewhere had suggested he might be a double agent.'

Cotton raised his eyebrows. 'Why would the Minister of Education have that information and feel it necessary to talk to the Home Secretary about MI5?'

Ayrtoun shrugged. 'Because Morrison is an ambitious, womanizing shit and Miss Wilkinson is rather needy and wants to serve him and have him be Prime Minister.'

Cotton nodded. Not particularly at Ayrtoun's language. He knew Ayrtoun was rarely as offhand or dismissive as he sounded.

'If they have reservations about Liddell why is he still there?' he asked.

Ayrtoun laughed. 'I did say I was trying to depress you. The Yanks were not too keen on him, either. In late 1941 the poor man got a report from Germany that the Japanese were intending to attack Pearl Harbour. He immediately passed this on to the FBI. They claim to have handed it on to the White House, who claim they never got it.' Ayrtoun looked round. 'The Yanks now say he should have sent the report to the Department of

19

Defense. Power means you get to be very particular about addresses and the right avenues.'

'All right,' said Cotton. 'And what was the third thing against him?'

'Ah. That's a bit murkier and has something to do with our wretched class system,' said Ayrtoun. 'Social balance. Sir Stewart Menzies was born into the very rich. Liddell isn't quite in that league but he was married to the Hon. Calypso Baring – yes, that's Baring Brothers Bank – until she divorced him in 1943. The PM thought that choosing someone less advantaged as head of MI5 – a sweet-shop owner and ex-chief constable like Sillitoe, for example – would balance Menzies better, or at least a little more obviously.' He paused. 'You know, you've either been damned clever or extraordinarily lucky.'

'Really?' said Cotton. The last time he had seen him, Ayrtoun had sneered that by joining the Colonial Service, Cotton was choosing 'the second eleven'.

'I didn't appreciate something you obviously did.'

'What's that?'

'The extraordinary extent to which colonial structures pertain in the mother country. Sillitoe's predecessor at MI5 was also a colonial policeman, a man who brought the techniques of Empire to deal with troublemakers here. Even the Labour Government thinks the Trade Unions are better treated as tribes, some more warlike than others.'

'The miners are hardly Zulus,' said Cotton.

Ayrtoun reached down into his briefcase, extracted and flipped open a file and handed him a piece of paper. It was the copy of a marriage certificate issued in Lusaka, Northern Rhodesia in July 1943. The groom's name was John Sillitoe, born in 1918 and his father was named as Sir Percy Sillitoe, Chief Constable of Glasgow.

'Now that really is a secret,' said Ayrtoun. 'The boy's mother is Mary Museba of the Bemba tribe. Oh, Sir Percy paid for the boy's education, but his white wife and children have no idea. Nor, of course, does the Prime Minister.' Ayrtoun held up a hand. 'And just to balance this out, don't forget that Sir Stewart Menzies' first wife made the most gruesome accusations about his sexual tastes before she ran off with someone else, that his second wife is a depressive, an invalid, and that he is currently taking advantage of one of his secretaries, described in the latest report on her as 'highly unstable with suicidal tendencies'.

Cotton handed back the birth certificate. 'Why are you telling me all this exactly?'

'To give you some perspective, old man,' snapped Ayrtoun. 'Sillitoe has run slap bang into resentment at MI5 and has come amply supplied with the stuff himself. On his first meeting with the Prime Minister, he was given the wrong file and made to look a complete fool. He took it as a declaration of war by his own staff. You were at Cambridge, weren't you?'

'Yes.'

'He'd loathe you, of course, as "book-learnt".' Ayrtoun smiled.

'Sir Percy is fighting a war of attrition. Did you know the poor bastard is no longer privy to Cabinet minutes? Menzies is.' Ayrtoun shook his head. 'Attlee is much tougher than people think. Sir Percy may be the poor boy but he's going to have to earn his minutes.'

Cotton winced. 'I take it the Americans are aware of his difficulties?'

Ayrtoun laughed. 'Let's say Sir Percy has quite enough on his plate at the moment. That priority card you have in your pocket is your passport. Keep it safe.'

'And Sir Stewart Menzies?'

'He also has his hands full, I assure you. But both of them are au fait with something that is about to happen.'

'Would that be something to do with Brylcreem? Open season on homosexuals?'

'Right. The American pressure for us to tighten security is a gift to a pansy-crushing department run by a man called Robert Starmer-Smith. He's assisted in legal and policing matters by an Inspector Radcliffe of Special Branch. Sir Percy is in no position to stop any of this but the Americans on the other hand are pleased to see any sort of action. MI6 is happy to stay out of it as long as their own buggers are left alone.'

'What would my job be?'

Ayrtoun was in no hurry. He lit another cigarette and puffed. 'Damage limitation, I suppose you could call it.'

Cotton sighed. They were on Streatham High Road. Ayrtoun pointed at the Goose pub.

'And where does the Greyhound fit in?' Cotton asked.

'The love that dares not speak its name has watering holes and meeting places,' said Ayrtoun.

'All right,' said Cotton.

'What have they been giving you to do?' asked Ayrtoun.

'Colonial stuff,' said Cotton unobligingly.

Ayrtoun let out one of his spectacularly loud, snorting laughs. 'Are you on for something a little more interesting?'

'I've just been reading about Malaya,' said Cotton. 'I quite liked the sound of that.'

Ayrtoun frowned. 'Do you even know how long it's been since I slept?'

'No idea at all,' said Cotton.

Ayrtoun grunted and closed his eyes.

At one level, Cotton was relieved. He preferred the uninterrupted whine and rumble of the vehicle to Ayrtoun's voice. Ayrtoun had aged in a year, looked pasty, had put on some more weight. Never tall, he now looked like some spiteful, long-nosed Buddha. Someone in Washington had said 'the problem with Ayrtoun is that he doesn't so much brief you as lambast you. You have to pick through all that violence and translate.' Cotton looked up.

The driver had run into problems, got his directions confused. The Triumph made several turns before they got on to North End.

Croydon had a bottleneck, caused by a narrowing of the road at the Whitgift almshouses. While they waited, some way back from the traffic-lights, Ayrtoun came to and looked across at a full triple window display of Snow White in the arcade of a department store.

In its own way it was a remarkable thing, of solid wood beds and chairs and automaton figures, including blue birds moving on a wide halo-type circuit round Snow White herself, and the crackling sound of 'Whistle While you Work' from a loudspeaker.

'Not much of a Christmas,' said Ayrtoun, pointing at the window. 'That's pre-war, barely dusted off. The show's grubby and the tinsel's sad.'

The lights changed and the car moved on. It did so slowly but did not stop, creeping along after the traffic-lights towards the High Street corner of the Surrey Street market.

Ayrtoun sat up and made a beckoning gesture. A slight young man, dressed in a pale-tweed suit and brown brogues that could only have come from the black market, ran across the road and opened the front passenger's door of the slow-moving car. He brought in chill and a faint smell of toffee apples, roasting chestnuts and something like overripe oranges.

The young man jumped in beside the driver,

slammed the door and removed his hat. He had blondish curly hair that had been much oiled.

Ayrtoun sighed and pointed. 'May I introduce you to Derek Jennings,' he said. 'The boogie-woogie bucal boy from Company Bum.'

The boy had already shrunk down in his seat and was twitching his hat in front of his face as if it were something between a fan and a wide-brimmed mask.

'Derek is affecting discomfort that he might be seen with us in a chauffeur-driven car. Absolute horse shit, of course. Unless, of course he doesn't think the car quite grand enough.'

Ayrtoun pointed again at Derek's small, curly head.

'I should inform you, Colonel,' said Ayrtoun, 'that Derek tells the Inland Revenue he works as a free-lance journalist or stringer. At one level at least, one of the liberal or muck-raking professions, isn't that right, Derek?'

Derek did not answer.

Ayrtoun cleared his throat and turned his head a little towards Cotton. 'He also works for us, of course. Five quid a week, isn't it, Derek?'

Derek did not reply. They passed the Swan and Sugarloaf pub.

'Now that is a nice name,' said Ayrtoun.

When they reached the Red Deer, Ayrtoun spoke again.

'I've been thinking of giving you a raise, Derek,' he drawled, 'commensurate with some new things you're going to have to do. What would you say to . . . seven pounds ten?'

'Better a tenner,' said Derek.

Ayrtoun laughed, apparently delighted. Even the driver let out a snigger.

'Don't be silly, Derek,' said Ayrtoun. 'I'm offering you fifty per cent more than you're getting now. Do you understand that?'

Derek nodded.

'Of course, you also understand the offer is entirely conditional,' Ayrtoun said. 'You do realize that, don't you? Let me repeat – there are some new things you're going to have to do to earn it.'

No one spoke. After about five hundred yards, the road turned again by the Royal Oak.

'The person beside me,' said Ayrtoun, 'is Mr Cotton. Colonel Cotton as was. A real soldier, Derek. While you were fumbling with nylon stockings and ducking down alleys to get away from the police, he was hunting down and killing our enemies. You will be reporting to him. Now how can I put this? Whether dither or necks, Mr Cotton cuts through things. Is that clear to you? And he has assistants for less lethal work. One is a rather fearsome Jock, from Glasgow, who keeps piano wire and razor-blades in his hatband. Mm? I imagine for you a fate worse than death would be to have that waifish little face chopped up, wouldn't it, Derek?'

Cotton had never been cast as the bogeyman before, knew of no razor-wielding Jock assistant and was not sure how effective Ayrtoun's words would be until he saw that Derek had been unable to resist glancing at him in the rear-view mirror. They were approaching a place called Purley.

'Pull up near the cinema, will you, driver?'

Ayrtoun got out a small pad the size of cigarette papers. 'Jot down your telephone numbers, will you?' he said to Cotton. 'All right, Derek, out you get.'

Cotton wrote, Derek got out and Ayrtoun wound down his window. He took the paper and handed it to Derek.

'Commit those numbers to memory,' he said.

Derek looked somewhere between surprised and nonplussed.

Ayrtoun looked at his watch. 'Shit. We'll give him a minute,' he said. 'What were those numbers again?'

Cotton told him.

'Good,' said Ayrtoun. 'One more time perhaps.'

Cotton shrugged. He repeated his telephone numbers again slowly and clearly.

'All right Derek?' asked Ayrtoun. 'Eat the paper, will you? It's rice paper, man.'

Derek blinked. Ayrtoun snatched the rice paper out of Derek's hand and stuffed it into his own mouth.

'You see? It's not bad at all. Rather sweet.'

Ayrtoun swallowed and so did Derek.

'You have those numbers in your head?'

'Yes.'

27

'Say.'

Derek told him what the numbers were.

'Good.' Ayrtoun got a ten-shilling note out of his wallet. 'Go and get something you *can* eat, Derek. Isn't there a Dorothy's Café here?'

Derek let out a noise like a rabbit sneezing. 'And there's a Palm Court for those who like dancing with fat women!'

Ayrtoun pretended surprise. 'Oh no,' he said, 'not those awful footguards from Caterham barracks? I am so sorry. Well, how about the cinema back there?' He looked round. 'Yes, the Astoria. That'll be ladies for the matinée and some sort of mixed grill.'

Derek looked uncomfortable. 'My mother goes there sometimes,' he mumbled.

'Then invite her to lunch, man!' said Ayrtoun. 'And an ice. Oh, look!' There was real delight in his tone. 'I see they have *Great Expectations* coming on Boxing Day and *A Matter of Life and Death* after that.'

Derek looked round at the posters, as if checking those were real titles.

'You will call Mr Cotton next Tuesday morning at 10 a.m. You will arrange a meeting – so you can get to know each other a bit more.'

'All right,' said Derek.

'No,' said Ayrtoun. 'Colonel Cotton will tell you what he wants and you will do everything you possibly can to comply with his orders. Have you got that? It's your choice. Seven pounds ten

28

a week, Derek, or your face like a bloody fishing net.'

Derek looked more resentful than impressed, as if he did not need that much insistence.

'Do you understand that, Derek?'

'Yes, sir.'

'And no tales, Derek, no mean tricks on people you dislike, mm? No faffing around. Don't be lazy. And don't ever dream of hiding. Driver.'

CHAPTER 3

The driver put the car in gear and drove off. Ayrtoun sighed. 'I'm not actually sure whether Derek can read,' he said, 'so I make allowances.' He snorted, for Ayrtoun quite softly. 'I do know we're awash with rice paper someone ordered. Do you want some?'

'No, thank you.'

Ayrtoun laughed. 'Derek's rather older than his boyish looks may suggest. He may even be as old as you. He's utterly terrified of ageing, of course. He started as an apprentice mechanic but acquired a taste for the life some of the car owners had. Soft cheeks, soft cashmere rugs and a hamper in the dickie seat. He was turned down for military service – "character defect". Then, rather wittily, the police picked him up for trying to be a spiv rather than a rent-boy. Derek can be a very quick learner if he's desperate. He dug around and shopped one or two bigger wide-boys and then we took him over.'

The Triumph had continued past Purley Cottage Hospital, a parade of mock-Tudor shops, and then swung right to get on to Purley Way. They were heading back to London. There was a rise in the road. The sky up and ahead, the usual dull grey pall over London, had taken on faint tinges of tobacco brown and some touches of faded sulphur yellow.

'Looks like snow,' said Ayrtoun.

Cotton thought it lacked pink.

'You obviously don't know London,' said Ayrtoun. 'Snow almost never lies in London. Too much coal, too many bodies.'

To the right of Purley Way were rows of light-engineering factories, warehouses and car showrooms and garages. Along on the left was the entrance to the white, half-art deco Croydon Airport and the similarly styled Airport Hotel. They turned in and parked.

'Take my bags in, will you, driver?' said Ayrtoun.

The driver got out. Ayrtoun turned towards Cotton.

'I'm sorry you're on the Tinkerbell detail,' he said. 'But the Americans want you. And I agreed. Perhaps not for the same reasons. They think you're honest and direct.' Ayrtoun paused. 'I have the impression they may even think you're slightly prickly and puritanical – like woollen underwear. They're quite frantic about traitors, fifth columnists, the enemy within, and they're particularly frantic we're not doing much about ours. They're also brewing up a witch-hunt of their own, an unholy alliance of ambitious demagogues, politicians – you should see some of the crop just elected – unscrupulous newspapers, various evil-minded churches anxious to save their choirboys for

31

themselves and, of course, any number of intelligence agencies.'

Ayrtoun paused and lit a cigarette. 'Have you ever seen an American gangster film? They spray bullets, turn cars into a lot of holes with bits of metal round them? Sometimes there's quite a lot of collateral damage. Shop windows shattering, passers-by going down.' He shrugged. 'These days if we riddle a queer instead of a traitor, that's aim enough for them.' Ayrtoun stubbed out the cigarette. 'You should also look at our own warlocks, of course. Did you know how long MI5 and Special Branch have been hunting pansies? Since 1939.'

Cotton frowned. 'As part of our war effort?' he said.

'Quite,' said Ayrtoun and opened his car door. 'Let's go in.'

They went into the airport, past the Propeller Bar and directly to a private room.

'Sandwiches for two and a pot of coffee,' Ayrtoun told the steward. 'As soon as you can, please.'

He sat down, got a folder out of his briefcase and put it on his knees.

'You're on the fairy squad for another reason however.'

He gave Cotton the folder. Cotton opened it. At the top of the page was a head and shoulders photograph of a middle-aged man wearing a striped tie and a hard collar that cut into his ample neck. His chin formed little more than a thin tier or ledge above his jowl. His nose was sizeable

32

enough to make his eyes look narrow-sct, but above those he had barely any eyebrows. His hair was scraped back, and it took Cotton a second or two to realize that the parting was rather low and to the left side of his head. His ears were large and his earlobes were pushed up by the fat round his neck. The man was smiling. The lips were thin and the smile was lopsided, but he gave the impression of being almost squint-eyed with contentment and pride. Cotton looked up.

'Major Albert Briggs MP,' said Ayrtoun. 'Major Bertie.'

Cotton did not know him.

'A new kind of MP, of course. But quite interesting.'

Cotton waited.

'MI5 have agreed that they can't be seen to be investigating our own MPs, can they now?'

'And MI6?'

'Yes, that would be me,' said Ayrtoun, 'for now anyway. Major Bertie is building his own little intelligence service, something Members of Parliament are not supposed to do. However, the Labour Government has considerable suspicions about our Intelligence Services, some of them I should say amply justified, and is certainly not kicking too much about Major Bertie's information-gathering activities.'

'Does he have a special interest?'

'Oh yes. Major Bertie is an excitable and prurient chap. I suspect he finds even the word "smut" exciting. He collects the dirt on the Tory Party

33

– but is also building a little photographic library on his own party members, preferably in a state of arousal.'

'Does he have an aim?'

Ayrtoun nodded. 'Yes. I'd imagine there's a certain sniffing of ambitious dogs' bottoms involved. He'll be able, at the very least, to cash in on his collection later, perhaps be a small kingmaker or even wag his tail in a junior Cabinet post. Where the hell are those sandwiches?'

Cotton read the report that was not supposed to exist. Albert Cedric Bellamy Briggs had been born in November 1900 in Portsmouth. His father, George, had been described on the birth certificate as 'first mate'. His mother Peggy was recorded as a piano teacher. As Ayrtoun had said, a new kind of MP.

An only child, Briggs had been educated at Portsmouth Grammar School. He had joined the Army Education Corps in 1920 where, being a trained teacher, he was immediately promoted to sergeant. It was not clear where he had been trained but he had recently mentioned the town of Havant in a newspaper interview in which he had also said his training had been 'Froebel-based'.

Cotton looked up. He did not know much about educational theory but knew that Froebel had come up with the term 'kindergarten' about a hundred years before and that the term translated literally as 'children garden', a concept not normally associated with military school.

'Havant and Froebel?' he said.

Ayrtoun smiled. 'That's Major Bertie's idea of humour.

Cotton saw that Briggs had spent almost all of his peacetime army career at the Duke of York's Royal Military School in Dover, retiring in 1938 with the rank of sergeant-major. He had married his wife Doris (née Gibson) in 1934. They had no children. The same year that he was married, however, Briggs had fathered an illegitimate child, a girl called Evelyn. The girl's mother, Rose O'Sullivan, remained his mistress and he had recently set them up in a villa he had bought in Bognor Regis, where she described herself as widow and called herself Sullivan. In 1934, Rose had been sixteen and employed as a skivvy or serving-girl. Evelyn now attended a college for young ladies.

As the steward arrived with a tray, Cotton paused. Presumably the tale of Sir Percy Sillitoe's domestic arrangements in Africa had been meant to put Major Briggs' own family affairs in perspective. Cotton looked down at the report again but was interrupted by a noise that combined protest and something like retching.

'Dear Jesus!' Ayrtoun exclaimed staring at a sandwich. 'What the hell is this?'

'Fish paste, sir. I believe it has salmon and shrimp in it, sir.'

'Then I have to say your faith is considerably greater than mine,' said Ayrtoun. 'Do you have anything at all to mask the flavour?'

The steward looked doubtful. 'We do have some chutney, sir. And there is a tin of piccalilli but . . . on that side of the plate the sandwiches are liver-paste, sir. You might prefer those.'

'I very much doubt it.' Ayrtoun shook his head and sniffed at the coffee pot. He sighed. 'This is mostly chicory waved over a coffee bean,' he said.

The steward nodded.

'Just bring me a whisky.' Ayrtoun looked at Cotton.

Cotton shook his head.

'And a plain biscuit if you've got some.'

'We have Rich Tea biscuits, sir.'

'Good, I'll have some. Yes, please take this tray away.'

The steward did so. A man in uniform approached.

'Twenty minutes to take-off, sir.'

'Thank you,' said Ayrtoun.

He looked at Cotton. 'We've given your name to the Major. He'll be in touch.'

Cotton closed the file and handed it back. 'And what will we talk about?'

'Your mutual interest in security matters. My guess is he'll be quite flattered. By the way, he has only what I'll call a mild interest in flushing out fairies. I mean he's a politician, not a first-class moral humbug. But if he thought it would help him, he'd do it and do it indignantly, especially if he could find a security angle to dress it up in.'

'"It" being a security scare involving a homosexual?'

Ayrtoun nodded. The steward returned with a single measure of whisky and two biscuits.

'Two?' said Ayrtoun.

'Rationing, sir.'

'Thank you,' said Ayrtoun. He sighed when the steward had turned away. 'The Americans seem to think we're class-ridden, daft, queer or incompetent, sometimes all four together. I often think they have a point.'

Cotton said nothing.

'I have the impression you're waiting for something,' said Ayrtoun.

'Yes, I am,' said Cotton.

Ayrtoun took a sealed envelope out of his inner jacket pocket.

'The driver will take you home. He knows where you live.'

Cotton opened the envelope. In its own way his letter of appointment was a marvel of obscurity. It appointed him as 'acting liaison officer' in an operation codenamed 'Sea-Snake'. This operation was covered by the Official Secrets Act. The heads of both MI5 and MI6 had initialled it but the signatory was Ayrtoun.

'Am I right in thinking neither MI5 nor MI6 will really cooperate with me?'

'Yes,' said Ayrtoun. 'That's about it.'

'What other letters do you have for me?'

'The driver has them. There's no point in hanging around. What do you say?'

'I haven't signed anything.'

'There is nothing to sign.'

'What about Colonial Intelligence?'

'Sir Desmond has been informed you've been seconded.'

'Anything else?'

Ayrtoun smiled. 'No.'

'Let me see if I have this right. You appear to want me to soften MI5's efforts at queer-bashing and to emasculate an MP.'

'That's not a bad way of putting it. *Great Expectations* can be our codebook. What do you say? The UK can also be a land of opportunity, you know.'

'Fuck you,' thought Cotton, but he smiled instead.

'Have a good flight,' he said.

The driver offered Cotton a tartan rug. Cotton shook his head. A few moments later they were heading back to London.

At Cotton's address the driver got out and opened the door.

'I have something for you, sir,' he said. He went to the back of the car and came back with a heavy cardboard box. It was from Cotton's sister Joan in New York. Evidently Ayrtoun had thought a Christmas package stood more chance of actually arriving if it came through diplomatic channels.

'Thank you,' said Cotton. The driver took off his cap and placed his card on top of the box. His name was Hans Bieber. He had straight dark hair that flopped naturally into a middle parting, brown eyes, and something of the chin-raised, ready-to-smileness of the ballroom dancer.

'My nickname is Eager Beaver,' said Hans. 'A joke. Bieber sounds like the German for "beaver".'

Cotton smiled politely. 'POW?'

Hans Bieber shook his head, but did not answer the question. 'I don't want to go back to Germany. Ever,' he said. 'Mr Ayrtoun suggests this car and this driver should you need them.' He paused. 'I think you will. I'm changing my name soon. I will be John. John Driver.'

'Is that another joke?'

'No,' said the driver. 'Deed poll. The paperwork is going through now.'

Cotton nodded. 'Really? Where do you live?'

'At the moment, I'm living in Kensington.'

'Are you telling me that is temporary?'

'It depends. He's director of a football club. Very jealous.'

Cotton shrugged. 'Chelsea?'

'Or Fulham,' said Hans, as if Cotton were being a little naughty and indiscreet. He put his gloved hand on Cotton's forearm. 'Thank you for not saying Arsenal.'

Hans giggled and put on his cap to show that personal banter was over. He took an envelope out of his inside pocket and dropped it on to the gift box. It was addressed to Cotton in Ayrtoun's handwriting. He then assisted Cotton inside the block and saluted.

CHAPTER 4

Cotton lived in Wilbraham Place off Sloane Street. The five-storey block of apartments was stolid red brick marginally relieved by white stone edgings. He chose it because the flat was conveniently placed for Sloane Square Tube station. His bank was near the first stop, at Victoria. He usually got off at the second stop, St James's Park, and walked across the park to work. It was just another stop to Westminster.

The block had a porter, an ex-sergeant from the First World War called Reginald Hill, with polished boots and a bristling moustache. By the lift was a names-board showing which residents were in or out. Cotton hardly knew any of them. Three never appeared to be there. A retired general's middle-aged daughter used her father's flat when in town, and when Cotton got back from work, he would sometimes see her in evening gowns and fur stoles when she was off to the theatre and Major General G. B. D. Fenwick was shown as being IN. Some of the flats were rented out – to a shy, film-star handsome man called Shalhoub from the Lebanese Embassy with a never-seen wife and two plump, demure little daughters; and a couple from Canada called Grimes, he having something to do with aluminium. Another was occupied by a Harley Street dermatologist's female 'cousin', called Brenda, who had a small dog and who winked when she said the word 'cousin', and another to a dentist called Silver who lived in Manchester but was on all kinds of committees.

Cotton had bought the place in early 1946 from an ex-army colleague. Even allowing for a depressed market, the price was reasonable, and Cotton just had enough cash, from his late mother and his wartime savings, to complete the purchase of the flat and everything in it quickly. The service charge was rather high and the property was leasehold – his father did not approve of leasehold though the term of the lease, Reich style, was only slightly short of a thousand years – but central heating and hot water were included in the fee.

The flat had ceilings rather too high for the size of the rooms and draughty metal windows. The décor was pre-war, about 1933, done for an actress Cotton had never heard of, apparently influenced by the designer Syrie Maugham. This turned out to mean that the walls were plain and off-white, the large rug on the parquet floor was similar, and the two sofas were grubby white. He was told the curtains might have started off as a colour called celadon but had faded to eau de Nil. By the time he moved in, the walls had picked up more than ten years of smoke and shadows. He was

41

particularly fond of what looked to be small elephant tusks – apparently they had contained a mirror – above the mantelpiece in the main room. But the bathroom was robustly plumbed, entirely tiled in white, green and black, and had a shower-rose the size of a soup plate.

There was a sizeable if rudimentary kitchen with glazed double doors to the living room. On the left, down a corridor, were a bedroom with two single beds, the bathroom and, on the other side, a small room giving on to an internal courtyard-cum-lightshaft that he guessed had been for a maid. At the end of the corridor was the bedroom he used, with a window that gave on to D'Oyley Street.

There was a gas supply to the kitchen and to the main bedroom, where there was a fireplace containing a structure resembling punctured rolls of parchment that lit up with a plosive puff, at first with a blue-tinged flame that then turned yellow. If used for more than a few minutes, the stack of broken parchment turned red and caused headaches. The electric fire in the sitting room was a mix of ceramic and metal, squares of pristine honeycomb and various wires, some coiled, some protective.

Cotton put Joan's food parcel on the kitchen table. He opened the letter. Ayrtoun told him his American contact was Ed Lowell. Lowell would be in touch 'very shortly'. He might find a journalist called Miles Crichton useful. 'He camps out at the Garrick Club. I have told him to contact you.' The handwritten letter was initialled. There were two postscripts: 'It is not a question of stopping Briggs or getting rid of him – more showing him his limitations in as kindly and as cooperative a way as you can.'

The final note told him to keep the original appointment card and destroy the letter. He did. He then took the paper off Joan's parcel and found two envelopes, one to his father, one to him. He opened his. It was a Christmas card. On one side Joan had written: 'Do try to get Dad to cross the Atlantic and visit us. He has never even seen his grandchildren.'

The parcel contained American plenty, mostly in cans. There was canned tuna, canned clams, a large can of ham, and of asparagus, spinach, peaches, pears and pineapple. There was also coffee and something called Turbinado sugar. It was pale brown, and looked to Cotton like Demerara. He made a list of the items and wrote a thank-you letter. 'We're awfully grateful,' he began.

On his desk on Monday, Cotton found an invitation from Ed Lowell to have lunch the next day and, on Garrick Club paper, a suggestion from Miles Crichton that they meet on Wednesday.

Cotton had to spend the rest of the day calming an agitated Portman.

'There's a whole selection process to go through!

43

It will take two, perhaps three months to choose Lloyd's successor. Whitehall won't speed up but they hold me responsible for finding an acting replacement.'

They talked about possible candidates.

'Is what you're doing so awfully important?'

Cotton showed Portman his card.

'Damn!' said Portman. 'Pity. I'd have preferred you.'

'Why?'

'You always give the impression you're about to give someone two fingers.'

Cotton smiled. 'I'm sorry,' he said. 'It's not something I mean to do.'

On Tuesday, Cotton met Ed Lowell for lunch at the Connaught in Carlos Place, Mayfair. The five-star hotel had something of a reputation as the local for Americans, only a short stroll away from the Grosvenor Square Embassy.

Lowell struck Cotton as looking more like a State Department diplomat than an intelligence officer. He had the small affectations of style that Cotton had seen in British rather than American diplomats, to show they weren't run of the mill – two buttons of the left sleeve of his suit undone, his wristwatch worn over his shirt cuff and – he was sitting in an armchair by the fire in the bar to the left of the entrance – showing dark green silk socks. Ed Lowell rose. His tie was also green silk but many shades lighter. Cotton was six foot one.

Lowell was taller, a little stooped if only out of politeness, and had the slightly embarrassed manner, not quite of a junior master about to instruct the boys in the facts of life, but of a patrician academic who had, by bank account and brain, inherited considerably more than his fair share.

He did not shake Cotton's hand. He tugged at it, as if at a velvet bell-pull.

'Shall we?' he said.

In an era of strict rationing, restaurants had been spared. At one level at least, supply and demand worked for those with money to eat out. Prices had been set, but restaurants had shown great ingenuity to cater for those prepared to pay more. Cotton had once been taught that restaurants came about because of the French Revolution. The chefs at suddenly headless great houses had decided to spread their delicacies to a wider and, though living, still limited market.

Lowell and Cotton were led across the entrance hall through another bar and into the panelled dining room. An actress Cotton could not quite place was having a crystal flute of champagne with an elderly man. His pate and face were tanned the colour of brandy, setting off the strip of white hair above his ears. Her face was the colour of single cream, her lips cochineal. Both were wearing new suits, hers shiny, satin, black; his double-breasted pale grey.

Cotton and his host were given a table for those less anxious to be recognized, towards the windows.

Lowell sat down, then abruptly held up his arms as if surrendering.

'Now wasn't that just a wonderful speech Winston gave in Missouri earlier this year?' he said as a waiter draped a napkin over his lap.

He meant – another waiter was flourishing a napkin for Cotton – Churchill's Iron Curtain speech delivered on 5 March 1946.

'But Winston's gone,' Lowell went on. 'And then poor old Maynard passed.'

John Maynard Keynes had died in April.

'Leaving us with our skirts up and our knees trembling at the prospect of Soviet rapine?' said Cotton.

Lowell paused. His face showed polite pain but not a great deal of enquiry.

'Shall we order then?'

Cotton was not that good at distinguishing different American accents but was fairly confident Lowell was from the Brahmin, or what his sister Joan called the cold-roast side of Boston. There was something husky and constrained about his voice, as if his throat was getting hoarse from being obliged to be sociable. These sounds did not so much vary as waver and jump. The *o* of old, for example, sounded probably more English than Cotton's, but the *o* of order was like 'awda'.

Lowell chose paté de foie gras, a rare steak, and mint ice-cream on a praline tart. Cotton chose scallops, turbot, and a lemon sorbet. The choice of wine was not a problem. Ed Lowell dismissed the sommelier's wine list with a wave of his hand.

'I have to work this afternoon,' he said.

Cotton raised his eyebrows. 'Really?' he said.

Lowell smiled, again as if unsure, and then chose a Virgin Mary.

The sommelier spoke up. 'Might I suggest a chaste Bellini, sir,' he said to Cotton. 'Without the Prosecco? But with alternative bubbles?'

Cotton was doubtful. 'Do you think that would work?'

'Yes, sir,' said the sommelier. 'I assure you. I can give you my guarantee.'

There was a story in Whitehall that the Foreign Secretary, Ernest Bevin, had just persuaded Cabinet that Britain should proceed with developing the atom bomb regardless of whether or not they could afford it, because he had just had US Secretary of State James F. Byrnes on the telephone and was not going to be spoken to like that ever again. Evidently the sommelier was having a similar, if more masked reaction to Ed Lowell.

Imperturbable, Lowell decided on another tack, but continued to insist on British weakness.

'When do you think your government will honour the agreement to make the pound sterling convertible?'

Cotton shrugged his shoulders. 'No idea.'

'How long after that before you devalue?'

'Likewise,' said Cotton. 'You wouldn't like to get to business, would you?'

Lowell smiled. 'You have a reputation for being straightforward,' he said.

The Bellini arrived. The sommelier had simply used champagne instead of Prosecco.

Cotton tasted it and tried to look apologetic. 'I know nothing about you or your reputation.'

To Cotton's surprise Lowell looked discomfited, though perhaps out of embarrassment at Cotton's bluntness. For some reason the first name of the actress across the room came to Cotton. It was Patricia, but he could not decide whether her surname was Roc or Medina because both were half-known to him from billboards, perhaps a magazine, and a notion that both tended to act in off-the-shoulder costume dramas.

'Mr Lowell—'

Lowell held up a large, manicured hand. 'Oh, call me Ed, please. By the way, that is not short for Edward, but Edwin.'

'Is it?' said Cotton. 'Well, do please call me Peter.' He cleared his throat. 'In the US you have more experience of a variety of security agencies than we have. Do you have any senators or representatives who run their own operations?'

Lowell considered, probably, thought Cotton, as to whether or not this approach to business was acceptable. Then he nodded.

'No, not in that way,' he said. 'We have committees. In any case, we don't consider Major Briggs to have an organization as such.'

Cotton smiled. 'We use the phrase "a keen interest in certain aspects of security" I think.'

Lowell did not smile but he did nod. 'Something like that.'

'Would you know how he's financing this interest?' asked Cotton.

Lowell shook his head. 'It's not Communistic.'

'Are you sure about that?'

Lowell paused. 'We're not funding him either.'

Cotton nodded. At least Lowell was beginning to choose his words with obvious care. 'Have you met him?'

'Not directly, no,' said Lowell. 'Our reading of him is that he's an English nationalist.'

'You're using English for British?'

'No,' said Lowell. 'The Major doesn't like the Scotch.'

'For any particular reason?'

Ed Lowell blinked. 'It may be his first commanding officer was a Scotchman and didn't cut him much slack.'

Cotton smiled. He agreed he should have known. 'I haven't met Major Briggs yet,' he said. 'But I understand I'll be doing so shortly.'

Their first courses arrived. Cotton cut into a scallop and placed about a third of it on his tongue. To his own surprise, he almost moaned. The last time he had eaten anything so good was some three months ago when he had been given a real ham sandwich.

'Is that satisfactory?' said Ed Lowell.

49

'Yes, it is,' said Cotton.

'Mine could be a little warmer,' said the American.

Cotton decided to eat another bit of scallop before he spoke again. It was wonderful.

'Tell me what worries you,' he said.

There was a pause. Ed Lowell seemed to be considering whether the foie gras was acceptable or not. He nodded.

'We consider some members of the Labour Government to be either pro-Soviet or anti-American.'

'Is there someone in particular you have in mind?'

'Some concerns have been expressed about Sir Stafford Cripps.'

Cotton was genuinely surprised.

'Why? He's not a Communist. His objection to a British atom bomb is purely on the grounds of cost. He's not trying to curry favour with you – or with the Soviets.'

'Rolls Royce,' said Lowell.

Rolls Royce had developed a centrifugal jet engine, the RB41 or Nene, designed by Frank Whittle. When approached by his own jet engine scientists about this, Stalin had expressed doubts that anyone in the West would be stupid enough to help them out. He had not counted on Sir Stafford Cripps. Cripps had not only invited a Soviet delegation to Britain to see the engines, but, as a gesture of good faith, he had even gifted twenty-five of the engines to the Soviets, apparently thinking this would encourage them to sign up for a licensing agreement that would bring in much

50

needed cash. The Soviets had gratefully accepted the jet engines but had not signed any commercial agreement. Instead, they had promptly started to 'reverse engineer' the gifts with a view to manufacturing their own jet engines for a new fighter plane. The British Cabinet, under the guise of collective responsibility, had decided to close ranks round Sir Stafford and back his decision.

'Exactly,' said Cotton. 'That kind of thing has a cost.'

'You really would think so,' said Ed, 'but we understand there's a movement to replace Prime Minister Attlee with him.'

Cotton shook his head. 'It won't happen.'

'Why not?'

'There was a movement for Cripps to replace Churchill a couple of years ago.' Cotton shrugged. 'This is merely the peacetime echo. Foreign Secretary Bevin doesn't like him. That is why, just like Churchill, he keeps sending Cripps away on visits to India to talk to Gandhi. Gandhi was inelegant enough to suggest to a journalist that his visitor was akin to an old-fashioned bank manager unaware his bank is bust.' Cotton shook his head. 'Sir Stafford is not the kind of man to stoop to know this. That's why Churchill said "There but for the grace of God, goes God".'

Lowell frowned. 'I never quite understood that. What does it mean exactly?'

'That were he to perform a miracle it would be to make wine into water. As better for us, you see.

Most down-to-earth Labour politicians know that the electorate would prefer more bread and dripping to more austerity. Sir Stafford has the principled innocence of the prohibitionist.'

Lowell considered. 'What's dripping?' he said.

'Animal fat left over from roasting. It congeals as a sort of greasy memory of meat for people who don't often get to eat it.'

Their first-course plates were removed and replaced by the second course. Lowell bent over a large steak and breathed in. He picked up a knife and fork and cut into it.

'Yes,' he said. 'It's rare. You British are not so good at that.'

Cotton watched Ed Lowell cut the steak up into smallish pieces before putting down his knife and changing the fork from his left to his right hand. Though Cotton was impressed the Connaught had even been able to provide steak, he was a little more intrigued that Lowell had not mentioned Herbert Morrison, the Home Secretary, as a candidate to take over as Prime Minister, particularly as a much stronger Westminster rumour than anything to do with Cripps, had Morrison on the US government's payroll. His turbot, though not as shockingly good as the scallops, was excellent.

'MI5 is hamstrung,' said Lowell.

'It is,' said Cotton. 'Apparently that's one of the reasons I am talking to you.'

Lowell moved on to MI6. 'Sir Stewart Menzies

is a great bureaucrat and infighter. But he has a tendency to leave security work to others.'

Cotton nodded. 'Possibly.'

'Too many loose ends, Peter. We want to see things tightened up.'

'But who doesn't, Ed? The USA have just spent more than a year on ferocious domestic wrangling while everybody else waits for a successor to the wartime OSS.'

'It'll come,' said Lowell. 'There is no doubt about that.'

'I'm sure it will. But one of our problems is that you Americans are extraordinarily forgiving of your own slow processes but rather demanding that we speed up. Since we are trying to keep in step with you, but you haven't yet fixed on quite what you are doing, this is not as easy as you might like.'

'Another chaste Bellini, sir?' said the sommelier.

Cotton was not much of a drinker. But he decided to accept.

'Yes, thank you. Very refreshing.'

'And I'll have another Virgin Mary,' said Ed Lowell. He sat back. He smiled.

'Do you hunt, Peter? Fish?'

'No,' said Cotton. 'Do you?'

'I was in Norfolk over the weekend. Pheasant.'

'Interesting?' said Cotton.

Ed Lowell smiled. 'I think it was. Your class system is—'

'Silly, nasty, and crippling,' said Cotton.

Ed Lowell smiled again and leant forward. 'You

do know I have no interest in homosexuals per se? It's security risks we're after.'

'Per se,' said Cotton.

'It's vital you keep me abreast of things.'

Cotton thought about that. 'No,' he said, 'it's not. You mean it's convenient for you. But I can't give you any guarantees, Ed. I haven't started yet, and to promise anything now would be absurd.'

Ed Lowell nodded. 'I do need a form of words, Peter.'

'Try "full and willing cooperation" then.'

'Words matter.'

'Of course they do. But today you're not getting any words that could inconvenience me.'

Ed Lowell raised his chin. 'Are you asking me to trust you?'

'I'm not sure I am, Ed.'

Ed Lowell laughed. Cotton had the impression he had just, satisfactorily from Ed's point of view, conformed to type. He didn't know what that type was.

Cotton could not recall many difficulties in understanding Americans when he had been in Washington. Ed Lowell, however, had been difficult and then, almost as if a timer had gone off, wanted to appear as much chummy as demanding.

'Are you enjoying your meal, Peter?'

'Oh yes, Ed,' said Cotton.

Lowell smiled. 'Good. I think I understand you better.' He wagged a finger. 'We should do well.'

'I'm glad you think so, Ed.'

CHAPTER 5

Cotton had agreed to meet Derek Jennings that evening in a cocktail lounge of Derek's choice. It was called 'The Beaufort Club. Private Members Only'. Before the war, the chairs had been painted a pale green but they now looked tired and scratched. The waiter wore a faded red bum-freezer type jacket. The patterned carpet had as many stains as swirls. Derek was wearing another new suit. It looked big for him and Cotton understood that Derek was really very thin. The wide-shouldered, wide-lapelled suit formed a kind of screen from which there were not quite in place projections of elbows and knees.

Derek ordered 'a Chelsea sidecar'.

'What's the difference between that and a sidecar?' said Cotton.

'Gin, sir, instead of brandy. The Cointreau and lemon juice stay the same,' said the waiter. 'Going to a show, Mr Jennings?'

'Not tonight,' said Derek. He shrugged. 'I've seen everything.'

The waiter glanced at Cotton. 'Sir? May I tempt you to the same?'

Cotton shook his head. 'A whisky and water,' he said.

'Any particular brand, sir?'

'A malt. The Glenlivet? Would you have that?'

'Of course, sir.'

Derek looked slightly surprised. When the waiter had gone, he frowned and leant forward. 'It'll be Glen Hackney, you know.'

'I know that but I haven't come for the drink, Derek. And I'm not here for pleasure.'

A man wearing make-up approached them. Derek shook his head. 'I'm busy now, Basil,' he said. 'I'll speak to you later.'

Cotton smiled very briefly. 'Derek, you have a choice. I can use you or not. I'm indifferent. It's up to you.'

'I'm the best there is, Mr Cotton. Far more than Mr Ayrtoun knows.'

'Really?'

Derek giggled. 'Mr Ayrtoun said I had sucked more lordly cock than lollipops. He's got it all wrong.'

'In what way?'

'It's not me who is doing the sucking, Mr Cotton. It's the lords on their knees.'

'Well, I'll certainly tell him that,' said Cotton.

Derek was in explanatory mood. 'Mine is like alabaster, they say.'

Cotton couldn't help it. He laughed from his chest. It was a genuine laugh, something he had not felt for some time. He was a little surprised by Derek's reaction. Derek turned his chair

56

sideways and crossed his legs. He showed a stretch of very white, very thin, hairless shin and moved his head rather jerkily.

Cotton frowned. He was aware Derek had been trying to impress him with the Mr Jennings and man-of-the-cocktail-lounge business. Now something else was going on. Cotton tried. The light was more than dingy but somehow, as Derek worked his profile with the abruptness of a chicken, Cotton caught a glimpse of something unexpected. From one thin angle, Derek presented a waifish version of Michelangelo's David, a David-Derek with a much smaller skull and a small rabbit-pink upper lip from the effects of a cold. Cotton nodded. Derek was explaining his attraction to back up the status he claimed.

'All right, Derek, tell me what you can offer.'

Derek pulled his chair round again. 'London south of the river, through Surrey and quite a bit of Kent, there isn't an important homo I don't know about. And in Sussex I can do you for Brighton, Eastbourne and Worthing.'

'A "homo" in this context being?'

Derek giggled. 'Well, not *me*,' he said. 'I mean the homebodies, the family men. There's a lord-lieutenant with five children, a couple of judges—'

Cotton shrugged. 'I know this,' he said. 'What's your point?'

Derek blinked. 'Well, there's an etiquette, you know.'

Cotton closed one eye. 'There's a *what*?'

Derek was uncertain. 'Is it pronounced like that? Etiquette?'

'More or less. Why are you mentioning manners now?'

Derek was uncertain about something. 'It's all rather private,' he said. 'I mean, they go places but they don't go as the lord-lieutenant or the judge, do they? I mean, well, there's an element of incognito involved.'

'But not entirely. Are you talking about discretion?' Cotton asked.

'Yes,' said Derek without sounding too sure. 'It's like a protected area, you know, where identities are – not so important.'

'A bit like carnival, is that it? But without masks?'

'Ooh. That's quite good, Mr Cotton,' said Derek. 'Carnival is about it.'

'So what are you saying?'

'Well, they're not, you know, unrealistic. I mean they know where they've been and they're not silly.'

'You're talking about blackmail?'

'No! It's an arrangement, Mr Cotton. The etiquette! I help them, they help me.'

'And this help consists of?'

'Information, Mr Cotton. Let's say I tell them where good things are happening. They tell me bad things they know.'

'Your etiquette is a system of mutual favours.'

Derek looked doubtful.

'It's a kind of club,' said Cotton. 'A society that prefers secrecy.'

'Well,' said Derek, 'you might say that. I mean look at the Scrubs.'

He meant Wormwood Scrubs, one of His Majesty's Prisons in London.

'That's where they send us. We make up about half the prison population there. Queer Hall they call it.'

Cotton had not known that Wormwood Scrubs specialized. He nodded. 'Have you been there?'

Derek shuddered and shook his head. 'I've managed to keep out.'

'All right, Derek. I'm going to ask you for four things. You know MI5 and Special Branch are not keen on "carnival".'

'I don't like Special Branch.'

'You don't have to. The first thing I want is information of their involvement in anything you hear. That has two sides. First, what and who are they looking for? Second, how many of them are – involved.'

Derek frowned. 'Are using the etiquette, you mean?'

'All right,' said Cotton. 'We'll call it that. Is that the first thing clear?'

'Yes.'

'The second thing is this. I'm not talking about the etiquette here, I'm talking about honest to God blackmail. There are people in other sensitive jobs who could be pressured if it was known—'

'That they liked "carnival",' interrupted Derek.

'All right. Civil Servants in the War Office, a number of people in the Armed Forces—'

'I understand, Mr Cotton. I do. You mean the vulnerable amongst us.'

'That's it. You hear of anyone in trouble, you tell me. Is that clear? That's not just people with more money, it may be those without.'

'Yes, sir.'

'The third thing I want from you is to keep an eye on people snooping around. They may not be employed by the Government to do that.'

'What, Mr Cotton? Foreigners?'

'Not just foreigners. They may be working for private clients.'

'Right. What's the fourth thing?'

'That you're honest, Derek. Don't pretend you know when you don't. I'll take hunches, I'll even take inklings, but don't give me information just to give it. Is that clear? If you have nothing to say, you have nothing to say.'

Derek was polite if a little patronizing. 'It *is* Christmas,' he said.

'Meaning?'

'The police aren't well paid, you know. Some of them get helpful when they have to buy presents for their kiddies. The arrangement I had with Mr Ayrtoun was what you saw. The ten bob goes five bob to me and five bob for Sergeant Statham.'

Cotton went home on the Tube. He always found the Underground at night depressing. The other travellers looked weary and passive, too tired to pretend, rocking as the carriage rocked.

60

Cotton closed his eyes. He realized he was treating Derek's world as a foreign country. There had been times when Derek had, with some care, treated him as a worthy innocent.

He was. At Cambridge he had studied macro-economics. The less measurable parts – corruption, barter and other unrecorded, sometimes imposed, transactions – had fallen into micro-economics and not been on the syllabus. He had then joined the army where activity was furious, movements controlled and information little.

Cotton thought that here in London he was at the very least dealing with a second economy. In the cocktail lounge, Derek had told him that his brother-in-law 'was quite a big player in Croydon, really. He's a greengrocer.'

'Is that a euphemism? A special name?' Cotton had said.

'What? No, he has a stall in Surrey Street Market. You know, sprouts and stuff.'

'Sprouts can't make him a player.'

Derek had looked pityingly at him. 'Not just sprouts,' he said. 'A counter has two sides you know. Over and under. How many sides has a stall got? Jim can get a lot of things for the constable's kiddies. He's got storage in Wallington and use of a van.'

Derek had fingered his own striped tie. 'See this, Mr Cotton? Silk. Pure silk.'

'Yes,' said Cotton. 'Pre-war I take it.'

'Oh yes,' said Derek. He smiled. 'My guess is – it's about twenty years old. Do you recognize it?'

Cotton squinted. The tie was brown, grey and a silvery white. A memory of a school sporting match stirred, but not too clearly. 'It might be Lancing College.'

'Lancing?' said Derek. 'That's a good school, isn't it?'

Cotton shrugged. 'I take it you didn't go there.'

'No, but somebody who did left a trunk of clothes in a depository.'

'It won't be missed?'

Derek had looked more pitying than abashed. 'Some of the trunks aren't going to be reclaimed, Mr Cotton.'

Cotton forgot, almost drank from his glass. 'You're wearing a dead man's tie.'

'Well, I'd have worn his shoes if they'd fitted! Beautiful shoes, Mr Cotton, hand-made, really top-class.'

Cotton reached across the table and grabbed hold of the tie. 'You shouldn't do that, Derek. Don't ever do that again,' he said.

'What? Make use of a dead man's clothes?'

Cotton twisted his wrist and the tie. There was a faint squeak from the silk as old threads parted. 'No "etiquette", Derek. No more delicate advice and helpful tips on manners and lips round alabaster and ex-Lancing men like Mr Tom Driberg MP. No back stories, no coy jokes, no cute little secrets and no fucking games. You don't play dead man's clothes with me. Have you got that?'

Derek was having some difficulty breathing.

'We won't meet here again,' said Cotton, 'nor anywhere like it. Clear?' He let go.

'That's good, Mr Cotton,' said Derek. He started nodding. 'It's good to clear the air.'

'I'm glad you think that,' said Cotton. 'You really must never forget it. Clear?'

'Look, I've had contact with Mr Driberg once, but I didn't know his old school. I swear.'

Cotton sighed. 'Then you have to be very careful, Derek.'

The waiter, alarmed by the turn of things and ties, was approaching.

Derek sat back and smiled. 'Is what Mr Ayrtoun said true, Mr Cotton. You've killed?'

Cotton nodded. 'Yes,' he said as quietly as possible.

'What about that Jock?' said Derek. 'The man from Glasgow!'

Cotton had been surprised but played along. 'You really don't want to meet him,' he said. 'Derek? I have great expectations of you.'

The waiter, in reflex at the tone, smiled. Derek nodded.

'Thanks, Colonel. I really appreciate that.'

At his stop on the Tube, Cotton got up and groaned. He shook his head. He couldn't think of a single thing that might make the job enjoyable but could think of several that would make it anywhere from unpleasant to miserable.

CHAPTER 6

On Wednesday, 18 December Cotton was surprised to find Hans Bieber waiting for him by the Triumph to take him to the Garrick Club.

'This isn't necessary,' he said.

'Mr Ayrtoun wanted you to have these,' said Hans, giving him two folders.

Cotton got into the car. He opened the first folder. The report on Hans Bieber was a thin, single page and had huge gaps. He looked up. Hans was watching him in the rear-view mirror. Cotton read that Hans had been born in Hanover in 1910, the third son and seventh child of a baker called Klaus and his wife Gerda. He had received an elementary education. By 1923 he was helping in the family business as a delivery boy on a bicycle. By 1932, Hans had been a drag artist 'of some renown' in Berlin. His version of Lili Marlene was described in the report as 'quite exceptional, probably a classic' – probably by Hans, thought Cotton.

Hans was paying close attention to Cotton's reading. 'It was a question of assuming the part and the longing,' he said. 'The dressing up part wasn't so difficult.'

'I really don't mind,' said Cotton.

'Do you mean you don't care, sir?'

'No. I mean I don't mind,' said Cotton. 'I take it Mr Ayrtoun knows a great deal more than this?'

'Yes,' said Hans. He sighed. 'I am good at mechanical things, Mr Cotton, but not written things.'

'Why on earth are you writing this in the first place?'

'Because if I have a report I exist! Reports are what you work on in this business.'

'I had already understood that you were more than a driver, Hans. I will tell you, however, that you have to give more information.' Cotton looked down. 'It says here that you joined the Nazi Party in 1934. Is that true?'

'To hide!' said Hans. 'The best place to hide! In the mouth of the wolf!'

'Really? What did they teach you?'

'To drive, Mr Cotton. Real driving. Response to ambush, smooth driving, pursuit driving—'

Cotton held up his hand. 'It says here you got married,' he said.

'Mutual advantage,' said Hans. 'I knew her from Berlin. Ping-pong girl, you know. Dyke.'

Cotton looked up at Hans's eyes in the rear-view mirror.

'It says you drove for someone important during the war. You don't say who.'

'But Mr Ayrtoun thought –' Hans paused '—it wouldn't be advisable to say who.'

'Wonderful,' said Cotton. 'Mr Ayrtoun has you on a string, right? Residence? Work permit? And now you're writing your own report in an attempt to do what exactly?'

'I need papers, Mr Cotton. Papers will help establish me.'

'Tell me about the person you're living with.'

'Robert. I don't want to give his surname. He's a—'

'Director of a football club, yes, you said.'

Hans looked apologetic. 'And a Tory London County Councillor too.'

Cotton frowned. 'Right. Would he be married?'

Hans grimaced almost as if he was curtseying. 'He left his wife and two children for me.'

'My. That's quite something. You must be very special for him to take that kind of risk,' said Cotton. 'How did you get away from Germany?'

Hans coughed. 'I drove,' he said. 'Mercedes. I drove for Bremerhaven when I knew the British were there.'

'You had information to trade.'

'Yes.'

'Have you met Robert's children?'

'No.'

Cotton looked at his watch. 'I have to get to the Garrick Club,' he said.

'Yes, sir. Of course, sir.' Hans started the Triumph. 'Down Pall Mall, round Trafalgar Square, up St Martin's Lane and right into Garrick Street.'

Cotton nodded and began to read the file on Miles Crichton. MI6 was covering the Garrick Club membership and expenses for this 'freelance journalist, theatre critic, author'. Cotton learnt that Crichton had a cruel nickname, 'The Cat and Bagpipes'. Apparently this had been the name of a pub 'popular with Scotch and Irish MPs' in the eighteenth century in the alleys between Downing Street and Charles Street before they were demolished and built over by government departments. But it really referred to his appearance. As a child, Crichton had contracted polio and now used crutches. 'He has the legs of an eight-year-old boy,' said the report.

Whatever Crichton's physical disadvantages, he was not timid in print. As a theatre critic he had apparently made enemies of G. B. Shaw ('Mr Shaw never tires of hearing actors speak even his most turgid thoughts back to him') and T. S. Eliot ('Mr Eliot's play *The Family Reunion* failed in 1939. Unchanged, it has now been revived. Has the intervening war improved the play? No').

The son of a barrister and with a law degree himself, Miles also wrote on legal matters, particularly miscarriages of justice. He had recently attacked the Attorney General Sir Hartley Shawcross. Shawcross had prosecuted William Joyce, Lord Haw-Haw, famed for his wartime broadcasts on behalf of the Nazis, on a technicality. By accepting Haw-Haw's false obtainment of a British passport in the thirties, Shawcross argued that he was then British and had been guilty of treason. Haw-Haw had been hanged.

Crichton had also had a go at Shawcross's opening statement at the Nuremberg Trials: 'To talk of the rule of law and then to sit down with Soviet legal luminaries from the show trials, with all examination of Allied crimes excluded, is utter humbug.'

In 1938, Crichton had found out that his legal training didn't matter. He had been taken to court for reporting, accurately, that a press baron's son had attended a charity supper with some friends, including a Lady Violet Hunsford. Some lines down, he mentioned that the press baron's son had bid 36 guineas for a vase. The press baron's lawyers claimed that the article was defamatory because it suggested that the son had in effect been bidding for Lady Violet. While dismissing the suit as verging on the malicious, the judge had shown his irritation by omitting to award costs to either party. To pay his legal fees, Crichton and his wife Rosemary had lost their house in John Street, and had ended up 'camping out in two rooms overlooking theatrical warehouses in Macklin Street, off Covent Garden, where the prostitutes used to live'.

The car pulled up. 'This is it,' said Hans.

Cotton had never been to the Garrick Club before. He found a large, stolidly grey, pseudo-classical building in Garrick Street. Inside, various male staff exuded a hush of respect for their charges.

With a white bust of Shakespeare to his right, Cotton gave his business to a porter. 'Peter Cotton, to see Mr Miles Crichton.'

'Mr Crichton is expecting you, Colonel.'

He was ushered up the main stairs. Cotton had never liked eighteenth-century colours, particularly what he thought of as stagnant cesspool green. There were portraits on the walls. These included the images of one or two women. Otherwise, the Garrick was an entirely male preserve.

Miles Crichton was in the cocktail bar, fast asleep in a round-armed chair in a dark corner. Arranged in a line on the table in front of him were three empty champagne glasses. Tucked between himself and the arms of the chair were his crutches. From a distance, Cotton saw how the Cat and Bagpipes name had come about. Crichton was dressed in an ancient blue chalk-stripe suit and wore a red bow tie just visible below his slumped chin. Add on his small-featured face, his roundish head and smoothed back hair, a hunched, neckless look, and the crutches, and there was something of a cat sitting on bagpipes with the chanter and drones sorted out.

The porter cleared his throat and Miles Crichton woke instantly. He had large blue eyes. He smiled.

'Colonel!'

'Not any more, Mr Crichton.'

'Don't you believe it,' said Crichton. He held

out his hand. Cotton shook it, and found that the cripple had a deliberate and exceptionally powerful grip. Crichton smiled again and summoned the barman. 'Same again all round, please.' And then to Cotton, 'Won't you sit down?'

Cotton nodded and sat. The report had said Crichton's legs were like an eight-year-old's. Not true. They were as thin as an eight-year-old's, but longer and twisted.

'An advantage to being a cripple is the tremendous saving on shoe repairs,' said Miles Crichton. He leant towards Cotton. 'The advantage of having a tall young man from Intelligence come to see you is . . . well, I shall of course over-egg you, in a portentous and shadowy way. But I will not give your name. I will call you my Colonel from the Secret Service. It adds steel. The Garrick is not noted for its physically courageous members, but a few of them have imagination or suspicion or easily stirred fears. What do you say?'

'I'd prefer some discretion,' said Cotton.

Miles shook his head. 'Not part of my valour, sorry. I like the idea of protection and I will make shameless use of you to get it.'

Cotton smiled. The champagne arrived.

'Cheers,' said Miles. He downed his glass like medicine. 'How can I help?'

Cotton came straight to the point. 'Major Albert Briggs MP has a salary almost exactly the same as mine. I know how I'm getting on so I'd be interested to know how he can afford to own a house for his wife in his constituency, another for his mistress in Bognor, and how he can have his daughter privately educated – all while keeping a flat in Dolphin Square for himself and running what is described as a private intelligence service. Eight years ago he was a retired sergeant-major without any property or prospects.'

'You're suggesting that's quite a short time and there's been a war in the middle?'

'A short time certainly. The war, on the other hand, provided some with opportunities.'

Miles Crichton smiled. 'Didn't it just!' He paused. 'I think to do what Major Briggs has done,' he said, 'you have need of an awfully good solicitor. Might I suggest Alfred Perlman?'

Cotton waited. 'Just one man? Nobody else?'

Miles Crichton started. 'Dear God, you can't say "just Alfred". For one thing he's quite phenomenally stout, legs like a hippo and the lugubrious, hangdog face of someone just breathing to get to his next meal. Alfred is the same age as Jesus at the crucifixion, looks quite twenty years older, but probably has more down-to-earth influence. Are you going to drink that champagne?'

Cotton pushed the champagne glass towards him. 'Go ahead. What brought them together?'

Miles lifted Cotton's glass. 'Oh, I really think we can give Herr Hitler the credit for that, don't you? Whatever else Adolf did, he contrived to start a social revolution here, sent the class cat amongst the privileged pigeons, blurred many, many boundaries. Lawyer Alfred and the man to be Major Bertie met in the very same gunnery unit and, surrounded by sandbags, over mugs of tea, buffing up a 3.7-inch QF gun or two, from time to time loosing off a shot at a Nazi bomber plane, realized they could help each other out. Now Briggs is Alfred's "in" to Parliament and much bigger contacts, and Alfred takes care of Major Bertie's finances.'

Cotton nodded. 'I take it he is not just a good manager.'

'Alfred looks after one of the biggest property estates in London, has discretionary powers, can sign cheques, that sort of thing. He's also awfully good with rich widows.'

'You're reading between the lines?'

Miles Crichton frowned. 'I don't deal in gossip,' he complained. 'I deal in the omitted history.'

'Forgive me,' said Cotton, 'there's a lot of that about.'

'But not in the real world!' said Miles. 'Understand. Alfred takes care of people. He gets rid of his clients' "impurities", he oils their self-importance. Behind that gross exterior is a slim, elegant legal Fred Astaire. His wits are as quick as Fred's feet.'

Cotton smiled, but Crichton thought he was not taking this seriously enough.

'Take the Inland Revenue,' he said. 'I don't know about you, but they scare the shit out of me. To Alfred they are splendid chums in the struggle for fairness and social justice. If they're lucky they keep up with him, as Ginger does in "Cheek to Cheek", and don't notice the feathers coming off her dress – quite enough to line several nests. They are happy, the widows really want to be happy and I'd suggest there's a profitable gap in the middle. More champagne?'

Cotton nodded and Miles Crichton waved at the barman.

'Alfred allows his widows to feed him what he calls "delicacies". He's also rather fond of good-looking young men but limits himself to having them watch him as he toys with dainties. There's a wonderful story of him just after the war in France. Do you know what an ortolan is?'

Cotton remembered *ortolano* in Spanish. 'It's a tiny songbird. A kind of bunting?'

The champagne arrived. Miles took a sip to refresh himself, and leant back in his chair.

'Exactly. And a very great delicacy. You have to prepare it though. You catch it, you prick out its eyes, put it in a dark box and feed it on millet, grapes and figs. After a month it has swollen to about the size of a goutish thumb. You then kill it. You drown it in Armagnac, pluck it, season with salt and pepper and pop it into a high oven for eight minutes. You then use your napkin as a kind of wimple, wear it over the head to form a private cocoon – or as if you had a head cold – so that nothing of the exquisite aroma and taste escapes. You eat it whole, though some bite the head off

73

first, bones and all. I imagine there is, for the very sensitive, a kind of evaporated puff from those minute Armagnac-soaked lungs.'

Cotton's eyebrows had come up. 'I see,' he said.

'No, you don't,' said Miles. 'Think about it. How long do we normally chew? A few seconds at best. An ortolan takes about two minutes to eat. That's a very long mouthful of bliss. Of course, it is all a bit High Church for me. A two-minute orgasm for a man would, I think, be rather alarming.' He paused. 'When the war was over, Alfred found it expedient to go to France to check out a client's vineyards. He gave six weeks' notice and brought his own embroidered napkin.'

'Have you met him?'

'Very briefly. Here actually.'

'What did he say?'

'Whisky is always kosher.'

'Is that a joke?'

'No, no. Apparently whisky is kosher whoever prepares it.'

'What about songbirds?'

'I don't think they are prohibited by a dietary law,' said Miles, 'but I imagine certain decencies are observed. I don't think they'd be eaten when children or maiden aunts were present.'

Cotton smiled. 'What's his background?'

'His father was an immigrant, from Lithuania, a tailor. A hard-working invisible mender, if you know what I mean, quiet and careful to the point of timidity. But his mother! Doughty as unleavened

74

dough, indulgent as sugar mice! He has a half-witted brother, you see, who soaked up most of the family money. So in the family arithmetic Alfred became a brain and a half. Won scholarships. I never understand why people don't see that scholarship boys can be imaginative and perceptive as well as obedient and bright. They must be associating scholarships with charity. But Alfred saw very early on that his clients' ability to be charitable had often been preceded by a crime. And crimes are always crude, however they are dressed a couple of generations on.' Miles Crichton waggled a finger. 'Don't underestimate Alfred. He knows you get one life and does not care about his reputation after his is over, just as long as his clients in this life are kept happy and he gets to eat ortolan.'

He paused. 'There is some suggestion he assigned his soul to the devil before he even reached puberty – and then beat him to the dinner table. Alfred knows what he is. He's a very talented, extraordinarily practical lost soul.'

CHAPTER 7

Cotton's contact at London Metropolitan Special Branch was a Sergeant Dawkins. Cotton was told his name was Dickie, that he dressed in plain clothes and consequently should not be addressed by rank 'in public situations'.

Dickie Dawkins suggested they meet at the church of St Martin-in-the-Fields, on the north-east side of Trafalgar Square. Cotton was unsure whether or not this was Dawkins's idea of neutral ground. In his mid thirties, quite short, Dawkins had a fresh, slightly chubby face that made him look fatter than he was, and a lot of straight, dark hair that flopped when the water he used when combing it had dried out. He was standing outside the church two columns along watching, without signs of obvious enjoyment, a Chinese family celebrate a christening and drew Cotton's attention by the spit and polish of the toecaps of his shoes.

'Mr Dawkins? My name is Cotton.'

Dawkins nodded. 'Colonel,' he said.

'No, no,' said Cotton. 'That was only during the war. My name is Peter Cotton now.'

He paused, smiled, and held out a hand to Dawkins.

Dawkins gave his hand a quick tug. 'Dickie Dawkins,' came in a mumble.

'Delighted to meet you,' said Cotton. 'Are we going in?'

Dawkins blinked. 'Do you want to?'

'Not particularly.'

'Right,' said Dawkins. 'It's a famous piece of architecture,' he added.

'Yes,' said Cotton. 'James Gibbs, wasn't it? The architect, I mean.'

'I believe so. Very influential.' Dawkins paused. 'In the US particularly.' He frowned. 'Do you have an interest in church architecture?' he asked.

'None at all,' said Cotton. 'Nil.'

Dawkins laughed. 'Right,' he said.

'We'll walk then.'

'Just one second.'

The Chinese family was going down the steps.

'Do you see the baby has a board at the back of his head? The Chinese like that bit of a boy's head flat. It's their idea of beauty. So they encourage it while the skull is still soft.'

Cotton nodded. 'You've worked with the Chinese?'

'My first job,' said Dawkins. 'Before the war in the East End. They got bombed out and moved to Soho – Wardour Street and round there.'

'And what have you been doing recently?'

'Black market,' said Dickie Dawkins. 'We've just closed a clothing coupon operation. But we're still swamped, you know. You've seen the figures, I suppose.'

77

Cotton nodded. It had been made public that the level of recorded crimes had increased tenfold in a period of twenty years. That obscured the point that the bulk of the increase had taken place during and particularly in the eighteen months after the war.

'Yes, I know. What you're involved in now is more to do with national security than criminal activity. I think you could take it as a vote of confidence.'

Dawkins looked doubtful.

'What have they said to you?' asked Cotton.

'That you'd fill me in.'

'Anything else?'

'Sir?'

'Please. My name is Cotton.'

'Yes, Mr Cotton.'

'There's an officer called Radcliffe in Special Branch.'

'Inspector Radcliffe? Yes. He works there.'

'Do you know what he does?'

Dawkins looked less uncomfortable than disapproving that he was being asked about a colleague. 'I don't rightly know,' he said.

'What he does or whether you can say what he does?'

Dawkins blinked.

'It's all right,' said Cotton. 'What I really want to know is whether or not Mr Radcliffe has spoken to you or whether he knows of this meeting.'

'He hasn't spoken to me. Why would he?'

Cotton smiled. 'Good. Mr Radcliffe and a Mr Starmer-Smith of MI5 are about to start a campaign aimed at . . . discouraging the homo-sexual community in sensitive jobs.'

Dawkins made a face.

'I know. I wasn't thrilled either,' said Cotton. 'Part of our job, however, is to see that this doesn't occupy too many men or prove too much of a distraction.'

Dickie Dawkins shut his eyes for a moment. 'Can I be honest?' he said. 'If I had a choice, I wouldn't touch this with a barge pole.'

'Agreed,' said Cotton. 'What can you tell me about Radcliffe?'

'Not much. He went to a minor public school.'

'What does that mean?'

Dawkins blinked. 'Most of us didn't.'

'Right. Anything else?'

'He has an interest in Greyhound pubs.'

'Yes. In Croydon, for example.'

Dawkins nodded. 'I understand he has a man there. But there are other Greyhounds, you know. There's one in Carshalton, quite high class, another in Streatham. And in Battersea, of course.'

Cotton's eyes widened. 'What? Find a Greyhound and you find succour and a male friend? Are you serious?'

Dawkins shrugged. 'Well, it's not entirely Radcliffe's choice, let's be fair.'

Cotton sighed. 'Would you know his man in Croydon?'

'You're joking?'

79

Cotton shook his head, mostly at Ayrtoun's method of communication. He wondered whether Derek was working two agencies. It wouldn't have surprised him.

'We have been given a name,' he said. 'Operation Sea-Snake. I'm described as a liaison officer. We'll have to find out what that means. At present I'm taking that to mean I work with you. You have close knowledge of London. I don't.' Cotton was not sure Dawkins believed him. 'I'm familiar with the bit between Whitehall and Sloane Square.'

'Ah. Right,' said Dawkins.

'I've also been asked to keep an eye on a certain Member of Parliament. Major Albert Briggs.'

Dawkins shook his head. 'No. Whatever else he is, Briggs is not like that.'

'Apparently his interest is in smut in general and photography in particular.'

Dawkins groaned. 'Do you have children?' he said.

'No. You?'

'I have two little girls. April and June, six and four.' He made a face.

Cotton nodded. 'I understand. But we don't actually know what is going to happen.'

Dawkins frowned. 'You're telling me to wait?'

'Something like that. Will that do for now?'

Dawkins thought. 'Yes. All right.' He sighed. 'You're being honest.'

'Yes.'

Dawkins winced. 'Honesty has its drawbacks.'

'I know that too,' said Cotton. 'So far I've spoken to a patrician American who's difficult to understand, a heavy-drinking journalist who may just embellish his anecdotes, and a driver I've been given who is German and now lives with a Tory councillor who is also director of a football club.'

Dawkins smiled. 'Can I be honest too?'

'Of course.'

'Queer business is never good for a career.'

'That's probably true.'

Dawkins smiled. It looked like an involuntary reflex, a twitch. He offered his hand and Cotton shook it. The handshake was brief and polite. Dawkins shrugged.

'Do you use your sweet ration?' he said.

'No,' said Cotton. 'I'll bring them along after Christmas.'

Cotton watched Dawkins walk away. He thought Ayrtoun might have had a point in trying to depress him. He was able to think this while not thinking any better of Ayrtoun.

CHAPTER 8

Cotton had already told his father of Joan's present. He carried the box down to Peaslake after work on Monday, 23 December. The morning of the 24th he had taken off.

'This is all a bit Red Cross,' said James Cotton.

'I didn't see any meat at all when I passed the butcher's here. There was a "closed for the holidays" sign.'

His father shook his head. 'Damned bad show,' he said.

Cotton began removing tins and placing them in piles. Meat, vegetables, fruit. His sister had even included a tinned cake.

'She's stealing from me,' said James Cotton.

Cotton frowned. 'Who is?'

'No, not her. Her daughter.'

It turned out that the lady who cleaned and cooked for his father, Mrs Douglas, had developed what James Cotton called a 'bad leg. I don't know what it is exactly.' To help her out, she had brought along her daughter Maisie.

'How old are we talking?'

'I don't know.' James Cotton paused. 'She must

82

have left school,' he added. 'She's quite buxom in a vulgar sort of way.'

Cotton considered his father. Having become a widower in 1938, he had retired from Mexico in 1939 into a world war. At sixty-seven he was beginning to look pinched, bent and old. His speech, when not being mean, had started to dither as if he needed a little acid to be clear.

'Why are you saying this?'

'I'm a banker,' said James Cotton. 'I tot up. I began to notice – deficiencies.'

'From your wallet?'

James Cotton shook his head. 'Coinage,' he said primly.

Cotton stifled a sigh, but his father had not finished.

'She's quite clever, you know. I left the milk money in the hall. She didn't touch that, oh no. But I put a shilling on the mantelpiece in the drawing room beside the Christmas cards. That went, all right.'

'Did she dust under the cards?'

His father looked more confused than offended. 'What *do* you mean?'

'Either you were checking on her dusting or putting temptation in her way.'

James Cotton did not like this interpretation of his behaviour. 'I defy you,' he said, 'to find the shilling.'

'Have you given Mrs Douglas a Christmas present?'

'Under the circumstances I felt—'

'I don't like tinned peaches. Do you?'

'Not particularly. Why do you ask?'

'I thought I'd drop in on Mrs Douglas. I'll give her the peaches from Joan's Christmas hamper and have a little chat.'

'I see,' said James Cotton. 'All right. You do understand, don't you? I don't want to be taken advantage of. This kind of thing did not happen when I was your age.'

Cotton did not bother to reply. Later he found a Christmas card, got his father to sign it, added his own signature and expressed good wishes to the Douglas family. After a second's doubt he enclosed a pound note instead of ten shillings – he thought Mrs Douglas probably deserved more than Derek Jennings outside the Astoria in Purley.

On Christmas Eve he picked up the tin of peaches and drove down to the village in his father's Riley.

Mrs Douglas lived in one of a short row of small, brick and flint cottages. Without the roses and sweet peas of summer, the place looked wilfully crooked and bleak. Cotton knocked at the door.

'Oh, Colonel Cotton,' said Mrs Douglas.

'No Colonel now, Mrs Douglas. I've come to wish you and your family a very merry Christmas.'

He handed over the card.

'I'm sorry about this,' he said, offering the tin of peaches, 'we're not very good at wrapping. This is from my sister Joan in America. I'm sorry too

84

that we're doing this so late. My father's getting a bit forgetful.'

'This is very kind, sir,' said Mrs Douglas. 'Would you – like a cup of tea?'

'You're very kind, Mrs Douglas.'

Cotton went in. Mrs Douglas shifted the kettle on the range.

'Tell me about your leg, Mrs Douglas.'

'Oh,' said Mrs Douglas, 'it's a silly old leg.'

It was considerably swollen and had been wrapped round with a crepe bandage from ankle to knee.

'Do you know what the problem is?'

'Varicosities,' said Mrs Douglas. 'I caught one of them and it leaks a bit. Nothing grand.'

'Have you seen a doctor?'

'Well, not really,' said Mrs Douglas.

'You haven't, have you?'

'It is an expense, you know, sir.'

'Are you waiting for the new Health Service?'

'That was my intention, sir.'

'You don't think you might need treatment before that?'

Mrs Douglas made a face. The kettle whistled. Mrs Douglas made some tea.

Cotton sighed. 'Mrs Douglas, my father's getting on and he's become a little reduced and worried about himself. I had an aunt who wanted to give everything away when she got old. My father is the reverse. Do you understand me?'

Mrs Douglas frowned. 'I think so, sir.'

85

'I mean he's anxious about losing control of things. He's even frightened of people taking advantage of him. Can I be honest? He can be insecure enough to sound a little mean-spirited. He can be forgetful. And since he used to look after other people's money, he keeps counting his own.'

Mrs Douglas looked rather pained. 'But he is a good, kind man,' she said.

'That's what I'm saying. Just that he gets a little forgetful and can be even a little ratty about it. He doesn't like change. He forgets where he put things, often imagines the worst.'

Mrs Douglas looked as if she no longer knew what to say. Cotton took advantage of that.

'He finds it difficult to respond to other people,' he said. 'He gets emotional and upset. He doesn't like seeing you like this. But on the other hand he gets unsettled, even suspicious, if there are other people in his home. So what I'm going to do is this. Call in on the doctor and get you an appointment. My father will gladly pay for the treatment.'

Cotton smiled. 'In one way, it's a little selfish. I'm only sorry this wasn't done before.'

'Oh,' said Mrs Douglas. 'It's a lot to ask.'

'But you haven't asked, have you?'

'No, sir. Milk? Sugar?'

'Neither, thanks,' said Cotton.

Mrs Douglas was surprised but poured. She liked, Cotton saw, very strong tea.

'Thank you, Mrs Douglas.'

Mrs Douglas also liked lots of milk. Instead of rationed sugar she used honey as a sweetener. She appeared a little more relaxed or at least relieved and talked about her husband, Walter, a farm worker, her son, an apprentice at the local butcher's, and her daughter who wanted to be a hairdresser. She also said her children wanted to move to Australia.

'My husband's not so keen,' she said. 'It's a big change.'

'I'm sure it is worth thinking about,' said Cotton.

'And I've got your father.'

Cotton shook his head. 'My sister Joan is trying to get him to move to the USA.'

'Is she now?'

Cotton had found Mrs Douglas almost grue-somely deferential. The local doctor was not. A tweedy old party called Powell, fond of shooting, with considerable faith in phrenology and his own bluff dignity, he showed no surprise to see Cotton.

'Ah, Cotton,' he said. 'I was wondering if your father would say anything.'

'About what?'

'My guess? Congestive heart failure.'

'Did you tell him that?'

'Not in so many words. I just said his ticker was showing its age. He'd been complaining of breathlessness, you see. And his legs don't work so well any more.' He looked up. 'It's not operable. I am keeping an eye on him. I'm giving him a little rat poison to thin his blood. You should keep an eye on his legs. If they swell up or anything like that—'

'Does that mean he's liable to suffer a heart attack or a stroke?'

Dr Powell made a face. 'If I'm right and it is congestive heart failure, it's other organs you have to worry about. The kidneys mostly, though there is always the liver.' He looked up. 'Can't really give you a timescale. He could chug on for quite a bit yet. On the other hand, if he is lucky, he could pop off quite quickly.'

'All right,' said Cotton. 'Thank you for that. Now I have another question. My father is looked after by a Mrs Douglas.'

'Down in those cottages?'

'Yes. She has a problem with one of her legs. As far as I understand, her varicose veins leak and she caught one vein on something sharp.'

Dr Powell shrugged. 'Those damned socialists are bringing in a health service. Why doesn't she wait for that?'

'Because I work in town and need her to be looking after my father.'

'Right,' said Dr Powell. 'Right you are. Are you taking this matter on then?'

'I am,' said Cotton. He got out his card. 'This is my address. You will bill me, please.'

Dr Powell took the card but then looked doubtful. 'I hate to mention this but, well, your father – how shall I put this?'

'Hasn't posted his cheque?'

'I imagine something like that.'

'Thank you, Doctor. I'll find out what's happened and get it dealt with. My telephone number is on the card in case you need to contact me.'

'You see?' said Dr Powell. 'This health service thing can't hope to compete with the doctor–family relationship already in existence.'

Cotton nodded but did not answer. 'What time will I tell Mrs Douglas her appointment is for?'

Dr Powell looked startled.

'She hasn't got a telephone, you see.'

'No, quite.' Dr Powell looked at his diary. 'I'm shooting on Tuesday,' he said.

'Monday then.'

Dr Powell flicked back a page. 'Four thirty?' he said.

'That's absolutely splendid,' said Cotton. 'Thank you so much, Doctor. I really want her in top form as soon as possible. My father needs it.'

'Yes, of course,' said Dr Powell. 'I can see your point of view. Quite.'

Cotton drove back to the cottages, told Mrs Douglas her appointment with Dr Powell was at four thirty on Monday afternoon and that his father was paying the bill for the doctor and any prescriptions, but asked her not to say anything about it since she knew how withdrawn and sentimental he was getting.

'Oh, he's a proper gentleman,' said Mrs Douglas. She put her hand on Cotton's forearm. 'Thank you, sir,' she said.

Cotton shook his head.

'No,' said Mrs Douglas. 'Thank you for handling this matter so tactfully. I've been thinking about what you said. Maisie won't be going again.'

Cotton told his father he had arranged a doctor's appointment for Mrs Douglas.

'Why?'

'So she can get better.'

'I'm not paying.'

'I am.'

'What do you mean?'

'I said I'd meet the costs.'

'But you have other things to pay.'

'I do. But you don't want Maisie here again and Mrs Douglas is not fully fit, I thought we could at least get her better before she went off to Australia.'

'What are you talking about?'

'That life is changing. People are getting other choices. They're thinking of emigrating.'

'In Maisie's case, I imagine Australia would welcome her with open arms.'

Cotton ignored this. 'You do know you've never met your grandchildren? Joan has been asking you for years to visit them. Why don't you sail over when spring comes? In a couple of years' time you may find it too arduous.'

'I don't want to be any trouble.'

'Then the sooner you go the better.'

James Cotton frowned. 'Did the doctor say anything else?'

'About what?'

James Cotton grunted. 'No, no,' he said. 'That's all right.'

'Oh, he did say something about a bill.'

His father shook his head. 'I don't think he's a very good doctor. He *pretends* to understand, you know.'

Cotton smiled. 'Yes, he does give the impression of being happier shooting pheasants than treating patients.'

'All right. I'll deal with it. I say—'

'What?'

'I'm thinking perhaps someone should take a look at the basement. I haven't been down for years.'

Cotton went down to the basement and groaned. Electric wires hung from the rafters as if ready for Christmas decorations but carrying generations of spiders' webs instead. The large boiler, never used, was rusty, resembled some aged apparatus from the industrial revolution. He opened a hatch and peered in. The size of two cement mixers, the burning chamber contained some elderly silver ash. Cotton tracked the chimney. He was unsure whether or not the thing would still function, certainly with any safety, and did not know what fuel had originally been burnt. His father had stocks of wood but Cotton knew wood did not burn like coal. He was also aware the thing would need to be fed, something his father could not do.

He found some old packing straw, lit it and tossed it into the furnace. A few seconds later smoke issued from a crack in the furnace itself and a little after that from a crack in the flue. The house needed a new boiler, new wiring and probably new plumbing.

He went upstairs, washed dust off his hands and face and told his father.

'Yes,' said James Cotton calmly. 'I imagined that would be the case. I'm thinking of having the place improved, now that the war is over and things should start getting back to normal.'

'Good idea. Why don't you go ahead?'

Cotton wrote a letter to his sister:

Dear Joan

Once again, very many thanks for the Christmas parcel. Very much appreciated, since supplies here are even worse than last year.

The local doctor has told me he thinks our father has heart problems – congestive heart failure is his initial diagnosis. It is not clear quite how bad this is but he is looking thin and tired and his temper is not too festive.

Of course I am aware that you and Todd have been encouraging him to visit you for a long time. May I suggest we organize it for him, get him a passage on a liner for spring, April say, so that he can spend a couple of months with you? The weather at that time of year shouldn't be too hot for him and, you never know, once he sees your children, he may get out of himself more. We could also get another medical opinion, from a doctor with a more positive interest in his patients and some grasp of the relationship between fee and the quality of his professional attention.

Cotton felt some relief when he had sealed and addressed the envelope, probably at the prospect of being free of his father for a spell.

On Christmas Day – they had agreed not to exchange presents – they ate tinned chicken soup, tinned ham and tinned asparagus from the USA. They managed to blind bake some pastry and fill it with tinned pears.

'A long time since we've eaten like this,' said James Cotton. 'The Americans do have a sweet tooth though, don't they? I feel sorry for your generation, you know.'

'Why?'

'You're having to grow up rather late.'

Cotton smiled. 'What exactly are you talking about?'

'That while wars are drastic, gruesome, brutal and all the rest of it, they are also rather simple. Live or die, really. What you've all missed is the kind of experience of the world that allows you to judge people when they're not hiding behind uniforms. It's not a good training for the rest of your life.'

'Do you resent us?'

'On the contrary. Rather grateful, of course. I'm merely pointing out the drawbacks or costs involved. You've got to start all over again and your references are out of date.'

As James Cotton spoke the sound of wavering singing started up outside.

James Cotton groaned. 'It's those bloody carol singers again.'

He got up and went out. When he came back he shook his head.

'I gave them money rather than punch.'

Cotton nodded. 'Are you now advising me to get out of what I am in?'

James Cotton considered. 'No. I was just thinking you're looking rather drawn. I wondered whether or not it was stress. Dealing with the great and the good, I suppose.'

'Not so great and not so good.'

His father smiled. 'There is something to be said for a quiet life, you know. A quiet life is usually quite stressful enough. There's something I want to listen to on the radio.'

'You do that,' said Cotton.

CHAPTER 9

Back at work on 27 December, Cotton found that Miles Crichton had been right to suggest that Major Briggs had a manager. Alfred Perlman had sent him a note. Perhaps Colonel Cotton would like to call in at his office at 6 p.m. that evening.

At 5.50, Cotton walked up the hill from his office and into Jermyn Street. The Turkish baths the novelist Trollope had frequented in the nineteenth century had been bombed in 1941. There were a couple of tiles still left on the cleared bombsite. The other Turkish baths in the street, at 92 and still functioning, was almost opposite Alfred Perlman's office or chambers. There was a discreet but highly polished brass plaque for Perlman & Eaves. He rang the bell and was let into the building.

The office was on the main floor. A trim, white-haired lady let Cotton in. She accompanied him to a double door, knocked and went straight in.

'Mr Cotton to see you, sir,' she said and withdrew.

Alfred Perlman was on his feet and mostly

dressed in formal evening wear. A middle-aged lady was in front of him, one knee on a chair, trying to tie his white tie. The lawyer did not shake hands, instead held out his fingers as if about to put them in a finger bowl. The fingers made three wearily small shooing gestures.

'Do sit,' he said. 'I'm late for an important function. I'm always late.'

Alfred Perlman sounded as if he had a blocked nose.

'I think we need that chin up a bit,' said the lady.

Alfred Perlman held up a hand.

'What would be the direction of any conversation you might have with my distinguished client?'

He then pushed his chin upwards. The lady used one hand to push up his jowls and sighed. She needed two hands for the tie.

'Largely to avoid misunderstandings,' said Cotton. 'We also want to avoid possible embarrassment or working at cross purposes. And, of course, to assist in the resolution of any conflict that might arise involving national security interests, party interest and the sovereignty of Parliament.'

Cotton thought his mother would have described what he had just said as 'absolute, if reasonably fluent, tosh'. He would have agreed, but was interested to see whether or not this was Alfred Perlman's sort of language.

Still with his face towards the ceiling, Alfred gave him to understand he was not displeased but needed more. That hand gave a languid cranking gesture.

'You will know, I hope,' Cotton went on, 'that I'm neither with MI5 nor MI6 but have been seconded from another intelligence agency. I'd also point out that your distinguished client's keen interest in security matters is known to other, foreign agencies, including the Americans and the Soviets. A meeting would allow me to run over certain checks – entrapment and other dangers. I'm not saying your client is unaware of these dangers, simply that if the Intelligence Services are clear he knows of potential pitfalls, there will be less possibility of misunderstandings.

The lady had finished with the tie. She stood up.

'Mirror,' said Alfred Perlman.

It had taken a little time for Cotton to see that Alfred Perlman was not tall, perhaps five foot eight, because he was so corpulent. Now that the lady had moved he could see how extraordinarily stout the lawyer's legs were. He had a belly certainly but then tapered to quite small shoulders. There was then that dewlap, the large head and a slack lower lip.

'That looks fine,' said the lady.

'If you say so, Miss Marx,' said Alfred Perlman. 'Tails.'

The lady helped him get into his tail coat. This took some time. The room was clubby. There was a large whitish fireplace, a partner's desk, three walls were dark green, the other dark red and there was some art. An etching, possibly by Rembrandt, of Jews in Holland, a painting of a horse, certainly a potential Stubbs, and a portrait of a lady in the style at least of Gainsborough. There was also an example of modern art but not very brightly coloured – Ben Nicholson perhaps? – and a large number of silver-framed photographs of Alfred and one, sometimes two, of the great and good. Cotton realized they were arranged according to activity. There were a lot of politicians on a rectangular table. On an oval side table were a number of financiers and refugee royalty. But on another, round table there was Alfred Perlman with Chaim Weizmann, then with the contralto Kathleen Ferrier beside a microphone and, right at the front, with Anna Neagle, the actress in a flying outfit when playing Amy Johnson in a film.

'Are we ready?' said Alfred Perlman.

Miss Marx stood back and examined.

'Yes, we are, sir.'

Alfred grunted. 'I'm late,' he said again. He nodded. As he moved forward his hand came up again. Cotton had the impression he had passed some test, though also thought he was being told to wait.

When Alfred had left the room, Miss Marx moved the chair she had knelt on.

'May I get you anything, sir?'

From the other room Cotton heard 'The car is waiting for you, sir.'

'I was thinking of leaving,' he said.

'One moment, sir.'

Miss Marx left and came back with a card. One side bore Alfred Perlman's official telephone numbers. On the other, handwritten in pencil, were two more.

'The top one is Mr Perlman's private telephone number. The lower is my own.' She paused. 'Given Mr Perlman's commitments—'

'It might be better to telephone you first should the need arise?'

'Yes, sir.' She fetched a blank index-sized card for Cotton to put down his own telephone numbers.

'O for Office, P for Private and S for Secretary please.'

Cotton shared a secretary. Her name was Phyllis and it was very easy for her to feel overworked.

'I'm going to leave off the S for now,' he said.

Miss Marx beamed. 'Entirely as you wish, sir.'

In Jermyn Street Cotton looked around and stepped down.

'I say! Is that you, Peter?'

Cotton looked up. Coming out of the Turkish baths on the opposite side of the street was someone familiar but not by name any more. Cotton briefly tried to place him.

'Hang on! I'll be directly over.'

'Hang on' did it. This was what George Dyce had said when they had been training near Dumbarton about four years before. George was a younger son of a wealthy family and had cheerfully described himself as 'bone from the neck up'. He had found map-reading difficult. Tall, about six three, he had wavy fair hair, a strong jaw line and very pale blue eyes. He pointed at them.

'I went in this morning with bags under my eyes like a Great Dane's balls. How do they measure up now, do you think? Labrador? Jack Russell?'

'Pekinese,' said Cotton.

'Christ!' said George Dyce. 'Have my eyes closed up?'

'Would you accept chihuahua?'

George Dyce laughed. 'Chihuahua,' he repeated. 'That's good. The man put on some greasy stuff. Professional boxers use it apparently.' He blinked, then frowned. 'I have to go out again tonight.' He paused. 'Is your club round here? You're not a Carlton Club chap, are you? White's?'

'No clubs,' said Cotton. 'My office is nearby.'

'Who do you work for?'

'The Colonial Office. Sterling Area.'

George looked impressed. 'Would that be brainy stuff?'

'I'd hardly say that, George. How about you?'

'Schmoozing for the family bank,' he said. He blinked. 'I'm sacrificing my liver for profit.'

Cotton smiled. 'It's nearly seven,' he said.

George frowned. 'What? I say, you're not trying to get rid of me, are you?'

'No,' said Cotton. 'I was wondering what time you were meeting your clients.'

George looked at his watch. 'Oh damn,' he said. He groaned. 'I really do have to be off. But look, I'm having a Hogmanay party. Should be lots of fun. Where do you live?'

'Wilbraham Place.'

'Wonderful! I'm nearby, in Cadogan Square! That's settled then. You really must come.' George paused. 'Shit,' he said.

'What is it?'

'I can't remember. Am I going to Quaglino's or to Mme Prunier's?'

Cotton nodded. 'That's easy, George. Bury Street is just down here. Call in – if you don't have a reservation at Quaglinos, you'll know it's Mme Prunier's.'

George frowned. 'I'm not entirely Bertie Wooster, you know.'

'And I'm not Jeeves,' said Cotton. 'I'm going that way. My office is only a few doors down from Prunier's.'

Cotton began walking and George followed.

'All right,' said George. 'I do have a card, you know.' He fiddled in his waistcoat pocket and took out a business card.

Cotton gave George Dyce his own.

'I'll send you an invitation,' said George.

'That's very kind,' said Cotton.

'No buts,' said George. 'None at all. I insist.'

'Are you all right?' said Cotton.

George groaned. 'I had a snifter, well two, after the steam.'

101

'Get some water into you.'

'Right,' said George. 'Of course, you are.'

Cotton went back to his office and wrote Ayrtoun a message: 'I need an excellent Secretary.'

CHAPTER 10

The next day around eleven in the morning Cotton received, on House of Commons stationery, an invitation to have luncheon with Major Albert Briggs MP at Fontwell Park on Saturday, 4 January 1947. 'Noon – sharp please.'

He wrote back and accepted. He booked Hans Bieber.

At 2 p.m. he received a reply from Ayrtoun. 'Agreed. Pick well.'

He had a meeting in Whitehall about the Sterling Area. As he was coming out he saw a young woman he recognized but could not place.

'Excuse me, Miss?' he called.

'Yes?'

Cotton remembered where he had seen her – in his old boss's office just before he had left for Washington in September 1945.

'How's D?' he said.

She frowned. 'I don't rightly know,' she replied. She grew a little more disapproving. 'He has retired to private life, you know.'

Cotton liked that. 'Yes. I did know that,' he said.

He took one of his cards out of his pocket and gave it to her.

'My name is Peter Cotton. I work at CI ops in St James's Street but have been seconded to something at home. I'm looking for a secretary who can be tough, discreet and who knows all the ropes. The operation has priority status, and I need someone to start in the New Year. I have no idea how long this will be for. Might I suggest, if you are interested, that you make your enquiries – but please, do let me know as soon as you can. Is that fair?'

The young lady considered. Cotton remembered now. Her first name was Moira. He did not know her surname. 'I don't know yet,' she said.

She struck him as solidly built. She gave off an air more of containment than contentment and was in no way ingratiating. Probably about his age, she had a set to her mouth that spoke of brisk no-nonsense, particularly where men were concerned.

'Thank you very much,' he said.

That evening he received her note. Miss Moira Kelly would, in principle, be pleased to accept Colonel Cotton's offer of a job but wished to clarify some matters before making a formal acceptance.

He asked her to meet him after work next day and she chose tea at the Ritz. In the event she asked for coffee – 'it's some time since I had a proper cup' – and suggested that they be 'Miss Kelly' and 'Colonel Cotton'.

'I understand,' said Cotton. 'The only thing I'd point out, Miss Kelly, is that I'm no longer a Colonel.'

She looked at him as if he were being whimsical.

'I don't like being called Moira, sir, not at work. The advantage of keeping to the proprieties is that a degree of respect is also involved.'

She meant rank as much as proprieties. She had the tone of voice that Cotton knew as 'cut-glass'.

'Of course.'

Miss Kelly said she was from Devon, in the south-west of England. She described her father, rather airily, as 'the third son, the Vicar', and said she had had two brothers, both 'fighting men'. One had died of malaria and dysentery in the Burma campaign. The survivor was 'a submariner'. Her pronunciation sounded almost scornful, but Cotton understood she was proud of him. She herself had been recruited by D during the war from 'Navy maps' after 'a stint in Gibraltar'.

'Did you like that, Miss Kelly?'

'The work yes, Gibraltar no.'

'What have you been doing recently?'

'I'm not at liberty to say,' she replied.

'Good,' said Cotton. 'Why have you decided to accept this job?'

Miss Kelly's manner changed abruptly. 'It's a bit more sharp end than my present work, sir! And I hope it gives me a lot more to do.'

Cotton looked at her. It was not just her accent. Her choice of vocabulary was akin to a slap on a skittish horse's rump. He supposed that made a kind of sense.

'You are aware that the job may involve some delicate and some possibly unsavoury matters?'

She looked slightly shocked. 'I am not a prude, sir. Absolutely not.'

'Why didn't you like Gibraltar?'

'Too hot, sir. The weather, I mean.'

He nodded. 'Good, Miss Kelly. I look forward to working with you.' He held out his hand and, still with her gloves on, she shook it.

They agreed she would start on 2 January and that Cotton would see to what she called 'the transfer of my responsibilities'. Cotton had two main doubts: one, that he was taking advantage of her, giving her the chance to put her job above anything else; the second was that she might be furiously rather than calmly patriotic.

'I'm sorry to bring this up,' he said. 'While I don't know how long this operation will last, I am aware that we have lost valuable people to marriage and other priorities, children and so on.'

Miss Kelly blinked. 'I assure you, Colonel, I have no intention of marrying at present.' She smiled. 'It would take a very special man to make me think I needed him.'

Cotton did not so much nod as bow.

'I've had an invitation,' said Cotton. 'Luncheon at a place called Fontwell Park. This Saturday.'

Miles Crichton was sitting in his usual chair.

'Ah,' he said, 'Briggs is giving you the racing man. Cloth caps and thoroughbreds. Of course, he has a local but rather proprietary interest in Fontwell.'

Cotton sat down. 'Is he on the board or committee?'

'No, no,' said Miles, 'he doesn't need that. Deference towards an MP is enough. It's his local racecourse, as it were, when he's in Bognor. In his constituency he goes to Uttoxeter.'

'Is that in Staffordshire?'

Miles smiled. 'So I believe. When he's here in town, he's fond of Sandown.'

Cotton gave up. 'Sorry. I have no idea where that is.'

'Esher in Surrey. You're not giving the impression of being a man of the turf.'

'I know horses are measured in hands. That's about it.'

'How delightful. You're not a gambler then.' Miles frowned. 'But you're not a Methodist or anything, are you?'

Cotton smiled. 'No, no. My mother taught me that small men in coloured jerseys on quadrupeds were not at all interesting. And then I studied economics.'

Miles Crichton laughed. 'Sport of Kings. And Major Bertie, of course. I think this deserves some champagne.' He raised a finger for service. 'Now how can I help you?'

'I thought you might be able to fill me in. How did Briggs contrive to make the move from retired sergeant-major in the Army Education Corps to an MP with an interest in security matters. What were the steps?'

Miles nodded happily. This was what he did. 'I suppose, I certainly hope, that you were far too busy during the war to register the book Sir Richard Acland published with Penguin in 1940. He gave it the title *Unser Kampf.*'

Cotton's eyebrows came up. 'As opposed to *Mein Kampf?* Our Struggle rather than My Struggle?'

'Exactly! Some notion of that decent, old collective "we" chaps against that awfully selfish "I" person. It sold 150,000 copies.'

Cotton shook his head. 'I missed it,' he said.

Miles laughed. 'Sir Richard, you see, has a talent for conversion. While he was Liberal MP for Barnstaple, he became first a Christian and then a socialist. That means he prefers the term Common Ownership to Socialism, and for moral rather than economic reasons.' Miles shrugged. 'He's basically a patrician getting his tweeds into a very sincere twist in a way I usually associate with older men. He's only about forty now. Terribly against private property as the root not only of evil but of untoward behaviour. In 1944 he gave away his own country estate at Killerton in Devon. Over six thousand acres and two hundred cottages.'

'Who to?'

'Well,' said Miles, 'we don't really have peasant farmers, do we? So he gave it to the next best thing in this country, the National Trust. The have-nots can visit what the haves used to have. I imagine his family is absolutely livid. There has been a suggestion it was something of a publicity stunt for his new party.'

A waiter brought two glasses of champagne and a small dish of cashew nuts. Cotton smiled. 'Go on,' he said.

Miles picked up a glass and drained it. 'Sir Richard also founded a political movement. Forward March – I don't know if you've heard of it? Scouting for those of voting age. All rather serious if knobbly-kneed. He even announced that Hitler had stumbled on some good points – he rather liked the idea of camps for shirkers.'

Cotton nodded. 'I've heard of Forward March,' he said. 'How does that fit in with Briggs?'

'When Sir Richard was trotting around the country scattering his well-meaning disciplinarian fairy dust, some of it settled on Major Bertie. He'd done his eighteen years in the army. He had a little pension and was getting nostalgic for some sort of command and imposed respect. He also liked concepts like professional ethics and an ideal of service to describe his own past. He had nothing against a rousing hymn either. For a man looking for a dignified future and a bit more money, he found himself uplifted and welcomed its grass roots politics.'

Miles paused and started on the second glass of champagne. 'You can't actually make this stuff up, you know.'

Cotton smiled. 'No, no. I appreciate that,' he said.

'Good,' said Miles. 'Well, Forward March joined the 1941 Committee to form a political movement called Common Wealth. In 1942, Common Wealth put up a candidate in a by-election at Maldon in Essex. They weren't actually doing quite the done thing, of course. The idea was that, during the war, by-elections were not contested. But they did and their bugger got in.' Miles paused. 'I use the word "bugger" advisedly. You've heard of Tom Driberg MP?'

Cotton nodded. 'Yes. I have.'

Driberg had been in the Communist Party until 1941 when an art historian called Blunt had exposed him as an MI5 agent. The reason Blunt knew, one he omitted to mention to his fellow Communists, was that he too was on MI5's payroll. Miles raised his eyes towards the discoloured eighteenth-century ceiling.

'Blunt is as pernickety as a butler checking a carriage clock for dust,' he said, 'and he rather agreed with Winston that Driberg was giving sodomy a bad name. Blunt was, of course, speaking up for all decent, art-loving, Communist sodomites everywhere.'

Cotton smiled.

'Driberg is absolutely reckless,' said Miles. In religion it's all communion and heavenly scented incense, but in matters of the flesh it's directly downstairs to the public urinals. He has his own

110

version of "a night on the tiles" but he's certainly not impractical. Comfortably before the '45 election he had moved to the Labour Party. The only thing Driberg and Acland share is a discomfort with the cantankerousness of the common man when he doesn't do what he is told and behave nobly. Sir Richard is now angling for a safe Labour seat for himself.'

Miles was thirsty. 'More champagne?' he suggested.

Cotton nodded. 'And Major Bertie?' he asked.

'Oh, he had moved on too, of course. You can't blame him. But most important of all, he had met Manny Shinwell, now the distinguished Minister of Fuel and Energy. Manny also helped him understand how voters might choose an MP who had come through the ranks.'

'Ah,' said Cotton. 'You're saying he's entirely Manny's man?'

'Oh yes. At the beginning, of course, Major Bertie couldn't speak for toffee,' said Miles. 'He sounded, I was told, as if he was trying to read a *Times* leader with the help of an invisible ouija board. Manny helped him with that. But I think it was Alfred Perlman who actually got him listening to Stanley Holloway.'

'Do you mean the actor?' said Cotton. '*This Happy Breed, The Way to the Stars*—?'

'More his salt-of-the-earth character monologues,' said Miles. 'Albert Ramsbottom. Sam Small.'

The champagne arrived. Miles drank his glass

and shrugged. 'The British are like everyone else. They don't want justice. They want more for those who deserve it. Themselves, usually. And lashings of sweet sentiment for everybody else. All Major Bertie had to do was make a few flattering adjustments for his constituents: "Are you ready? Lads! Are you ready? Ready for fighting men and working men to get what they fought and sweat for?" Pause. A small growl. "It's about f-f-flippin' time!" He had quite a witty line about crusts, you know, tired of "crusts tossed by toffs".' Miles looked up and smiled. 'Are you going to drink that champagne?'

'No,' said Cotton. 'Thanks, Miles.'

Miles laughed and took the glass. 'The Establishment moves. The only thing that really changes, however, is the style of the gold leaf laid on the rich British ordure.'

CHAPTER 11

On New Year's Eve Cotton went along to George Dyce's house in Cadogan Square. He found he had not been paying attention, and had failed to understand that on the death of his elder brother in the Battle of the Bulge, George had, as well as the London house, inherited very many Scottish acres of grouse moor and deer forest.

Cotton's mother had been Scottish, from Aberdeen, and had once told him that there was one thing worse than a snob. That was 'county' – 'Anglo-Scots landowners of an intelligence somewhere between feral and feudal'. She had mentioned a description Henry James had given of one of these men dancing in Highland dress. While it was true Henry James might have been easily upset, she thought the description 'terrifyingly accurate'.

George Dyce's house was like something out of a Henry James novel, full of heavy drapes and Victorian paintings, some of wildlife on moors, some of fairies in woods. Cotton had been told it was black tie but was one of the few men in black trousers. A lot of the others did not have ties at all but bits of white lace on velvet jackets above dress kilts. There were a number of women with tartan sashes.

Cotton also found George had a Happy Valley side to his family in Kenya. On arrival, a whisky was pushed into his hand and he was introduced to a group round a man in tartan trews called Hector, who was telling a story.

'Well, I woke,' Hector was saying. 'Bloody dark! But there's a strange shape by my bed. I hit it hard, damned hard, with the butt of my pistol. And what do I hear? "Oh, sah! Make you no hit me. Jacob he be sick. I bring you in his place!" It was his nephew with my morning tea. Twelve years old. Balls like a bull. Know what? Didn't spill a drop. I can't wait to get back.'

Hector held up his glass for a toast. 'Happy days!'

'When are you going?'

'Ten days!'

'Good for you,' said Cotton.

George – or Georgie – had organized what was called a traditional Scottish dinner. A dish of haggis and 'neaps' (turnips) was piped in and followed by venison and Atholl Brose.

At dinner Cotton was placed by an elderly gentleman dressed in black.

'How do you know George?' he was asked.

'From the army.'

'What was he like?'

'He had difficulty map-reading.'

The old man laughed. 'What do you do now?'

'I'm an economist in the Civil Service.'

'But why?'

'Just over a year ago I was in the US in Lord Keynes' baggage train. The woman I was going to marry died and I was offered a job here.'

'Have you thought of banking?'

'Only in the US. Here some banks have a lot of family in them.'

The old man smiled. 'I know what you mean,' he said. 'Oh, you'll be all right. I say, George's friends are rather rowdy, don't you think?'

For some of the party Cotton was shadowed by a heavy-footed girl in a buttercup-yellow gown and tartan sash who kept fiddling with her hair. At midnight she pressed him against a wall and browsed on and around his lips. At half past midnight the girl leered at him.

'Have you got a big cock?' she asked. 'I bet you have!'

'Damn!' said Cotton. 'I knew there was something I'd forgotten to put on my list of New Year resolutions.'

The girl stepped back and blinked. 'There's no need to be unfriendly, you know.'

Cotton saw his elderly dinner companion was leaving. 'No,' he said. 'It wouldn't be fair. I'm having a little medical treatment. But that's a secret, of course.'

The girl stared at him, raised her eyebrows

and then guffawed. 'Oh Christ,' she said. She then called out. 'I say! Peter's got the clap!'

'Sorry about that,' said George Dyce when he was seeing Cotton out. 'Should have warned you about my cousin. We call her Mimi Trousers, you know. A couple of drinks and her interest in male appendages comes to the fore.'

'Thank you,' said Cotton. 'It's been a lovely party.'

'You're a terrible liar.'

Cotton smiled. 'Not at all,' he said.

But George Dyce did not let it go. 'I meant it's odd that someone like you doesn't lie well.'

'Come on, George.'

'No, no. I understand you're involved in what they call the dark arts, hush-hush stuff.'

Cotton laughed. 'Life can't be that dreary for you, George.'

'No? The family bank – that old man you were talking to at dinner – has just said they don't want me any more. He could have waited till I wasn't drunk, don't you think? Now there's talk of my becoming the lowest of the low.'

'What's that?'

'A stockbroker.'

'My heart bleeds for you, George. I get to work for the Colonial Office and spend a lot of time on the Sterling Area. Drop in and see me. We can have stewed tea and divide a biscuit some time. And you can see how fascinating all those columns of figures are.'

116

George sighed. 'That's better,' he said.

'Happy New Year,' said Cotton.

'I say,' said George, frowning very sincerely, 'you will look after us, won't you?'

Cotton looked at him. Was this a joke? George looked maudlin.

'For fuck's sake, George. You've got a family bank to keep you warm.'

Cotton walked home. It was not far. He began the walk irritated and depressed, irritated that he had allowed himself to be depressed, thinking there had been times during the evening when he would have posted in his passport. By the time he arrived in Wilbraham Place he was looking forward to sleep and no work for the rest of 1 January 1947.

But when he let himself into the building he found Monsieur Shalhoub and his two little daughters downstairs. Monsieur Shalhoub worked in the Lebanese Embassy, had a square jaw, a thick moustache, but large, rather soft eyes. He spoke very quietly, with a breathy, slightly flat-tongued restraint. He was dressed in a dark blue velvet smoking jacket and was wearing monogrammed slippers. The girls were in coats, had rugs, a doll and a teddy bear.

'I am quite at my wits' end,' said Monsieur Shalhoub.

Cotton had to strain to hear him but did not really have to ask why. Shrieking noises and loud music were coming down the stairwell. He frowned and pointed at the board. The General's daughter, Margot Fenwick, was the Shalhoubs' neighbour.

'My girls, you see, are becoming a little alarmed, even agitated.'

Cotton looked. The tired little girls, about five and three years old, were huddled together on a sort of settle. Their eyelashes looked wet.

He held out his hand. 'Peter Cotton,' he said.

'I know. My name is Shalhoub, Michel.' Michel Shalhoub performed a minimal bow from the neck.

They shook hands. Monsieur Shalhoub did not believe in firm grips.

'Are you down here because you've called the police?' asked Cotton.

Monsieur Shalhoub considered this. 'I have been very near to calling them.'

'But you've forborne to do so until now?'

Monsieur Shalhoub shrugged. 'I had some doubts about whether, tonight of all nights, your admirable police force would have the available manpower for a caller with a foreign accent.'

'Have you spoken to Miss Fenwick's guests?'

'That was not successful,' said Monsieur Shalhoub. 'They opened the door but my suggestion that they reduce the level of noise was not welcomed.'

'I'm sorry?' said Cotton.

Monsieur Shalhoub almost mouthed. 'Well, they slammed the door, you see.'

Cotton nodded and looked at his watch – it was

118

one fifteen. He tried a smile on the little girls. 'They must be getting awfully tired,' he said. 'Would you like me to have a try?'

Monsieur Shalhoub was a diplomat. 'I can see that might be quite a good idea,' he said, 'but I should hate to put you to any inconvenience or impose on you when there might, after all, be a degree of personal risk involved. I have the impression that some of the guests have drunk a very great deal.'

'Too bad,' said Cotton.

Cotton went upstairs. He could hear Margot laughing as if she were being mercilessly tickled. Artie Shaw's *Everything is Jumpin'* was being played very loud. Cotton leant on the doorbell to Margot Fenwick's flat.

The bell was one of the shrill, peremptory kind, as penetrating as an alarm, but it took a good half-minute before the door was flung open. Cotton did not stop ringing the bell.

A small, red-haired man, wearing, with the help of a chin strap, an extraordinarily pink dildo on his head, white make-up on his face, and a black patch round his left eye staggered slightly and then squinted at him.

'Mr Faun?' asked Cotton. 'Or are you trying to be a unicorn?'

'What the hell do you think you're doing?'

'Isn't it obvious? I'm ringing the bell.'

The man winced. 'But what do you want? Do you want to come in?'

'No, no,' said Cotton. 'I was hoping to get Margot's attention.'

'I'm not sure I like your tone.'

'Good. We're making progress. Go and get Margot. Is she still upright?'

The man swayed and frowned. 'Oh God,' he complained, 'you're being manly.' He raised his chin. 'That's all over, I assure you. I was a conchie, you know. Mm? What did *you* do in the war?'

As he said this he tried, rather clumsily and slowly, to swing the door shut. Cotton moved forward and blocked the swing. The door juddered.

Cotton leant forward until he could see just how bloodshot the little man's eyes were.

'Whenever I was slitting children's throats, I always gave them a sweet beforehand so that they could go out on a happy gurgle. Have you got that? You're frightening children, Mr Peaceful. Time to stop.'

Behind him Margot appeared looking flushed and sweaty and uncomfortable. Though at least ten years older than Cotton, she behaved as if he were scolding her.

'I didn't invite quite so many people as this,' she said.

Cotton took his finger off the bell.

'I know you didn't.' He straightened up. 'Do you want any help? Moving them out, that is?'

Margot was confused or possibly just sulky.

'I thought he was going to punch me!' said the little man.

'Do you want any help, Margot?'

'No,' said Margot very quietly. 'No.'

'Good. Then get someone to stop the music, will you? If you want, I can come back, all right?'

As Cotton went downstairs the music stopped, though the record got scratched.

'I think we're nearly there,' he said to Monsieur Shalhoub. 'What would you like to do? I imagine revellers will start appearing quite shortly. You carry one child. I'll carry the other. What do you say?'

Cotton picked up the plumper child, smiled at her and started up the stairs. On the first floor they were passed by a swaying middle-aged lady in a costume that included medieval sleeves to the floor and kind of gauzy train. She paused.

'Children are spoilsports,' she said. 'I simply can't abide them.'

'Now that, girls, is a veritable sourpuss,' said Cotton. He called after her. 'If you're driving, madam, be careful of the Isadora Duncan neck snag – at least until you are out of earshot.'

Monsieur Shalhoub looked quite shocked. Cotton did not mind. He put the little girl down outside the Shalhoub front door, smiled and wished Monsieur Shalhoub a happy New Year. He looked down the corridor at Margot's progress – a small group of people were being seen off by the small red-haired man with the white face and doggy black patch, who had removed the very pink dildo – and walked upstairs to his own flat.

121

Cotton let himself in, loosened his tie and collar and went to the kitchen to drink a glass of water. He wasn't sure. Had he fallen asleep on his feet? A buzz sounded, possibly again. Cotton went to his front door and opened it.

The little red-haired man was now accompanied by a girl dressed in an outfit of parachute green that had patches of paint on it. Cotton had no idea what she was dressed as. She looked like a knowing elf in camouflage she had long grown out of. Her very large eyes showed she had drunk a very great deal.

'Falcon wants to speak to you,' said the little man.

Cotton looked from the little man to the girl. Both were about five foot four. The girl looked as if she was about to speak but suddenly frowned. She turned and knuckled the little man on his upper arm.

'Ow! That hurt!'

'My name's Anna Melville,' she said.

Cotton shrugged. 'All right,' he said.

'But that's what I was saying!' said the little man. 'She's a Czech refugee.'

'Apart from the Anna, Melville is my new name for Britain.'

'And what was your old name?' said the little man.

'Sokol.'

'That's what I said! It means falcon, sometimes falconer.'

Cotton sighed. 'Why not Anna Falconer then?'

'Ooh, consonance,' said the red-haired man. 'F and K, old man. She doesn't want people to think she's a girl who ruts on kitchen floors.'

The girl laughed and hit him again on the upper arm.

'I was a Jew there,' said the girl. 'I'm certainly not going to be a Jew here.'

'All right,' said Cotton. 'I'm pleased you feel you have the choice.'

'Don't you think her English is fabulous?'

She shook her head. 'I've learnt on the hoof.'

'Really? Who do you speak like, darling? Who was your model?'

'I tried Edith Evans but settled for Margaret Lockwood.'

'Christ! I thought you were imitating Wendy Hiller but adding a dirty snort.'

The girl looked as if she was about to hit him again, but as soon as Cotton started closing the door she spoke up. 'We think Margot might invite you to dinner – to make amends, you see. She sent us to make peace. She's so awfully sorry.' Anna Melville paused and frowned. 'She says you're rather upright. Have I got that word correct?'

'No. But you're talking to the wrong person. It's the Shalhoub girls you want and I'm sure they would prefer a little tea party. Banana sandwiches, pop, that kind of thing. I suspect that at this time of night they'd prefer a written invitation though. Why don't you post it to them?'

'Buggeration!' exclaimed the girl. She sounded admiring. She fumbled in her small bag, found and put on a pair of spectacles and leant forward.

'I had wondered if you were hard all the way through. He said you were like seaside rock but salty.'

'And you actually believed him?' said Cotton.

The girl laughed and poked her head through the half-open door.

'I say! Do you live here all on your own?'

'Not quite like Margot. You concentrate on the Shalhoub girls.'

'I think she's going to send them presents.'

'Wonderful. I'm sure they'll love them. Can we end this now? Time to go home.'

'You're lucky,' said the girl. 'You don't even know how far we have to go.'

'No, I really don't,' said Cotton.

The girl paused, then giggled. 'You really don't care what people think of you.'

Cotton smiled politely and looked at the little man. The eye surrounded by black greasepaint was closed. 'Hey!' he said. 'Take her home.'

'Oh come off it!' said the girl. 'I've seen you! You've been ogling my breasts the whole time!' She raised her eyebrows. 'You can play with them if you give me a bed.'

'Oh dear God,' said the red-haired man. 'I do apologize. We're theatre people, you see.'

'I had understood that. Why don't you rescue her?'

The girl looked down at her feet. Cotton winced. He recognized that sway as she tried to focus.

'I'm *not* being melodramatic,' said the girl. 'I'm just out on my feet.'

The little man started to put an arm round her. 'I know you are, darling. But I'm worried about you snoring.'

The girl laughed and then passed out. The red-haired man caught her. Cotton checked. She was not pretending.

'Take her to Margot?' said Cotton.

'I think she's rather overrun by sleepers on the floor already.'

Cotton carefully took the girl's spectacles off. They brought her in and put her on the sofa. Cotton got a blanket and put it over her.

'Don't you pass out,' he said to the red-haired man.

The man frowned. 'I don't pass out,' he said. 'Ever. I'm Gus.'

Cotton nodded. 'Is she going to be all right?'

'God knows. I think she just needs to sleep it off. I say this is all a tad embarrassing. Can I go?'

'You're leaving her with a complete stranger?'

The red-haired man had a go at thinking. He looked put upon and slightly sick. After a while, he spoke. 'I can't think of a reason. She's not my type, if you understand me?' He giggled.

'Then you'll have no problem staying with her,' said Cotton.

'Damn!' said the red-haired man. He sighed. 'You wouldn't mind if I just nipped out to—'

'Yes, I would mind,' said Cotton. 'In fact, if you go on like this, I'll help you downstairs with her.'

Gus made a face. 'Would you have a telephone?'

'Yes.'

'Good! Would you mind if I used it?'

'Yes.'

'Why?'

'You won't get a taxi. The evening is over. And I'm truly fed up with this. Stay here with the girl. Or you both leave. What do you say?'

'For God's sake. I barely know her. We met at the Arts Theatre. She does something behind the scenes there. Usually has a paintbrush between her teeth.'

'Is she really Czech?'

'I don't know. She says she is. But she could be from Bootle for all I know.'

'Fine,' said Cotton. 'I'll get you a blanket.'

When Cotton came back Gus had sat down, closed his eyes and opened his mouth. Cotton dropped the blanket on him. He went to the kitchen, poured two glasses of water for them and set them down beside each one. He also got a salad bowl. He prodded Gus.

'If you vomit, you vomit in here. Have you got that?'

Gus groaned.

Cotton went to the front door, locked the door and removed the key.

He looked at them. The girl looked to be out, unconscious rather than asleep. The man was twitching. Cotton thought. They could hardly be part of a honey trap operation for someone whose sexual tastes were not yet recorded. He went to bed.

At eight something woke Cotton. He got up, put on some clothes and went to the bathroom. The door was locked.

'I'm having a bath,' the girl called. 'I'm having a lovely bath.'

Cotton went through to the kitchen. He looked through the doors into the living room. Gus was still fast asleep. When he turned round he saw the girl had been busy. She had found some soap flakes, spilt them but washed out her stockings and knickers in the sink. The knickers were on the towel rail, the tea towel tossed on to a chair. She had taken the cord of the kitchen blind, stretched it out and tied the loose end over a cupboard doorknob and used it as a short washing line for her stockings. Neither stockings nor knickers looked remotely new.

Cotton put on a kettle to boil and cleared up the soap flakes. He unlocked the front door. He cut some bread to toast.

The girl appeared smiling with her hair still wet.

'Absolute bliss!' she said. 'You have no idea. I hope you don't mind but I used your shampoo. Oh, and I borrowed your razor.'

'Did you change the blade?' said Cotton.

'No,' she said. 'Do you own this place?'

127

'You have a keen interest in property?'

'In consumption, darling. What were the paint-ings on the wall?'

'I understand there was once a Matisse, a Dufy and a Derain.'

'Wow! You're rich. Or at least you were. Did you have to sell them?'

'No. I never bought them. They belonged to a previous occupant. I think she was an actress.'

'What was her name?'

Cotton shook his head. 'I have no idea.'

He went to the bathroom. Anna Melville had omitted to clean the bath. She had left his razor out. He changed the blade – it was his last – and brushed his teeth and his hair. He half expected her to have gone but she was sitting at the kitchen table with her glasses on and her eyes shut. The underwear and stockings had gone.

'Who cleans the bath in your house?' he asked.

The girl opened her eyes and looked up. 'Who said we had a proper bath?' My God, you're a bit of a stickler, aren't you? We just had a party, that's all.' She frowned. 'Don't you have a maid?'

'No,' said Cotton, 'I don't.'

She shook her head. 'You're not an intellectual, are you?'

'As against what? An actor?'

'Did you go to university?'

'Yes. It doesn't mean you're an intellectual though.'

'Where did you go?'

'Cambridge.'

'Are they more intellectual at Oxford?'

'Even less.'

She laughed. 'Are you saying you don't need to be clever to go to Oxford?' she said.

'Intelligence is negotiable. You always need funds.'

'Good. That's useful information.'

'Is it? I'm glad.'

'Tell me about Cambridge.'

'Why?'

'That man through there is still asleep.'

Cotton nodded. 'I studied economics.'

'You're telling me you're clever.'

'I didn't say that. I had a friend in college on six hundred pounds a year. There were even a few on a thousand. Strings-of-pearls money we called it.'

'Why?'

'Because of the presents to girlfriends.'

She laughed. 'I like this country.'

'Why?'

'It has opportunities.'

'Surely America has more.'

'Not theatrically, darling. What's the time?'

Cotton told her. It was a little after nine.

'Damn. I'm supposed to get home for lunch.'

'Is it far?'

'My parents live in south Croydon. My father managed a factory in Brno. Now he's a bookkeeper.'

'I'm sorry.'

'Why? When we first arrived we were sent to Wolverhampton! They're very pleased with Croydon.' She looked up. 'They're hoping my brother becomes a professional violinist.' She shook her head. 'He's twenty-three. That's too old and he's not tough enough. He's the youngest.'

'And you are?'

'The oldest of three. My sister lives in Bradford. She married a dentist called Green and breeds.'

'You don't want to do that?'

'Darling,' she said. 'Don't joke.' She smiled. 'I'm quite ambitious, you know. I have plans.'

'Good,' said Cotton.

'Mind you, people like him,' she said pointing in the direction of Gus, 'don't take women seriously. Unless they suffer, of course.'

Cotton was not sure how old she was. There was something of her playing younger, as if that might be winsomely attractive.

She and Gus, finally woken, left about eleven to go, they said, to Lupus Street in Pimlico. Cotton telephoned his father, cleaned up the flat – Gus had left a smear of black and white greasepaint on the sofa he did not know how to get off – and went for a walk. At about five he took an aspirin, made something to eat, read a little, listened to some Art Tatum music and wrote a letter to his sister in New York. Around nine he had a bath. He was asleep by ten.

CHAPTER 12

On 2 January Cotton found Miss Kelly already at work. There was no sign of Phyllis and he did not ask what had happened to her. Miss Kelly had made other changes, to the position of her desk, for example; he thought she had probably cleaned the windows as well.

He started her off by suggesting she contact Alfred Perlman's secretary.

'Mr Perlman is a lawyer. He represents, among many other distinguished clients, Major Albert Briggs MP. Major Briggs has a keen interest in security matters.'

Miss Kelly nodded. A few minutes later she returned.

'I have spoken with Miss Marx and we have exchanged private telephone numbers,' she said.

After that, they sat down and Cotton explained what he wanted and why. By the end of Friday he had what Miss Kelly described as 'an informal map' of the departments within the agencies. There were a couple Cotton had never heard of. Miss Kelly had also identified a list of vulnerable government departments, military research establishments and associated private companies. A draft sketch looked like a fly-clogged cobweb. There were over 130 addresses.

On Saturday, 4 January Hans Bieber drove Cotton to Fontwell Park in the Triumph to meet Major Bertie Briggs. The day was cold but the sun was bright, strong enough to break up most of the mist in the air and reveal the glint on the frost on the ground. Hans flipped at the sun visor as they headed towards the south coast. They arrived shortly before noon and were met by a young man.

'Major Briggs is on the racecourse, having a look at the going, sir,' he said. 'This way.'

The main building at Fontwell looked rather American to Cotton, a white structure like a demure plantation house on the South Downs. The young man led Cotton round it. Fontwell was a national hunt course. Hurdling was on a simple loop course, steeplechase on a figure of eight. The course was small – the figure of eight no more than a mile – and to Cotton's eye rather odd; the small grandstand had a thatched roof.

Major Briggs was at the finishing post. Cotton was not sure what he was dressed as, possibly a trainer, perhaps a starter. The MP was wearing a bowler hat and a stout, whitish officer's coat and was carrying a shooting stick. It had never occurred to Cotton before that the seat part resembled stirrups.

'Nothing like it, eh?' said Major Briggs, holding out an arm and offering a view of the course.

Cotton looked. He thought the view was spoilt by the white railings. They shook hands. 'This is my first visit to a racecourse, Major Briggs.'

'Well, you *have* led a sheltered life then.' Briggs smiled. 'Or perhaps not. Is that what you are saying?'

'No,' said Cotton. 'Just that I've never been to a racecourse before.'

'No nags today, I'm afraid,' said Major Bertie sadly. 'Still it is a lovely place. England at its very best.' He turned and they strolled on the turf. 'Do you think I should drop the Major?'

Cotton smiled. 'The Prime Minister is often called Major Attlee.'

Briggs nodded. 'What were you?'

'A half-colonel, sir.'

'You're a clever beggar, is that it?'

'No. I was given that rank when I went to Washington DC, and never felt very comfortable with it. I was a soldier for about half my service. And I was a captain then.'

'But you saw action.'

'Only in Sicily.'

Briggs raised his chin. 'Wounded?'

'Just some broken bones.'

Briggs nodded, then squinted and then enquired, 'You're not actually a toff, are you?'

Cotton shook his head. 'No. My father was a bank manager but in Mexico mostly. There were advantages in that.'

Briggs abruptly smiled. 'All right. And who do you think you are now?'

'An intelligence officer talking to a member of His Majesty's governing party who has a keen interest in security matters.'

Briggs smiled and nodded. 'You are a clever bugger then,' he said. He sniffed. 'I also like military strategy,' he said. 'You?'

Cotton shook his head. 'No. I was never involved in that and I suspect I lack the necessary talents.'

Briggs was shocked, as if he had never heard anyone admit similar before. 'What do you mean by that?'

'Some people are born with a good ear for music. Or we say a surgeon has "good hands". It's not just analysis. That's relatively passive. A good general needs grasp, sees ways and usually has a gift for self-publicity. Learning is involved but a basic talent is required. I deal in much quieter things.'

Briggs stared at him. 'Are you a team player? Did you play sports at school?'

Cotton nodded. 'Yes. And at university.'

'What did you play?'

'Football.'

'Rugger?'

'No. Round ball.'

'What position did you play?'

'Goalkeeper.'

'Right,' said Briggs. 'Why was that?'

'Oh,' said Cotton. 'I think that came from

Mexico. Goalkeepers are viewed as rather heroic there.'

Briggs laughed and nodded. 'Play anything else?'

'I was an undistinguished member of the tennis team.'

'What was the problem?'

'An erratic backhand and a very belated realization that the strings on the racquet need to be tighter than I ever had them.'

Major Briggs paused, nodded, then wagged a finger.

'I'll tell you what it is,' he said. 'You're not a toff but you're not like me. Do you know the difference between us? People like you can afford to be self-deprecating. People like me can't.'

Cotton did not ask what Briggs meant by 'afford'. Nor did he say he disagreed.

Briggs nodded. 'How did you get your MC?'

Cotton sighed and told him. He realized as he was doing so, that he was more or less repeating what he usually said when asked. He had been lucky to escape the worst effects of a blast. According to the citation, his medal had been for assisting others when under heavy fire. The citation did not mention that most of the fire had been from offshore.

Briggs nodded. 'Friendly fire, was it?'

'An American shell started it,' said Cotton.

'Are you married?'

'No. But I've been engaged. Twice.'

Briggs frowned. 'I don't like the sound of that. You shied at the last fence, is that it?'

'No, they both died. One in a bombing raid in Clerkenwell during the war, the other in a car accident in Washington DC just over a year ago.'

Briggs blinked. 'Christ, lad,' he said. It was the first time that Cotton felt he was hearing Briggs' real voice. 'There's bad luck and there's—' He paused. 'What's that handbag woman called? In a play?'

'Lady Bracknell? *The Importance of Being Earnest?*'

'Yes. Something about misfortune can account for one mishap, but two can only be carelessness?' Briggs looked round and stared at him.

It was, thought Cotton, in the nature of this job to have his sexuality considered, however peremptorily while standing on a racecourse.

'Nah,' said Briggs confidently. 'You'll find somebody. There's a girl out there waiting for you. I'm sure there is.'

Cotton nodded politely.

'But two!' said Briggs. 'Are you lucky? Or those around you unlucky?'

'I'm not superstitious.'

Briggs laughed. 'Right,' he said. 'I bet you're fucking not.'

Major Bertie had a young assistant called Swayles in attendance. The young man accompanied them but was always about twenty feet away.

'How are we doing, Tommy?' Briggs called.

'I'll check, sir,' said Swayles. The boy ran off towards the house.

Briggs turned and they began walking towards the finishing post.

'That's my electoral agent's boy,' said Briggs. 'He had a bad time at the Battle of the Bulge. Only eighteen then. Suffers claustrophobia, fears enclosed spaces. And flames. He was in tanks, you see. Has nightmares about getting cooked. I look after him as best I can.'

Cotton nodded. Major Briggs was showing himself to be a gracious, charitable man and conscious of human misfortune.

Briggs grunted and stamped a foot on the ground. 'The going would be a bit slippery today. The ground underneath is hard but the surface looks like it would cut up.'

'I see,' said Cotton. Major Briggs, however, knew his stuff and was no push-over.

Shortly afterwards Swayles waved from the upstairs.

'Major Briggs! Major Briggs! Everything's ready, sir!'

Briggs waved back. 'That's the spirit,' he said to Cotton. 'Now, what would you say to some bubbly, eh? Pol Roger. Winston's brew.' He laughed. 'I never saw why a socialist can't like champagne. Why the hell not?'

They went inside and upstairs. A buffet lunch had been arranged for them.

'Quite a spread, eh?' said Major Bertie. 'That's

smoked trout there. A gift, you know. MPs get treated like doctors.' He laughed. 'Pile your plate, lad, and tuck in.'

Cotton had the trout. Major Bertie chose ham and chutney. They sat down.

'Right,' said Briggs. He poured from the bottle of Pol Roger. 'What's all this stuff about queers?'

'It's more general, Major. It's about the possibilities of blackmail and extortion.'

Cotton was not sure that Briggs was actually winking. He shut one eye and raised the other eyebrow.

'And what do you think? Mm? Should they be legalized?'

Cotton nodded. 'Yes. At present the illegality gives our enemies an unnecessary lever and confuses us. Outside a group in MI5 and the Special Branch, that's the common view amongst intelligence people I've talked to because they deal with the practicalities. It's when you introduce spurious moralities that things become impractical and often grotesque.'

Major Bertie was unimpressed.

'Do you know what I dislike about them?' he said. 'That air they have of being nature's specially blessed cases. You tell me this now. Do you really think that those who betray nature would have the slightest qualm about betraying their country? They're like that fellow who wrote *A Passage to India*. What's his name?'

'Do you mean E. M. Forster?'

'Yes. He's the superior pansy who said he hoped he'd betray his country before his friends. That's private income talking before he calls for someone else to pick up the bill. Do you think that's going to wash coal in Seaham?'

Seaham was Manny Shinwell's constituency in County Durham, a mining area. Cotton understood Shinwell's constituency was being invoked to remind him of Briggs' contacts and also took it as shorthand for what would wash with honest to God public opinion. Cotton had taken Forster to mean that patriotism and loyalty were not necessarily identical, that patriotism could be a sham and most people's loyalty was directed at a few people around them. He decided not to answer Briggs directly.

'I understand Forster voted Labour,' Cotton said, though he had no idea whether he had or not. 'A lot of people in the arts did, I believe.'

For a moment Cotton did not know how Briggs would react – but he let out a gruff laugh.

'Right! And votes are votes,' he said, 'even if they're from snobbish buggers and toffee-nosed perverts.'

Cotton thought Briggs probably took some comfort and some thrill in the notion of a weakness in the upper classes. Presumably he did not think privileged and/or effeminate men were good at washing coal. The coal industry had been finally and formally nationalized at New Year. Cotton suspected that for Shinwell, and so for Briggs, they

139

were now on the coal standard, as it were. This standard was about honest justice for workers, was way above any considerations on homosexuality, prejudice or potential coal shortages. At one level, from Briggs' point of view, adultery and homosexuality were the same: secrets to be exposed if doing so were to his advantage.

'There is a precedent, you know,' said Major Bertie.

'I'm sorry. What do you mean?'

Briggs sat back in his chair. 'Vansittart,' he said.

Cotton said nothing. In the thirties, Robert Vansittart, in the Foreign Office, had run a private intelligence service out of frustration with appeasement. His concern had been exclusively anti-Nazi. For Briggs to compare the two was, as kindly as Cotton could put it, optimistic. He did not ask who Briggs was fighting.

Major Briggs laughed. 'What's this word "honeytrap"?'

Cotton remembered the word 'smut' from his conversation with Ayrtoun in the car. 'Well,' he said, 'the Soviets – and others, of course – are keen on compromising people. A girl finds you amazingly attractive – or, if they think you're like E. M. Forster, a boy does. A few photographs and you're caught between losing your position and status or helping out with the Soviet cause.' He looked up. He was entirely aware of Briggs' own interest in compromising photographs. Briggs did not look at all abashed.

'And of course,' Cotton went on, 'another problem is that photographs of indiscretions can become currency, can be sold on.'

Briggs shook his head. He was very confident. 'I only deal in exclusives,' he said. 'I can tell you that.'

'Exclusives don't tend to stay exclusive,' said Cotton.

'No, no. I always get the negatives.'

Cotton shrugged. 'Of course there's always the business of wanting people to *think* you've got them.'

Briggs smiled. 'Now that's a thought, eh?' He looked directly at Cotton. 'I suppose what you really want to know is how I finance things.'

Cotton did not answer. Briggs pierced a chunk of ham and covered it with chutney.

'I don't have to tell you the Government has some leeway with funds. You know that. I'm not sure I'm not being backed by "The Fund for the Relief of Sundry Female Objects in Distress".'

'Ah. Those poor girls again,' said Cotton.

Briggs laughed. 'That's it.' He put the ham and chutney into his mouth.

Cotton knew that this dismissively named fund really did exist. He also knew Briggs was lying to him in the sense that he was trying to get him to collude with a fiction that implied that Major Albert Briggs MP had Government backing for his snooping.

On one level the lie was astute enough. Briggs was merely bringing up the various bags of

Government money that were excluded from the accountants' attentions. Cotton knew that Ayrtoun, for example, had access to money that officially came from nowhere.

On another level the lie was depressing. Briggs wanted Cotton to accept the lie, either because he shared a view of how snooping was done or because he was too stupid or deferential to question it.

Both men agreed after lunch that the meeting had been 'extremely useful' and shook hands. They would 'check on things', in Briggs' phrase, every month.

'He's a bully,' said Hans when the Triumph was running.

'Yes, he is,' said Cotton. 'What are you basing your opinion on?'

'He kerb-crawls.'

'He does what?'

'Drives along the kerb talking to whores.'

'I know what kerb-crawling is! How do you know this?'

'I've watched him do it.'

'All right, Hans,' said Cotton.

'Sir?'

'Wait.'

Cotton waited until they reached Dorking. He then asked Hans to park and suggested a walk. Cotton knew Dorking a little. It was where he often arrived by train to visit his father, though he rarely strayed further than the station forecourt.

'Mr Ayrtoun suggested you follow Major Briggs. Right?'

Hans nodded. 'I asked the girls on Park Lane. The Major insults them and tells them what he would like to do to them.'

'Wonderful.'

'He does it when he's angry or frustrated.'

'Quite. After a hard day in Parliament, is this?'

'Yes. It's quite a well-known fact.'

'Not to me, Hans.'

Hans looked surprised. 'He is not a complicated man,' he said.

'Perhaps not,' said Cotton. 'But we have a problem.'

'Sir?'

'Were you given a time to tell me about this? After my meeting with him?'

Hans twitched. 'Well, no. Mr Ayrtoun didn't actually give a time. He just said I should tell you. I didn't want to influence you before you met him.'

'All right, Hans, I want you to tell Mr Ayrtoun something.'

'Yes, sir.'

'Don't you know what it is?'

'No, sir.'

'Dear, dear. Take me home, now, would you?'

Cotton got back to Wilbraham Place in the dark at shortly after five. At 9 p.m. he got a call from Washington DC.

'What precisely is the problem?' said Ayrtoun.

'What's Hans's job, apart from driving that is?'

143

Ayrtoun sighed. 'He does some surveillance work for me.'

'Ah,' said Cotton. 'Would that include watching me?'

'I haven't got the time for this.'

'Neither have I,' said Cotton.

Ayrtoun paused again. 'You accepted the job.'

'No I did not,' said Cotton. 'I agreed to the job description you gave me.'

'What do you want?'

'More information and better timing.'

'Explain.'

'For a start, at least equality in the information my ex-Nazi driver gets.'

'There are wider issues, you know.'

'Kerb-crawling isn't one of them. I'm entirely happy to go back to St James's Street and show enthusiasm for the potential problems in Malaya.'

There was a pause. 'MI5,' said Ayrtoun, 'have launched their push. Right now. They're on a queer hunt.'

'Hans knows about this?'

'You should be prepared,' said Ayrtoun.

'Have you any specific information?'

There was a pause.

'No,' said Ayrtoun. 'That's your job.'

'What else does Hans do for you?'

'He's well connected.'

'Ah.' Cotton wondered if Hans's Robert had been targeted.

'He does a drag routine. Lili Marlene. He's very popular in some circles,' said Ayrtoun.

'I know.'

'How?'

'He showed me his own draft of his own report.'

Ayrtoun grunted. 'Have nothing to do with that,' he said.

Cotton put down the telephone, lifted it again and left a message for Derek to call him. About an hour later, Derek called Cotton from a telephone box.

'We've got a snooper. Usually does divorces in Brighton. Just stopping off earlier on the line.'

'Do you know who he is?' asked Cotton.

'He's some sort of photographer out of Soho.'

'MI5?'

'I doubt it. More a Special Branch kind of person. Takes portraits of prostitutes for call-girl directories and catches adulterers in bed when they tell him to.'

'Have you seen him with a camera?'

'Nah. He says he's trying to track down some woman's brother.'

'He's fishing?'

'And clocking. You know, getting familiar with the faces.'

'Amateur?'

'At this. He's not kosher, is he? He's small porn.'

'Do you have a name?'

'Joe. I think he's Italian. I mean his parents are. He's just here, sweating a little bit from all that rail travel and the smiles he gets.'

'All right. Keep him in view. And look around. Oh, next time you see him, ask him if Major Briggs is well.'

'Major Briggs? All right. I'll do that.'

CHAPTER 13

Around six in the morning of Monday, 6 January Cotton received a telephone call. He had been woken by the shrill bell and the sound was still in his ears.

'It's Derek,' said Jennings. 'You've got one, a man called Watson. He's been arrested. He's an atomic something. He's in Croydon police station.'

'Thanks, Derek.'

Cotton called Hans Bieber, who was already up and remarkably cheerful. They agreed he would pick Cotton up at 6.45.

Cotton stood under the shower, shaved, dressed and was boiling the kettle when the telephone rang again. It was Dickie Dawkins.

'We've had a security alert,' he said.

'From Croydon?'

'Yes.' Dawkins sounded disappointed.

'I'll be going there directly,' said Cotton.

'So will I,' said Dawkins.

Cotton smiled. 'I only have his surname.'

'Alexander Ashley Watson,' said Dickie Dawkins. 'He's a specialist in something called plutonium enrichment. Works at Harwell. Was on his way to Fort Halstead near Sevenoaks in Kent.'

'What's the charge?'

'Gross indecency under Section 11 of the Criminal Law Amendment Act of 1885.'

'Do you have the details?'

'When I see you,' said Dawkins.

'Right. Can you put a block on everything you can until we get there?'

'I think so,' said Dawkins. 'I don't know what plutonium enrichment is.'

In January 1947, beyond a very general notion, neither did Cotton. Though British and refugee scientists had been involved, even initially been at the forefront of what became the Manhattan Project, the McMahon Act, unanimously passed by the US Congress in August 1946 to avoid nuclear proliferation, had made it clear that British scientists did not have a complete understanding of the atom bomb production process. One of the gaps was in plutonium enrichment.

'I think we can say it's important,' he said.

He decided however to test Alfred Perlman. He called his secretary.

'This is Marion.'

'I'm sorry I didn't know your name.'

'No,' said the lady. 'You want Olivia. One moment.' There was a pause and another voice came on the line.

'This is Olivia. Is that Mr Cotton? How can I help?'

Cotton said he had to go to Croydon police station and wanted to ask Mr Perlman a question.

'Does it involve a possible criminal charge?'

'Section 11 of the Criminal Amendment Act.'

'Will you be there by nine? I'll have Mr Perlman telephone then.'

'Thank you very much.'

Cotton and Dawkins arrived at Croydon police station almost at the same time. They found Watson was being held but had not yet been formally charged. The draft charge sheet said that Watson had been found in the grounds of a local school, Whitgift Middle School in North End, close to the OTC armoury with its supply of First World War rifles, by a night watchman who was quoted as saying he had heard 'the rattle of chains'. The watchman, fearing an IRA robbery, had contacted the police and then spied on what he was quoted as describing as 'an unnatural act'. Disturbed by police whistles, Watson's companion had run across the playing fields and escaped in the direction of Wellesley Road. Watson had merely done up his flies and asked what the racket was about.

The police sergeant was helpful. 'We could also get him for trespass, you know.'

'Where is he?' said Dawkins

The police sergeant was surprised. 'In the cells, of course.'

'Get him out,' said Dawkins. 'Change the records.

149

Put him in an interview room and make sure he's always been there.'

Dawkins turned towards Cotton.

'Who is the head man here?' Cotton asked the sergeant.

'Well, that would be the chief constable, sir.'

'Contact him,' said Dawkins.

A police constable went off to deal with Watson. The sergeant telephoned the chief constable.

'What's going on?' he asked, having left a message that the chief constable was urgently required.

'You'll find out when and if necessary,' said Dawkins.

The police constable came back.

'Transfer completed, sir.'

Cotton and Dawkins went to see Watson. He was standing in his socks putting the laces back in his shoes. One of his socks had a hole in the toe.

'I have an appointment near Sevenoaks,' he said. 'And I'm going to be late because of this.'

Dawkins nodded. 'Do you want me to call anyone, sir?'

'Don't be absurd,' said Watson. 'This is something only I can deal with.'

Cotton considered him. Alexander Ashley Watson was about five foot nine. He was square-shouldered but thin, and had strands of hair so blond they were almost white combed over his scalp but not enough to cover the crown of his head, blue eyes and a rather shapeless nose. He was flushed, his eyelids were twitching and he spoke with an almost asthmatic emphasis.

'Given the circumstances, Mr Watson,' said Cotton, 'you seem remarkably calm.'

'I'm not. This is intolerable.' Watson paused and swallowed. 'Really, neither of you have the slightest idea who or what you are dealing with.'

Cotton nodded. 'Are you quite sure about that?' he asked. 'Do you normally get visits from Special Branch and the Intelligence Service when you're in a police cell?'

Watson looked instantly bored. 'I'm under a great deal of pressure,' he said, 'and I need occasional release. It's not particularly interesting. It certainly isn't important.'

'Agreed. But given your work, you didn't think a more private arrangement for the obtainment of release might have avoided this?'

Watson shook his head. 'I really am not in the slightest bit interested in your morality,' he said.

Cotton nodded. 'I'm not sure I've got enough morality to be interested in,' he said. He sat down. 'But I would draw your attention to the pertaining law and to certain unpleasant consequences that flow from it.'

Watson blinked. 'I don't think you know what I do.'

'I'm pretty sure I don't. But I do know that it involves plutonium, symbol Pu – a sort of joke I understand, amongst scientists. I know that

Plutonium 239 was synthesized at Berkeley in California in 1940 or '41.'

'It's pronounced Burkley, not Barclay.'

'Thank you. The problem that you don't appear to appreciate is that the fallout from the American McMahon Act stretches all the way to Croydon.'

'What on earth do you mean?'

'That incidents like this, if known, might lead to grim consequences. For you, that is. The Americans passed the act to stop others developing the atom bomb but – this is called real politics – have retained the ability to blackball some of our scientists. They get particularly anxious that information might be passed to the Soviets.'

'But that's utter humbug. For all I know, the Soviets may even be ahead of us. The Yanks can't be that hypocritical.'

'Oh yes they can. Just like us. Because they're not exclusively concerned with plutonium enrichment. Don't you understand? If this gets out your security clearance will be removed.'

'Then don't let it out.'

'That's why chain rattling is such a bad idea.'

'What chains?'

'Good,' said Cotton. 'I can use that. What happened?'

'For God's sake! All I did was go for a walk with a young man I met in the bar at the Greyhound. He suggested we duck into the school grounds. That's all. No one else was involved. It was pitch dark. We hurt no one. And no one but a peeping Tom would have known what we were up to.'

'You're still being charged with breaking the law.'

'But I am not a criminal!' said Watson indignantly. 'I am not a burglar or a spiv, you know, and I refuse to be treated as such.'

'I understand,' said Cotton. 'Could you leave this with me for a few minutes?'

'What can you do?'

'I was thinking of trying to get the charge quashed and unrecorded,' said Cotton. 'Is that acceptable to you? If you're prosecuted your career will be over anyway. Can we start with that?'

It took a little time, but Watson nodded.

The chief constable was a man called Kitson. Cotton did not know whether or not he was one of Derek's 'homebodies' or Ayrtoun's 'colonials', but could see that, behind his crisp uniform and shining buttons, he was flustered and unhappy. This was not simply because of what he called 'this distasteful matter'. The chief constable said he had just received a phone call from a Mr Alfred Perlman.

'He's some sort of fancy lawyer. I don't even know how he got my number.'

'I asked him for advice,' said Cotton.

The chief constable blinked. 'The man's a shyster,' he said.

'On the contrary,' said Cotton. 'He's offering help.'

'I beg your pardon. He suggested a charge against Mr Watson was . . . inadvisable was the term he used.'

'Did he give any reasons?'

'He talked about what he called the Driberg Defence. Whatever that is.'

'It's a variation of the Portsmouth defence,' said Dawkins. 'When a man charged with assault claims he thought his victim was making an unnatural suggestion. In Driberg's case there was an incident involving two unemployed miners in London in 1935 and in 1943 there was another with a Norwegian sailor in a bomb shelter in Edinburgh, and in both cases Driberg got off through what was also called misunderstanding due to difference of accent. Neither case was ever made public because Mr Driberg worked for a newspaper magnate.'

'Which magnate?' said the chief constable.

'Lord Beaverbrook,' said Dawkins. He nodded. 'This lawyer was saying you'd be wasting your time, sir, and it's a question of whether this goes down as a Driberg or as the other cases in between that are not public knowledge.'

'But I am here to uphold the law,' complained the chief constable. 'That's my responsibility.' He looked up. 'This is all more than highly irregular, you know!'

'It only appears to be irregular,' said Cotton. He wondered if he was blushing but realized he was past that. 'Without entering into specifics, I can tell you that Mr Watson is involved in top secret work. Whatever his private tastes, our instructions are to ensure he continues to contribute

154

to national security without undue demur or hindrance. We shall certainly mention your collaboration and discretion. We are not talking about the power of a newspaper magnate but the national interest.'

'I'm sorry. You can't be asking me just to make this thing go away?'

Cotton decided he had flattered enough. 'Correct me if I'm wrong, sir. Mr Watson's alleged companion has not been arrested nor has he been identified. We are relying on the word and vision of an elderly night watchman on a dark winter's night. He may have been asleep. He certainly thought at first that the IRA was attempting to rob the school armoury. Something to do with chain rattling. Later, however, the watchman shifted his story, while it was still as dark as ever, from the IRA to what he described as an unnatural act between two men. Under no circumstances do I want to suggest that an honourable old man could be mistaken or perhaps have been agitated in his imagination and the drama of shadows. But put, say, against a night-time stroll by an overworked scientist of repute involved in top secret work in the interests of national security, perhaps not as worldly as might be convenient, who wanders away from the street into a quiet scholastic environment through a gate we do not even know was closed, let alone locked, and then unfortunately decided to relieve himself quite near a pile of coal I understand, I'd suggest there were good grounds for doubt. I'm not a trained lawyer,

Chief Constable. But imagine what a real, first-class lawyer, like Mr Perlman's barrister for example, could do with that. The IRA are not known as a hotbed of homosexuals.'

'What are you asking me?'

'That given the possible difficulties in obtaining a conviction, the cost of a public hearing is not simply financial but could be very unfavourable to something affecting the security and defence of the realm.'

'I'd want guarantees.'

'Your cooperation would definitely be mentioned.'

'I meant—'

'I know what you meant, sir. May I ask you a question?'

'What kind of question?'

'Do you know what plutonium enrichment is?'

'I haven't the foggiest idea!'

'Neither have I, sir. But that's what Mr Watson does. And it's not about what an elderly night watchman thinks, it's a Cabinet level matter.'

The chief constable asked for a few minutes to consider. Cotton and Dawkins left him to it.

'What are you doing?' said Dawkins. 'What's all this Perlman stuff?'

'Just a test,' said Cotton.

'Of what?'

'I wanted to know how long it would take him to find out what was going on and whether or not he knows the difference between discretion and secrecy. He won't tell Briggs, not yet anyway.'

Dawkins looked disbelieving. 'You're trusting him?'

'Oh yes.'

Dawkins was a little embarrassed. 'You're not going to be able to keep this secret, you know.'

'That's what Perlman just demonstrated,' said Cotton. 'If an informant can call me at six in the morning with the news of an arrest, I imagine others will have received that information too.'

Perhaps Dawkins was trying to think on the bright side. 'But it's not as if he was an actor or someone famous.'

'No, but Watson has just become a high-level commodity to trade. Poor, if rather snippy, bugger. The demand for queers is strong at present and the supply limited and erratic. What are you going to say to your people?'

Dawkins sighed. He did not answer directly. 'Could we make him the victim? Or make the charge more acceptable – drunk and disorderly, say?'

'You have a queer hunter in Special Branch.'

Dawkins nodded. 'Radcliffe. He's higher up than me. He's religious. Goes on a lot about purity. Oh, and a woman's crowning glory being her hair.'

'You're not joking?'

'No. He's involved with the Crusader lads, you know.'

'No I don't. What are they?'

'Well, an organization like the Boys' Brigade has a bit of religion, you know – tacked on. The

Crusaders starts with the religion, then adds on the boys' bit.'

Dawkins paused, unsure whether he had quite been fair. Cotton ignored that.

'I take it Radcliffe has been informed about this.'

'Oh, yes,' said Dawkins. He paused. 'He's on his way here. He'll have told MI5. Mr Starmer-Smith. He and Radcliffe are close. They even live close by.'

Cotton nodded.

'How long do you think the chief constable needs?'

'He'll be making a telephone call. I'll wait here.'

Cotton went for a walk. Within a few yards he heard footsteps two strides behind him keeping to his step.

'Derek?' he said without turning round.

'The boy's name is Bambi Bosworth,' said Derek.

Cotton nodded. 'Where is he?'

'He's decided to have a little holiday with friends in Brighton.'

'Good. Have you anything on the chief constable?'

Derek sounded puzzled. 'No. He's officer class, the kind of man who thinks polished boots and buttons make for a good officer. He likes systems and he doesn't like problems. Believes his men are honest. Used to be in the Punjab. Somewhere like that.'

'All right,' said Cotton. 'Any press around?'

'Only a stringer who works for the *Daily Sketch* and the *People*.'

'What's the local newspaper?'

'Just one of the *Advertisers*,' said Derek. 'Mostly flower shows and second-hand cars. Croydon doesn't even have a football team, Mr C.'

'How much did you agree to pay for the tip-off on Watson?'

'Five shillings, sir.' He paused. 'It is January, sir.'

'What does that mean?'

'People are hard up after Christmas.'

Cotton nodded. 'I'm going to turn,' he said. 'I'll hand you a ten-shilling note as I pass. All right?'

'Very good, sir.'

Cotton stopped and put his hand into his pocket.

'Has Watson been here before?' he asked.

'He's been one of Bambi's regulars once, maybe twice a month for three or four months,' said Derek.

Cotton did as he said. Information on Watson was proving depressingly cheap.

CHAPTER 14

While he waited for the chief constable to finish fiddling with papers, Cotton looked for signs of the Punjab in him, or perhaps just somewhere warm. He found none. The chief constable was all pale, put-upon restraint.

Dawkins caught his eye and nodded. Cotton got up and went down to tell Watson he was going to be released without charge quite shortly. Watson was still in the interview room, now doing *the Times* crossword.

'I suggest you telephone Fort Halstead as soon as you can.'

Watson surprised Cotton. 'What'll I say to them?'

'That you've been delayed. You don't have to invent anything. Or are they going to insist on a reason?'

'No,' said Watson. 'Yes. I suppose I could do that.'

Cotton considered him. Did Watson have a problem with the truth in that he usually told it? It was the first time Cotton had had any impression Watson had taken on even a little of the delicacy of his position, enough to be confused or at least momentarily uncertain. Pity. Cotton knew

Watson's position was not in the slightest bit delicate.

He gave Watson his card.

'For now, anyway, this has some value. Should you find other security forces want to interview you, may I suggest you contact me at once?'

Watson was unimpressed. 'What? On the grounds that you've handled this business?'

'Doesn't that seem reasonable to you?'

'I am certainly not going to apologize.'

'I haven't asked you to apologize. But I would suggest you choose another route, that is, give Croydon a miss on any further trips.'

'My mother lives in Sanderstead.'

'That's not quite Croydon, is it?' said Cotton.

'It's just by South Croydon.'

Cotton nodded patiently. 'But I take it you are able to pass the Greyhound Hotel without going in,' he said, though he instantly realized he did not sound very patient. He tried again. 'Mr Watson, we have contrived to persuade the chief constable this time. We won't be able to do this again. Do you understand me? He believes he has principles too.'

Watson shrugged. 'I have absolutely nothing to apologize for.'

'That's not the point,' said Cotton. 'A number of people disagree and want to punish you by invoking the law. Do you understand? However unreasonable you think them, the law is presently on their side. Underestimate them and you will suffer.'

'Are you threatening me?'

'No. But some of the people who are threatening you will be arriving shortly. And I want to get you out of here before that happens.'

Dawkins came in, waving a couple of sheets of paper.

'That's it! Let's get you out of here.'

Watson stood up. Dawkins raised his eyes heavenward at Cotton.

'I got a lecture,' he said. 'I don't think the chief constable would even speak to you. Radcliffe will be here any minute.'

Cotton nodded. 'Mr Watson! Mr Dawkins here is going to accompany you to the Greyhound Hotel. Make your telephone call from there, pay your bill. Mr Dawkins will see you off. All right?'

'Am I to be given an apology?' said Watson.

'Do you want one?' said Cotton.

'Yes, I do.'

'Then I apologize, Mr Watson. But you don't seem to understand that I'm about to see someone who would never dream of apologizing. He wants your security clearance removed and you yourself in jail. I apologize again. But I can only apologize for what is in my power. Do you understand that? Mr Dawkins here—'

'That's enough,' said Watson. 'I don't need any more.'

'This way, sir,' said Dickie Dawkins. He looked at Cotton. 'Where are you going to be?'

'I think I'll stay here.'

Dawkins was uncomfortable. 'I don't know how long I'm going to be.'

'That's all right. Your priority is to get him on the road.'

When they had left, Cotton sat down in Watson's chair. He was no longer sure what he was doing. Given the leaks and the interest of Special Branch and MI5, it was unlikely anyone could save Watson. The scientist had not been charged but that hardly mattered. The incident would be noted and, in security terms, he had been flagged as a risk, possibly serious. About the best Cotton could do was to submit a report about the 'mistake' and recommend Watson's security clearance remain. It would be his perception of risk against two reports questioning Watson's fitness.

Annoyed, Cotton picked up the copy of *The Times* Watson had been looking at. The scientist had been doing the crossword and appeared to have done most of it except for one clue at the lower right-hand corner. It took Cotton a moment to understand the poor devil had not answered the clues. Instead he had written down some lines of Tennyson's poem 'Ulysses':

Come, my friends,
'Tis not too late to seek a newer world.
Push off, and sitting well in order smite
The sounding furrows, for my purpose holds
To sail beyond the sunset, and the baths
Of all the western stars until I—

Watson had not written the next word – 'die'. Cotton grunted. Evidently Alexander Ashley Watson was rather more dramatic and less confident than he wanted to appear.

Radcliffe arrived with three other men. He did so noisily – and went to see the chief constable. That did not take very long. To Cotton, Special Branch was an annexe to the Metropolitan Police, its employees invariably ex-policemen. Employees in MI5 could not arrest anyone – that was always done by Special Branch. After some ten minutes Radcliffe barrelled into the interview room. He was younger than Cotton expected, perhaps forty, with a square, curiously flat face, partly due to a Churchillian thrust of expression and a habit of walking with his hands behind his back. His face was flushed. He was a barker.

'Who gave you the right to interfere, laddie?'

Evidently Cotton too was younger than Radcliffe expected.

'Mr Radcliffe?' said Cotton. He got up and offered his hand. 'Peter Cotton. I'm delighted to meet you.'

Radcliffe pushed back his shoulders and raised his chin. 'I said—'

Cotton interrupted him. 'I know what you said.' He spoke quietly. 'But two things. One, for someone with an interest in this, you've arrived awfully late. Two, I am not, under any circum-stances whatsoever, your laddie.'

'I can't imagine you know who you are talking to!'

164

'Radcliffe? Special Branch? Keen interest in homosexuals?'

'Do you know what insubordination is?'

'Yes. And it's certainly not this.' Cotton got out his pass, the paper signed by Sir Percy Sillitoe and by Sir Stewart Menzies. He offered it to Radcliffe.

'What's this supposed to mean?'

'That MI5 and MI6 are involved and the heads of both have signed off on it. I don't know about Special Branch.'

'Starmer-Smith has said nothing about this.'

Cotton shrugged very slightly. 'Forgive me. Starmer-Smith has not been informed.'

'What's going on?'

'There was a misunderstanding,' said Cotton. 'It's been cleared up.' He paused. 'Do you know what they do at Harwell? And at Fort Halstead?'

Radcliffe did not reply directly. He took one hand from behind his back and pulled on his nose. He sniffed.

'Bad timing for your man.'

'He's not my man,' said Cotton.

'I've been making enquiries,' said Radcliffe. 'I don't rush into things.' He sniffed again. 'We'll get him, you know.'

'Very possibly.'

'What do you mean?'

'Just that. I take it I represent one effort to make this country's development of an atom bomb a priority. I daresay you have others. Priorities, that is. To do with ejaculations rather than explosions measured in megatons.'

Radcliffe wagged a finger at him. 'You don't even know what your own people are saying.'

'What people?'

'MI5 and MI6.'

'Strictly speaking I'm with neither. That's the point of this, Inspector.'

Radcliffe laughed. 'You'll see.'

'Of course I will.'

'What do you mean by that?'

'That our Intelligence Services lack consistency and coherence and are prone to empire builders in offices and cubbyholes, a number of them working at cross-purposes.'

'Are you trying to be offensive?'

'No. Just accurate in my descriptions.'

'Are you calling yourself an empire builder?'

'Not at all.'

Cotton took Radcliffe's expression as either pity or contempt.

'But even if I were, I'd hardly say so, would I?' said Cotton.

Radcliffe pushed out his lips and nodded. 'You think I'm just a humbug.' He shook his head. 'I'll tell you something for free. I've learnt that morality is the basis of everything. If a man has no decency or discipline, he is unreliable, he is weak. If he cannot control his urges, he becomes prey. Everything else stems from that. He takes his excuses where he can. Politically and in every way. He has betrayal in his bones.'

'I'm not aware the Soviets themselves are particularly kind to homosexuals but that doesn't stop them trying to take advantage of our attitudes.'

Radcliffe shook his head. He held up two fingers.

'Is that victory?' said Cotton.

Radcliffe smiled. 'You'll see. You'll find two things happen.'

'And you are not going to tell me what they are.'

Radcliffe smiled again. 'That's up to you. Maybe we'll meet again.'

Don't know where, don't know when, thought Cotton. 'Good,' he said. 'I look forward to it.'

Radcliffe crossed his arms behind his back and barrelled off.

Cotton sighed. He had, probably unavoidably, just made an enemy. He also thought Radcliffe was probably right. Two things, he had said. Cotton was almost surprised there were so few.

As soon as he got back to his office he put in a request for information. Everything on Watson. He knew this would be difficult for Miss Kelly because Watson was, as far as he knew, working at the highest level of secrecy. He also talked to her about Starmer-Smith and Radcliffe. She said she'd dig, and advised him that he might find the E & E, or Ears & Eyes, the department in charge of 'listening devices and cameras', useful.

'There's a small department in London,' she said. 'Close-up work really.'

On his way home, Cotton bought an evening paper. Sixteen hundred pits and 700,000 miners were well short of fulfilling the coal production needed to get British industry going again and to keep British houses heated. A lady in Blackburn was quoted as saying it was not just coal. There had been no bread, no bacon and no fat that day. In Manchester half the cotton mills were silent. In the Midlands car production was half what it should be. The paper suggested the miners were only interested in a five-day week.

On 8 January Miss Kelly gave Cotton a file and a pair of tweezers.

'Please do not touch the paper,' she said. 'Use the tweezers.'

Cotton opened the file. Inside it were two sheets of paper that reminded him of carbon paper at first, but were not. Their colour was more like the petal of the African Violet.

'This is what is called a psychological profile of Watson,' said Miss Kelly. 'The idea is it can't be photographed and that it picks up fingerprints from anyone who handles it.'

'Does it work?'

'Your risk, sir.'

Cotton smiled. 'Do you know who wrote it?'

'There are some initials, sir. Look. MC. I understand he's associated with the Tavistock

168

Institute and sat in on security interviews with the subject.'

'OK. How long have I got?'

'About two hours, sir.'

'Thank you, Miss Kelly.'

'Colonel.'

To read the report Cotton had to hold each sheet of paper up to the light. He learnt that Watson was an only child, born in Liverpool in 1910. His father, a doctor, had died in 1915. In 1921 his mother had remarried. Both mother and son had adopted the surname of her new husband, and moved to Birmingham. He had attended a Catholic grammar school and then taken a first in Physics at Imperial College:

> He described himself as having been 'arrogant, unforgiving and ambitious' at that stage in his development. On being pressed he admitted to feelings of contempt towards many sections of society, including a number of scientists. When asked about his political leanings, he laughed. He had been initially attracted to the order apparent in totalitarian theories. These brief political stirrings ended when he returned to his childhood home to pursue his doctoral studies at the university there – in Watson's own words 'a disastrous decision but one that was the making of me'.
>
> He found his mentor at grammar school,

a Father Patrick McCleverty, 'unable to countenance the fact that young men pass the age of eighteen'. Worse, he had soon entered into a furious dispute with his supervisor and professor, who he described as having 'little science and fewer morals'. The result is that he was never awarded his doctorate.

'I was right,' he said several times. But his work was noticed elsewhere, and by 1937 he was working on the initial steps towards the Atom Bomb.

He spent the war in North America and both the Americans and the Canadians describe him as very hard working – the Americans even use the word 'mono-maniac' – and he had good, even excellent reports from them on the quality of his work.

It is clear, however, that he is what the Canadians termed 'prickly'. He is not sociable. In the little spare time available he says he listens to Bach and Mozart. He claims recently to have started reading Dante's *Divine Comedy* in Italian. He says he uses a dictionary and his school Latin. On being asked, he admitted that the previous book he had read was T. E. Lawrence's *The Seven Pillars of Wisdom* in 1935 or thereabouts. 'But only the introduction.'

Cotton paused. He could hardly remember Lawrence's book apart from an impression of overwrought prose and something about clean young male bodies in the introduction. He grunted and went back to the report.

> The subject said he was inspired by Lawrence to buy a motor-bicycle and goggles. He described this as 'a phase that lasted for about five years' and that he had 'enjoyed maintaining the machine'.

There was a little more about his work in the US and at Harwell. And then MC had delivered his verdict: 'Narcissistic invert with pederastic tendencies. Good worker. Approved.'

Cotton shook his head – at reports in general – and replaced the purplish sheets.

'Thank you, Miss Kelly. You haven't risked trouble for this, have you?'

'No, sir.'

'Good,' said Cotton.

What Cotton did not know until a week later was that on the same day he read the report on Watson, at a Cabinet meeting in Downing Street it was decided to appoint William Penney, the scientist who had written the report on the development of the British atom bomb, as head of the development itself. There was nothing remarkable or unexpected about the appointment.

It was simply confirming what was already happening.

But it did automatically trigger a security review of those working on it.

CHAPTER 15

When Cotton got home he found two unstamped envelopes on his mat. One contained an invitation from Margot Fenwick to an after-theatre dinner party on the 17th of January.

'Please do come,' wrote Margot. 'It will mean a lot to me and should be fun and exciting for you.'

Cotton grunted. The other note told him his shoes had been repaired. He accepted the invitation and went to collect his shoes the next day. Inside the shop he looked at the new soles. They resembled compacted and glued sawdust.

'Is this leather?' he asked.

'It's the quality that's available, sir,' said the cobbler.

Cotton stroked a sole with his index finger. A dank line appeared.

'Let them soak something up,' said the cobbler. 'Even shoe polish will help.'

Cotton trudged and queued for his rations. In the grocer's however he saw some glass jars containing three pounds of green beans in a saline solution. He bought one.

Cotton took his purchases home. He put his stores away and tackled his repaired shoes. He did not have much black shoe polish left so he rubbed in some brown that he had left over from military service. After three applications the sole had become only slightly darker. He did not think he was in danger of slipping. He wondered more if they were quite waterproof.

On Monday, 13 January, he put them on and went to work. On his way, he read that troops had been called in to substitute for striking lorry drivers. In his office, he had barely seen the first item on the morning bulletin – the day before, in Haifa, the Stern Gang had driven an explosive-laden vehicle into a British police station, killing four and injuring 140 – when he got a phone call from Derek.

'I'm in hiding,' said Derek.

'What are you talking about?'

'I'm in hiding, Mr C! In Whyteleafe.'

Cotton had no idea where Whyteleafe was. 'Who are you hiding from?'

'Maurice, of course!' said Derek. 'He catches me and I'm in trouble, Mr Cotton. He's still got six chairs left! I need your help, Mr Cotton, I really do!'

'All right,' said Cotton. 'I'm listening.'

It took Cotton some time to calm Derek down and get enough clear information to understand what his informant was talking about. Then he needed Dickie Dawkins's help. They met at a tea room off Piccadilly and Cotton learnt that Whyteleafe was a village 'past Kenley', to the south-east of Purley in Surrey.

'Maurice is Maurice Bly,' said Dawkins. 'He's a loan shark.'

'Are you telling me that Derek owes him money?'

'No. Maurice doesn't give a shit about Derek.'

'So what's going on?'

'Our business in Croydon stirred things up. And that lawyer contact of yours didn't help.'

'Perlman? What did he do?'

'He had Major Briggs mention to a couple of newspapermen that the Croydon police had corruption problems. Chief Constable Kitson was livid and started a review.'

'Not to Maurice Bly's taste?'

'Not at all.'

'Are you saying he identified Derek as part of his problem and threatened him to get a response? You're saying he knows what Derek does?'

'Of course. I imagine Derek mentions his contacts quite often.'

'Christ,' said Cotton. 'So now Bly wants to know if Derek is bluffing or really does know people who could help.'

'That's about it,' said Dawkins. 'I'll go down to Croydon tomorrow. You should come.'

'Why?'

Dawkins shrugged. 'You'll actually see how things are.'

After a while, Cotton nodded. 'All right. Now tell me about the chairs Derek mentioned.'

175

Dawkins smiled and shook his head. 'Derek is talking about a man called Vernon Carter. He disappeared in December 1945. The story is Maurice beat him to death with a solid wood chair from a Snow White display. Probably Dopey's.'

Cotton blinked. He remembered the window display he'd seen on his first visit to Croydon with Ayrtoun.

'Maurice works for the store,' said Dawkins. 'He's certainly not going to deny the story. It makes his debt-collectors' jobs easier.'

'What did this man Carter supposedly do?' asked Cotton.

'Carter dealt in "shrinkage". That's when stores "lose" some of their goods before they go up on the shelves. All stores have to allow for it. But not Maurice Bly's. The management there is very happy.'

'You're telling me that a loan shark works for a department store?'

'Yes. He works in the basement. This is one of the stores that "entertain to sell" as they put it. It's for the kiddies. They've got a grotto, a little stream – oh, and an Indian Emporium. We may find tomorrow that Maurice smells a bit. It's incense – sandalwood and all that stuff.'

Dawkins and Cotton went to Croydon by train the next day. From Victoria on a fast train it took barely twenty minutes to get to East Croydon station. They walked down past Whitgift Middle

School to North End, crossed it and then tackled a steep, downward-sloping cobbled alley.

At the bottom of the slope they came out into light. On a corner, about fifty yards away to their right, standing entirely alone was a tiny, two-storey pub called the Duke of Wellington. The painting of the Duke was based on Goya's with some added colour. Little remained of the buildings that had once stood around it except for a few scattered grey bricks on an area of about half a football pitch.

'Bomb damage?' said Cotton.

'Doodlebugs,' said Dawkins. 'Croydon lost about seven hundred people to Doodlebugs falling short of London. In a way it has helped with the slum clearance. The remaining buildings were easier to condemn. Shaken up, you see.'

Just before they went into the pub a butcher's boy on a bicycle pulled up.

'After you,' said Dawkins.

They followed the butcher's boy inside. He made directly for a table and slapped down something wrapped in soft brown paper in front of a portly little man. The little man tweaked at the paper and revealed a little blood and kidneys. He nodded. Another man removed them from the table and the boy left.

'This is Mr Smith,' said Dawkins, indicating Cotton.

Maurice Bly lifted a finger in acknowledgement and smiled a little. 'If you feel that's incumbent upon you, it's all right by me, Mr Dawkins.'

Bly was wearing a brown dustcoat. His cheeks were as crusty and cracked as cooking apples, he had a little white hair and, as he smiled, he exposed a number of gaps in teeth almost as small as milk teeth.

'Is Mr Smith a man for bitter? Or does he prefer mild?'

Dawkins cleared his throat. 'Mr Smith doesn't drink beer, Maurice.'

'A spirits man, then? But I don't know that they can do you a pink gin here, Mr Smith.'

'I'm on duty, Mr Bly,' said Cotton. He could smell no exotic incense, just old beer.

'I feel honoured,' said Bly. 'I do. But this is not a place for champagne, Mr Smith. They might have a bottle or two of cider here. They wouldn't rise to draught.'

There was something Uriah Heepish about his manner, but it was evidently in no way serious.

'I asked Mr Smith here as an observer,' said Dickie Dawkins. 'You don't object to that?'

Maurice Bly shrugged happily. 'Not my call, sir,' he said. 'This is a free country.'

They were interrupted by another butcher's boy.

'What's this?' said Bly.

'Crown of lamb, sir.'

Cotton thought Maurice had to be spending very little on food and very little time queuing with his ration book.

'Good,' said Maurice. 'Send this to – Mrs Statham. Yes, Mrs Statham.'

And, of course, food had become a currency. And power.

Maurice looked up. 'You've heard I've been a bit unhappy, have you?' he said.

'Came straight down here as soon as I knew,' said Dickie Dawkins.

Maurice Bly smiled. 'Oh, it's no laughing matter,' he said. 'We've been getting way too much attention since they had that poof kerfuffle at the Greyhound.'

'What kind of attention?'

'Bobbies on the beat at New Addington.'

Cotton only found out what Maurice was talking about on the train back. A lot of Maurice's prime market, the poor, had been moved to the Boot Estate, built on what had been a farm, in New Addington. Although several hundred houses had gone up by 1938, the war and lack of money had isolated the estate and there was little in the way of infrastructure. There was no public transport and no other facilities, except a pub. No school, no doctor, no library. The estate was locally known as 'Little Siberia'.

'It's right up a hill. There's no midwife. They don't even have trees,' Dickie Dawkins told him. 'I think there's some word of a church being built as a contraceptive measure.'

Maurice was complaining that his debt collectors could no longer act with impunity.

Dawkins nodded and turned towards 'Mr Smith'. 'Have you seen enough?'

Cotton understood he was being asked to leave.

Maurice Bly smiled. 'Only if it is quid pro quo,' he said.

Cotton smiled back. 'In return for what?'

'Just my little joke,' said Maurice. 'Really for Mr Dawkins here. Is there anything I can do for you, sir?'

'Yes,' said Cotton. 'Do you know someone called Derek Jennings?'

Bly feigned thought. 'I might do.'

'He's off limits. You talk to Mr Dawkins. But don't touch Derek.'

'Why should you think I would?'

Cotton shrugged. 'Do you have a lot of competition in your line of work, Mr Bly?'

Maurice frowned. 'Are you talking about that fucking Greek in West Croydon?'

'I wasn't really. I was trying to get over to you that my interests are a little wider than local, and I and my team don't have the . . . constraints, shall we say, or the limitations or needs that the local police do. Do you understand me?'

Cotton thought he had probably alarmed Dickie Dawkins more than Maurice Bly. Maurice smiled.

'Yes, I've got that,' he said. And then to demonstrate he understood. 'You already drink champagne, right?'

Cotton smiled. 'I was hoping to appeal to your patriotism.'

Maurice was delighted and possibly flattered. 'Always, Mr Smith. Always.'

Cotton left them to it. On his way out he stepped aside for a boy bringing a box of groceries. Later he would see a delivery of vegetables.

Dawkins did not take long, but in the meantime Cotton watched the children, off school again, playing in the wasteland. Some had arranged blackened bricks into gun posts. A hopscotch game had been drawn in black and girls were skipping. A boy with ragged shorts, bare legs and plimsolls was using a battered pram wheel as a hoop, apparently excluded from the main game. Dawkins came out and they started walking.

'Why isn't Mr Bly in jail?' said Cotton.

'Nothing is in his name,' said Dawkins. 'Do you want to know more?'

'Why not?'

'We think he has an arrangement with a Tory baronet in East Grinstead – a backer.'

'He'd be a champagne drinker, I take it?'

'Yes,' said Dawkins.

'What's going to happen?'

'Oh, I imagine there'll be the odd mechanical problem with police vehicles. It's quite a climb to New Addington on a bike.'

'Quiet law?'

'Something like that. I called you Mr Smith because—'

'I know. Why has there been no progress in finding Vernon Carter? The police have had more than a year.'

'You need informants,' said Dawkins, 'and there

are some things informants don't think worth the cost.'

'What about the Greek?'

'He's a bookie. He's called Randall. He was born in Greek Street, that's all.'

'And Mrs Statham, recipient of the crown of lamb—'

'A police wife,' said Dickie Dawkins.

Cotton nodded. 'Someone in Motor Division?'

Dickie Dawkins grunted, more an acceptance of shabby realities than a yes.

On their way back on the train to London, Dickie Dawkins asked Cotton a question.

'Are you armed?'

'No. It's not allowed. Are you?'

Dawkins tapped Cotton's forearm. 'Here,' he said.

'What is it?'

Dawkins put his hand in his side pocket and brought something out. He looked around.

'Put out your palm.'

Cotton did. In a variation of a handshake, Dawkins transferred something warm and heavy into Cotton's hand. Cotton opened his fingers.

The knuckledusters were made of brass, looked like four hexagonal nuts welded together, the inside edges smoothed off and the leading edges hammered down. On the small finger side there was a small curl that Cotton had seen on some scissor handles.

'Does damage all right,' said Dawkins, 'but it's really to protect your knuckles, you see? You don't want to break your hand, do you?'

Cotton closed his fingers over the knuckledusters and looked at Dawkins.

'Look,' said the Special Branch man, 'when I was a uniformed policeman I protected property and I was protected by the uniform. It's not like that now. I'm plain clothes and that confuses, as any lawyer will tell you. I am not going down without inflicting damage first.'

'Mr Bly?'

Dawkins tapped the knuckledusters. 'Do you want some of these yourself? You have to be measured, you see.'

Cotton shook his head. 'No thanks,' he said. 'Can I tell Derek to stop hiding?'

He handed the knuckledusters back.

'Oh yes,' said Dawkins.

Back in his office, Cotton called Derek and told him he should wait twenty-four hours before he returned to Croydon.

'Did you go to see Maurice?' said Derek.

'Yes, I did.

'Oh, Mr Cotton. That's class. Thank you.'

CHAPTER 16

At four o'clock, Cotton went to the Garrick Club. He found Miles Crichton in reflective mood.

'Are you religious, Colonel?'

'No,' said Cotton.

'Then who do you ask for forgiveness?'

'People I have unwittingly offended. Have I offended you?'

'No, no. I was speaking in a larger, more spiritual sense. And I think you probably know that.'

Cotton smiled. 'I usually try to stick to practicalities.' He told Miles what he had been doing in Croydon.

Bit by bit and with a couple of glasses of champagne Miles Crichton began to cheer up.

'Don't disappoint me!' he said when Cotton had finished. 'Don't say you don't adore corruption. Wonderful thing. We are probably behind the Americans at present but trying so hard to catch up. Rationing is after all merely a form of prohibition. There's nothing like rigid rules for ornate wriggle room. We're no longer fighting a war. We have peacetime with harsh restrictions and no

184

enemy. We British don't have morality, we have behaviour, class and oodles of profitable humbug. Your Mr Bly has his bankrolling baronet. Some of our Dear Lords are mingling with gangsters, sometimes up against a wall. It's inevitable that such intimate contact should lead on to business arrangements. Our Establishment was never for those people who believe the propaganda about decency and fair play. And we're getting genuine gangsters! Not just the fighting gangs of the thirties.'

Cotton looked at him.

Miles Crichton frowned. 'Oh. Am I getting overwrought again?' he asked.

'There's a risk.'

'Right. I think I'll take myself off to the Stab in the Back and chat with other hacks. Do you want to come?'

'Any particular reason?'

Miles smiled. 'A reporter called Tom McEwan.'

A pub near Fleet Street called the White Hart was more frequently known as the Stab in the Back, or just the Stab. It was a favourite with *Daily Mirror* journalists. After Cotton had got Crichton downstairs, they took a taxi. The pub turned out to be rather plusher and more like a Victorian gentlemen's club than Cotton had expected. At first glance, Tom McEwan looked trim and well dressed. On a second glance, he began to look almost frail. He had the index and middle fingers of his right hand stained yellow down to the knuckles, and one of his eyebrows drooped as if permanently on guard against smoke. His neat moustache was slightly discoloured.

'We're dispensing with introductions I take it,' said McEwan. He sighed. 'Let's be Pip and Squeak and Wilfred, then.'

McEwan had a thick Scottish accent that he alleviated by speaking quite slowly. He laughed very quietly, with almost no sound to the breath. The cartoon characters he mentioned were in a popular *Daily Mirror* strip, a dog and a penguin who acted *in loco parentis* to a long-eared rabbit who was only capable of two elementary sounds, one being 'gunc'.

'Of course, Tom,' said Miles Crichton. 'Just a little chat.'

Cotton offered them a drink. Both journalists chose double whiskies, McEwan specifying Bell's. Cotton went to the bar and bought them.

'Miles tells me you've an interest in Robert Starmer-Smith,' said McEwan, when he came back.

Cotton nodded. McEwan lit a Kensitas cigarette. 'Sorry about this,' he said, 'they're supposed to cool the throat. You're welcome to try one.'

'No, thank you,' said Cotton.

McEwan frowned and tasted his drink. 'You're not a pious, clean-living person, are you?'

Cotton smiled. 'No.'

'But you're not drinking either.'

'I have,' lied Cotton, 'a fairly heavy night ahead.'

'All right,' said McEwan. 'I take it you haven't had much luck getting hold of Starmer-Smith's file and you have found people a tad reluctant to talk about him.'

'Something like,' said Cotton.

McEwan tasted his whisky again. 'The key point of Starmer-Smith's life,' he said, 'was that he did his war service before Oxford. He lasted a fair bit but then had a complete nervous collapse in 1916 and had to spend a year in a sanatorium in Guernsey. There they stitched his mind back together again and sent him to Army Intelligence.'

McEwan stubbed out his cigarette with some vigour.

'Does that explain why he thought his greatest service to his country in 1939 would be hunting down homosexuals? Surely he had other options,' said Cotton.

'Now you're talking,' said McEwan. 'What he is, is a man who has been to the brink and cannot bear the notion that it was for nothing. It's made him unforgiving and determined.' McEwan sipped his whisky. 'I suppose most people would describe him as somewhere between a stuffed shirt and a hair shirt. Wrong. He's not the kind of man who feels he has to tell you in private that he hates the sin but not the sinner. He's more castrate the sinner and look – the sin's gone because I've got his balls in my hand. Not that he'd ever say that in public. He'd stress the paramount

187

need for societies to be homogeneous, and his loathing of adulterate culture.'

Homogeneous? Adulterate? Cotton recognized that special use of language from Spain.

'He's a National Catholic?'

McEwan laughed. 'That hasn't really caught on here. So Starmer-Smith has found he's had no choice but to consider the Church of England as "moral mortar",' he said. 'But just look at the Archbishop of Canterbury. He believes buggery to be beyond the pale as well as unmentionable – but, come on chaps, a little boyish tinkering is not really worth pursuing with the full weight of the law.'

'You're telling me a high-ranking Intelligence Officer believes his job involves a religious stance?'

The journalists looked happy.

Cotton sighed. 'Is Starmer-Smith married?' he asked.

'Oh, yes,' said Miles. 'There's a story that his first girl gave him up when he broke down. Later he married the daughter of his spiritual adviser, the Reverend Gilbert Caskie's girl, Violet. They have two daughters, also named after flowers.'

Cotton nodded. 'All right, gentlemen. Tell me something. Mr Starmer-Smith is part of MI5. He works in what we'll call delicate matters. You are prohibited by law from writing about him. Do you normally follow such people?'

McEwan held up his finger. 'In the thirties,' he said, 'I worked at the *Glasgow Herald*. Gang correspondent, you might say.'

'Ah. When Sir Percy Sillitoe was Chief Constable.'

McEwan smiled. 'Good. What do you know about the Billy Boys?'

Cotton shook his head. 'Not much. They were a powerful fighting gang. And I understand they were Protestants.'

'Oh, Prods, yes. Billy had them drilled, with bands for the Orange marches. Glasgow is Protestant against Catholic and vice versa. Let's say Billy and his boys hid behind sectarianism. In exactly the same way as the Catholic gangs like the Norman Conks and the San Toi did. When Sir Percy began working his magic a number of other people began to think the Billy Boys might have their uses. As fighting men, that is. First Sir Oswald Mosley offered them black shirts and Billy was quick to take that up. And when the war broke out, the army always has jobs for semi-trained brutes. Robert Starmer-Smith took two razor boys – Frankie Sinclair and Jackie Boyle.'

'Why would Starmer-Smith want men like that?'

McEwan looked at Miles Crichton. 'Shock therapy?' said Miles.

'I think,' said McEwan, 'that he'd say it's because the enemy has the Devil's ways and you need men who know those ways but are now working for the common good and the moral mortar of society.'

Cotton nodded and sat back. Did Sir Percy Sillitoe know about Sinclair and Boyle? He thought probably not. Was there the threat of a sentence hanging over them? He thought there probably was. It was likely, then, that they had if not police backing, at least police forbearance. Presumably that was what Radcliffe was for. He also made a mental note of the anti-Semitic flavour of what he had heard.

'Are you going to do something?' asked Miles.

Cotton smiled. 'First, I'll think. Thank you very much, both of you.'

'You're not going already?' said Miles Crichton. 'Another round, gentlemen?'

Cotton got them new whiskies. He held out his hand to McEwan. 'Thank you,' he said. 'You have been very helpful. If I—'

'Contact in the same way. Good luck.'

'One last thing. How mean is Briggs?'

McEwan looked doubtful. 'What would you say?' he asked Miles Crichton. 'He'd certainly hit a woman, he's spiteful but he's most spiteful when he is being loyal, of course.'

'What are you talking about?'

'Omitted history,' suggested Miles Crichton. 'Things that didn't happen or are not useful to recall.'

'As in?'

Crichton turned to McEwan. 'Wentworth Woodhouse?'

Wentworth Woodhouse was a palatial Georgian country house on a huge estate in south Yorkshire. Manny Shinwell had not just given permission for open-cast mining of coal in a Humphry Repton park right up to the back door, he had insisted on it, despite protests from the local miners.

190

McEwan nodded. 'Briggs worked for Manny. He came down here to tell anyone who would listen that the miners had been manipulated by the Earl, that the poor bastards were still tugging their forelocks.'

On his way home on the Underground, Cotton gave in to generalities. He wondered what kind of security service could be run on reports and opinions on character. Mostly, however, he wondered at a department in MI5 that employed Glasgow criminals. Seven years was an unbelievably long time for a razor boy not to have put his mark on someone and have it recorded. He thought what his own report would be like. It would have a number of contributions, from Ayrtoun, for example, and then have been given a show of coherence by someone else. It would not mention he had stabbed a young man to death in Cadiz in 1944.

On Wednesday morning, 15 January, Cotton met up with Dawkins at the Victoria Station bar and told him what he had learnt from Tom McEwan about Boyle and Sinclair.

'Have you ever heard of these people?' he asked.

'No,' said Dawkins.

'What are the chances you can find something on them?'

'What? Honestly?' said Dawkins. He made a face. 'Very poor. If what this journalist says is true, I doubt there'll be any records.'

'Unofficially?'

Dawkins shook his head. 'No. A couple of Jocks with razors is the kind of thing I'd have heard about, even if the queers weren't pressing charges.'

'Will you ask around?'

Dawkins thought, then shook his head. 'No. Do you want reasons?'

'Yes. Why not?' said Cotton.

'Either your journalist is wrong – in which case I'm drawing attention to myself. And if he is right someone's got a very tight lid on it – and questions will cause me more bother than any answers I can get are worth.'

Cotton smiled. 'You don't trust journalists?'

'It's not that. It's just that they can be a bit free and excitable with their conclusions.'

'All right,' said Cotton. 'Let's keep the names in mind in case they crop up.'

'Agreed,' said Dawkins.

CHAPTER 17

On the night of the 15th/16th at about 1 a.m. Cotton's telephone rang.

'Yes?'

'You're the cotton man,' a voice mumbled.

'This is Cotton, yes.'

The person at the other end sighed. 'They've removed my security clearance.'

'I'm sorry to hear it, Mr Watson.'

'You knew.'

'No, I didn't,' said Cotton. 'You've just told me. What happened?'

There was a pause. 'It's not – fair.' Watson said this very quietly, without emphasis on 'fair'.

'No,' said Cotton. 'Tell me what happened.'

'They took away my security clearance. And they say there's nothing they can do about it. It's out of their hands.' Watson groaned. 'I have – and I am saying this in the most literal sense, you know – absolutely nobody to appeal to.'

'Then choose something else.'

'What do you mean?'

'Go back to your university, for instance.'

Watson sighed again. 'Oh, I don't want to do that any more.'

'Why not?'

'Because I'm a researcher. I don't want to teach.'

'You can still do research.'

'No,' said Watson. 'It's not the same.'

'Of course it isn't. But you really need to find something different, something preferably that suits you, but you really need to do so quickly.'

The next pause was so long Cotton wondered if Watson had passed out.

'Easy to say.'

'I know.'

Something between a snuffle and a laugh came down the line.

'I'm in a phone box,' said Watson.

Cotton heard what might have been another mumbling voice or just the cabin door opening. 'Mr Watson?' he said.

'Oh, damn,' said Watson.

The line started beeping, then clicked and went on to a continuous drone. Cotton groaned. He put down the telephone and waited. He did not think Watson would call back and he did not.

In the morning Cotton contacted Dawkins and told him of Watson's telephone call. By ten, they knew Watson had left his digs in Oxford.

'I mean he's given them up and paid off the landlords,' said Dawkins. 'He gave his forwarding address as his mother's, piled his stuff into a small Austin and left. That was on the 14th in the evening.'

'Didn't he say his mother lived in a place called Sanderstead?'

'Yes, we're getting on to that. And I am trying to get hold of the car registration number,' said Dawkins.

By two in the afternoon they had the car registration. But there was no sign of the car and it was clear that Watson was not at his mother's and had not visited her in the last few days.

On Friday, 17 January Cotton reluctantly went to Margot Fenwick's 'post-theatre supper'. Though Margot's note had said black tie, he found himself to be the only man in evening wear. Margot herself was the only female in a gown. It was emerald green, pre-war but she had simply let out some of the tucks to allow for her expansion in the time since. It gave her an unfinished rather than a bohemian look, as if off stage there would be a seamstress with pins in her teeth. The six others there had come directly from the theatre. One girl still had streaks of green and white on her face and an edge of flesh and orange crust. In Margot's lamp-cluttered drawing room her poses sometimes gave her the look of wearing a mask or of representing someone like Toulouse-Lautrec's absinthe drinker.

Cotton was reminded of the swoops and swirls of Mexican street processions he had experienced as a child, but without the colours. Gus, the small red-haired man who had slept on a sofa in Cotton's flat on Hogmanay, swept in and produced a paste tiara for 'Queen' Margot. Margot giggled, apparently unaware that his caresses and chucks were intimate without being interested in much more than this meal and others to come.

'You don't approve,' a girl said.

Cotton turned. Anna Melville, previously Sokol, was not wearing a fancy costume but a black dress that was at least one size too small for her.

'Of your taking advantage of her?'

Anna Melville laughed. 'Come on. She enjoys herself. She gets the attention she wants – and the juicy gossip. Nothing's free. I know that. If you're interested, of course.' She did not let Cotton reply. She put her hand on his arm. 'Please don't think of the future. I don't know how long Margot has got but then neither do you. If in ten years she feels old and abandoned, well, she had this.'

Cotton shook his head. 'I don't feel responsible for her.'

'What do you feel?'

'Mildly uncomfortable. But probably only for this evening.'

The girl laughed and went to embrace Margot.

The other guests included a female costumer who was running a sideline in clothes – 'usually, undergarments and nightdresses, darling' – made out of parachute silk, and a bald man called Eric Sangster who described himself as 'the poet' and immediately asked Cotton which side he was on in the 'ferocious battle' going on at the Poetry Society.

'Blood everywhere,' said the poet grandly.

Gus popped up from behind Eric's bald head and whispered.

'I say, have you heard that Alec Clunes has given Christopher Fry four hundred and fifty pounds to write a new play?'

Eric stiffened. He looked at Cotton. 'Did you know Fry's real name is Arthur Hammond Harris?'

'Mr Cotton here thinks Eric is not a good name for a poet,' said Gus.

'Is that true?' asked Eric.

'Not in the slightest. I don't see that George Orwell is a better name than Eric Blair.'

'What do you think of Orwell?' asked Eric.

'He's not a poet, is he?' said Cotton.

'Well,' said Gus, 'aren't we opinionated?'

Eric blinked. 'I'm against the aesthetics of bare fact,' he announced.

'I see,' said Cotton without understanding or, after a moment's pause, any desire to enquire what Eric meant. 'Are you a playwright as well as a poet?'

'Certainly,' said Eric. 'I profess the muse. But I also consider theatre to be social poetry. Catharsis, not tranquillity, is my aim.'

Cotton had been a little anxious that he would be asked what he himself did but now saw very clearly that there was no need.

Margot had an elderly female servant she called

Nanny who was cooking the meal. Nanny kept coming out of the kitchen to complain to Margot that she wasn't a cook.

'Come on,' said Gus, 'I'll make the gravy. You all love my gravy.'

The meal was chestnut soup, a brace of tough pheasants accompanied by very burnt onions and a purée of Jerusalem artichokes, and then some Cheshire cheese and quince – all from the country. It was amazingly bad but no one gave any sign of noticing. The drinks were mixed, according to what people had been able to bring. Eggnog mixed with phrases like 'the future of mankind', port with names like Stanislavski, and brandy with gossip about people Cotton did not know.

'You don't like theatre,' said Gus.

'I much prefer film,' said Cotton. 'The boards don't squeak and the thing is edited, scenes are reshot if required. That might be tedious for the actors but it does suit the spectators.'

Gus laughed. 'You just like the lack of rapport, the lack of contact. You want to ignore the uncertainty, the danger in live performance.'

'I absolutely love it. A film actor can concentrate on the role rather than appealing for applause or getting put off by a cough. On film an actor can get more chances. On stage the audience is stuck with a mistake, a badly cast actor or a fluffed or forgotten line.'

'My dear chap, theatre is much closer to life.'

'But not always well-acted or convincing,' said

Cotton. 'Ham it up on film and you run out of work. I'm sure you are thinking of David Hume. He described the mind as being like theatre – but seen far more rapidly. Film is actually getting there. The actors don't have to exit the stage. The frame can cut. More important, it allows for whispers rather than bellows. On film the smallest movement of a face can be important. On stage it's a windmill of arms and voices getting hoarse as the greasepaint melts.'

'But that's the point! Theatre wants catharsis,' said Eric. 'We don't want to be observing shop girls or people on the Tube!'

Cotton smiled. 'But catharsis on stage is usually bombastic, false or frenzied. The actor intrudes. On stage the actor's relationship with the audience is too important to the actor. It can look as if he's too involved in self-expression, wants a reflection. A film actor has to concentrate on the role.'

Cotton stopped speaking. The tough pheasant and burnt onions were beginning to cause his stomach problems.

'Have you ever seen a film called *Ecstasy*?' said Gus. 'It's Hedy Lamarr being naked before stardom. It's sometimes called "The Burning Bush".'

Cotton nodded. 'I saw it in Germany in 1945.'

'What did you think?'

'Do you really want to know?'

'Yes!'

'OK,' said Cotton. 'Miss Hedy Lamarr is very

beautiful. However, the nobility of physical work in the film is much overrated and the story, elderly mind, educated impotence, young, uneducated muscle, all those symbolic clouds, trees and horses become tiresome.'

'I rather liked those gleaming muscles,' said Gus. He laughed. 'But do you know how the director got those looks of ecstasy on Miss Hedwig Kiesler's beautiful face? He jabbed her in the bottom with a safety pin!'

Cotton smiled. 'But the pin was off screen, surely?'

'My!' said Gus. 'You prefer your acting in real life, don't you?'

'I've never been on stage,' said Cotton, 'so I have never had to come off it.'

Cotton had barely got up from the table when he was punched on the arm.

'Are you telling me I'm too fat?' said Anna Melville.

'No.'

'The film may have been made in Czechoslovakia but she's an Austrian Jew, you know, from Vienna.'

'All right.' Cotton frowned. Did she normally compete with film stars who had changed their names?

'You *are* a bastard,' she said.

'Why exactly?'

'I have worn my black grape dress.'

In case he failed to understand, she pointed at her plumped breasts.

'Lovely,' he said, 'but I'm afraid I have indigestion.'

'I could squeeze it out of you.'

Cotton leant across and kissed her on the lips. She was momentarily surprised, then pushed her tongue into his mouth and moaned. He broke the kiss.

'You're very sweet and ripe,' he said.

'Jesus, don't say that. I want to be tart.'

Cotton grunted before he smiled.

'I'm going to go now.'

'Suit yourself, Mr Stiffy, but when you get *very* frustrated, I'd be happy for you to bear down on me.'

Cotton went to Margot to thank her for 'everything'. Margot giggled. Then giggled some more. He walked to the front door but was pursued.

'I don't think it's your generous soul Anna's after,' said Gus Mallory.

'I see,' said Cotton. 'You're a kind of interpreter, is that it?'

'My dear chap, as Stanislavski said, you go in and you go out of a character to get the rounded whole.'

'You're a poet, Mr Mallory. Tell Margot again, it's been lovely.'

Cotton went back to his flat. He had a headache but groaned mostly because he had been stirred and irritated.

He grunted. 'Black grapes,' he said. A moment later he tasted burnt onion on his teeth and went to brush them.

★ ★ ★

In the afternoon of Monday the 20th Cotton received a telephone call from Geoffrey Ayrtoun.

'Any news of Watson?'

'No.'

Ayrtoun sighed. 'Is it wise to let Watson handle this himself?'

'I'm not sure we have much choice.'

'Good,' said Ayrtoun. 'Glad you got that off your chest. Of course you are right. We have few resources and, as you say, probably less choices. You're on a "do what you can with what you've got" kind of job.'

'Are you saying I should expect something else, something new?'

'I have absolutely no idea. You did your best for Watson, kept him out of jail. I'm not holding you to more, just asking you to keep your eyes peeled on this – and anything else that crops up.'

'And?'

Ayrtoun made a noise. 'The problem with the Starmer-Smiths of this world, the would-be moralists, is that the stupid bastards don't understand the effects of their righteousness.'

Cotton waited. Ayrtoun cleared his throat.

'Are you in a position, Colonel, to give me a guarantee that A. A. Watson has not responded to his abrupt banishment by going with what he has to a foreign power?'

'No, I'm not,' said Cotton. He raised his eyes towards the cornice. The pattern in the plaster was a sort of cut-off oval, like a beheaded egg with swags.

'You see?' said Ayrtoun. 'Do try to find him, old man. It would be better for everyone.'

But Cotton had no success when he called the other agencies. Nobody had any information at all on Watson's whereabouts. For what it was worth, MI5 in their watch on Soviet buildings and people had nothing either.

Cotton talked to Dawkins. Dawkins had nothing to report either.

'He must have the car off the road,' he said.

'Perhaps. How far have you enquired?'

'If we're lucky,' Dawkins said, 'he'll have holed up in Devon or Shropshire or somewhere while he thinks of what to do.' He paused. 'Look, unless we step this up, making him a wanted person and put out a nationwide alert, we're pretty well stuck. He's not actually wanted for a crime, is he?'

'No,' said Cotton. 'Thanks. One last thing. Today I was asked whether or not I could guarantee Watson hadn't gone to the Soviets. Of course I couldn't.'

'Yes,' said Dawkins. 'But I can't guarantee these Jock razor boys the journalist told you about haven't got anything to do with Watson's disappearance. I don't believe they do, though. Why would they bother now that his security clearance has been taken away?'

Cotton grunted. It was a sort of 'yes' but was hardly happy.

★　★　★

On Tuesday, 21 January the temperature dropped very sharply. At about three thirty in the afternoon thick snow began to fall. In London at least there was very little wind. The snow settled and began to layer. For a spell people looked cheerful in all that white. But Cotton noticed on his way home that the screeching of the Tube wheels had become sharper, as if there was a knife grinder nearby, and by the time he had crunched the short way to Wilbraham Place from Sloane Square station he could barely feel his fingers and feet except as vague areas of ache. 'A bad night for water pipes,' someone had said on the Tube.

Cotton drew the curtains in all the rooms and put on the electric fire in his sitting room. He prepared some leek and potato soup and listened to the news on the radio while it was cooking. The storm was very bad and snow was drifting 'in eastern areas and the Midlands'. Drifts as high as twenty feet had been reported. In certain parts of the country temperatures between 10 and 15 degrees Fahrenheit were expected overnight.

He telephoned his father who told him the snow was deep all right but he was well wrapped up and sitting by the range in the kitchen.

Cotton then ate the soup and some bread and a scrape of butter. He listened to some music but gave up because Art Tatum sounded particularly crackly, and began reading a book called *Laughter in the Dark* that he had picked up in a second-hand bookshop along with one called

Miss Lonelyhearts. Around nine, he checked on his bedroom. Despite the fat central heating pipes, he could see his breath. He unplugged the electric fire and took it through to warm the bedroom, opened the doors to the kitchen and put on a gas ring.

Later he heated some milk, put a small shot of whisky in it and drank it before he went through to his bedroom. He got out another blanket, and just before he got into bed he parted the curtains and looked out on D'Oyley Street. There was about two feet of snow on the road and the snow, though less, was still falling. This was London and the complete silence felt strange.

CHAPTER 18

On Wednesday, 22 January 1947 one of the guests at the Greyhound Hotel in Croydon did not respond to his wake-up call at 7 a.m. Unable to get any response or hear anything inside the room, the bedroom door was opened by hotel staff at about 8 a.m.

The police and the ambulance service were called at once. The first to arrive was a police constable on foot at about 8.15. He closed the room again and waited.

The heavy snow – it was still falling – and the extreme cold were causing mayhem. The train, Tube and bus services were fitful and slow when they operated at all. Snowploughs and gritters were out on the roads but new snow was falling on what they cleared. By the time the security alert was given it was 9.30 a.m.

Cotton received a telephone call from Dickie Dawkins of Special Branch at 10.15.

'Your man Watson would appear to have topped himself. In the Greyhound Hotel, of all places.'

'Are you there?'

'You're joking. I've only just heard myself.'

'Are the trains running?'

'Nobody seems to know.'

Cotton telephoned Hans Bieber. The driver was unimpressed by the winter weather.

'I will collect you,' he said. 'I have snow chains.'

'I don't know how they'll work on Streatham High Road.'

Hans made a tutting noise. 'I have driven in snow before,' he said. 'Give me ten, maybe fifteen minutes.'

Cotton called Dickie Dawkins to offer him a lift.

'Your Kraut driver? No. I'm trying the train. They've got the snowploughs out.'

Hans Bieber took twenty minutes to arrive.

'Not tyres, weak windscreen wipers,' he complained. 'They stick on the snow.'

They experienced a tremendous skid however, both sliding sideways and turning right round as soon as they started, ended up facing the wrong way a couple of inches from a white mound secreting another vehicle.

'*Scheisse!*' said Hans.

Cotton said nothing. He thought he should leave Hans to his job.

'What kind of stupid snow is this anyway?' said the driver, but the skid had done its job and Hans Bieber got them facing the right way with a sort of determined delicacy and then concentrated on his job, without speaking.

What surprised Cotton was that Watson should

have gone back to the Greyhound Hotel to commit suicide. He had found Watson to be stubborn, naïve but also very decided. Was this really as crude as 'This is where my career ended. Look what you have made me do!'?

They drove over the Thames. The river looked the colour of milky tea and the texture of wallpaper glue. Cotton had never seen the Thames freeze over. He wondered what kind of temperature it would take to make it icebound.

He put the tartan rug over his knees and settled back. After a while watching the snowflakes stream past, he closed his eyes and found something similar moved under his lids.

'Can you see?' he asked Hans.

'Not much. That is why I am going slow.'

'It's not a criticism, Hans.'

'There are flurries,' said Hans, 'at any speed.'

'You're doing well,' said Cotton. He opened his eyes. The needle of the speedometer was flickering between ten and fifteen miles per hour.

It was 12.45 when they arrived at the Greyhound. There being so many official vehicles and no space left in the courtyard, Hans dropped Cotton off and went to look for somewhere to park. Standing by an oddly conjoined grandfather clock in Reception, put together from two different historical fashions, Cotton learnt Dickie Dawkins was still not there. He decided to wait and took up the offer of a mug of soup and a chicken sandwich and the same for Hans Bieber when he arrived. He was shown into the hotel manager's office and briefed by a police inspector.

The manager of the Greyhound said that Watson had arrived 'with the snow' the evening before. Since October he had stayed there several times, arriving in the afternoon or evening, before leaving quite early the next morning.

'He drove himself, sir,' said the police inspector. 'It's a little Austin. Parked in the courtyard.'

'Have you looked at it?'

The inspector did not answer directly.

'Make sure nobody touches the deceased's motor vehicle,' he said to a constable. He looked at Cotton. Cotton moved his hand as if about to speak.

'No, check the inside. See if there's anything there.' He paused. 'The keys will be upstairs. Just check if there is anything visible.'

Watson had gone to his room and stayed there. He had asked for a fire to be lit and had ordered room service – whisky, a ham sandwich with mustard and an apple. He had tipped the waiter sixpence.

'The next anybody knew was this morning,' said the inspector.

'Where's the body?'

'Still upstairs, sir. The doctor's up there now.'

'Are you calling this a suicide?'

'Not until we have all the information.'

'Did he leave a note?'

'We haven't found one so far, sir.'

'All right. I'll wait for Mr Dawkins. Have you any information on when he'll get here?'

'No, sir.'

Cotton went out to the reception area. Hans Bieber raised his chin.

'What?' said Cotton.

'The nancy boy is here.'

'Where?'

'In the bar. I'm not going there.'

Cotton shrugged. 'I don't mind.'

He went through. Derek Jennings was on a bar stool with a pink gin in front of him. He stood up.

'Sit down,' said Cotton. 'I want to know whether Watson saw anybody last night. The Greyhound says no.'

'Well, they would, wouldn't they,' said Derek.

'The police and Special Branch will certainly be asking around to see whether or not the management is correct. Take care, of course, but I want you to speak to the staff as well. Clear? We need to know of any patrons who might not want to come forward. Not just nice young men. Include those who might have had difficulty getting home to their wives and children last night. Go wider than the Greyhound.'

Derek nodded.

'Have you eaten?' asked Cotton.

'No.'

'My driver is in reception. They're offering soup

and a chicken sandwich. Tell him I say you're on our tab.'

It was 1.25. There was a disturbance in reception caused by Dickie Dawkins's arrival. He, his hat and coat were entirely covered with snow. Cotton went to see him.

'I had to damn well walk from East Croydon station,' said Dawkins unnecessarily. He was beating his hat against his leg.

Cotton took this as a complaint that the police had not collected him by car and saved him the walk.

'Bloody Brighton train,' said Dawkins, struggling to get out of his coat. 'We got stuck at Wandsworth Common. Right,' he said. 'Have you seen the body?'

'No,' said Cotton. 'I've been waiting for you.'

'All right,' said Dawkins. He paused. 'Is there anything to eat?'

'Soup and a chicken sandwich.'

'I'll have some of that,' said Dawkins. 'Thigh meat!' he called out.

'I'm sorry, sir, the chicken is over.'

'What do you mean?'

'The chicken is finished, sir.'

'What have you got?'

'Some Argentinian corn-beef, sir.'

'With mustard,' said Dawkins.

They went upstairs. Watson's room had a policeman outside. Inside they found the doctor, a detective sergeant and the body. Watson was still in the four-poster bed, on his back. His eyes were closed. Beside him on the bedside table was a plate, a rat-tail knife and the remains of an apple on it. Watson had eaten about half. Beside the plate was an empty syringe.

'Can you smell that?' said the doctor, pointing at the plate on the bedside table. 'Sometimes people describe the smell as being like bitter almonds. But they may have bitten an apple seed. That's got a small amount of cyanide in it too.'

Dawkins sniffed.

'This is in the apple,' the doctor said. 'The deceased would appear to have injected it with the syringe and found half an apple enough.'

Dawkins winced. 'Shit,' he said, 'he looks grim.'

Cotton looked at him. Then at Watson. In a dark room on a snowy day the dead man's face was grey with blue tinges. A moving, spotted effect from the snowflakes provided no animation.

'Have you moved him?' he asked the doctor.

'No. He was tucked up like this. All very neat.'

'Will you be doing the autopsy?'

'Oh yes,' said the doctor.

'What's that?' said Dawkins, pointing.

'An erection,' said the doctor. 'It happens. There's a Latin phrase. Amorous death, something like that.'

'Jesus,' said Dawkins.

For a man who had seen other bodies, some of them a great deal more gruesome than this neat arrangement, Dawkins looked queasy. Perhaps it was the tidiness that upset him, that someone could clear themselves away.

Cotton went to the window and looked out. He had to bend to do it. Below was the courtyard. There was a fire escape outside. He checked the window frame. It was of the sash type, not too big. The catch arrangement on the upper frame was drawn over the lower.

'Has anyone touched this?' he asked.

'Not as far as I know, sir,' said the sergeant.

Cotton looked round the room. Despite himself he found he was judging Watson's taste in choosing this room to kill himself. The style was what Cotton thought of as Victorian-Tudor. There was the four-poster bed that, although it had Elizabethan-type posts, did not look very old. The drapes were a dank-looking red, a sort of material flock. The needlepoint rug on the stained floor-boards was decorated with flowers.

Cotton walked over to a blackened door. It gave on to a bathroom. He noted that Watson had left nothing in there, no toothbrush or shaving kit.

'Have you cleared up here?' he asked.

The police sergeant shook his head. 'No, sir,' he said and walked across and opened the wardrobe door. Watson had hung up his shirt, suit and tie on the same hanger. Below them were his shoes, each containing a rolled-up sock.

'He has a small suitcase,' the police sergeant said and moved to that. The case contained a toilet bag, a linen bag ('his dirty underwear'), a fresh

213

shirt and fresh underwear. There was also a translated edition of *The Odyssey* and a book not of matches but of toothpicks.

Dawkins looked as much disapproving as puzzled. 'What is this?' he said. 'A boffin, some sort of expert in deadly science, comes to a hotel in a place where he was arrested about a fortnight ago, tops himself with cyanide and carries on like bleeding Snow White? Why did he need the apple if he had the syringe?'

'The ingestion of cyanide can be used to obtain a rapid decrease in blood pressure,' said the doctor. 'Of course, in high doses it attacks the central nervous system and heart.'

Dawkins turned. 'Are you saying it's better eaten?'

'It's what Goering did a few months back. And the man who invented nylon. He drank his with lemon juice, I believe.'

Dawkins grunted. 'No note?'

'No,' said the detective sergeant. 'I haven't found anything.'

Dawkins sighed. 'I'm hungry,' he said.

Cotton nodded and they left the room.

'Am I going to be seeing Radcliffe again? Or perhaps Starmer-Smith.'

Dawkins shrugged. 'I doubt it.'

Downstairs, Cotton left Dawkins with his soup and corn-beef sandwich and went to look for Derek.

Cotton had to wait but Derek had news.

'Mr Watson was drinking with a tall, tanned, good-looking fellow, greeny tweed suit, greying hair, not a homebody in any way, in the Swan and Sugarloaf. My source saw him give Mr Watson something like a tobacco pouch. They shook hands. Mr Watson then went to the Greyhound.'

'Good source?'

'Bambi Bosworth.'

Bambi was the person who had fled across school playing fields in early January.

'Nothing for old times?'

'Bambi says no. Mr Watson was a bit fragile. He gave Bambi a fiver and wished him well.'

'He didn't think something was wrong?'

'Well, he wasn't going to turn down a fiver, was he? That's a lot more than he usually gets. And he was getting it for old times' sake.'

Cotton went back to Dawkins. 'You're looking for something like a tobacco pouch, apparently.'

'Why?'

'That's what the syringe and the cyanide came in.'

Dawkins called a policeman. 'Look in the rubbish,' he said, 'A tobacco pouch is what you are looking for.'

'Leather?' said the policeman.

'It could be waxed cloth,' said Cotton.

The policeman left. 'What's this about?' asked Dawkins.

'Where would you get a syringe and cyanide?'

Dawkins sighed. 'I'm not a scientist,' he said.

'I don't think cyanide is an essential part of the atom bomb process.'

'We're looking for a supplier, then.'

In Watson's little car in the glove box the police found a small canvas roll, the kind of thing field hospitals have to hold scalpels and instruments. The police took it away.

'Next of kin?'

'I think he told me he had a mother in Sanderstead,' said Cotton.

'I'll do that,' said Dawkins. 'But give me a policeman to come along.'

CHAPTER 19

On Monday, 27 January, under a note announcing that the British Government had agreed to give Burma independence, Cotton found an urgent note from Ed Lowell, the US liaison officer, requesting a meeting. There was no mention of lunch.

He called Ed Lowell and they agreed to meet, at Lowell's suggestion, at the Royal Academy of Arts within half an hour. Cotton told Miss Kelly he was going out.

'Did you see Al Capone was dead, sir?' she asked.
'Syphilis apparently.'

'Right.'

Ed Lowell met him with an aggressive hush, tilting in to whisper.

'I'm disappointed, Peter. This man Watson was a Trotskyite!'

Cotton blinked. 'Is that some sort of fucking euphemism?'

'What are you talking about? I am talking about his political leanings.'

Cotton shook his head. 'I don't have that

information, Ed. What we do have is a report of someone who initially considered himself far too clever to respect the politics of democracies but who managed to frighten himself during the thirties by seeing how a desire for order could turn out. If you want to describe his politics, it was science for science's sake. He was touchy, proud and socially inept. He wasn't a joiner. If he had been he might have got more support from his colleagues.'

Ed Lowell got angrier. 'This man spent time in the States!'

'And what have you got on him during his time there? You have nothing, correct?'

'This isn't our information,' said Ed Lowell. 'It's from your side.'

'Really? And what does that say?'

Ed Lowell paused.

'Either it's surmise or—'

'What?'

'We're being played, Ed.'

'Are you saying he wasn't a member of the Communist Party in the early thirties?'

'I have seen no record of it.'

'That he wasn't in the Trotsky-Bolshevik-Leninist group, a Peace League man?'

Cotton closed one eye. 'No he wasn't. Watson wasn't a pacifist. He contributed to the Manhattan Project. That caused thousands of deaths. He was working on our bomb. You're lumping people together. And you are missing the point.'

'What's that?'

'We have a male witch called Starmer-Smith in MI5 who hunts homosexuals. I'm not saying it's him, but someone has taken the trouble to think homosexuality wasn't quite enough to identify a posthumous security risk. So they've added Trotskyite. Can you say who? I'll bet you can't. That brings us on to the question – why would someone want to confuse us.'

'It came from your side!' said Ed Lowell. 'You can't be suggesting someone with you is deliberately misleading us.'

It was very cold and Cotton was becoming irritated. He calmed himself with a small smile.

'No,' he said. 'All right. As I understand it, Ed, part of my job is to act as a cross-check so that people don't run away with themselves. In this case, we may merely be victims of gossip. It may be more. Someone may have been over-enthusiastic. They may have been providing a sop to American pressure. Or it may be someone is manipulating things, making a dead man far more politically threatening than he was, possibly even lending him some threat that belongs to someone still with us. That would be the real point, wouldn't it? The one to look into.'

Ed Lowell frowned again. 'You can't be suggesting your intelligence services are that porous.'

'Who cares?' said Cotton. 'I've seen the effects of the word "Trotskyite" on you. We don't know if there is a motive and if there is one, what it is.'

Ed Lowell paused. 'What can we do?'

'Find out where the information came from and consult later.'

Ed Lowell shook his head. 'It's your management systems,' he complained.

'Possibly. Will you try to trace back?'

Ed Lowell nodded. 'OK. But my people are alarmed. They want answers.'

Cotton had had enough. 'Have you heard anything about any of your people from us?'

'No,' said Lowell. 'What are you suggesting?'

'Just a query,' said Cotton. 'I'll get back to you when I really know and have evidence for what I say.'

Back at the office, Cotton got directly in touch with Ayrtoun.

Ayrtoun replied at once. 'Our indistinct old friend, "European sources", tagged Watson as a Trotskyite. That information automatically passed to the Yanks because it is information, it bulks up the reports and Watson can't answer back. Watson condemned his name by committing suicide. I am tracing it – but will accept any contributions. Look at the time factor – did this tag surface after his death or was it there before?'

On Wednesday, 29 January the freeze worsened. The temperature in central London dropped to about 16 degrees Fahrenheit. In other parts of the country it was even lower. It was almost possible to hear the country icing up. Whereas the London press had previously said 'Scotland cut off' by twenty-foot snow drifts and thousands of livestock were feared dead, they now said 'North and Midlands cut off'. It was estimated that two million workers had been laid off without pay from Birmingham to Sheffield.

In Pont Street that weekend Cotton saw women in fur coats queuing up with buckets to get water. There were NOes everywhere on shop signs. No bread. No fish. No potatoes. No firewood. No soap. No clothes.

On Saturday evening, 1 February, Cotton made sure the windows were blocked. He pinned blankets over the frames.

Around 9 p.m. his buzzer went.

'Yes?'

'Anna Melville here.'

'Isn't Margot at home?'

'It isn't her I want to see. It's you I want to see. I have a problem.'

Cotton failed to speak quickly enough.

'For God's sake, I'm freezing my tits off out here.'

Cotton pressed the entry buzzer.

Anna Melville appeared out of the lift carrying a small cardboard suitcase, looking as if she was wearing everything else she had. Over a black felt headpiece, removed from a props department, she had an elderly brimmed hat and over that a scarf she had tied round her chin. Another scarf had been wrapped round her neck. She was wearing so many clothes under her coat she could not do the lower buttons up. She pulled the scarf away from her mouth.

'I could pretend,' she said, 'I had entirely fallen for you. But I also need somewhere to sleep tonight. It makes you doubly attractive and this would be cheaper for me, particularly as I barely have any money. And it's absolutely freezing. You have very interesting lips, you know. An interesting mouth. I've brought some cheese. Can I come in?'

'No Margot?'

'She went home. The theatre is barely operating. Not enough money to pay my wages.'

'I'm sorry,' said Cotton.

She shook her head. 'I had to damn well walk. From Pimlico. I fell over. Twice. My bum must be black and blue.' She frowned. 'I can't tell if it's really warm or not in here.'

'It's not really warm,' said Cotton.

'Have you got hot water?'

'The boiler is just ticking over, not more. What about your parents?'

'There's my grandmother, my brother, as well as my parents. There are three rooms. And one has a stove. The loo is outside and it has frozen solid. They're thirteen miles away.'

Cotton put her in the spare room.

'Are you serious?' she said.

'Yes, I am.'

'Are you one of those men who like to sleep alone?'

'It's a bit of a store room,' he said. 'But it should do.'

He moved some boxes he had never unpacked and considered the bedding. He took the bedspread off one of the two single beds and pinned it over the window. He took bed linen out of the cupboard and draped it in front of the open oven in the kitchen. He also found the trunk with his army kilts in and took out two to provide extra blankets.

'You wore these skirts?' she said.

'They're heavy and they are warm.'

On Sunday he was woken by the cold and the sound of scratchy music. Since about 1937, Cotton had not so much collected as picked up some gramophone records, no more than twenty and almost all piano jazz. There were several each by Art Tatum and Fats Waller, *Boogie Woogie Dream* by Albert Ammons and Pete Johnson, *Honky Tonk Train Blues* by Meade Lux Lewis and a Louis Armstrong *Tiger Rag*.

Cotton went to the window. Behind curtains and blanket, there was no view. The pane was white, not with Jack Frost type patterns, this was more like ice filings. When Cotton went through it was the *Tiger Rag* she was playing. Sitting beside the electric fire with a blanket around her, she laughed when she saw him.

'You like this stuff?'

'Very much.'

'But it's barely music! It's hardly together!'

'You don't have to listen to it.'

'Don't tell me I've offended you!'

'I'm saying if you don't like it, don't listen to it.'

'It's not exactly Bach or Beethoven.'

'No, it isn't,' said Cotton. 'But aren't you at all interested in the improvisational side of it? No two performances are the same in jazz. Didn't someone say that was what happened in theatre?'

She laughed. 'No,' she said. 'No theatre audience is going to like "To be, double bubble beep, or not boop to be".'

Cotton smiled. 'Have you done anything about breakfast?'

'No. I don't cook,' she said. 'Well, I can do dumplings, I suppose.'

'Porridge then,' said Cotton.

It took time. The gas pressure was low and both the water and milk were near freezing.

Around noon Michel Shalhoub rang at the doorbell. He was dressed in a fur-collared coat and homburg hat.

'Mr Cotton, I implore you,' he said. 'I'm having problems getting signatories for my petition.'

'What's it about?'

Monsieur Shalhoub leant forwards and spoke even more quietly.

'Through diplomatic channels I have what I will describe as access to fuel supplies. I have been offered a delivery of coke, enough both to keep the boiler alight and perhaps provide a greater degree of warmth than now. There is unfortunately a monetary charge for the delivery that, apparently, comes outside the normal charges we all pay.'

'Are you asking for a contribution?'

'You weren't in yesterday. Some residents, Miss Fenwick, for example, refused. She has gone home, I understand. Another problem is that I wish for the throat of the boiler to be opened, to provide more heat, you understand. I have spoken to the porter but he tells me he needs permission to do this.'

'Permission from whom?'

'The residents' association. But that is not due to meet until March. Mr Cotton, have you seen the water?'

'What do you mean?'

'It's *thickening*!'

'Yes. Where is this delivery?'

'Round the corner,' said Michel Shalhoub. 'They tell me I have ten minutes before they move on.'

'How much?'

Michel Shalhoub told him. 'I only have three pounds,' he said.

Cotton looked. He had just over five pounds. 'They won't accept eight pounds?'

'No.'

'Have you tried Brenda? The old lady with the dog?'

'Well, exactly,' said Michel Shalhoub.

'We'll try Brenda.'

Brenda looked delighted to see them. 'It's

thirty-eight degrees in here,' she said, 'and my dog's paws are cold.'

Within a minute she had opened her safe and from a large roll had extracted two five-pound notes.

'They're thieves, aren't they?' she said. She sounded perfectly cheerful.

The coke was delivered, the gravity feed opened up and within a few minutes the heating had begun to tick as the water circulated. Within a couple of hours Brenda's thermometer was up to forty-eight degrees.

'It's almost toasty,' she said.

CHAPTER 20

Government agencies did not have access to black market or 'diplomatic' fuel. In St James's Street there was no heat in Cotton's office and lighting was by evil-smelling candles.

'Please don't say anything about Dickens,' said Portman. 'Bad for morale.' One man, in the Africa section, was wearing a hat over a balaclava along with his overcoat.

'Can you see like that?' said Portman.

'Perfectly,' said the man. 'Why do you ask?'

Cotton did have a note from Ayrtoun, though.

'Are you all right?' he asked Miss Kelly, before he left.

'The typewriter keys are sticking in the cold,' she said. 'And the liquid in my eyes is making me see double.'

The E & E, also known as SP or Snoop Patrol was not based in St James's Street or Whitehall but in Soho in Wardour Street. They were due to move but were making do with four rooms up a steep staircase with a tread so narrow Cotton had to walk on the balls of his feet. His contact there, a bored-looking man with very straight eyebrows that almost met in the middle and a lot of curly black hair coming out of a hat with ear flaps, took him into a makeshift listening booth.

Despite his name, Freddie Igloi had no hint of a Hungarian accent. He explained the presence of a car battery. 'It's the electricity supply. It wobbles.' He looked round and pointed at a gas ring. 'That's about quarter normal pressure,' he said. 'I'll have to turn it off. Sorry. It hisses.'

Igloi did that. He gave Cotton some earphones.

'We have something that might interest you. Two British subjects, a man and a woman, in a restaurant in France. Near Versailles actually, on Saturday, 11 January this year.'

He looked round. Cotton nodded. Freddie Igloi raised one of his ear flaps and put one side of his earphones to his ear.

'The conversation is the usual febrile, self-important stuff between adulterers. Headphones.'

Cotton put them on and listened. There was quite a lot of background noise, a knife scraping on a plate, some laughter, then, very close, a startlingly loud sigh.

'Oh, this wine is heaven,' a woman said. 'Truly.'

Despite himself Cotton felt a twinge of embarrassment. He could hear her swallowing.

Freddie Igloi tapped Cotton's arm. 'She's stroking his hand now,' he said.

There was some desultory mumbling about 'the long term'. That gave way to diary consultations and a date for sex nine days forward.

'I'm looking forward to it already,' she said.

'Does your husband know about us?' said the man.

'He's jolly well going to have to grow up! Divorce is damned serious! He's going to have to pay the financial consequences! He really will!'

To an outsider, it was clear her companion's reaction was more realistic or perhaps mealy-mouthed, certainly less insistently exclamatory when he described his own wife.

'She's a clinger, you see, gets weepy and senti-mental and keeps talking about the investment we've put in.'

They were then interrupted by a child speaking in French, saying it was his ninth birthday. He was offering them some *bonbons*. The couple were polite, the woman taking the time to congratulate him in French words unaffected by any sort of French accent.

'What a pretty boy!' said the woman to the man.

'Ah,' said the boy in English, 'you are British. My father says I should be most grateful to you for all your country has done for mine.'

Freddie Igloi stopped the tape and lifted one earpiece. Cotton did the same.

'Pretty good, don't you think?' he said. 'Wait.'

They listened to some more, through sorts of chocolate, before the boy excused himself.

'Goodbye,' he said.

'Speaks very well!' said the woman.

Freddie Igloi stopped the tape again.

'That is because his name is Robinson. Son of our man in Paris.'

Cotton registered that love, or at least adultery, had failed to recognize a native speaker speaking English in France. He frowned. 'What are they doing to the boy?' he asked.

Freddie Igloi shrugged. 'He got chocolates, didn't he? His father bribed the waiter to put a bug under the table, said he was a divorce detective.' He clicked the tape on.

'Now,' he said.

'I'm pretty sure I'm on for a lot more trips,' the man said. 'Of course, I can't tell you about it, my sweet, but I've been being useful recently. Tipped our people off about a security risk. It can't have done me any harm, that's for sure.'

Freddie Igloi clicked the switch again.

'This man is your European source,' he said. He got out a card. 'His name is Andrew Vine. He spends a lot of time in Paris talking to the French on atomic matters. He's a liaison officer.'

'God,' said Cotton. 'Who isn't? What does it mean in his case?'

'That he's a civil servant, a stickler, not a scientist,' said Freddie Igloi. 'Will I go on?'

Cotton smiled. 'Yes, do.'

'The stuff about Watson is what we call backdraught. Somebody talked about him to Vine in France. Vine then talked about him to the French and the French authorities kindly conveyed their security worries back to other British Intelligence departments.'

'Why would he talk about Watson to the French?'

Freddie Igloi shook his head. 'I don't think we can trace where the instructions came from. That would be more your job, wouldn't it?'

'Quite.' Cotton remembered that Ayrtoun had been flying to France from Croydon airport in December. 'Tell me about the woman Vine is sleeping with.'

Freddie Igloi looked at another card. 'She's a secretary in the British Embassy in Paris. Julia Tennant as was, now Julia Gardener. Her husband is in the military, based in Paris, spends a lot of time in Brussels, carrying briefcases mostly.'

'His rank?'

'Just a captain.'

'How long has the affair been going on, do you know?'

Freddie Igloi shrugged. 'I don't rightly know. She only went to Paris last May. But that conversation didn't sound quite first flush of lust, did it? I'd guess they started last summer.'

'What do you know about Vine?'

'That he's a lot older than the girl. She's twenty-eight, he's forty-two. He is married, three children under twelve. His own wife is forty. I can't tell you if she has spread or anything. They live in a place called Purley.'

Cotton remembered Purley. It was where Ayrtoun

231

had dropped Derek off before going to Croydon airport. 'Purley?' he said.

Freddie Igloi nodded. 'Yes. It's a hilly place in Surrey, on the fringes of London. He commutes in.'

There was a photograph, not that clear, taken by the boy's father from just under tabletop level. Vine looked chubby but frail in a pompous sort of way, Mrs Gardener slender and with the strained look of trying to find a strong man she could direct. It was a question of body shapes and postures. Cotton was aware that his reaction and summary judgement had been only fractionally slower than the camera shutter. He'd placed Vine as easily manipulated. Was Julia Gardener his source? Or had he been encouraged by blackmail?

'Thanks,' said Cotton. 'You've been very good. Now I have to be boring.'

'How do you mean?'

'No moonlighting,' said Cotton. 'If anybody here does work for Major Briggs MP, they'll end up in Wormwood Scrubs.'

Freddie Igloi shrugged. 'You want Giuseppe, also known as Joe – he does artistic photographs and agreed divorces. He's eight doors down from here, same side of the street.'

It was lunchtime. The weather was raw, Cotton had just been listening in on a good meal and he needed a break.

'You have a choice,' he said to Hans through the window. 'Lunch – or eight doors down you can meet a photographer called Giuseppe.'

232

'What kind of lunch?'

'I thought Chinese,' said Cotton.

Hans shook his head. 'I'm not a man for sauces,' he said.

Cotton smiled. 'How many times have you eaten Chinese food before?'

Hans did not answer directly. 'I'll grab something,' he said. 'In any case, it is not fitting that we have lunch together.'

'All right,' said Cotton. 'It seems Major Briggs uses Giuseppe. You don't have to warn him off, but tell him we know. He can give us copies. Make the arrangement.'

'I'm not sure,' said Hans.

'Yes, you are,' said Cotton. 'You want to be useful, don't you?'

'Mr Ayrtoun—'

'Agrees with me.'

'Where will you be?'

'I was told to go where the Chinese are going.'

'Where's that?'

'Where there are other Chinese eating. That means it's good and doesn't cost too much.'

Cotton found the restaurant he was looking for close by, on Brewer Street, simply by following a group of Chinese. Hans did not go until Cotton went in. He was the only European in the place. It was crowded and what with the voices, the sounds of eating and the clatter from the kitchens, filled with quite a racket.

A waiter spoke to him. It took Cotton a second

to sort out the words. He had said something like 'Are you with Dawkins?'

Cotton didn't know that he had seen the man outside St Martin-in-the Fields but decided he should have.

Cotton nodded. 'Sometimes,' he said.

The waiter nodded. 'Sit here. Squid? Crab? Yes.'

He left. Cotton was sitting on a stool at the end of a longish table. At the other end a family was eating without looking up. He closed his eyes. The place was steam-room warm and ear-buffetingly noisy, hardly an exotic holiday. But he enjoyed the smells, particularly the garlic and chilli, which reminded him of Mexico.

The food did not. The squid had been wok-fried and scattered with hot red flecks of chilli pepper. The crab was more complicated.

'How much do I owe you?'

'For you?' said the waiter. 'Five shillings and six pence.'

This was the standard restaurant charge. Cotton paid and thanked the waiter.

'You tell Dawkins you got good treatment, you hear?'

Cotton found Hans Bieber in the Triumph, carefully eating some bread and salami.

'How did it go?'

'No problem,' said Hans.

'Did you pay him?'

'I don't have access to money, sir, only a garage and petrol account.'

234

'Do we need to pay Giuseppe?'

'No need.'

'What did he say?'

'He admitted he did some work for Major Briggs.'

'Does Briggs pay him?'

'If he does, it's not a lot. Giuseppe's had a little trouble in the past with the obscenity laws. There was a book, he said, confiscated. He's not happy with this recent business of going to Croydon. He's more an old whore-and-divorce-in-Brighton man.'

'He'll give us copies of what he takes for the Major?'

'He already has.'

Hans opened the glove compartment and took out a Manila envelope. He gave it to Cotton.

'Giuseppe says Major Briggs calls the last few of these "not to be seen by girls" photographs.'

'Are they all compromising?'

Hans shook his head. 'Most are men being where they shouldn't but there's a few through the keyhole and a bit of jiggery-pokery.'

'Great. Did you threaten him?'

'I didn't have to. He really needs a little help with the obscenity charge.'

'I can't do that.'

'I think this would be more for Mr Dawkins,' said Hans.

'That would be up to him,' said Cotton.

When he had checked on Andrew Vine's whereabouts, Cotton phoned Dickie Dawkins.

'I ate at a Chinese restaurant today. The waiter wanted you to know they treated me well.'

Dawkins laughed. 'Where was this?'

'Brewer Street.'

'Good?'

'Not bad.'

'How much?'

'The usual.'

'Ouch,' said Dawkins. 'You'll need more visits to become a friend. What can I do for you?'

'There's a man called Giuseppe—'

'I know,' said Dawkins. 'A divorce photographer.'

'Yes. Major Briggs is using him.'

'All right,' said Dawkins. 'What's he got on Giuseppe?'

'Something about obscene publications. Giuseppe is now collaborating with us too.'

'That's good, isn't it?' said Dawkins. 'We can leave it where it is, if you want.'

'Could you tell Giuseppe that you're working on his problem but need time?'

'Yes,' said Dawkins. 'I could do that.'

'I've got a lead on how our dead friend acquired a reputation for left-wing politics. The source. I'm about to look into it.'

'All right.'

'How are you getting on?'

'So-so,' said Dawkins. 'Radcliffe came by to ask me what I was doing. I said I was just obeying orders. To the letter.'

'Was he friendly?'

'Not really,' said Dawkins.

'I can imagine that,' said Cotton. 'I'll keep you up to date.'

CHAPTER 21

Cotton called Hans Bieber and told him where and when to collect him in the Triumph. He left his office at 5.45, ate a spam sandwich and drank a cup of tea that tasted flowery, and at 6.43 took a train from Victoria to Purley station. The train was not fast. It took thirty-three minutes and stopped frequently. After East Croydon, there was South Croydon, Purley Oaks and then Purley itself.

Snow was falling, but only in the white equivalent of a drizzle. He got out of his compartment, walked down some stairs, through a dank red-brick tunnel and came out on to a small station forecourt. The lights there were poor and were attached to single-storey shops. A passenger in a bowler hat made his way towards a small Morris, got in and was driven off. Cotton ignored the solitary taxi and walked.

Out of the forecourt, he turned left. The slope was uncomfortably steep and he had to walk carefully, with quite small steps. After about seventy yards he turned right. Cotton kept going, past Dorothy's café, the Jolly Farmer pub, and waited at traffic-lights to cross the Brighton Road.

He then walked up the Banstead Road, past the Palm Court Derek Jennings had mentioned. There were a few footguards from Caterham waiting outside. Then there was Purley library, a low civic thirties structure. Directly past that was a small park of about half an acre in the shape of a round-headed triangle, where the road forked, ready on the other side to turn into Purley Way.

Cotton crossed and kept going. About eighty yards further on, he turned left into Woodcote Valley Road. This road was narrower, there were a lot more snow-covered trees and less light. The only sounds he could hear were his feet and his breath.

Nearly opposite Purley Knoll he came across the corner plot he wanted. The house on it had red tiles on the roof and down the walls. It was low and long. The gate to the garden had a wooden porchlike arrangement, also tiled and there was something similar, presumably a false well, to one side of the crazy-paved path. On the other was a wooden bird table. Snow-covered rose bushes in diamond-shaped sections took up most of the rest.

Cotton walked to the front door. There was a lot of blacksmith's work on it. He raised the knocker and rapped it three times. In the cold, the knocks sounded brittle enough to crack. An icicle from the eaves came down. It did not pierce the snow. It broke on the ice and rattled.

Cotton had become used to people on the inside

of doors opening them dressed for the outdoors. This lady, cautious because of the weather and the time, was wearing a silk headscarf and what looked like a baby's shawl round her shoulders. She frowned and Cotton decided how to speak.

'Colonel Peter Cotton to see Mr Andrew Vine. Sorry about the time but it's urgent and official.'

Mrs Vine let him in. The hall contained an unlit fireplace but had a Moroccan-looking column of metal in which a flame flickered. It looked like low lighting but was evidently meant to provide some heat. Cotton noted Mrs Vine's breath showed white when she spoke. The placed smelt of beeswax polish and something like pea soup.

'I'll go and get him.' She was then struck by another thought. She moved across the hall and pushed at a door and clicked the light switch. A couple of wall lights came on in a small reception room. She went in and drew the curtains on the leaded lattice windows. In the fireplace was some rolled paper and kindling. She pointed very briefly and Cotton shook his head. The waiting room was even chillier than the hall. They were using it as a buffer round a core.

'Do please sit down. I won't be a moment.'

There were two armchairs by the fireplace but there was hardly room for any more furniture. There was a thin glazed bookcase on one wall containing small leather-bound books. Cotton had just picked out the titles *Rasselas* and *The Rape of the Lock* when his attention was taken by some whispering.

'How would I know? Really! He's come to see you!'

There was a pause. Though shorter, Mrs Vine had struck Cotton as quite similar looking to her husband's lover, slim but with a more determinedly defensive jaw line. On the tape, Vine had called her sentimental and weak but to Cotton she looked much stronger than her husband.

Outside, Vine cleared his throat. Shortly he appeared, with Mrs Vine behind him. He was wearing a tweed jacket, university scarf and gloves. It made him look flabby and nostalgic.

'This is most highly irregular,' he said.

Cotton had not expected much better.

'Mr Vine, I have come to see you about a matter that has a codename,' he said.

Vine blinked. 'What codename?'

Cotton paused to give him a chance. He looked at Mrs Vine. Her husband appeared to have been stunned into non-thought entirely.

'What codename?' insisted Vine.

'Codename Julia,' said Cotton.

Vine grunted. It was a low, almost soggy sound. He swallowed and cleared his throat. 'Yes. It's all right, dear. I'll handle this.'

Mrs Vine was determined to be polite.

'Colonel, may I offer you some refreshment?' she said.

Cotton smiled. 'You're very kind, Mrs Vine, but no, thank you. This won't take long.'

She closed the door. Andrew Vine made an

241

attempt to look indignant but when he spoke he whispered.

'Now look here! I don't know who you are but you invade my home, you upset my wife, you—'

Cotton waited. But Andrew Vine had run out of words. 'What?' he asked.

There was no reply.

'Two questions, then. First, who was it told you Watson was a security risk because of his politics? Second, was your affair with Mrs Gardener used to oblige you to inform the French of what you had been told about him?'

'But it wasn't like that! Good God, I was trying to help, do my duty!'

'Really? That's commendable, I suppose. Did you check on the information before you passed it on?'

'That's not my job,' said Vine. 'I acted in good faith, I assure you.' He blinked. 'I reported what I had heard. It would have been remiss not to do so.'

'Did you know anything of Watson before this?'

'I knew he was very prickly and difficult. I knew he could be very arrogant.'

'So you could say you merely responded to a suggestion about something you already knew or suspected?'

Vine looked unhappy. 'Well, I wouldn't put it quite like that,' he said.

'I see,' said Cotton. 'Do you know, Mr Vine, that Watson is dead? And that he might not be if you had kept your mouth shut.'

'I certainly don't accept responsibility.'

Despite himself Cotton smiled. 'I'm absolutely sure you don't. Who suggested you talk about him to the French?'

'It wasn't like that,' Vine said again. 'It was far more – normal! Almost social.'

Cotton gently waved the fingers of his right hand, then lightly clenched them.

'Who?' he said.

'It's complicated,' pleaded Vine.

'No it's not,' said Cotton.

There was quite a pause before Vine spoke. There was appeal in his voice. 'I was flattered,' he said. 'This was high up!'

'Who?' said Cotton.

'For God's sake! I got it on rice paper. I was told to eat the damned thing.'

Cotton started to turn away.

'MI6!' said Andrew Vine. 'That's all I can say.'

Cotton raised his eyebrows and shrugged. 'Mr Vine, I don't have to threaten you. Your wife is on the other side of the door.'

'A man called Mair gave me the rice paper and then told me to see a Frenchman called Bodard. It was Bodard who told me they were worried about Watson. The man's a Trotskyite!'

'Was,' said Cotton. 'He's dead. Why did you believe Bodard?'

Vine was incredulous. 'Why would he say that if it wasn't true? Mair's MI6, for God's sake! And we were in the British Embassy!'

243

'It didn't strike you as odd that Bodard was speaking to you rather than someone in Intelligence. Like that man Mair, for example.'

'But I'm on the committee,' said Vine. 'I can't say more about Anglo-French cooperation on certain matters. The work is classified.'

'Of course,' said Cotton. 'And you were flattered. What about Codename Julia?'

Vine winced but did not speak.

'The affair is over,' said Cotton. 'You will make no contact with Mrs Gardener again. You will not respond should she try to contact you. You will not tell her of this meeting.'

'Do I have a choice?'

'Yes. You can do what I say. Or not.'

'Are you threatening me?'

'I'm telling you, Mr Vine. It really couldn't be simpler. Do you understand me?'

Vine nodded.

When Cotton came out of the house, he found the Triumph parked outside. It was snowing again, this time quite heavily. Hans Bieber got out and opened the door for him.

'London, sir?'

Cotton nodded.

They started off. Hans turned the car right and moved towards Purley Way, but then pulled up.

'Damn!' he said. He looked behind. 'That's quite a steep slope.'

It took Cotton a moment to catch on. He moved to get a better view.

Down the Banstead Road by the Palm Court, men in uniform were sliding about all over the road, falling, punching and grabbing. There was blood and glass and fresh snow.

It was like some perverse Christmas card except that, behind the fight, a torch light flashed and flashed again. The police were there with a black Maria but were not intervening.

Cotton looked a little to the left. In the small park in front of Purley library shadows moved, as if on some night hunt. Three smallish men brought down a larger fellow.

'The Jocks will win,' said Hans Bieber.

Cotton had not looked at who was fighting or how. Now he picked out that it was the Guards from Caterham and what looked like Highland Light Infantry. The Scots used a tactic like dancing girls, linking arms and spinning – even when someone spun off he was sliding at some speed with a broken bottle in his hand.

'We can get by,' said Cotton.

'One moment, sir,' said Hans.

A few seconds later a jeep with military police and a dog sped past them.

Hans checked the rear-view mirror and let the car creep forward. The fight was already melting away. The headlights illuminated a Guardsman on the pavement in the pose of the Dying Gaul. His cheek would need a lot of stitches and his nose would need to be reset. Broken glass gleamed on black ice.

Hans Bieber shook his head. 'These shit police have permitted too many escape routes,' he said. As they turned left, he pointed at a couple of soldiers hiding by a bush across from a sign that said Coldharbour Lane.

'Yes, they have,' said Cotton. 'Hans?'

'Yes, sir?'

Cotton waited till they were on Purley Way.

'Where is Mr Ayrtoun?'

He saw Hans Bieber glance at him in the rear-view mirror.

'He's in Paris.'

'All right. Is he still there? Or is he there again?'

'He came back from Washington yesterday, yes, Sunday.'

'And how long will he be there?'

'I don't really know but certainly all this week.'

'Tell him I'm coming to see him, would you?'

CHAPTER 22

According to regulations, Cotton should have caught the boat train to Dover, the ferry across the Channel, and the French train from Calais to Paris, all first class. That was the so-called first option after the most recent government cuts. To his relief – Cotton loathed cold, choppy sea – the weather forecast in the Channel was too bad. So Hans drove him in the Triumph to Northolt in Middlesex. He flew from there to Paris on a BEA unpressurized Vickers Viking, one of only three passengers, after a delay of four hours. During the wait, he saw ice being scraped off the wings and the pilots let air out of the tyres. Apparently this meant a softer landing in Paris. On the plane the stewardess asked him if he was on business.

'Government business,' he replied.

'We have an awful lot of sandwiches. Would you care for some, sir?'

'No, thank you,' replied Cotton. 'Unless they're real.'

'No such luck, sir.'

Below him, the south of England was grey-white,

broken up by sketchy, wormlike hedgerows. They flew so low that he was just able to pick out the Brighton Pavilion as they went over the south coast. It was quite difficult to do. The gleam of the Pavilion domes had been iced over.

To Cotton's surprise Ayrtoun was waiting for him at Le Bourget airport. Paris felt quite as cold as London.

'We'll have supper later,' said Ayrtoun.

'All right.'

'There's something of a myth that you always eat well in Paris,' said Ayrtoun. 'It's not true. Too many grey steaks and cut corners. But naturally they prefer horse meat to the ersatz. And they do have quantity.' He looked up. 'Tell me.'

Cotton summarized his meeting with Vine.

'Do you believe him?'

'I'd like to interview Mrs Julia Gardener.'

'Who wouldn't?' said Ayrtoun. 'We'll do that.'

They went directly to the Embassy at 35 Rue de Faubourg Saint Honoré in a Citroën taxi. Cotton was interested to see how Ayrtoun would tackle Mrs Gardener.

'Scoop Julia Gardener from the pool,' he said to a young man, 'and deliver her to me.'

They did not have long to wait. Cotton had seen a photograph of her seated. She was tall, probably taller than her lover, and very slim. She raised her chin and stood up very straight. Cotton saw that her legs were trembling and that her stockings were silk.

'Do sit down,' said Ayrtoun.

The young woman almost dropped into the chair.

Ayrtoun squeezed out a smile. 'Mrs Gardener, my name is Geoffrey Ayrtoun. I am based in Washington DC. But recently I have had to make too many trips here.'

'Well, I've heard of you, sir, of course I have,' said Julia Gardener. 'It's a privilege.'

Ayrtoun paid no attention. 'The person beside me is Colonel Cotton. He catches people. He catches people out.' Ayrtoun looked up at her. 'He tells me you are an adulterer. The Colonel has already spoken to your lover.' Ayrtoun looked round at Cotton. 'Did you talk about this affair to the man's wife?'

'No,' said Cotton.

'You see,' said Ayrtoun. 'We're trying to help you. As further assistance, to help you desist entirely in ill-advised behaviour, you will find Mr Vine will no longer be enjoying jaunts to Paris and on you.'

The young woman blinked at first but then, perhaps, there was something of a flutter in her eyelashes. She flushed slightly.

'I really must beg your pardon!' said Julia Gardener. 'I have met Mr Vine but I can assure you I'm happily married to a splendid man.'

Ayrtoun shrugged, then breathed out. He began by sounding more weary than annoyed.

'It's entirely as you wish, Mrs Gardener. But

every time you lie to me I really will ask myself why I should spare you further humiliation. Next lie and your splendid husband's career will start to crumble. And as a bonus we will provide evidence for your husband to divorce you. And for Mrs Vine to prosecute her husband. Is that clear to you?'

Mrs Julia Gardener said nothing.

'Good,' said Ayrtoun. 'I want to talk about a man called A. A. Watson.'

That did surprise her. It is one thing to deny, another to be ignorant and frightened. 'I don't know him, I really don't.'

'Of course you don't. Mr Vine knows – or rather knew of him. Watson committed suicide, you see, because the French enquired as to his probity and reliability. Something to do with his sexual habits, I believe. They did this because they were tipped off. By Mr Vine, in fact. Mr Vine, as you may indeed have experienced, is not an instigator. He goes along for the ride, as it were. He has told us where the prod came from. What we want to know is whether or not you helped him with this prod. Did anyone tell you to have an affair with Mr Vine?'

'No! Of course not!'

'Oh do think, Mrs Gardener. Your mind is perhaps as open to suggestion and flattery as your legs, though you may find that difficult to admit. Where did you meet Mr Vine?'

'Here at the Embassy. At a reception, actually. It was—' She stopped.

250

'Do you know someone called Mair?' Ayrtoun blinked. 'Do you want another name? How about a local called Bodard?'

Julia Gardener blinked but stayed silent.

Ayrtoun let out a groan. 'I really do think I am being quite patient,' he said. He turned to Cotton again. 'Did you ever see those terrible bits of newsreel when poor French bitches ended up with their heads shaved and then had to run a gauntlet of indignant would-be Resistance heroes? There wasn't much anyone could do except feel appalled or sick.'

Cotton glanced at Ayrtoun.

'Most of those girls had just picked the wrong man, perhaps got a bit too comfortable,' said Ayrtoun. 'People hate that. But I suppose we could call them shop girls, village girls, innocent girls who didn't know better—'

'I've met Mair,' said Julia Gardener. 'I think he may have introduced me to Andrew.'

Ayrtoun nodded. 'All right, Mrs Gardener. This is what will happen. You will do your best to get pregnant—'

'I am.'

'Of course you are. Does your husband know?'

She shook her head.

'And Mr Vine?'

'No.'

'Splendid!' Ayrtoun scratched his cheek. 'Do we know who the father might be?'

'My husband,' said Julia Gardener.

251

'Really?' said Ayrtoun at his most incredulous. 'Well, good for you! Then I suggest you tell him your glad tidings and resign your position. Perhaps you didn't know it before, but you are now anxious to be a good, even excellent mother. He will receive an offer of a new job and a promotion. You will do your utmost to make him accept it. It'll be something colonial but, I can assure you, a very pleasant colony. Nothing rough, like Nigeria.' Ayrtoun turned and smiled at Cotton. 'Malaya perhaps.'

Mrs Gardener came to rather quickly. 'Job offer before announcement and my resignation?'

Ayrtoun smiled. 'Done,' he said. 'Mr Vine is due for Civil Service Siberia. Ministry of Pensions, I imagine.'

Mrs Gardener had already moved on. She showed no interest at all in the man she had shared chocolates with in Versailles.

'Can you get your husband to accept?' said Ayrtoun.

'It depends how it's sold,' she said.

And after she had gone: 'Quite a clever girl, really.'

'How did you know she's pregnant?'

Ayrtoun smiled. 'She went to the Embassy doctor. Almost had a fit, apparently.' He nodded. 'She'll play,' he said.

'I'm not so sure,' said Cotton.

'Why not?'

'She's self-regarding enough to be silly – or

possibly ruthless. She could bully her husband into a divorce and move on to someone with more prospects.'

'Shit,' said Ayrtoun. 'Are you just saying this to annoy me?'

'No. She lives very much in the present. I heard a recorded conversation she had with Vine. She can get excited by the tone of her own voice.'

'What about Vine?'

'He was the weaker partner. Weak doesn't dare but—'

'Quite,' said Ayrtoun.

Cotton shrugged. 'Who's this man Mair?'

'What our Communist friends would call an ingratiating lick-spittle in MI6.'

'Who is he licking?'

Ayrtoun shook his head. 'I didn't mean that. He's a good-looking pimp.'

Cotton did not know whether Ayrtoun was disturbed or unsettled. 'What about the Frenchman, Bodard?'

'He's in the arms-dealing business. He's all profit and account.'

'So why mention Trotsky and Watson, then?'

'That I don't know. But it will be part of a deal.' Ayrtoun smiled. 'He is, officially at any rate, resident in Switzerland. I'll get on to our people there, but let's be honest, the entire country is a safe. Will you look for Mair?'

'Why would I have to?'

'He was let go a while back.'

'How long a while?'

'Four or five months, I think.' Ayrtoun looked round. 'Why don't you think about that. Dinner at seven?' He gave Cotton the address of the restaurant.

'It's nothing too grand,' Ayrtoun said. 'But it's honest.'

In terms of temperature Cotton did not know whether Paris was more or less raw than London, but the cold cut through to his bones quicker, wind whipping the chill off the stone buildings on the short walk to his hotel in Rue La Boétie. He had never thought of London brick as being relatively gentle before. Cotton checked in and was taken up to his room in an ornate but trundling *ascenseur*. As he went he saw the decorators were working on the second and third floors. His room, on the top floor, was a substantial kind of garret. The wallpaper was of wide red and white stripes, not his taste but then not too off-putting. What was clear was that the room had just been decorated. The sheets on the bed were also new, like the cover on the round bolster the French used for pillows. There were fresh cut flowers in a vase and a bottle of carbonated water on a tray. And the French were keeping rather warmer. The radiators were hot to touch. Though not to drink, the cold water in the bathroom was not icy and the hot steamed.

Cotton showered. The soap provided was a little too perfumed for his taste but he had not felt quite that clean and comfortable for some time.

He took a taxi to the restaurant, a small place with once plush booths and *fin de siècle* lamps, to find Ayrtoun already ensconced there and halfway down a bottle of burgundy.

'We're having onion soup, then slices of duck with shallots.'

Cotton raised his eyebrows.

'It's what they recommend,' said Ayrtoun. 'And I never argue with them.'

'All right.' Cotton sat down.

'What time are you leaving tomorrow?'

Cotton told him.

'Good,' said Ayrtoun. 'You'll have time to call in on Fauchon. In La Place de la Madeleine. Get yourself some lunch. Have a little swim in Frenchness. All those glazed things.' Ayrtoun smiled. 'The French don't have porridge and water socialists. But they have what I believe is called a political *pourriture* or mess. Probably why they are recovering from the war quicker than us.' He lit a cigarette. 'My wife has even heard their fashion people are coming back.'

Ayrtoun had brought her up. 'How is she?' asked Cotton.

'Oh, not too good,' said Ayrtoun. 'I blame myself. For marrying her, you see.' He looked up. 'She's lost weight. Had a bad attack of jaundice in July.'

Cotton had carried the alcoholic and unconscious Penelope Ayrtoun out of a seedy Washington roadhouse about fourteen months before. She had been very thin then.

255

'She's been losing hair,' said Ayrtoun. 'Terrible thing for a woman, you know.'

Cotton nodded. Was this part of why Ayrtoun had mentioned shaved heads to Julia Gardener?

Their waiter brought them two large bowls of onion soup.

'You'll have to eat everything from Fauchon before you land in England,' said Ayrtoun. 'We now defend our fortress island against pleasure rather more effectively than we did against bombs.'

The waiter brought them bread. It was hot. Ayrtoun broke some, pointed at the rising steam and shook his head.

'Priorities,' he said. He snorted, then sighed. He poured more wine and drank.

'How are you handling things?' he said.

'I wasn't able to do much for Watson,' Cotton replied.

Ayrtoun shook his head and popped more bread into his mouth. 'No, your job was never to save queers from death or a fate worse than it. In any case you couldn't have saved Watson. He was far too arrogant and insecure to let anyone else have control. That's what suicide is for some, you know. Control. They make the decision, not you, me or anyone else. No, I think of you as part flak-catcher, part probe.'

Cotton smiled briskly, almost a twitch, but hard enough for a small grunt.

Ayrtoun blinked. 'I meant how are you handling the paranoia?'

'What are you talking about?'

'The natural tendency of spies to feel spied on. Everywhere. A waiter brings you a plate – in theory you understand what he's doing but your eyes check his fingernails, his shoes, if he's sweating. Is he sweating too little or sweating too much? Your lover brings you a cup of coffee and you wonder what her real motive is. A colleague scratches his cheek in public and you look around to see who he is signalling.'

Cotton laughed. 'No. I've met Major Briggs and Watson and did not have the impression either was spying on me.'

'Briggs is just a puffed-up amateur flirting with the edges of crime. He can't imagine that anyone is looking at him.'

'Are they?'

'No need. He can be stopped at any time. The only doubt is how he can be made useful before then. He's just another self-important little fantasy wandering about, unaware he is waiting for the final edit. Almost all the great and the good end up as queasy little footnotes. The successful get examined for their great flaws. The rest take up charity work or shame.'

Cotton praised the soup. This was the first time he had ever seen Ayrtoun tired and bitter to no practical effect. His face was flushed and he had already ordered another bottle of wine. Ayrtoun, however, was quick as well as paranoid.

'There's also the business of having to be a brute. You remember Tibbets, don't you?'

Jeremy Tibbets had died alongside Katherine Ward in what had been officially recorded as an automobile accident in December 1945 during a snowstorm in Washington DC. Cotton had been planning to marry Katherine and thus remembered very well.

'Damned stupid, really,' said Ayrtoun. 'I was told to pick a code-breaker but not told what for or what kind of characteristics they were looking for in my choice. I still don't know exactly, but it's perfectly easy to surmise from Tibbets's working at Arlington Hall that it involved efforts to decipher Soviet codes.'

'Tibbets told me the Soviets use a one-pad system but had been obliged during the Nazi invasion to repeat some of those pads,' said Cotton. 'He was frustrated because mathematics had very little to do with the job, and he was a proud mathematician.'

Ayrtoun shook his head. 'He shouldn't have said a thing, of course.' He shrugged. 'Very late last December something happened at Arlington Hall. I think it happened before, but that was when there was a shocked official intake of American breath. I can't swear to it, of course, but we think they had finally found definite and definitive evidence that the Soviets had not just infiltrated

258

the Manhattan Project – the project was riddled with happy sharers.'

Ayrtoun made a face, as if unimpressed the Americans had acted surprised when there were enough other indications to make the news expected.

'By early January the Americans were already getting very restless and anxious to react. One of their easier options, of course, was looking at us, the back-door boys, as it were.' He looked up. 'How are you getting on with Ed Lowell?'

'We get by, I suppose.'

'You mustn't underestimate him. Ed's a very sharp New England tack. By the way, you have something wrong.'

'What's that?'

'Ed's a Department of Defense man. He was in the Navy. In American intelligence terms almost royalty with all that that entails.'

'Which is?'

'Ed thinks he has more rights and common sense than more recent immigrants. He doesn't approve of the new agency. He thinks that will be for lethal buffoons in zoot suits and vulgar ties. That doesn't make him any less hard-nosed.' Ayrtoun shook his head and indicated a couple in the restaurant.

The couple was not particularly young. The man was in his thirties, dressed in a brown and white striped suit, and the woman was thin but with a lot of hair. They were preparing to kiss but had held off about six inches and looked somewhere between anticipation and manoeuvres, hers more than his but that may just have been her deep-red lipstick.

Ayrtoun cleared his throat. 'Most of our words for awkward things, from sex to subterfuge,' he said, 'are from the French. This new American agency, according to my sources, is going to concentrate on covert and clandestine things, instigate operations abroad.' He shook his head. 'We invoked the threat of violence and intimidation and did quite well avoiding trouble until we were rumbled, of course, during the war. The stupid side of America is actually going to take it all on, from bribery to assassination. They think it's their duty. Top dog means you don't just snarl, you bite.'

Cotton was getting depressed. Ayrtoun's grip was going in waves. He had looked bad before, but now the drink had made him look worse, and he was at the stage of sometimes closing his eyes as if that might help him to see better.

'Do you know something?' he said. 'If I were a Soviet agent in the British Intelligence Services I'd keep deliberately making mistakes, decent-sized mistakes, that is, and at not too regular intervals. We're awfully forgiving of mistakes. A slip-up? Rank stupidity? Colleagues rally round. The service matters most. These things happen.'

Cotton said nothing. Was this what Ayrtoun was doing? Hunting for someone who made mistakes?

'Just look at us here. A comfortable little dinner in Paris, we can appreciate these things. And of course you know where and what Burgundy is . . . but if you heard I was a Soviet agent you'd think, well, the man's a frightful shit, of course, but steady on. His wife's a drunk, he's going that way, but there's no need to be over-personal and he is under colossal strain from overwork. We all have our problems and flaws. He's one of us. We really don't want to think that something as fatuous as an ideology could win out over, well, we can't use a word like "comradeship" but certainly something similar, to do with our shared class.'

Though he had enjoyed the soup, Cotton was not feeling particularly chummy. The waiter served the duck.

'Take your own position,' said Ayrtoun. 'If you were to marry that Czech girl, people might wince at your choice but would probably be under-standing enough not to lift a finger.'

The duck was good. 'Who said anything about marrying her?' said Cotton.

'What if I were to tell you she's in the Jewish underground, involved in spiriting the pounds the Nazis forged into the Zionist cause?'

Cotton sighed. 'I'd say she was the best agent I had ever met.'

'But you can't rule those things out!'

'Sometimes you can.'

Ayrtoun shook his head. 'You're a confident bastard, aren't you? Are you thinking of marrying her?'

'I barely know her.'

'Then get rid of her.'

'I'd prefer to get rid of Hans.'

Ayrtoun shook his head. 'He's not entirely your chauffeur.'

'Quite. Is this the wider view you have pressed on me?'

Ayrtoun winced, tilted to one side.

'What is it?' said Cotton.

'I'm drunk,' said Ayrtoun. 'Are you chancing your arm?'

'Have you got a point to this?'

Ayrtoun belched. He blinked and shook his head. He belched again, this time with more evident relief. 'Yes,' he said. 'I need you to concentrate. I spend far too much time on women. Our new man in Istanbul, for example. He's a drunk and he's a depressive. The woman he married last year while she was pregnant with their fourth child, sometimes attacks herself. Cuts herself. Injects herself with her own urine.'

'Christ,' said Cotton. He stared at his boss.

'You're not going to have a lot of time for women, whoever they are. They can mess you around. And you have a lot of tracking down to do.'

For dessert Ayrtoun chose blue cheese. Cotton had the tarte Tatin. When they had both tasted what they had chosen, Ayrtoun smiled.

'We have been infiltrated to an extraordinarily high level. Not just one person.' He held up a hand and waggled his fingers. 'Several people.' He shook his head. 'Were I a Soviet agent, I'd ignore all that need-to-know stuff and our formal arrangements to ensure secrecy. No need. I'd simply keep an eye on us failing to move on from gentlemanly complacency and keep passing on documents, plans and secrets with something that must feel and look very like impunity. My cover would be other people's incompetence and another bottle of burgundy. Though claret would do, of course.'

Cotton enjoyed the coffee, then got Ayrtoun into a taxi.

When he got back to his hotel, the man on duty spoke to him.

'Colonel Cotton?'

'Yes.'

'Would you like some company, sir? Terms are very reasonable at present.'

Caught off-guard, Cotton stared.

'A little Algerian, delicious. A Chinese girl, very obliging.'

Cotton held up a hand. 'No, no,' he said.

The concierge was not put off. Cotton was still hearing the literal translation. 'One even has a black girl from Senegal, very supple. And excellent national produce, of course.'

Cotton shook his head. 'Very kind,' he said in French, 'but unfortunately I have work to do. Good night.'

Cotton went up to his room and from there he telephoned his own flat. There was no reply. He telephoned Miss Kelly.

'As discreetly as possible please, what you can

find out about a man called Mair. Exports let him go a few months ago, four or five is my information.'

MI6 was Exports, MI5 Imports.

'May I do that tomorrow morning, sir?'

'Of course. Sorry to have disturbed you, Miss Kelly.'

CHAPTER 23

On Wednesday, 5 February Cotton ate a croissant and drank coffee for breakfast and then went shopping. He bought some razor-blades and a toilet case about the size of a National Loaf of bread. He took a taxi to Fauchon and there bought himself food to eat on the plane. In the empty case he fitted two quails, individually and beautifully wrapped, and two croissants. The paper on the quail was secured by a sticker, the croissant paper by thin ribbons. The assistant serving him commiserated.

'*Ô monsieur, vous êtes anglais.*' It sounded like sympathy for a chronic condition.

By ten he was at the airport, by ten thirty, in the air and eating. He ate fresh bread and terrine of pork and pepper, what the assistant had called a *soupçon* of pheasant with truffles and Armagnac, and a clementine from Corsica.

At Northolt the customs men were talking amongst themselves.

'How long have you been away, sir?'

'A little less than a day.'

'On business?'

265

'Government.'

The customs man looked at him and put a chalk cross on his bag.

Cotton walked out and got directly into the Triumph.

'What have you been told to do?' he asked Hans.

'Look for a man called Mair.'

Cotton got back to his office at about twelve thirty. He told Hans to wait, went upstairs and gave Miss Kelly a croissant and a quail.

'Freshly smuggled this morning,' he said. 'Just a taste, I'm afraid.'

Miss Kelly flushed. 'Very welcome, sir.'

She put the food in her desk drawer and brought him a file.

Paul Mair had been born Paul Morton-Mair in Rome in 1907, and was the son of an Anglican priest. He had chosen to drop the Morton part when he reached twenty-one, had had a number of jobs, including stockbroker when he initially came down from Oxford, had even been a model in the early thirties, had then joined an oil company in 1935 'in an unspecified capacity to do with hospitality' and had been recruited to MI6 in 1941, spending the war mostly in Alexandria in Egypt, but with trips to Beirut in the Lebanon and to Palestine, mostly Jerusalem. He had also visited Baghdad and Basra in Iraq, Jeddah in Saudi Arabia and Istanbul in Turkey. He spoke French and 'some basic Arabic'.

'What did he do for MI6?'

'That's a bit unspecified too, sir. I haven't been in touch with MI6.'

'Right. You have lunch, Miss Kelly.'

Cotton went out and downstairs to the Triumph and got in.

'They say Mair is very good looking,' said Hans, as if not sure he was doubtful or envious. 'Older man type, you know.'

'Meaning?'

Hans had no trouble with the low-down. 'He likes slim girls, young girls. He's a cherry picker. In 1941 a lord who shall remain unnamed had him warned off his fourteen-year-old daughter.'

'Did MI6 get him for statutory rape?'

'In 1941.'

'Stables and doors?'

'Yes. He's supposed to have contacts in the Arab world, you know, from this pimp job he had with the oil company. Hospitality manager, something like that.'

'What did he do in the Middle East?'

'He had to take a little older. Wives of queers. He doesn't like too long with one woman. An in-and-out kind of man, unless she's very young.'

Cotton had meant Mair's job in the Middle East; he thought Hans probably knew that. He nodded.

'Didn't you say you'd been married?'

'Just the once, sir.'

Cotton looked over at him.

'It was an arrangement,' said Hans, 'of mutual advantage. I have had no cause to regret it.'

'Do you know where she is?'

'I have reason to fear she's in the Russian sector. Leipzig. The divorce papers came from there.'

Cotton nodded. 'I see,' he said. 'I'd quite like to meet or at least see your Robert. A Tory football director, didn't you say?'

'I don't understand, sir.'

'You've heard of tit for tat, haven't you?'

'Mr Ayrtoun gave me my instructions, sir.'

'And what did you find out about the girl in my flat?'

Hans made a face. 'Theatre. Poor. You are the younger. Did you know she's a Jew?'

Cotton nodded.

'Thank you, Hans. What's Mair's status at the moment?'

Hans leant forward. 'They have "transitory" on his file.'

'Right,' said Cotton. 'You don't know where he is, do you?'

'No,' said Hans. 'I am unsure of his whereabouts.'

'He could even be abroad?'

'Well, exactly,' said Hans.

'Do you know what a gooseberry is, Hans?'

Hans frowned. 'It's a fruit.'

'Also a chaperone. A third party. A killjoy.'

Hans grunted. '*Ein Anstandswauwau*?' He sounded put out.

'If every time I look at a girl you are going to sniff around and report back to Mr Ayrtoun, then you may also find Robert trips on something.'

268

Hans blinked. 'I obey Mr Ayrtoun,' he said.

'How do you think he's doing?' said Cotton. 'He's a busy man. Too much work. I thought he was looking tired. You might want to think of a plan B if you don't have one.'

Cotton tried Miss Kelly.

'What does "transitory" mean on someone's file?'

She shook her head. 'It is not a status I've seen or would recognize, sir. There are certain people who are called from time to time but they are usually described as "retained" or "temporarily inactive".'

'I want to know if Mair is in this country,' he said. 'How could I find that out quickly without using MI6 sources?'

Miss Kelly smiled politely. 'Are you requesting me to do that for you, sir?'

Cotton nodded. 'Yes, I am. If you can, of course.'

Within half an hour Moira Kelly knocked on his door.

'Totteridge,' she said. 'He's in Totteridge. That's about eight miles from here. It's on the Tube, the Northern Line, the penultimate stop, before High Barnet. And he's renting a house and used the name Paul Morton on the six-month lease.'

Cotton smiled. 'Excellent. I'm very impressed. How—?'

Moira was pleased. 'I tried the name Mair and thought I should include Morton and Morton-Mair. He needs a telephone. He's too recent to

269

be in the telephone book but there are records and bills. The telephone people are helpful, you know. His bank is Barclays. From his garage bills he would appear to have a Lagonda motor car.'

Cotton took down the address and contacted Hans.

'You believe Miss Hockey-sticks?'

Hans's English was coming on. 'You're joking,' said Cotton.

CHAPTER 24

In Totteridge they found a large family house, a late twenties or early thirties mix of mock Tudor and Arts and Crafts. It had not snowed for a couple of days but the night felt icy and bleak when they got out of the Triumph. The curtains in a bay window were drawn and a little light showed. To the right under the garage door was a sluggish little flicker of blue. Cotton stopped and pointed.

'For the Lagonda,' whispered Hans. 'Paraffin lamp under the car to stop freezing.'

Paul Mair was not the kind of man to keep the path cleared. Hans slipped and grabbed at Cotton.

'Sorry.'

They moved down the path at a careful shuffle. Cotton knocked at the door.

Nothing. Cotton knocked again.

This time there was a noise and then the sound of heavy, dragging feet approaching the door. The sound was oddly rubbery. The door opened. Either Paul Mair had been woken by the first knock on the door or was ill or was, in a phrase Cotton had learnt from his time in America, drunk as a skunk.

271

Options one and three had possibly combined in two. He gave them a queasy, anaesthetized look.

'Mr Morton? Mr Mair?' said Cotton.

Paul Mair thought. 'Do I know you?' he enquired.

'My name is Cotton.'

'Have I heard of you?'

'I don't know. Have you?'

Paul Mair shrugged and then abruptly found a taste in his mouth he disliked very much indeed. 'Who's the other man?'

'This is John Driver, Mr Mair.'

Mair frowned and leant forward. 'That sounds like a pseudonym, you know.'

'It's his new name,' said Cotton. 'He's originally from Germany.'

'Is he now?' said Mair. He tried to look reflective. I'll tell you what it is, Mr—?'

'Cotton. Peter Cotton.'

'Yes. I don't like two men coming to see me when it's dark.'

'In less wintery conditions,' replied Cotton, 'I'd agree. But if we had, for example, wanted to kill you, we would have done so already, wouldn't we?'

Paul Mair blinked. 'Who said anything about killing?'

'Have you heard of a man called Watson?'

Paul Mair frowned. 'It's rather a common name, don't you think?'

'Come on, you can do better than that. And it's cold out here.'

Paul Mair gave in. 'Oh, all right, all right,' he

said, already turning and beginning to shuffle along the hall.

Cotton and Hans stepped in and closed the door. The dragging noise Cotton had heard before the front door had opened was attributable to Mair's sheepskin-lined flying boots. He had not done them up. He had one trouser leg loosely tucked in, the other was merely rucked up.

They turned after him into the drawing room. Apart from two kitchen-type chairs and a small card-table, the room was bare to the light bulbs. There were some old newspapers on the floor-boards, a first underlay for a carpet no longer there. The fire was banked, however, with glowing coke. On the table was a nearly empty bottle of whisky and a Chinese-pattern teacup without a handle or a saucer.

Paul Mair rubbed his hands and turned to welcome them. He was dressed in what, in better light, turned out to be a pale green tweed suit and a camel-coloured scarf. At thirty-nine he was getting to the age of looking as much fragile as slim. His hair, particularly where the oil had worn off, looked white, but he retained something of the manner of someone rather charmingly looking around to see where he had mislaid the rest of his charm.

To the left were some double doors. Hans drew them back. On the floor of what had been meant as the dining room, slightly off centre, were a mattress and a heaped-up quilt.

Paul Mair waved a hand. 'I have no interest in the shrouds of respectability,' he announced. 'I'm camping in this ghastly place until the end of March.'

'What happens then?'

Hans had already moved on. They heard him walk into the kitchen, open cupboard doors and then go out and up the stairs.

'He's your sniffer dog, is he?' said Mair.

'What happens at the end of March?'

'Can I offer you something? We could eke out this bottle if I could find a glass or other receptacle. Oh, I know. I'll divide it between the cup and, well, could you drink from the bottle? Can you bear that?'

'March,' said Cotton.

'I leave these dreary shores.'

'Where are you going?'

'Only France. Well—'

'What?'

Paul Mair shook his head. 'Awful thing,' he said.

'What is?'

'I have a bank account in France. I had two hundred pounds in it. And then I got paid four hundred more.' He smiled. 'For services rendered, you see.'

'What happened?'

'It's all gone.'

'Four or six hundred?'

'The six. I mean that is beyond the pale, isn't it? Taking back the four hundred is one thing, cleaning me entirely out is pretty gratuitous and rather nasty, wouldn't you say?'

Hans came back. 'There's nothing at all upstairs except a sunlamp.'

'Yes,' said Paul Mair. 'It's a very small room. I turn it on and lie down on the floor, you see. I just fit.'

Cotton looked at him.

'Oh come on,' said Paul Mair. 'Let's not pretend too much. Call me a cad. I don't care. That's what I do. I am the Mozart of the suspender belt. I can even make a meal of a garter for a starter. But one's fingers can't loiter if they're pale, old boy.' He was in appealing, apparently confessional mode. 'It's the slope of a young belly I like. The tuck, you see, of the main course.'

Cotton nodded. Was Mair trying in a man-to-man way to find the right gear? 'So why do you stay here?'

'I've told you. I've barely got a bean. You see, my idea was I'd get a fresh start in France. Surely that's clear enough?'

Cotton shrugged. 'Sell the Lagonda.'

'Why?'

'They drive on the right in France.'

'I know all about that,' said Mair. 'But it took me such a long time to get her.'

'Tell me about Watson.'

'I abandoned any pretence to morals years ago. My father was an Anglican vicar. Ghastly snob. I was brought up in Rome, you know.'

'I know.'

'Gelato and breasts, that's what I remember.'

Despite himself, Cotton found Mair's manner, the badly acted stabs at remembering who he was, amusing, almost admirable.

'I'm good for syringes,' Mair said. 'And I can get hold of stuff to put in them. It's usually heroin or cocaine but I can, at a push, do you for other substances.'

'Cyanide?'

Mair looked pained. 'There's a positive glut, old man. The Germans had enough to kill an army.' He turned towards Hans.

'Try *under* the sunlamp, Fritz,' he said.

Annoyed, Hans left.

'He's not much of a sniffer,' Mair said.

'Tell me about Watson.'

'Dear Lord,' said Mair, 'it's really not so difficult. Most people aren't frightened of death, you know. They're frightened of *how* they will die. They prefer it to be quick and painless.' He shrugged. 'I'm pretty positive that makes sense.'

'You're probably right. What has that to do with Watson?'

Mair looked baffled. 'We're talking about a little man, some sort of plum scientist who allowed his taste for lads to, well, ruin his career?'

'You could say that. Was he very depressed?'

'Oh God yes,' said Mair. 'He was very down. He said he couldn't understand why the law was placing his robin above his scientific mind. Something like that.'

276

The word 'robin' threw Cotton for a second, until he remembered the poem 'Cock Robin'. The combination of baby talk, suicide and science was novel.

Mair shook his head. 'Do you know his own mother didn't know about his tastes? A damned shame, if you ask me. I'm with Lord Byron on this.'

'Really? What did Byron say?'

Mair looked doubtful. 'Any port in a storm?' he suggested.

'I'm not sure I remember that. What did you do?'

'I just kept him company for a bit, that's all. He didn't seem to have a lot of friends left. He was rather bitter about that. So we had chats and drinks. He had absolutely nowhere to go, you see. He was finished, poor devil, ambition dead, career over, nothing and nobody to live for.'

'So you helped him move on?'

Mair looked doubtful. 'You can put it like that. I don't think *I* would.'

'You facilitated his suicide.'

'I assisted his suicide,' insisted Mair. 'I'm not mealy-mouthed, you know. I provided the where-withal. Christ, he thanked me! You're a hard man, you know.'

'I wasn't there.'

'Everybody needs help. And he didn't want to cause a mess. You know, throw himself under a train, that kind of thing. He wanted to go quietly. And he wanted to leave his mother something.'

'What was that?'

'A little hope! At least a chance to deny it was a suicide. She'd probably prefer accident. Something not intended.' Mair blinked. 'And then I had to get back here. The weather was atrocious.'

'Why?'

'Why what?'

'Why did you do this for him?'

'For Christ's sake! I facilitate things! That's my job!' Mair suddenly looked doubtful. 'I have told you about the money, haven't I?'

'Yes, you have,' said Cotton. 'My next question is—'

'I've no idea who gave the order.'

Cotton nodded. 'I didn't imagine you did. But you can help me.'

Mair shook his head. His eyes moved towards the bottle of whisky. 'In late September last year I was, well, turfed out really. My particular skills were no longer needed in MI6.'

'Why not?'

Mair made a face. 'Do I have to go into that? It was administrative, really. Stuff about regulations.'

'Expenses?'

'I was several quid short on the Lagonda.'

'You did a little borrowing?'

'Yes,' said Paul Mair. He paused. He decided to carry on shedding pretence. 'I wasn't really thinking of paying it back, you know.' He shrugged. 'They took it off my last month's salary and settlement pay in any case.'

'Then what happened?'

'I went on a four-day bender.'

'Mm,' said Cotton. 'After that?'

'I couldn't pay my rent. I was overdrawn.'

'What about the two hundred in France?'

'That was my nest egg. It was then I got a note.'

'No address? No signature?'

'No stamp either. It said I still had the possibility of "unauthorized" jobs for MI6. It came on rice paper, edible stuff, quite sweet really. It did make mention of four hundred quid. And I rather fastened on that.'

'You didn't think it was a lot of money?'

Mair looked appalled. 'Jesus! I was just thinking of getting hold of some cash and then buggering off to France.'

'What happened?'

Paul Mair had begun to twitch. Evidently he found this troublesome.

'Go ahead, have a drink,' said Cotton.

There wasn't much whisky left but Mair slopped it when he poured into the cup. He drank. For a moment he looked relieved. Then he frowned.

'Have I told you about the Soviets?'

'No, you haven't,' said Cotton.

Mair shook his head. 'A man from their embassy got in touch with me.'

'Really?'

'Yes! He thought I might be –' Mair thought for the word '– disgruntled.'

'Were you?'

279

'No. I was a combination of pissed and pissed off really.'

'You sent the Soviets away?'

'I said I had another job.'

'I see. Do you want to tell me about that?'

'I needed somewhere to live, you see.'

'And your unauthorized contact suggested here.'

'I wasn't actually in a position to choose, you know.'

'How did you get the money to pay for it?'

'Envelope containing the deposit and six months' rent.'

'You didn't think that might be an advance?'

'They still didn't have to take the two hundred in France.'

'Did you think of buggering off then?'

Mair sighed. 'Only briefly. Anyway the envelope was delivered to the estate agent. He said the bank had sent it round for me.'

'Good,' said Cotton. 'Give me his name.'

'He has an office by the local shops. His name is Rig something. Rigsby.'

The telephone started ringing. Mair looked alarmed. He turned to Cotton.

'Do you really think I should answer that?'

'Yes,' said Cotton.

Mair picked up the telephone. He listened.

'Yes,' he said. 'There's someone else here.'

Mair held out the receiver. 'I think it's for you.'

'Thank you,' said Cotton. He had not been expecting any call.

'Sir?' said Moira Kelly.

'Yes.'

'You're at the number I gave you?'

'Yes.'

'The house has foreign diplomats as close neighbours. A cultural attaché lives at number 39. The Embassy has also rented number 41 though it is not clear who lives there. It appears to be run as a sort of B & B for several low-level staff, chauffeurs, that kind of thing.'

'How convenient,' said Cotton. 'What made you think of checking?'

Miss Kelly sighed. 'I don't know. The name Totteridge, I think. But the link didn't come until I was on my way home.'

'Where are you now?'

'I'm back at the office.'

'Good. Do you know what I'm thinking?'

'Yes, sir. Somebody's already on their way.'

'Thanks.'

Cotton put the phone down, then picked it up and listened. The tone sounded as the normal burr. No click. He began unscrewing the mouthpiece.

'What on earth are you doing?'

'Checking, Mr Mair. Do you have any contact with your neighbours?'

Paul Mair shook his head. 'Not much. They're rather dull, suburban sort of people.'

'Surely the Soviet cultural attaché across the road would be a little more exciting?'

Paul Mair groaned. 'Oh shit!' he said. 'I'm no

281

good at this kind of thing. I'm more perfume and girls and sherbet.'

'Sherbet?'

Mair winced. 'Fizz? After the garter. I dab a little on a finger, lick it and move up the thigh. Hell, it's not electricity but it acts almost as well.'

Cotton showed him the telephone.

'What am I looking at?'

'Nothing much. No aid to listening, for example.'

'They can put them elsewhere.'

'I know they can.'

Paul Mair made a face, even looked nauseous. 'What is it?'

'The notion of being observed, even being listened in on, is not very pleasant, not in private things,' he said. 'I'm not a voyeur, you know.'

'Do you have much of a social life?'

'Are you talking about girls?'

'Not only girls.'

'I haven't been doing much, not lately.'

'Do you think the garage has ears?'

'I beg your pardon.'

'I'd like to see your Lagonda.'

'Really? Oh, all right.'

CHAPTER 25

Hans was in the kitchen. On the flat surfaces he could find, he had laid out a selection of syringes and some small bags of this and that.

'It's mostly heroin and cocaine,' he said. He pointed at two small purses. 'Vials and pills. Food for Watson.'

'We're going outside for a breath of fresh air,' Cotton murmured. 'A man will be coming to check some things out. He shouldn't be here for a while but if he turns up let him in.'

Hans nodded. 'Can I stay by the fire?'

Cotton nodded. He unlocked the back door.

'God, it's cold,' said Paul Mair. He shuddered and rubbed his hands.

They went into the garage. There was a smell of paraffin. Mair took hold of a broom and dragged out the lamp.

'I don't want the radiator to crack,' he said.

The Lagonda was a V12 Drophead Coupé in grey and black. They got in.

'You have Soviets for neighbours,' said Cotton.

'Yes,' said Mair, 'but they do rather keep to

themselves, you know, as if they might get infected by something.'

'They're a bit near for comfort, surely?'

'Beggars can't be choosers.'

'Yes, that might worry some people, Mr Mair.'

Paul Mair blinked. 'I say, do you mind if I gun her up a bit? Get some engine heat going?'

'Not in an enclosed space.'

'We could go for a drive.'

'No, we couldn't.'

Paul Mair sighed. 'I'm depressed,' he announced. 'It's this country, you know. It's so damned grim. The weather's awful. The food's unspeakable. Even the little shop girls are a bit desperate for fun.' He glanced queasily at Cotton. 'I have absolutely no future here.'

'Have you thought about journalism?' asked Cotton.

Mair shook his head. 'I can't write for toffee.'

'What about your old boss in MI6?'

'Butler was his name. He called it a day after the war and went back to Oxford. He speaks lots of languages. Turkish, Arabic, Farsi, that kind of thing. I should have resigned when he did.'

'Why didn't you?'

'The oil company didn't want me back. Said things would take a couple of years at least to get back to normal after the war.'

'Would Butler recommend you for anything?'

'No! Of course he wouldn't,' said Mair. 'He's an academic. Awfully sharp, of course, but the kind of man who doesn't say a word now about what he was doing then. If he won't admit that, he's certainly not going to remember me.'

'What about France? You were planning to move there. What would you have done?'

'I hadn't thought. I just wanted to get out of here.'

'But you've been to France quite often, haven't you?'

'I've been,' admitted Paul Mair. 'After all, I was looking for somewhere to live. That was what the money was for. I was thinking of something not too big, of course.'

'Right,' said Cotton 'But I'm talking of a time before you left MI6 – perhaps May or June last year?'

Paul Mair made an effort. It did not last long. 'I'm not good at dates,' he complained.

Cotton smiled. 'You were at a reception at the Paris Embassy. You introduced a man called Vine to a young woman called Julia Gardener.'

'Oh yes,' said Paul Mair. 'You're right. I went over from London with him. He's something atomic. Rather the Englishman abroad.'

'What do you mean?'

'The timid husband looking for adventure, I suppose. He got quite excited when I picked up a girl. Her name was – Monique.'

'I see,' said Cotton. 'You were leading by example.'

Paul Mair looked as if he did not understand.

'I only introduced them, you know. I'm not responsible for what went on after that.'

'How did you know the girl?'

Paul Mair frowned and thought. 'Yes,' he said after a while. 'Julia. Quite slim, rather leggy? Pretty pert up top. Actually, you know, she turned me down. Said I wasn't the right kind of man for her but was perfectly charming about it.'

'What did that tell you?'

Paul looked nonplussed. 'Well, that she probably was open to another kind of man.'

'Someone like Vine?'

'I imagine someone she thought more reliable or long term. She gave me the impression of being quite ambitious. A stepping stone kind of girl.'

'What about her husband?'

Paul Mair closed his eyes long enough for Cotton to wonder if he had fallen asleep, but then he shook his head. 'Awfully sorry! Can't remember him at all. Just an impression of something doggy or perhaps dogged.'

Cotton nodded and looked across at Paul Mair. Gloomily, Mair was staring straight ahead through the windscreen.

'Pity you're going to have to sell it,' said Cotton.

Mair sighed. 'I know,' he said. 'I got her relatively cheap.' He shook his head. 'I'm not going to get a lot for her. I'm just too desperate.'

'Concentrate,' said Cotton.

'I could do with a drink.'

'I know. But I haven't brought any. Sorry.'

286

'I see. Yes. What do you want from me?'

'Do you know a Frenchman called Bodard?'

Mair nodded. 'He's an arms dealer. About fifty. Has jackets that button up too high. Wears his hair in that odd sticky-up sort of way.'

'*En brosse*?'

'Yes. That's it. Looks like a brush. He has a thin moustache. Has a chateau, shoots boar there.'

'Could he help you?'

Paul Mair laughed. 'Even I really don't think that would be wise.'

'But you've had dealings with him.'

'Hardly. I've done him a couple of favours. He's done me a couple.'

'What did he want?'

'Information, of course.'

'Any particular subject?'

'Not really. He vacuums information up. Anything to do with military equipment and supplies. He deals in anything. I mean the man has a Colonial War department already set up. Run by a Pole. He deals in helicopters, Sten guns, mines, jeeps—'

Cotton interrupted him. 'And witch hunts,' he said.

'What are you talking about?'

'Did Bodard ask you for an introduction to Vine?'

Paul Mair frowned.

'I'm guessing, you see, that Vine heard from Bodard there was a particular scientist in the

UK atom bomb development project who was homosexual.'

Mair raised his chin. 'Now you're talking about Watson,' he said.

'Yes.'

'I knew that,' said Mair.

'In May last year? Maybe June?'

Mair did at least look doubtful but then thought of something. 'The man was a Trotskyite as well.'

'Who said?'

'*I* don't know.'

'Bodard?'

'Jesus! It might have been. But . . . look, you make it sound all so planned.'

Cotton nodded. 'Let's see,' he said. 'In May 1946 you introduce a civil servant to a secretary and they start an affair. The civil servant, gonads at last unrationed, is then told something that can justify more trips to Paris in the national interest. A scientist is not only homosexual, he is also a Trotskyite. These things may mean the scientist is an awful security risk. You lose your job at the end of September and in January this year somehow end up with the very same scientist near the Greyhound in Croydon to assist him into the next world, having actually believed you'd be paid four hundred pounds for this service. I suppose if you believed Watson was a Trotskyite, you'd believe in the money. Have I got that about right?'

Paul Mair shook his head. 'I wouldn't put it like that. I mean hindsight is all very well.'

288

'Is it? I'd have said a minimal degree of foresight rather does for later excuses. Someone has been toying with you, Mr Mair, without you registering very much at all.'

There was a pause. 'Well, it isn't Bodard,' Mair said.

'How do you know that?'

'If he told Vine something, he wasn't doing it off his own bat.'

'Quite,' said Cotton. 'You've got that right. Let's go inside again.'

They got out of the Lagonda and Mair pushed the little lamp under the radiator again. They walked out of the side door.

'Did you know the word "avocado" came from the Greek for testicle?' said Mair.

'You're talking about the cold,' said Cotton.

'Yes, I suppose I am.'

They went into the house.

Hans Bieber was sitting on a chair by the fire. He jumped up at once.

'Where did you get this coal?' he said.

'It's coke,' said Paul Mair. 'I got a delivery last week.'

'How did you manage that?'

'Neighbours,' said Mair. 'The people in front got a lorry load and passed some of it on to neighbours, out of solidarity apparently.'

'The Soviets?'

'Yes. They're obviously on good terms with somebody. I've got about five bags left. I could let you have one, if you wanted.'

'Mr Driver doesn't need any fuel,' said Cotton.

The telephone rang. Startled, Paul Mair looked round.

'It's probably for us,' said Cotton.

Hans picked up the phone. He listened, then nodded.

'Two or three minutes,' he said. He put down the phone. 'That's Freddie,' he said. 'I'm going to collect him at the station.'

'Good,' said Cotton. 'See if there's anything open and get what you can in the way of food or drink.'

'There won't be,' said Hans.

'Try,' said Cotton.

'Good man,' said Paul Mair.

Both sat down at the card table though there was nothing to play. Mair glanced at Cotton, but seeing Cotton was not then going to ask him more questions, stared at the fire. Shortly after, his eyes closed.

Cotton had been told in September 1945 that the Intelligence Services were ridding themselves of the schoolboys, adventurers, more obvious conmen. What had D said? The louche and the farouche. Obviously this was taking time, though he could imagine that using someone like Mair could have its advantages. Cotton looked at his watch. It was just past eight. He looked at the newspapers on the floor. The one nearest to him was from the summer of 1928 and lamented the poor performance of the British team at the

Amsterdam Olympics. Only three gold medals: scant harvest in Holland. Cotton felt his lids drooping. He stretched out a leg and kicked Mair's foot. Mair grunted.

'What did you do after you gave Watson his syringe and his Goering juice?'

'I'm not entirely heartless, you know. I went on a bender.'

'Fine,' said Cotton.

'Who's coming now?' said Mair.

'Someone who is going to sweep the house for listening devices.'

'Is he going to bring any refreshments?'

'I don't know. Do you remember the name of the man from the Russian Embassy who got in touch with you when they thought you might be disgruntled?'

'Oleg something.'

'Great.'

'Give me a moment! Cherkesov?'

'Oleg Cherkesov. Are you sure?'

'Yes. Something like that. Tall, bit of a panto-mime villain, has hands from an El Greco painting.'

Cotton knew very few of the names in the Soviet Embassy but Oleg Cherkesov was one. He was a 'legal', that is someone protected by diplomatic immunity, but he was also supposed to be Beria's man in London, Beria being Stalin's man in charge of Soviet secrecy, and now the Soviet effort to produce an atom bomb.

'Shit,' said Cotton.

'Are you talking figuratively?'

'Not really,' said Cotton.

In the event, Freddie Igloi had brought a thermos flask of tea as stewed and sweet as pre-invasion stuff. Hans had managed to get a half-bottle of brandy.

'I'm really a whisky man,' said Mair.

'Take it or leave it,' said Hans.

Mair took it. 'It does make my liver twinge, you know.'

Freddie Igloi had already opened his small case. It did not take very long for him to check out the house, about twenty-five minutes. Cotton drank some tea, then washed out the cup-top and handed it on to Hans. Hans shook his head. The only hiatus was getting Mair to move. Cotton got him through to the kitchen, washed out his cup and offered him some tea.

Mair looked put-upon. 'I am not really a tea sort of person.'

'All right.'

'What's going to happen?'

'When the search is finished we'll leave.'

'But what am I supposed to do?'

'I don't know. You have this place for a bit longer, don't you? Perhaps something will turn up.'

'What would you do in my position?'

'Sell the Lagonda.'

'You're not much help,' said Mair. 'I'm feeling rather low.'

'Yes, I'm sorry about that. Do you want my card?'

Mair thought about this. 'All right.' He looked up. 'May I have one?'

'Of course.' Cotton gave him a business card.

Freddie Igloi came through. 'That's done, Colonel Cotton.'

'Oh Christ, you're a colonel,' said Paul Mair.

'I was a colonel,' said Cotton. 'We'll give you a lift back,' he said to Freddie Igloi.

'Will you?' said Freddie Igloi. 'That would be a help.'

'Good. Well, Mr Mair, that's it. If we need to be, we'll be in touch. I take it you are going to be here for a few days more?'

'What do you mean?'

'That if you find you are on the move, you check with me first. All right?'

'You can't just leave me here.'

'Why not? You're not being charged. You are no longer an employee of the Intelligence Services, not even informally from what you tell me.'

'Fuck it,' said Paul Mair. He gave a sheepish smile. 'I'll have to give my liver a twinge.'

'I could put him out of his misery,' said Hans Bieber when they were back in the Triumph.

Cotton stared at him.

'He has nothing left,' said Hans as if this was self-evident.

'Stop it,' said Cotton. 'You are not going to touch

Paul Mair, except to shake his hand and thank him for his contribution. Clear, Hans?'

'If you say so.'

'I will be in touch with Mr Ayrtoun about this. Have you got that?'

'All right, all right.'

'Good. We are leaving Paul Mair exactly where he is, that is, alive and in Totteridge, for two reasons. The first is that his neighbours might notice if he vanished. The second is that whoever is working with them on our side would also notice.'

'Yes, but—'

'By leaving him we make him their problem. Do you understand? He has only a few weeks left of his lease. We know where he is and that will do for now.' He turned to Freddie Igloi. 'What did you do?'

'It's not a bug exactly. We can't afford too many. It flags the telephone exchange, and the numbers dialled and connecting to his telephone are recorded. It's in the base of the apparatus.'

'Good. All right, Hans. Now we need to know a few things. One, where did Mair go after he saw Watson off.'

'Not here?'

'The weather was terrible. He didn't mention his Lagonda. Do you believe he drove back here from Croydon in the middle of a snowstorm? He also told me he'd gone on a bender. I'll have it checked. The second thing we want to find out is who supplies him with his drugs.'

'I don't understand that,' said Hans. 'If he's dealing in drugs, why is he poor?'

'Good question.'

'Drug dealers get paid up front,' said Freddie Igloi.

'Exactly,' said Cotton. 'That may be why losing the money in France has caused him so much trouble.'

'Are you saying he has a French dealer?'

'No, I am saying we have to find these things out.'

'He could be the kind who gives out a little free, the party man. Then the dealer moves in,' said Igloi. 'It's a thought.'

'Where do you want to go?' Hans asked Freddie Igloi.

'Top of Edgware Road? Marble Arch?'

'Fine,' said Hans.

They let Freddie Igloi out and made for Wilbraham Place.

'May I ask you a question, sir?' said Hans.

'What is it?'

'Have you thought Mair might take cyanide himself?'

'Yes,' said Cotton. 'That's up to him.'

Cotton saw Hans shiver.

'What's the matter?'

'It's this cold,' said Hans. 'It's cold in Germany but it's not like this.'

CHAPTER 26

At Wilbraham Place Cotton took his suitcase out of the Triumph and went upstairs. Light was showing under the door. He let himself in.

'Where did you go?' said Anna Melville.

'I've been in Paris.'

'Really?'

'I have proof.'

He gave Anna Melville the remaining croissant and quail.

'Have you eaten yours?'

'I gave them to my secretary.'

'What's she called?'

'Miss Kelly.'

'Are you telling me she's more than a secretary?'

'No, I'm telling you she is a very good secretary.'

Anna Melville laughed. 'A secretary is more important than a lover, is that it?'

'It depends what you're doing, surely?'

'So this food is not a romantic offering?'

'It's food not commonly available in this country.'

'You're a gourmet.'

'Hardly. In Paris I also bought some razor-blades

and this toilet case. The croissants and quail were chosen because they fitted nicely into the case.'

She laughed. 'Gus says you work for MI5, something like that.'

Cotton shook his head. 'That's the problem with people who like drama.'

'He says MI5 don't employ women and Jews.'

Cotton frowned. 'Think about it. That can't be true.'

She shrugged. 'Why did you go to Paris?'

Cotton smiled. 'Because I was sent there,' he lied. 'Exchange rates, the number of francs or dollars you get to a pound, make economists very excited. We and the French both have threadbare or moth-eaten empires. We have the Sterling Area, the French—'

She interrupted. 'You could have got me perfume or stockings, you know.'

Cotton shook his head. 'I didn't know what kind of perfume you liked, thought stockings a little flimsy in this weather. I thought you might like something good to eat for a change. And then I didn't know that you'd be here.'

'Meaning?'

'I would have eaten them myself if you hadn't been.'

She smiled. 'My, you're a practical chap.' She broke off a piece of croissant and put it in her mouth. 'It's a bit near the end of the day to be quite fresh but – that's butter I can taste, isn't it?'

'Probably.'

She smiled. 'Now I don't want to strain your gentlemanly qualities,' she said, 'but I do like sex. Women aren't supposed to say that, are they? Is that intimidating?'

'No.'

'Off-putting?'

'In my experience, it's unusual.'

She laughed. 'Good. I thought we could start with a kiss. Would you like it with quail or a little more croissant?'

The next day, Thursday, 6 February, Cotton and Hans visited Paul Mair's estate agent, a man called Harold Rigsby who worked for a chain in a shop-cum-office on what was called a parade. There was a greengrocer, a butcher, a baker, a newsagent and post office, a place that sold equestrian goods, and then there was a small bow window with some panes of glass tinged pale green. Inside, Mr Rigsby was sitting behind a desk on which was a silver-plated candelabra. Only one of the three candles was lit but he lit the other two as they came in. There was a single-barred electric fire, but it was not on.

Mr Rigsby was plump enough for his wedding band to look uncomfortable on his finger. On the small finger of his right hand he had a signet ring he rubbed when he talked. He tried, though his breath showed in the cold, to be pompous and business-like and to invoke client–agent confidentiality.

'Mr Rigsby, you're not a doctor and you're not a priest. You deal in the selling, buying and renting of houses.'

'We have a code of conduct, I assure you. We have a policy of strict adherence to ethical practices as a matter of course.'

It took a little bluster time but Cotton got through to him and heard largely what he expected to hear.

'I was contacted by the security forces of this country,' said Mr Rigsby. 'They told me they wanted to rent a house to keep an eye on the Soviets at 39 and 41. I hardly felt in a position to demur. I am, after all, as patriotic as the next man. But I must insist. We received all kinds of guarantees. And assurances that no damage would be done to the property.'

Cotton smiled. 'I am absolutely sure of it,' he said. 'My understanding is the deposit and a full six months' rent were paid in full and in cash before Mr Mair—'

Rigsby frowned. 'Morton,' he said.

'That's your name for him, is it?'

'What?' said Rigsby. 'Are you suggesting I was misled?'

'I don't know what references you took up.'

'I was under the impression I was doing my bit in the national interest.'

'But we are talking cash, aren't we?'

'Yes. It's not unknown and there was nothing untoward about the transaction. All monies are accounted for and the receipts in order.'

'Who owns the house?'

'We act as agents. I assure you the owners know nothing of this. They are abroad.'

'Where?'

'The owner is in the ICS, the Indian Civil Service, and was very pleased we had let the house in such difficult market conditions. And at the full asking price.'

'How did the money arrive?'

Rigsby looked down at his ring finger. 'Through the letter box,' he said quietly. 'There was a note saying Mr Morton would be calling in and to have the contract and keys ready.'

'Did you meet Mr Morton?'

'Of course, I did! One doesn't let houses lightly, you know.'

'Who else did you see?'

'The two gentlemen who came before.'

'And showed you identification?'

Rigsby looked nervous. 'Yes. I'm pretty sure they did.'

'That's all right, Mr Rigsby. What were they like?'

'Decent enough chaps. One was called Cunningham. I remember that. And the other one was called Crouch.'

Cotton nodded. 'Could you describe them?'

'Not very well,' Rigsby admitted. 'This is some months ago. One of them had a moustache, quite thick. The other looked younger, in his twenties perhaps. Quite fresh-faced. That was Crouch. The

300

older man with the moustache was the one who did the talking.'

'Do you have a copy of the contract?'

'Of course. I say, there are not going to be any problems, are there? The lease is up at the end of March and we don't want anything untoward.'

'The contract?'

It was standard stuff. Paul Mair had signed his side as Morton and given his previous address as being in the Avenue Foch in Paris. Rigsby had signed for the owner, John Campbell Muir, whose address was given simply as New Delhi, India.

'Do you want to see the inventory?' said Harold Rigsby.

'Inventory of what?'

'Why, of the contents of course! The furniture and everything. The house is fully equipped, I can assure you. Some quite good quality stuff there, and the odd painting.'

Cotton nodded. 'I see. I couldn't have a copy, could I?'

It turned out there was not a spare copy, but Cotton looked at it. It was several pages long. Canteen of cutlery, full dinner service, Regency-type dining table and eight dining chairs, silver candlesticks in the drawing room . . .

'Good,' said Cotton. 'Thank you.'

Mr Rigby was looking alarmed. 'I say, Mr Morton is still there, isn't he?'

'Yes,' said Cotton. 'Of course he is. In fact we saw him yesterday evening.'

'So what's this about?'

'It's a cross-check,' said Cotton. 'Whatever we are doing we have to ensure everything is above board. That no one is trying anything on. This varies from profiting to . . . well, we understand Mr Morton was given some fuel by his Soviet neighbours. They appear to have handed quite a lot out.'

Mr Rigby grunted indignantly. 'That's because the Soviets have friends in that damned miners' union. The rest of us are living with candles, for heaven's sake!'

'Thank you very much, Mr Rigsby. This conversation is—'

'Of course, not a word.'

Cotton shook Rigsby's plump hand and he and Hans left the shop and walked to the Triumph. Hans paused before opening the car door.

'Do you mean that Mair has flogged off the furniture?' he said.

'It certainly looks possible.'

Cotton was intrigued that Hans looked agitated, rather more than he had at the idea of someone providing syringe and cyanide to a suicide. They got into the car.

'But that would be a crime,' Hans said.

'Yes,' said Cotton.

Hans started the motor. 'Are we going to see Mair again now?'

'No,' said Cotton.

'That fat man might go and see him. I would.'

302

'Yes, Rigsby may go along but I doubt if he'll go in. We'll go to Wardour Street. I want to speak to Freddie Igloi.'

Hans frowned. 'You are having Mair watched?'

'No. That would upset the Soviets. And we don't want to do that, at least not yet.'

CHAPTER 27

In Wardour Street Freddie Igloi told Cotton that Paul Mair had made three telephone calls in the hour after they had left.

'I have the numbers here. Two of these calls were to London but the third was to a place called East Grinstead. That was a very short call.'

Cotton took down the numbers and went back to the office. Miss Kelly took some time.

'That East Grinstead number was the hardest. They don't like giving out the number of important people.'

'Who are we talking about?' Miss Kelly dropped her voice. 'Sir Cyril Healey-Johnson. He's the third baronet. I looked him up in *Debrett's*.'

Cotton knew the name but little else. 'He's not an MP any more, is he?'

'No. He stood down in 1945.'

'The other numbers?'

'One to his sister. About ten minutes. One to an Anglican priest. Long call, about half an hour. The third call, to Sir Cyril, lasted no more than a few seconds.'

Cotton thought. The sister would be for help or forgiveness or goodbye. The Anglican priest would be against self-slaughter. The third call either for help or appeal, doubtless cut short.

'What kind of priest?'

'What do you mean?'

'High? Low?'

'Society. English. From the north of England.'

'How are we doing for money?' asked Cotton.

'Petty cash?'

'Yes. Ten pounds, for example.'

There was a pause. 'Five would be better,' said Miss Kelly.

'Seven pounds ten shillings, then,' said Cotton.

'Payment to?'

'Paul Mair. By post. Preferably by tomorrow.'

Miss Kelly could convey disapproval without any obvious movement.

'Thank you very much, Miss Kelly.' Cotton picked up the telephone but had something to say before he called.

'Miss Kelly, I want to arrange a meeting with Oleg Cherkesov of the Soviet Embassy. This will need all kinds of clearances.'

'He's top class,' said Miss Kelly. She meant that Cherkesov came in the first rank of Soviet representatives in the UK.

Cotton nodded and called through. Paul Mair took a long time to pick up.

'Paul?'

'Ehm—'

'This is Peter here. Peter Cotton. I came to see you the other evening.'

Paul Mair grunted. 'What is it you want?'

'I have just arranged to have seven pounds ten shillings sent to you. You should get the money tomorrow morning. It will come by post and it will be in cash.'

There was a pause. 'It's not enough to get away, you know.'

'Yes, I do know that.'

'So why are you sending it?'

'In payment, Paul. You're going to write a report.'

'What about?'

'Wake up, Paul. I want a full statement of your relationship with A. A. Watson. Omit nothing. Is that clear?'

'I suppose so,' said Paul Mair. 'I don't have any paper, you know.'

'That's one of the reasons you're getting some money, Paul. You'll be able to buy some and a pencil if need be. Buy some food as well. If you want I can send a secretary. She could take down what you say, type it up and have you sign it.'

Another pause. 'How do you know I won't bugger off?'

'Because we know about the furniture.'

'That's not a problem.'

'Why not?'

Cotton could almost hear Paul Mair frown. 'I'll just say I went away for a couple of days, came back to find the house stripped. The neighbours won't have seen anything and the insurance will pay.'

'What on earth makes you think we'll keep quiet?' Mair grunted.

'Right,' said Cotton. 'Do you know anyone called Cunningham? Or Crouch? They might have been together.'

'I don't think so.'

'What about Sinclair and Boyle? They're Glaswegians.'

'I don't know Glasgow,' said Paul Mair.

'Paul, I'm asking if you saw them before you accompanied A. A. Watson. Perhaps they persuaded you.'

'No. My instructions came on rice paper.'

'When?'

'Beginning of January, I suppose.'

'Come on, Paul. Was it before or after the sixth?'

'I think it was about the tenth, actually.'

'How did you meet Watson?'

'Went to Oxford. Met him in a pub.'

'How did you get to Croydon?'

'Oh, that was entirely his idea. He turned up here, wanted to stash his car in my garage for a few days. We took it from there.'

'All right. Are you clear now? You have something to do. Write down anything you remember. And I mean anything.'

There was another pause. 'I'm going to wait until the money arrives,' said Paul Mair.

Cotton stifled a sigh. 'Fine,' he said. 'Is that clear now? You have something to do.'

There was yet another pause. 'I'm going to wait until the money arrives,' said Paul Mair again.

'That's fine,' said Cotton. 'You do that. But I want the report by Monday, clear?'

'Do hang on,' said Mair. 'You couldn't give me a Q & A with the money, could you? It would help structure my report, you see.'

Cotton nodded. 'Yes,' he said. 'I'll do that.'

Miss Kelly brought him a checklist. Apart from Ayrtoun, MI6 would have to give approval for a meeting with Oleg Cherkesov. And MI5 would have to be informed.

'We have to make a formal application,' she said.

'Mention this involves A. A. Watson, deceased, an ex-agent of theirs called Paul Mair who claims (a) he assisted Mr Watson in his suicide and (b) that he was previously and unsuccessfully approached by Mr Cherkesov and that they will know more than I do about Mr Cherkesov's relationship with Mr Beria, presently in charge of the Soviet atom bomb project.' He looked up. 'I think that's enough for now. I'm happy to be briefed and/or accompanied. I perfectly well understand I'm not part of the Soviet department nor privy to our own military developments. If MI6 agree, they should inform MI5.'

'Is that all, sir?'

'I'm going to write a Q & A for the man who's getting the money. They should go off together.'

Cotton called Dickie Dawkins and told him something of what was happening. 'I've just found out where Watson's car was. In Totteridge, apparently. Not that our ex-MI6 man comes over as very reliable. He's writing a report but needs help.'

'Ask him if he encountered Radcliffe,' said Dawkins.

'Any particular reason?'

Dawkins sighed. 'No, I suppose not. But God, it's cold here.'

'Is he giving you a rough time?'

'No,' said Dawkins. There was a pause. 'He's overbearing,' he said.

'All right,' said Cotton.

When Cotton put down the phone, Miss Kelly handed him a note. It was a government release. Miss Ellen Wilkinson, Minister for Education, had died earlier that day, aged 55, in St Mary's Hospital, London, 'of pneumonia'. 'It says the cause of death was really a heart attack brought about by an accidental overdose of barbiturates. Accidental my eye,' said Miss Kelly.

Cotton was aware Miss Kelly was agitated.

'I'll bet you, sir, Mr Morrison will not attend her funeral.'

Cotton blinked. 'The ground's frozen,' he said. 'They're using pneumatic drills to dig up potatoes. I think dead bodies are being stacked.'

'She was a socialist,' said Miss Kelly. 'She may have chosen cremation. That's got priority.'

'Are you all right, Miss Kelly?'

Moira Kelly shook her head. 'It's a damned shame,' she said. 'She sacrificed herself. If their affair had become public Mr Morrison would have been ruined.' She shook her head. 'He had no idea of her sacrifice. And now he will be too frightened to attend her funeral and will think she killed herself to get at him.'

Cotton thought about it, possibly even of saying Miss Kelly couldn't be sure Morrison would not go, but then thought of Morrison and the self-concern of politicians. He looked at his secretary.

'I'm sorry,' he said. It did occur to him to ask himself whether Miss Kelly had ever fallen for a married man. He didn't ask her.

She blinked at him. 'Thank you, sir. I shouldn't have said those things—'

'It's all right.'

'I didn't admire her politics but—'

'It's really all right.'

Miss Kelly nodded. 'I'll get on, sir.'

Cotton wrote out the Q and A for Paul Mair. He kept thinking he had missed something, but gave it to Miss Kelly so that it could catch the post.

The next day, Friday, 7 February, the Government had no need to keep insisting on the official history at least, that Miss Ellen Wilkinson had died of pneumonia. The Right Honourable Emmanuel Shinwell MP, Minister of Fuel and Power, read out to the House of Commons a list of measures meant to spread the effects of the lack of coal evenly and fairly. Domestic consumption of electricity would be forbidden between the hours of 0900 and twelve noon and also from 1400 to 1600. Anyone using electricity at those times faced a fine of one hundred pounds sterling or three months in jail. There would be no 'external lighting'. The television service would be suspended and radio transmissions cut. Newspapers would be reduced. The list was long and included the banning of greyhound racing. German POWs would be put to clearing the railway lines with their hands, if necessary.

When Cotton got back home that evening he found Anna Melville had laid papers all over the kitchen table.

'You have a marvellous table,' she said. 'It's big and it's flat.'

'I'm glad,' said Cotton. At one end of the table was a bottle of wine and a glass. The glass was empty, the bottle almost. 'What are these papers? Drawings?'

There was an element of strip cartoon or story-board about them. She had drawn twelve squares across each foolscap sheet, but in each square there were only one or two curves and, like some sort of punctuation, occasional blank squares. He recognized the paper as his, taken from a drawer in his desk.

'You should think of these as akin to photographic negatives,' she said.

'All right. Black background, lines as white?'

'There will be colours in the lines. Do you know what blacklight is?'

Cotton had taken off his overcoat and scarf. He saw her eyes looked a little bloodshot.

'I've heard of it being used as a means of checking whether a banknote is genuine or counterfeit,' he said.

'You really know how to make a girl's heart skip a beat, don't you?'

'I know. Is there any wine left in that bottle?'

She checked. She shook her head. 'Just dregs,' she said.

'I see.' He went to the cupboard and got out another bottle of wine. He had two left. 'You're talking of UV light, is that it?' He took a cork off the corkscrew and began opening the bottle.

'Yes, I am! Good for you! Are you thinking of getting me drunk?'

'I just thought I'd drink some before it disappeared.'

She laughed and held out her glass.

'Blacklight theatre,' she said. 'It's quite a Czech thing.'

The wine gurgled.

'I haven't seen it.'

'It's because we can't see black on black. Our eyes, I mean. An actor dressed in black can move unseen against a black background. Another actor can appear quite normally. But perhaps the objects around him will move. We usually use luminescent paint on those.'

'All right,' said Cotton. 'But am I right in thinking you probably wouldn't act *The Cherry Orchard* in this way?'

The girl laughed. 'You could, you know! But you're right in a way. Do you know Méliès?'

'A moon with a face and a rocket in one eye? Surely he was a film-maker?'

'He was playing with our perceptions! Making jokes, surprising us.'

'I'm not sure I have grasped what your blacklight is yet. Right now I am somewhere between optics and tricks of light.'

'You make the stage into a black box, sometimes called a cabinet. You use blacklight and luminescence.'

'Do the actors speak?'

'Ah. There's a lot of blacklight theatre that likes mime. But you could, you see, simply have luminescent lipstick and have mouths speaking.'

'And you could just have them cover their mouths rather than turning away.'

She looked surprised.

'I mean that Méliès cut the film. It's the speed of the change that confuses. In blacklight you can be more fluid. Is that right?'

She closed one large eye on him.

'What's the matter?' he said.

'You might be getting hold of this.'

He laughed. 'Don't bet on it.' He indicated the papers on the table. 'What are you working on?'

'A dream, I suppose. My dream, that is, not dreams in blacklight.'

'Difficult.'

'Very,' she said. 'There's the expense. With a venue, actors, the light and all the rest, I'm estimating about four hundred and fifty pounds.'

Cotton had no idea of theatre finances or whether this was a large amount or not. He did remember Christopher Fry was supposed to be getting paid exactly that sum to write a play.

'And there is the actual play,' she said.

Cotton nodded. It had occurred to him, for example, that speaking mouths might find it difficult to maintain an audience's attention beyond, at a push, thirty minutes. Those glossy, moving lips would begin to upset or unsettle people in the stalls and look very far away to people in the gods, unless the words were good.

He poured himself more wine. The wine was still chilly but he could feel his face warming.

'Have you written it? Or is somebody else doing it?'

'That would be even more money.'

'Not if you collaborated with someone else trying to make a name.'

'I'm not sure the English, despite their experience of the blackout and even the candles now, wouldn't need something they could relate to.'

'You've just given it, haven't you? Set it in the blackout. A bomb-shelter. Or the Tube. Crump and thump of bombs in the distance. The

314

audience could be in the tracks, if you know what I mean.' Cotton leant forward and turned his head left as if looking out for a train.

'Don't act, darling,' she said. 'Tell me more.'

Cotton laughed, 'I don't know. Are you thinking of a comedy? Something sharp? Something sad? You could pick out various characters. You could have children. Even ghosts if you wanted. Bomb victims.'

'I'm impressed. You're more imaginative than I thought.'

'It's just Mexico. I had a nurse who didn't marry a man because her dead mother told her not to.'

She beckoned him and kissed him. 'Thank you. You'd be surprised how ungenerous theatre people can be.'

'No,' said Cotton, 'I don't think I would.'

She smiled. 'I think we could make Welsh rarebit. Well, we've got bread and there's a smidgeon of cheese and if we diluted the little bit of Lea & Perrins you've got, we could stretch things.'

CHAPTER 28

On Sunday, 9 February a thaw set in. By the next day, the slush had frozen into a thick layer of ice.

About three o'clock in the afternoon Cotton received a visit from a man often called the Court Circular, to brief him for his meeting with Cherkesov. Allen Beresford was a Kremlin reader for MI6 and, in the same way that previous British spies had studied and interpreted what was happening at the courts of kings such as Philip II of Spain or Louis XIV of France, he examined the Soviet leadership. Dressed in a deerstalker hat and with an Inverness cape over his town clothes, he came with a thermos flask wrapped in its own scarf, his own supply of biscuits and a hipflask.

'You do realize Stalin is nearly seventy,' he said, 'and suffers from high blood pressure? There are several indications that a degree of jockeying is going on amongst those who fancy their chances of succeeding him. All of them claim to recognize that reforms will be needed. Beria undoubtedly wants the job, but his position is not as strong as it may look. I take it you know Stalin called him "my Himmler" at Yalta?'

'Yes, I had heard that,' said Cotton.

'It's tricky coming on as a reformer if your power base is the secret police,' said Beresford. 'I mean, people may not mention it but they do remember the thousands of executions and millions in camps. Despite this, Beria has suggested some loosening of the State's grip and is standing up for some Jews, letting them out of prison so that they contribute, and so on. He's finding that rather sticky. Stalin is a visceral anti-Semite, you know, and the other would-be reformers are playing to that. Beria's not a natural reformer and is almost as paranoid as Stalin. So he's put his own men where he can. We were led to believe that your Mr Cherkesov might be one of them.'

'You're not sure?' said Cotton.

'Well, recently a number of stories have been in circulation about Mr Beria's sexual proclivities. He's supposed to send his men out to kidnap women off the streets. He then rapes them in the comfort of his own home and has a flunkey give them a bouquet of flowers when they're shown the door.'

Beresford looked up. 'Of course, this rape thing may well be a trumped-up charge. We don't know. But there have also been rumblings about the execution of ten thousand in Georgia in the early twenties, apparently without a fair trial on a case by case basis. And very recently, the faintest whispering in Leningrad, but not so far Moscow, that it was in fact Beria who ordered the killings the Soviets claim the Nazis did in Poland at a place called Katyn.' Beresford held up a hand. 'Beria's opponents are rehearsing accusations that might stick to him.'

'What has Cherkesov to do with this?' said Cotton.

'We're not entirely sure, but one of our analysts has suggested he had something to do with the rape story, that if it does not come from him, it was at least edited by him. He has a certain literary panache rare in Soviet rumour, a turn of phrase. That bouquet of flowers to the unfortunate women is his style, apparently.'

Cotton looked doubtful. 'Why does your analyst think that?'

Beresford made a face. 'Because during the purges Cherkesov is supposed to have suggested that the condemned be given a bouquet before execution and the instruction "Pass it along".'

'It's hardly the Scarlet Pimpernel,' said Cotton. 'Is your analyst seriously suggesting Cherkesov has a monopoly on the word "bouquet"? How does Beria take this?'

'If he knows, of course, I imagine he'd understand Cherkesov is retaining his options. Cherkesov also knows Malenkov very well, by the way. He's another runner.'

Cotton nodded. 'Right.'

'Cherkesov began in TASS, the Soviet news agency, in the twenties. He was sent to the US in

318

the early thirties. He speaks excellent English, as you'll see. In late 1939 he was rather abruptly packed off to Canada. He went back to the Soviet Union in late 1940 or early 1941 and is given great credit for his work organizing aircraft production. This is what brought him into contact with Beria and with Malenkov.'

'How old is he?'

'About the same as them. All born around 1902.'

'But Cherkesov is not a contender for the throne?'

'No, no. By Soviet standards he's something of a dandy, at least in manner and appearance. But he has a first-class mind.' Beresford paused. 'He'd certainly know that the reformers would not immediately reform Stalin's methods of eliminating enemies real or perceived.'

'What was he doing in the US, do you know?'

'Something that had already made him, unofficially, *persona non grata* in 1939. The Soviets were very quick and early in getting agents organized and into place in America. Cherkesov is given a lot of credit for that. He's quoted as saying "The Great Depression was a great opportunity for us. We were able to react even before the Americans voted for F. D. Roosevelt." As well as a skilled, insinuating propagandist, he's a considerable strategist.'

'So what's he doing in London?'

'Apart from us showing the Americans we don't do everything their way? He's supposed to be looking at the consequences of the money that will be coming to Europe from the US as part of the Economic Recovery Program. The Soviets are being offered help but have no intention of accepting it. Amongst his jobs, Cherkesov appears to be acting as a liaison, squaring this with Communist Parties in France and Italy, mostly. But we also know he's been meeting some people from Palestine as well, both Arabs and Jews. You'll see for yourself what he's like when you have luncheon with him tomorrow at Simpson's in the Strand.'

'Who on earth chose Simpson's?'

'He did,' said Beresford.

Pre-war, Simpson's had specialized in traditional fatted plenty, roast beef, saddle of mutton and steak and kidney pie. The problem in 1947 was that, even allowing for the privileged position of restaurants in a world of rationing, their famous ingredients, like Aberdeen Angus beef hung for a lunar month, were in short supply. Cotton had also heard there was a labour dispute in the Savoy Group to which Simpson's belonged.

'He's not going to lecture me, is he?'

Beresford blinked. 'I shouldn't have thought so. It's his favourite place, apparently.'

After Beresford had gathered up his flasks and wrapped himself up again and left, Cotton stretched and felt stiff and weary. He wondered if he was going down with something. He asked Miss Kelly if she had an aspirin for him.

'Well, I do, sir but—'

'What's the problem?'

'They are difficult to get now.'

'What do you mean?'

'Apparently coal comes into their manufacture and we know what's happened to coal.'

'I have aspirin at home,' said Cotton. 'I have a bottle of fifty pills. I'll replace it.'

He took an aspirin and decided to have a drink with Miles Crichton. Miles was, Miss Kelly found out by telephoning the Garrick Club, 'in his usual chair'.

'I was at the theatre last Saturday evening,' said Miles. 'Little Christopher Isherwood was there looking good enough to eat. Nobody could take their eyes off his new clothes. So the thread-bare audience huddled round him like sheep surprised they had survived. He was quite witty. The actors had heroically stripped off their coats and moved about the stage as if in the last stages of the shakes or arthritis. They had vapour to accompany their words, a curiously misplaced cartoon effect. Christopher said he had not before appreciated that suffering for art meant equivalent sizes for the male penis and the female nipple.'

Cotton nodded and looked round at the fire. It was bulked up by wood from broken wine boxes. He wondered how Rosemary, Crichton's wife, was managing in Macklin Street.

'You're not laughing today? Mm, you're beginning to look a little like our members who come here to hide from their wives,' said Miles. 'It's in the eyes. It's not quite the same as in those who have to earn a living and have seen awful things. It's sadder.'

Dutifully, Cotton smiled.

'They're not having a lot of trouble keeping the champagne on ice.' Miles beckoned the steward.

'Oh, you're still tall and young and with that expression of looking and knowing just where to cut at the neck.' Miles Crichton laughed. 'Did they feed you stodge at school?'

'Suet pudding?'

'Yes. It's training for Whitehall and Empire, old man.' The champagne arrived. 'Ah. My kind of cold shower!'

'Do you know of Sir Cyril Healey-Johnson?'

'Hear-Hear Johnson? Of course,' said Miles.

In 1938 during a vociferous foreign policy debate in the House of Commons an MP called Commander Robert Tatton Bower had advised Manny Shinwell 'to go back to Poland'. Above the ensuing uproar, a fraction before Shinwell crossed the floor of the House to slap the commander's face, the advice had received an enthusiastic 'hear, hear' from Sir Cyril Healey-Johnson.

'I have absolutely no time for Bob Boothby,' said Miles, 'but he was perfectly correct in accusing Sir Hear-Hear and other half-witted egotists of appeasing their own privileges even more than they appeased Hitler.'

'And now?'

'He's slipping, feels upstaged by the war.'

Cotton smiled.

'Oh, that's rather more common than we like to think,' said Miles. 'One of his favourite insults is "upstart". Oh yes, there's "jumped up" as well. Frightful snob.'

'What about drugs?'

'Ah. A little pinch of cocaine, I understand, at the tip of the knightly member. He is sometimes called the Earl of Sandwich. Mm? Young girl to the front, young boy to the back. He has what he calls conga parties.'

'In East Grinstead?'

'Oh. You mustn't underestimate market towns or British degenerates,' said Miles.

Cotton wondered whether champagne worked quicker at very low temperatures. He pushed his champagne glass towards Miles Crichton.

'Tell me how Sir Hear-Hear could be involved in other criminal activities.'

'Really?' said Miles. 'I suppose that would be better returns on investments. He might be what is called a banker. Criminals are hopeless at money. They need investment all the time and are used to paying very high rates of interest. If they have some nefarious scheme, they need a backer, you see, to fund them.'

'Right,' said Cotton. 'But wouldn't that work on nobody knowing who the backer is?'

'Absolutely. There's a chain involved in which

the perpetrator is beholden to someone he does not know.'

'In this case—'

'If you know about it, he really is slipping.'

'What if a drug dealer telephoned him?'

'He'd cut him off, of course.'

Cotton frowned. 'Does he have a wife?'

'Oh yes. Madeleine. Lives at the Savoy mostly. Quite fond of musicians, I understand, often from the West Indies. Now you give me something.'

'I'm having lunch with Oleg Cherkesov.'

Miles clasped his hands together and looked up. 'Bless you,' he said.

Cotton smiled. 'He insisted apparently on Simpson's in the Strand.'

'Of course,' said Miles. 'The roast beef of old England!' He looked round, made a contrite face. 'I've just got a thrill, you know, hearing his name.' He shook his head. 'We do get impressed by men responsible for all kinds of horror. He's Beria's man here, isn't he?'

'Apparently we're not sure about that. In any case we're not going to be talking about Beria.'

'Mum's the word,' said Miles. He raised a crutch at the bar for more champagne and put on his confiding face. 'I'm not at all interested in what people get up to in bed, you know. But over the lunch table! Mm? You will feed me a few scraps, won't you?'

Cotton nodded. 'I'll do my best but—'

'I suppose they'll be debriefing you, things like that. But there might be something left over?'

Crichton looked at Cotton for a moment and frowned.

'You're looking a little peaky,' he said. 'What I do in these cases is bury myself under blankets and sweat it out. Take a hot toddy as well.'

Cotton took the advice and went back to the flat. Anna Melville neé Sokol was not there. In the morning he felt lighter and cleaner than he had for some time. He took five aspirins to Miss Kelly wrapped in a twist of paper.

'I didn't need interest, sir.'

'I was thinking of an office supply.'

CHAPTER 29

At 1 p.m. on Tuesday, 11 February, Cherkesov appeared at Simpson's in the Strand with two squat, thick-necked guards. Cherkesov was much taller than either of them, languidly autocratic, and very, very thin. He had, rare in any Soviet Embassy, a definite theatrical side, was wearing an overcoat draped over his shoulders that he shrugged off. His shrugging reminded Cotton of Ed Lowell raising his arms at the Connaught to allow the waiter to drape a napkin over his lap. Cherkesov too raised his arms so that one of the bodyguards had to stoop and lurch to catch his coat. His fur hat he tossed to the other. His hair was dark enough to be dyed but lank and thinning and all the same length, quite long, down to his earlobes. Cherkesov pushed his hair back and waved the guards away.

'They say I look like your Sir Stafford Cripps,' he told Cotton, 'but it must be the similarity of antithesis.' He smiled. 'I hate all vegetables except radish and mustard. I like fermented grain and am addicted to chopped tobacco leaf.' He held out a large, cold, tobacco-stained hand and squeezed once. 'I'm delighted to meet you. Shall we, my dear?'

Cotton understood he was translating or pretending to translate from the French – *mon cher*. Cherkesov looked nothing whatsoever like Cripps. He had a strong, high-bridged nose and a quarter-moon look from the side, and raised his chin as he turned to make his entry into the dining room.

Years before, in 1936, on their last visit to the UK before his mother's death, his parents had taken Cotton to dinner only to find they were obliged to share the restaurant with the actor Donald Wolfit. Wolfit had posed at the door and used his reaching-to-the-gods-above voice to greet his dining companion.

Cherkesov simply spoke loudly enough for all the other people in Simpson's to hear.

'I like this place,' he announced. 'It reminds me of somewhere in Petersburg when it still was that. On the Bolshoya Morskaya. My father had had to make a delivery and as we trudged along I remember this vision through a window. I was about ten. The light was the colour of champagne. The wood panelling gleamed. There was a sizzle of lamb chops from somewhere downstairs and the hot, fat, sweet smell of privilege granted.'

Cotton remembered a Soviet in Washington DC who had quizzed him on his knowledge of Russian literature. He smiled. 'Pushkin,' he said.

Cherkesov laughed rather low. 'You're right. Have you read Gogol yet?'

'*The Overcoat* but I haven't got round to *Dead Souls*.'

The restaurant had given them a table in the centre of the room. Cherkesov took the first chair and waited for Cotton to go round. He picked up a knife.

'Feel the weight of that,' he said. 'It reassures in a way prayers can never do.'

Cherkesov waited for Cotton to sit before he did but there was nothing comrade-like about his instructions. He snapped his fingers for attention. The wine glasses on his side of the table were removed and replaced by a solitary small tumbler. An ashtray was placed on either side of him. There was no question, as with Ed Lowell, of not drinking. The waiters provided an ice bucket for Cherkesov's bottle of vodka.

He told the maître he would have his 'usual. Rare. With horseradish and bread sauce.' 'I eat one course,' he said, 'but a lot of it.'

The maître then turned his attention to Cotton.

'We have venison, sir, from Cameron of Lochiel. And perhaps his excellent smoked herring to start with.'

Smoked herring would be a kipper, thought Cotton, but he was interrupted.

'Please don't have the herring,' said Cherkesov. 'My father would return from work gleaming. The silver scales, you see. At a distance almost a beautiful sight. But I can't abide the smell!'

328

Cotton looked up at the maître. 'Is Cameron of Lochiel a famous Scottish provender?'

'No, sir. *The* Cameron of Lochiel, sir.'

Cherkesov smiled. 'Your aristocrats know how to survive,' he said. 'They become grocers.'

Cotton examined the short menu. 'Is the salmon also Mr Cameron's?'

'Loch Fyne, sir.'

'Salmon, then. Just grilled, please.'

'A Pouilly-Fumé to accompany it, perhaps?' suggested Cherkesov.

'All right,' said Cotton.

Cherkesov lit an American Camel cigarette and threw the packet into one of the ashtrays. He let the waiter pour him some vodka.

'You were in Washington,' he said.

'Yes,' said Cotton. 'For a short time, in late 1945.'

'We lost a good man there. Well, he actually died elsewhere but he probably picked up an infection when he was in DC.'

Cotton thought it more than likely that he was referring to a man he had met on the steps of the Lincoln memorial and who had begun with the name Slonim before he had been scratched to death during a handshake at a memorial service by someone Cotton liked, who was earning his freedom from Ayrtoun. As far as Cotton could work out, the scratch had at the very least encouraged a heart attack in a place as high as Mexico City. He was less sure that the substance used had been a derivative of belladonna or deadly nightshade.

'I'm very sorry to hear that,' said Cotton. 'Do you have his name exactly?'

Cherkesov made a cheerful, chesty sound. It was a kind of pre-laugh, as if he was shifting tar in his lungs before actually laughing. 'There is absolutely no need to apologize,' he said. He pushed back his hair and wagged a finger. 'They tell me you are a Keynesian of the purest sort.'

Cotton scratched his ear and shook his head. 'I'm not aware purity and Lord Keynes had much to do with one another. Surely his talent was for adjusting to the facts?'

'My dear,' said Cherkesov, 'a Keynesian is someone who steps back and rubs a little ice on their eyelids. It refreshes the vision, lends a wintery calm. I understand he saw nothing of intellectual interest in the Soviet experiment, thought we should have been allowed to get on with it and collapse on our own.'

Cotton smiled. 'You're dramatizing for effect, comrade. Keynes also talked about everybody being dead in the long run, but I really don't think he was referring to the shortening effects of war or even the efforts of Mr Yezhov.'

The purges of the late thirties in Soviet Russia, called the Yezhovchina, had been so severe that even Stalin had found it expedient to replace Yezhov with Beria and have Yezhov executed and his image expunged from all official photographs.

Cherkesov grinned. 'You know,' he said. It sounded somehow both happily complicit and accusatory.

He frowned. 'More vodka,' he said. The waiter poured.

Cherkesov sipped. 'Ten years ago, we were on our knees. I mean that almost exactly. Late January 1937. Collapse of the entire Soviet experiment was days off. Agriculture had failed, people were starving to death. Industrialization had ground to a rusty halt. The revolution had entirely seized up due to idiot plans, lies, paranoia and incompetence. I remember conversations – in New York, I was in New York – when we talked openly about what to do. I don't mean about how to reverse our failures at home, I mean what we would personally do, where we could take our families, how we would survive when Soviet Russia collapsed. My first choice would have been Spain – but there was a war going on there in 1937. My second choice would have been Mexico. I am told it is an extraordinarily varied and very beautiful country.' He wagged a finger. 'I must admit I thought of settling in Cuernavaca, von Humboldt's "city of eternal spring".'

Cotton nodded. 'Yes. It's about fifty, fifty-five miles south of Mexico City.'

'You've been there?'

'Only as a child. It's something of a resort for people escaping the capital.'

'You see! I always thought it would be a wonderful place to bring up children.'

Cotton made a face. 'I was only there for a few days. I remember my father complaining of the expense.'

Cherkesov smiled. 'Where did you live?'

'Normally? In Mexico City. By the country club.'

Cherkesov nodded. 'Nature made golf, eh?' He sat back, downed another shot of vodka and indicated the glass be refilled. 'So what impressed you most about Cuernavaca? For my part, I'm in no way an ornithologist but I thought I'd like to sit on a verandah as the sun sank behind the volcanoes, sip coffee and watch all those exotic, brightly coloured birds finish their day. I understand, though I don't know whether it is true or not, that the birdsong is akin to starlings roosting, a sort of pouring into a night jug.'

Cotton smiled and shook his head. He had had time to appreciate he had last been in Cuernavaca nearly twenty years ago, weeks before he had started prep school in England. His parents had gone on holiday there with his sister and himself and, amongst other things, had checked on what they called his attainments. To their consternation, they had found he could not tell the time. This had been corrected, big hand, little hand. And they had made other efforts. He had, for example, been taught chess.

'I don't remember the birds,' said Cotton. 'Perhaps I wasn't paying attention. I do remember the butterflies, though. I don't know what the collective name is. A flock, perhaps – in this case a cloud hovering over a flower-bed, a strange kind of mirror image, the butterflies paler than the flowers, the flowers not moving. But mostly, I remember when I was with my sister, in the rest-house garden and my shoelace was undone. I bent, and suddenly an enormous butterfly nearly blundered into me. As it pulled away those wings were big enough to make a soft rushing sound. Have you ever heard a pulse in a stethoscope?'

'Marvellous!' said Oleg Cherkesov. 'Everyone should have wonderful childhood memories.' He smiled and sighed. 'Pity. I really think I'd have liked Mexico. Well, if Trotsky hadn't been there, of course. But then we woke up and realized something had happened.'

'And you're going to tell me about it,' said Cotton.

'After this,' said Cherkesov. Somewhere between trundle and ceremony, a trolley arrived. On top, a metal dome the size of a nearly full-term pregnant belly slid back to reveal a smallish joint of beef. The carver removed some of the surface. Underneath, the meat steamed to show it was not quite raw. Cherkesov's red beef was cut thin, hung over his plate and then, the carver could not avoid a sort of curtsey, let down as if it were cloth.

'More,' he said.

His plate began to look like a red meat flower.

'Enough.'

Cotton had waited with his grilled salmon in front of him.

'Eat, my friend,' said Cherkesov. He cut a strip of beef and while his teeth gnashed at it, used a finger to scoop up some horseradish.

'Good?'

The salmon itself was a little dry but the chef had added butter. 'Yes,' lied Cotton.

Cherkesov smiled and cut himself more meat. He pointed his fork at Cotton.

'The *dream* of our revolution had turned out to be our most successful export. Your version of what we used to call the intelligentsia, when there were some around – and I include the Americans in this – were displeased with capitalist society. They thought it brutal, wasteful and unjust. They behaved reactively, without doubting or examining the Soviet regime, and began to think of us as I thought of bright, Mexican birds. Except they called them "the people". Now we could have this conversation in Manhattan or Hampstead, Oxford or Yale, surrounded by distinguished and highly intelligent people. They would not hear us.' Cherkesov shrugged. 'They did not hear of the purges. They ignored the pact with Hitler. Or if they did, they made excuses and the more self-righteous became Trotskyites.' Cherkesov laughed. 'Trotsky preached the need for a permanent revolution. Permanent! Anyone who does such a stupid thing deserves an ice pick in the head.'

'The Mexicans have a permanent revolution party,' said Cotton.

'They do, don't they? It doesn't seem to help

their poor much, does it? What was it that old reactionary Goethe said – "everything is both simpler than we can imagine and more entangled than we can conceive"? From our point of view the purges were something to be going on with, I suppose, while we waited for events to turn our way. Of course, we knew they would. But in some ways I sometimes think we have, since then, set the tone. There are variations, of course, in severity, but the lessons transmit to those who are anxious to learn and collaborate in a debate.' He shook his head. 'There never was any debate, that's a western illusion. We had a purge. You, particularly the Americans, lag behind and begin to brew up a witch hunt. We Communists have become witches. It's rather flattering.'

'Are you really suggesting we are trying to respond to your brutal decisions?' said Cotton.

Cherkesov shrugged. 'Of course I am. We are winning now because you have picked up reflections from our mirror. They don't have to be exact reflections. Only emulative. A little lost silvering. A little nightmarish twisting. They don't, of course, have to be witting.'

Cotton shrugged back.

'You talked to a man called Paul Mair.'

Cherkesov held up a hand. Cotton recognized the gesture. It was exactly the same as someone apologizing for a lucky net call at tennis. 'Oh, only briefly, I assure you. Not the kind of weakness we look for.' He looked up and smiled. 'We need someone with at least some memory of the night before and preferably the night before that. Our information on him was . . . let's say out of date.' He paused. 'Our interest in him was based on his contacts in the Middle East. It had nothing to do with his relationship with a fairly recent suicide. The agent responsible for recommending him has already been sent home.'

Cotton looked up.

'Oh come now, why on earth would we be involved?' said Cherkesov. 'We want what works! Just ask two hundred thousand Japanese in Hiroshima and Nagasaki. We go for successful technology. Like your jet engines. We had the Manhattan Project riddled with agents from the start.'

'But you don't have a bomb yet.'

'At this stage that is just a detail. The prospect of it does tend to frighten people into silly actions.' He smiled. 'We don't need to do anything. In the Soviet taxonomy a foreign socialist hero – a person you might call a traitor – comes above any sexual or moral classification made by the bourgeoisie.'

'You really can't be saying,' said Cotton, 'that Comrade Stalin is one of the bourgeoisie.'

Cherkesov laughed. 'My dear,' he said, 'Stalin shares something with your Socialist Party. I don't think either finds homosexuality sits well with the dignity of labour. Something to do with what they imagine is bending over and unfortunately submissive postures.'

Cotton understood he was being given something to quote. He nodded in acknowledgement.

Cherkesov smiled. 'Your liberal democrats despise
your leaders. They enjoy that freedom to think
that encourages self-importance. Their pious
consciousness that workers are less fortunate than
themselves leads to sops and generalizations about
fairness and justice. But what really thrills them
is the application of power. Your Establishment
has fantasies that it knows best, loathes democratic
dither, appeases the logic behind violence. The
"people" have become an abstract that provides
them with an emotional excuse.'

He cut some meat on his plate and speared
it with his fork. 'The workers? The workers need
direction. Take your miners and dockers. Heroes
of the war.' He shook his head. 'The miners
made money out of the war. Twenty-five pounds
a week, I've heard. The dockers? Princes of the
ports. Would they load armaments? Persuasion
and negotiations were needed. British officers
were reduced to the ranks for daring to hurry
them on. The British Communist Party fought
the British! We spoke to them, explained that
we were, at least while we fought the Fascists,
allies.' He shook his head. None of this would
have happened in Soviet Russia. Money? Better
conditions? Here's a bullet instead.' He looked
up. 'Have you ever given orders to have people
killed?'

'Certainly not on my own side.'

Cherkesov leant forward. 'No, my dear! You *start* with your own side. It's practical and it's practice. You learn. And when you kill others, how can they possibly be worth the sacrifice your own side made?'

He looked at the vodka bottle. There was not that much left. He shrugged and decided for temporary abstention.

'I spoke for a long time to one of your big trade union leaders. He told me the British Communists have no future because they failed to understand that the class war had no future in Britain. The unions are now an entrenched part of the British class system. Your miners are now a kind of mass duke. They receive deference. Your Manny Shinwell now has a police guard on his house in Tooting because the Duke hasn't dug enough coal. But does the Duke care that people can't keep warm? No, he whines about how hard his ancestors had to work. Your unions have no concerns for the rest of society, only for their own petty bourgeois self-interest.'

'Keynes suggested there was a religiosity in the Soviet Union.'

'What did he mean?'

'I'm not entirely sure,' said Cotton, 'but I'd guess he was talking about both the fervour of the converted and the establishment of ferociously authoritarian structures that religions need to establish themselves and protect their institutions against heresies.'

338

'My dear,' said Cherkesov, 'religions are charac-
terized by the willingness of the faithful to sacrifice
others to their faith. Some of the faithful will even
sacrifice themselves. It does not contribute exactly,
except in a negative way, but it does give them a
sense of communion or belonging before they
vanish, a rather spiritual version of life on this
earth. But of course, there are religious
Communists. I'm quite clear about it.'

'Clear about what?'

'The definition of a fool? Someone who believes
in systems.'

'I don't know about that but I tend not to believe
you on Mr Mair.'

Cherkesov laughed very loudly. 'Excellent!' he
said. 'We were given information that Mair had a
good contact in Palestine, that he knew someone
powerful in Irgun. Interesting for us, you see, that
he was also supposed to have contacts with Arab
nationalists.' He shrugged. 'We found our information was wrong, that Mair was more immediately
amazed by his own sexual impotence.' Cherkesov
smiled. 'It does not matter now. You have an MP.'
Cherkesov paused, apparently trying to remember
the name.

Cotton said nothing. He took a sip of the Pouilly-
Fumé. It struck him as more chill than taste,
almost bitter.

'Mayhew,' said Cherkesov. 'Christopher Mayhew.
Pro-Arab.' He frowned. 'You do have a lot of T.
E. Lawrence romantics in the Foreign Office.'

'I know,' said Cotton.

'But Mayhew is not naïve. He has sold a scheme to Mr Attlee whereby a department will be created in the Foreign Office to counter our Soviet propaganda. Of course it will be ineffectual having been intellectualized, but it should be profitable for some. It will subsidize publications, pay Bertrand Russell to write something, arrange the translation of *Animal Farm* into Arabic, that kind of thing.' Cherkesov laughed again. 'I'll be intrigued to see how a parable set on an English farm and involving pigs goes down in Cairo or Damascus.' He shrugged. 'Money,' he said. 'Do you know your friend Ed Lowell has no budgetary limitations whatever? Attlee accepted because the Americans will be paying for this and it shouldn't be too offensive. I have told our Communist friends and sympathizers here and in France and Italy to accept all approaches if they involve payment. To some extent it offsets our opposition to American aid. And we do need funds, of course. The other thing is that it really points us towards our view of the Middle East. If the Jews get their state we'll have years and years of trouble. Mm? I am telling my Arab friends that this is the last cruel lash of colonialism. But do you know what the real thing is? If you British do not stand back on Palestine, if you do not abstain, your aid from America is in danger. How shocking power is when you have lost it.'

At the end of their meal, on their way out, Cherkesov patted Cotton's shoulder.

'I don't think I'll be in London that much longer,' he said. After an entire bottle of vodka he was just beginning to slur.

Cotton smiled. 'But I imagine your own side will take good care of you.'

Cherkesov laughed. 'Remember what I said about reflections. Or, as you prefer, the pulse of pale butterflies.' He beckoned his bodyguards. 'My dear, we have unspeakable colleagues.' He smiled again. 'Delightful lunch. But I assure you. Your butterflies are not ours. We have no need to break butterflies on a wheel. We knock them down and stamp on them, an incidental on our march forward.'

Cotton smiled. He allowed Cherkesov a pause to tone down what he had said or at least get his butterflies in order. It wasn't a long pause.

'You may be right,' he said. 'About Keynes. Well, his notion that Soviet machinery would run out of lubricant and seize up on bits of old mirror and butterfly wings.'

Cherkesov laughed and thumped Cotton on the back. 'Excellent,' he said. 'I hope we will be able to compare notes in the future. I've enjoyed myself very much.'

CHAPTER 30

Despite the cold, Cotton decided to walk back to his office, to give himself some time before any debriefing. 'Stagey Soviet' came to mind as a description of Cherkesov, as did 'a race between his liver and his enemies'. As he hurried past Charing Cross station he came up with 'journalistic flak'. By the time he had got round Trafalgar Square and on to the Mall he was a little less unsettled. There was always an element of language as a disguise, a medium to mislead and misdirect. But Cotton was rattled enough to think Cherkesov was the most impressive Soviet he had ever met. Charismatic, not having to bother even to threaten, he revelled in his reputation. What was the problem? Cotton felt Cherkesov was telling something of the truth.

In the event, Cotton found there was no debriefing. The fuss beforehand and the lack of follow-up seemed to him to sum up the state of British Intelligence. He wrote a staid report for MI6 and another, a lot more frank, for Ayrtoun.

'In retrospect I'm slightly intrigued that Cherkesov took the trouble to have lunch with me – though he may just have wanted his beef roasted at Simpson's. I increasingly incline to the view that he really didn't mind that we were sowing confusion for them. Why would he?'

Ayrtoun's reply was almost immediate.

'Oh, for Christ's sake!' he wrote. 'We're not the BBC pretending to have a balance. Cherkesov is the most brutal person you have ever met. That's all. Your job is to take control of what you have.'

Cotton laughed when he got this. The laugh took him by surprise, burst out of his lips as soft as cooked pearl barley.

There was a moment he was alarmed, but then he decided not to be.

Going to the Garrick Club on 12 February, Cotton read in a newspaper reduced to four pages that the day before, the Prime Minister, Major Clement Attlee, had been booed by people who had come to see Sir Winston Churchill's daughter Mary marry in an unheated candlelit church.

Attlee was reported as being 'visibly upset'. Churchill had put his arm round him and brought him over to sign as a witness to the wedding.

'I love this sort of stuff!' said Miles Crichton. 'The tragedy is, Clem is probably one of the most decent prime ministers we have ever had and yet he is hurt by what he sees as an over-personal element to the criticism. At least a couple of million children went to bed last night fully dressed but with their bellies empty. Why? Largely because their

343

government is incompetent. And what have they got instead of competence? Righteousness, or in Attlee's case, hurt.' Miles Crichton laughed again. 'Nobody is more authoritarian than a thwarted sentimentalist. I imagine Manny Shinwell has impressed his Cabinet colleagues in that line. After a decent interval of pretence that he was not a fool, he will be given a job where people will obey his orders – something military, probably.'

'I haven't seen Major Briggs recently,' said Cotton.

'He'll be loyally keeping his head down for Manny.' Miles smiled. 'You should visit Alfred Perlman.'

'Why?'

'To see whether or not he's wearing an overcoat, like us. I bet his chambers are as cosy as the innards of a hot muffin.'

Cotton smiled. 'I was rather hoping to see Tom McEwan,' he said.

'I'm sure that can be arranged. Do you want it soon?'

'If possible.'

Back in his office Cotton wrote a note to Perlman. 'I have a query for your client. The matter is delicate and I'd appreciate your advice.'

'I can do this by telephone,' said Miss Kelly.

Within five minutes he learnt that Perlman had asked him to call in after work on Monday the 17th.

A few minutes later he heard from Miles Crichton. Tom McEwan would see him in the

Bunch of Grapes in Jermyn Street 'a little before 3 p.m. tomorrow'.

'He's having lunch at Mme Prunier's,' said Miles.

The next day Cotton was in the pub at two thirty. Tom McEwan appeared at ten to three.

'Old times,' he said. 'I haven't been to eat there since 1937. Ten years. Have you been?'

'No,' said Cotton.

'You must go,' said McEwan. 'Looks like a fucking ocean liner, big chandeliers, banquettes like a creamy fish sauce. Wonderful.' McEwan lit a Kensitas cigarette and Cotton bought him a brandy. 'What can I do for you?'

'I don't know,' said Cotton. 'We've raised nothing on Sinclair and Boyle. I mean absolutely nothing. Apart from no addresses for them, we've not been able to find any report of their activities in the last seven years.'

Tom McEwan laughed. 'Are you appealing to sources outside the Intelligence Services?'

'Oh, we do that.'

Tom McEwan nodded. 'How can I help?'

'I'd be interested in any trace of Sinclair and Boyle at all.'

McEwan paused. 'What's in it for me?'

'You say.'

'How about a bottle of whisky? Something good. A Jura, if you can.'

Cotton was relieved. 'Done.'

'I'll need a couple of days,' said McEwan. 'Fair?'

'Of course.'

McEwan squashed out his cigarette and lit another one. 'Are you a socialist?' he asked.

'Are you?' said Cotton.

McEwan laughed. 'I'll go through Crichton, if you don't mind.'

'Not at all.'

On the 14th Cotton returned home to find he had had a delivery from Twiss, Browning & Hallowes, a case of Dry Monopole champagne.

'Christ, you *are* rich!' said Anna Melville.

Cotton opened the card inside. It was from his father, wishing him a happy birthday on the 20th.

'You look surprised.'

'I am,' he said. 'It's not my father's usual kind of birthday present.'

'Is your birthday today?'

'No. The 20th.'

'How old will you be?'

'Twenty-eight.'

'You're a baby.'

'In comparison to?'

'Me. I'm twenty-nine.'

'When is your birthday?'

'It's been,' she said. 'Last month.'

'Did you celebrate?'

'It was the 17th. Do you remember? There was a dinner at Margot's.'

'I remember something about poetry but not about birthdays.'

She laughed. 'I didn't announce it, silly. Nobody announces they are twenty-nine.'

On Saturday Cotton queued and Anna had work. On Sunday she continued what she called 'developing' her blacklight play. He was surprised that she was following his bomb-shelter in the Tube suggestion. He saw that she could draw with both hands. From time to time she'd ask him something. This was slightly strange. She had more experience than he of being in London during the bombings, but she appeared to have little memory of the sounds, searchlights and blackouts.

On Monday, 17 February Cotton went round to Alfred Perlman's chambers in Jermyn Street at about 5.45 in the afternoon. Miss Olivia Marx showed him in directly. The lawyer was dressed for dinner, his jacket double-breasted, his black tie barely visible under his dewlap. The fire was banked but not lit. Instead, there were five small electric heaters around the edges of the room, two of which were on. Though no sauna, it was considerably warmer than Cotton's own office.

'I'm late,' said Alfred Perlman, as if he were saying hello again. He made no effort to move. Instead, he rolled an unlit cigar between his fingers.

'I like the smell,' he explained, 'but I don't like the smoke.' He waggled the cigar under his nose and breathed in. 'I'm late for an opera meeting. Covent Garden. I'm on the board.' He put the cigar down. 'How can I help you, Colonel?'

'Since 1939 MI5 has had a small team that

347

pursues homosexuals. The justification for this is the security risk a homosexual in a sensitive job might present.'

Cotton wondered whether Alfred Perlman had entirely closed his eyes or not.

'This conversation is off the record,' he said.

'Of course it is. What I wanted to find out was the scope of your client's interests. We believe this group in MI5 employs criminals who were Black Shirts.'

Perlman had another sniff of his cigar. He nodded.

'Allow me to speak as one who knows about reactions to Jews in this country,' he said. 'Any attempt to demonstrate anti-Semitism in the Intelligence Services would backfire. I'd say it was not in the interests of the Jewish community even to try that line.'

'Thank you,' said Cotton. 'That's very helpful.'

For the first time Cotton managed to induce a fleeting frown on Alfred Perlman's lugubrious face.

'Don't misunderstand,' said Perlman. 'I'm in favour of a Jewish State in Palestine. I'm sure you already know I'm on committees to this end. Our biggest problem in this country is Irgun and the Stern Gang. In the US, despite Einstein's opposition to a Jewish state, they're not a problem at all.'

'Yes,' said Cotton. 'I spoke to Oleg Cherkesov about them.'

'What did he say?'

'He claimed to be delighted. If the US supports

a Jewish state, the Soviet Union will do what it can with the Arab nations.'

Perlman stared at him for a while, then shrugged.

'We will have a piece of Europe in the Middle East,' he said.

'Mr Cherkesov was apparently happy to agree.'

Perlman cleared his throat. 'Why did you come to see me, Mr Cotton?'

'To show you I had not forgotten your distinguished client.'

'He's a busy man, particularly with this coal crisis.'

'Of course. The second reason was to thank you for your help in the Watson affair in Croydon.'

'I did what I could,' said Perlman. 'A sad business.'

'Yes,' said Cotton, 'but apart from losing an expert in plutonium enrichment, we had a little distraction in Croydon.'

'What do you mean?'

'Following a tip-off, there was some press interest, I understand, in possible corruption there. The police cracked down.'

Alfred Perlman shrugged. 'I don't apologize,' he said. 'I consider it a lack of respect.'

'What do you mean exactly?'

'I do my best, Colonel Cotton. I believe that if I were to apologize to a client, it would mean I had not done my best.'

'It wasn't all bad, Mr Perlman. There is a possibility that an ex-MP – a Tory baronet – is involved in criminal activities.'

'As what the criminal fraternity calls . . . a banker?' said Perlman.

'Difficult to prove,' said Cotton.

That did not bother the lawyer. 'It would be difficult to get good publicity,' he said.

'I was thinking of giving your distinguished client practice,' said Cotton. 'Acquiring experience in another field, perhaps.'

Perlman shrugged. 'A sort of breaking-in, you mean? I'd have to consider that.'

'Of course.'

Alfred Perlman may have smiled. He picked up his unlit cigar and put it back in a black leather holder. He glanced at the clock and grunted. 'Now I really am late,' he said. He stood up.

'All right. I take your point, Colonel.'

'Which is?'

'That my distinguished client should decide on both the nature and the spheres of his interest in "security". Perhaps limit his interests. This will not include anti-Semitism or the deviance of inverts.' He gave Cotton a brief nod. 'Thank you for asking after him. I'll certainly pass your good wishes on.'

On Tuesday, 18 February Cotton found a note from Miles Crichton. Cotton telephoned him.

'The person you met in the Stab has something for you.'

'What kind of thing?'

Miles Crichton had decided to be arch. 'I believe,' he said, 'that it has a Scottish theme.'

At lunchtime, Cotton and Dawkins met Tom McEwan of the *Daily Mirror* in King William Street in the City of London. Cotton was becoming accustomed if not to the cold then at least to recognizing the different sorts of cold. There was numb and weary. This was cold to the shoulders, raw on the face.

McEwan loosened the scarf round his mouth. 'Your man works nearby,' he said. 'He's prepared to speak to you on the strict condition that the information he gives stays as that, information only. He's not prepared to give evidence, verbal or written. He must have that assurance or he won't speak.'

'So why is he doing this?' said Dawkins.

'He's prepared to help you in the hope that what he says will in turn help you deal with Sinclair and Boyle.'

Dawkins shook his head.

Tom McEwan reacted sharply. 'You haven't seen or heard him yet!'

'All right,' said Cotton. 'Information only.'

'I have your assurance?'

'Yes.'

McEwan looked at Dawkins. Dawkins nodded.

McEwan smiled. 'That's the spirit. There's a pub in Arthur Street—'

'I know it,' said Dawkins.

'He'll be there in ten to fifteen minutes.'

'And how are we going to recognize him?'

'I gave him a description of you,' said McEwan.

Cotton held out his gloved hand and McEwan shook it. 'Thank you,' he said.

McEwan laughed his breathy laugh. 'Enjoy yourselves, gentlemen.'

Cotton and Dawkins walked down to Arthur Street. The pub was in a cellar, poorly lit but, being in the City, served wine as much as beer. Cotton chose a claret.

'I'll stick to bitter,' said Dawkins.

The place was quite warm, though. They looked to be burning driftwood in the chimney place. They were given a short menu. There was soup of the day, steak and kidney pie, sausages and mash and Cornish pasty.

'Cornish pasties?' said Cotton.

'It'll be horse meat,' said Dawkins, 'with swede and carrots.'

Cotton knew nothing at all about the ingredients of a Cornish pasty. Dawkins seemed most displeased by the carrots.

'Two Cornish pasties, please,' said Cotton.

They went to a booth. 'What's the matter?' he asked.

'I don't know how we're ever going to get someone to testify against Sinclair and Boyle,' said Dawkins.

'Let's see what we get now.'

They sat in the booth and waited. Their Cornish pasties had just arrived when a tall young man stooped over and asked Dawkins to slide along.

'Which of you is Colonel Cotton?'

'I am,' said Cotton.

The young man banged his gloves together, took them off and rubbed his hands to warm them. He used one hand to take off his hat, the other he offered to Cotton.

'My name is Frederick Causley,' he said.

Because the light was so poor Cotton was not sure if he was seeing things. As if on cue, however, Causley lifted his face. On each cheek, someone had carved a saltire, the cross of St Andrew. The cuts were remarkably even, all four straight and the same length, about two inches. Cruelly – the national flag of Scotland is a white saltire on a blue background – the scars showed as whitish with blue-tinged edges.

'Would you like a Cornish pasty? Something to drink?' asked Cotton.

The young man smiled. 'No,' he said, 'I'll have my usual.' He lifted an arm and waggled his hand at the bar and someone there nodded.

'Tom McEwan told you of my conditions?'

'Yes,' said Cotton.

Frederick Causley looked round at Dawkins. Dawkins nodded.

'I was eighteen in 1943,' he said, 'and had just left school. I came up to London at the beginning of August and met a very charming bomber pilot, a Wing Commander Graham Hands.' He looked up. 'No? He'd just won another DFC and was something of a hero. There were receptions for him and lots of parties. There was talk of him doing a tour of the US. I don't really know what happened.

I suppose I may have had something to do with it, but he wasn't sent. Instead, he returned to duty and I hung about in London waiting for my orders to come through. I did get away to see him in Lincolnshire one weekend. It was after that things turned nasty.'

The young man's lunch arrived. It was sausage and mash and a glass of wine. He tasted the wine.

'It's supposed to be burgundy,' he said. 'It's rough enough to mask flavours, particularly of the powdered potato.' He cut into a sausage and steam rose up. He smiled.

'At least it's warm, eh?'

'What happened?' said Cotton.

'Graham had a flat and I was camping out there. One day I found a letter on the mat addressed to me. It said I was sullying a hero's reputation and if I had any nobility of soul I'd get out and leave a great man alone.' Causley shrugged. 'I mean, there were actually spelling mistakes. It was "leaf" for "leave" for example, and the writer had had difficulty separating the words "reputation" and "repetition". It was unpleasant, but I didn't take it very seriously.'

'Where was the flat?' asked Dawkins.

Causley smiled. 'In Bruton Place. But I don't think there is a spelling test to be able to live in Mayfair, is there? The next day there was another note asking why I was still there. It called me a few names as well.'

'You don't have these notes, do you?' said Dawkins.

'No, I don't,' he said firmly. 'The next day I got caught. Two men with strong Scottish accents, one of them perhaps some kind of dwarf, got hold of me in Cork Street and shoved me into Cork Street Mews. One of them punched me hard in the ribs and the next I knew I had a forearm across my throat. The speed of it all was very shocking, to me at least. I couldn't really see what they were doing but I could see the razor.'

Causley paused and ate some mash. He drank a little wine, then turned his fork over and drew the prongs across the mash. 'One of them punched me in the balls with a knuckleduster. That was by far the most painful thing. When I got out into Cork Street a woman screamed. They had cut my cheeks so deep she could see some of my teeth.' He sighed. 'It's a difficult set of scars to get. There's no sign of a bullet and the lines are too neat for war.'

'Did you report the attack?' said Dawkins.

'Yes, but I had some problems. They had ruptured one of my testicles and I needed treatment. A police constable came to the hospital but it was 1943 and saying I had been attacked by two Scotsmen in civvies didn't really provide the police with enough information they could work on. There was a war on and I didn't really want to tell the police why I thought I had been attacked.'

'What about Graham Hands?'

Frederick Causley shook his head. 'I didn't see him again. His Lancaster came down somewhere near Bremen. The entire crew died. 27 September.'

Cotton nodded. He could not think of anything fitting to say. 'What are you doing now?'

'After the war the BBME took me on as a trainee.'

'What's the—?'

'Sorry. The British Bank of the Middle East. I've just finished my banking exams. I'm being posted to Damascus in April. Of course, I've had to promise them I won't get married for three years.' Causley smiled. 'That's the usual condition for the first tour. I have also met some Syrians. I don't know why but the scars don't seem to upset them. Or at least they don't ask me about them.'

'How do you think this helps us get Sinclair and Boyle?' said Dawkins.

Causley drank some wine. 'Yes,' he said, 'Tom McEwan told me their names. I know one of his colleagues socially, met McEwan himself a few days ago.' He shrugged. 'You know journalists. He asked me directly if two boys from Glasgow had cut my face. He described them quite well.'

'Mr Causley, we're trying to get them put away,' said Dawkins.

Causley showed polite but decidedly restrained interest. 'I've explained already I think. I have chosen my career path. In a few weeks I'll be out of Britain. I'm not risking that. In terms of testicles, I am as I understand Hitler was. And I have these SFEs on my face.'

'You've got what?' said Dawkins.

'Sorry. SFE is Scotland For Ever.'

'Or Sod Fucking Englishmen,' said Dawkins.

'Quite,' said Causley. 'I've got quite a few other names. I've been called Lord Haw-Haw by children.'

Lord Haw-Haw, William Joyce, of 'Germany calling' fame during the war had had a scar from his earlobe to the corner of his mouth caused by a cut-throat razor attack in the twenties. Cotton had read that the scar had burst open when he had been hanged.

Dawkins groaned.

'Thank you, Mr Causley,' said Cotton. 'We appreciate your position and we appreciate your help.'

'Thank you,' said Causley. He put his hat on again and started putting on his gloves. 'I wish you luck, gentlemen.' He slid out of the booth, finished off his wine and left.

Cotton sighed and cut into his Cornish pasty. There was swede in it and carrot, as Dawkins had said, and some strands of grey meat. The mix had been heavily peppered but was now cold. He pushed the plate away. 'He's right,' said Dawkins. 'What a shower of shit!'

Cotton looked up.

'What's the matter?' he said.

'I've been trying to get an address for the boys from Glasgow.' Dawkins shook his head. 'Haven't done it. They'll have identity cards, ration cards – I've found nothing.' He grunted. 'They must be at the Radcliffe Arms,' he said.

'Seems likely,' said Cotton.

Dawkins looked up and sighed. 'That young man tells a bloody good story, doesn't he?'

'Meaning?'

Dawkins grimaced and shook his head. 'I'm not criticizing,' he said. 'I just wish he hadn't been quite so good.'

Cotton nodded. 'I'll do everything I can,' he said, 'to make sure that Sir Percy hears about Sinclair and Boyle.'

Dawkins narrowed his eyes. 'Why did you go to McEwan?'

'Because I thought he could help.'

'You could have told me.'

'I didn't know what McEwan had planned. And I knew you don't have a high opinion of journalists.'

Dawkins looked round.

'Do you want another drink?' he said. 'I'll pay.'

'Do you want to say something?'

'No,' said Dawkins. 'I just need another drink.'

CHAPTER 31

On Thursday, 20 February, Cotton's twenty-eighth birthday, the temperature dropped again. By the time he had got to his office, news was arriving that the cross-Channel ferries had been suspended because of pack ice. Somewhere, someone had tried to keep warm by burning a stack of old files. On his desk he found a note from Major Briggs:

'I have a dinner party this evening but would like to see you beforehand. Please be at my Dolphin Square address at 5.30 p.m. Briggs.'

Cotton was mildly intrigued. Was this Alfred Perlman's idea or had Major Briggs acted on his own?

At 5.30 he was at Briggs' flat. Briggs, despite his new pinstripe suit, was looking rough, had a cold sore on his upper lip.

The Major's first words were 'Fucking hell! We're taking a beating over this bloody weather! Eh? What do they want? For the miners to go on strike?'

Cotton did not reply.

'We need something, lad! We need to hit back with something!'

Cotton nodded. The meeting had evidently not been suggested by Alfred Perlman.

'At one level, I'm only a civil servant, Major,' said Cotton. 'We have to keep clear of party politics. It's our remit.'

Briggs reacted badly. 'This isn't politics! This is justice!'

'Yes, sir,' said Cotton. 'That may be. Unfortunately, perhaps, I'm strictly forbidden from involving myself in either politics or justice.'

'I could harm your career, you know.'

'Yes,' said Cotton. 'You could.' He shrugged. 'If you feel like that, by all means complain.'

Briggs narrowed his eyes. 'What's your game?'

Cotton shook his head. 'I have none, Major. There may be something but I'm afraid it's too early to say and it won't help your present difficulties.'

'Do you know who you're talking to?'

Cotton let this pass. 'Do you have anything for me, Major?'

The doorbell rang.

'Damn,' said Briggs. 'Can I ask you a favour?'

'Sir?'

'Could you leave by the back door?'

'Yes,' said Cotton. 'I'll be in touch. Probably through Mr Perlman.'

Cotton saw himself out. In the kitchen he passed two uniformed maids preparing canapés. He trotted down the stairs almost cheerfully. Alfred Perlman would not be pleased with his associate.

★　　★　　★

360

When he got home, he found Anna Melville had arranged a birthday party for him in which she was the only other guest.

She was wearing the tartan trews that he had last worn in Washington DC, the legs rolled up but, despite the cold, nothing else apart from what the British call braces and the Americans suspenders.

In the drawing room she had rigged up a kind of tent. It was made up of the four kilts he had had to buy as an officer in the Argyll and Sutherland Highlanders and now no longer had a use for. They had been in a trunk with mothballs. Substantial woollen items, they had been worn from his sternum to his kneecaps and had lead shot at the base of the pleats to ensure the correct swing and to avoid windy mishaps.

'A tepee? In tartan?'

She laughed. 'I was thinking more of a place in which to give you my present. I am putting my mouth where my money should be. I think the French say *faire la pipe*.'

Cotton's eyebrows came up.

'My French language may not be very good,' she said. 'But my French is universal. Or is that too near the bone for you?'

They drank champagne, she showed him luminescent paint in the dark, and they ate. Anna Melville had even prepared supper. It consisted of cubes of fried spam, green beans she had found in a jar and slices of fried bread dumpling. Cotton did not eat much but did open another bottle of Dry Monopole.

Before he had even left for work on 21 February the telephone rang.

'Mr C?' It was Derek.

'Yes,' said Cotton.

'I've got a question.'

'All right.'

'Well, it's not strictly speaking about our business, if you understand me. I'm thinking of my own position.'

'In what way?'

'It's about rewards.'

'What are you talking about?'

'Would there be a reward for information about Vernon? Vernon Carter?'

It took Cotton a moment to remember. Carter had been 'the expert in shrinkage' who had disappeared in or around Croydon in December 1945, possibly, even probably at the hands of Maurice Bly. There was the story Maurice had beaten him to death with a solid wood chair no longer amongst the seven in the Snow White display. The chair named for Dopey was supposed to have gone missing.

'Are you in hiding again?'

'No, Mr C, no. I'm offering information.'

'Why to me?'

'I was thinking of Mr Ayrtoun, sir.'

'Right. You want me to tell Mr Ayrtoun you've

helped the police in the hope that will help your own situation.'

'Christ, I haven't spoken to the *police*! Mr C, you're the first person I've talked to. But yes, I'd be wanting to do a deal. A murder is worth more than anything I could be had up for.'

'All right,' said Cotton. 'I'll try but you understand this is Mr Ayrtoun's business? And before I do that you tell me what you have.'

They agreed to meet at a bar in the Cromwell Road at noon.

'You're looking a bit peaky today,' said Derek.

'Just tell me,' said Cotton.

Derek's story came down to this: his brother-in-law had seen a small patch of scrubland behind three new garages in Beddington, 'about another three garages' worth'. His brother-in-law had made enquiries and found the garages had been built in December 1945 and that they and the scrubland belonged 'to a lady'. On visiting the lady, an old woman living on the housing estate at New Addington, she had become 'flustered but still quite stroppy'. The brother-in-law had told her he could put quite a bit of money her way, to which she replied she was already getting 'something every week'. And anyway, the property wasn't really hers to sell.

'She's just a name, Mr C. Do you see what I mean?'

'Yes, I do.'

A short time later, the brother-in-law was given a warning by Maurice Bly's enforcer, a man called

Turner. 'Big Mick bastard,' said Derek. Persist in pressuring the old lady and he might find a Molotov cocktail coming through his window.

'Bly feels protective towards the old lady,' said Cotton.

'No! That's overkill. All he had to say was leave it, son, I've got plans for another three garages.'

'Are you really suggesting that Vernon is buried there?'

'It's obvious,' said Derek. 'Life's not that complicated but it was hard to get building permission and harder to get building supplies in 1945.'

'Surely the building trade suffers shrinkage too.'

'Yeah. But three garages in December 1945? Maurice claims he doesn't even have a car.'

'He uses the garages for storage? He rents them out?'

'I'm saying he is storing what's left of Vernon.'

Waiting for Dickie Dawkins at Charing Cross station, Cotton noticed the news-boards were saying 'Mountbatten appointed Viceroy of India. Independence by June 1948.'

When Dawkins arrived, Cotton told him of Derek's story.

'What do you think?'

'I wouldn't be surprised.'

'Can you do anything?'

Dawkins made a face. 'I'm thinking,' he said.

Cotton let him think.

'Do you want Derek safe?' asked Dawkins.

Cotton nodded. 'Well, yes. Why not?'

'Then we'll have to go in another way. I'll tell someone the council planning committee is being investigated, maybe the planning officer. Anomalies. Possible corruption. I'll check who's who and get back to you.'

'Are you suggesting Maurice may have paid for his planning permission?'

'No. It's called influence,' said Dawkins. 'It doesn't have to be that direct. How much of a hurry are you in?'

Cotton shrugged. 'When you can. What's the matter? You look down.'

'My little one has a lazy eye,' said Dawkins.

'I'm very sorry to hear that,' said Cotton, though he was not sure what a 'lazy eye' was. 'Is there a treatment?'

'Yes,' said Dawkins. 'They cut out a disc of paper and put it over one lens of her spectacles. Over her good eye, that is. It makes the lazy eye work harder.'

'Do you know how long this will take?'

'We kick off with three months,' said Dawkins. 'Then we check again. My wife's a bit upset.'

'Of course.'

'I didn't know. She had the same thing when she was a girl. I think she feels a bit guilty.'

'Give her a present, then.'

Dawkins looked up. 'Yes,' he said, 'maybe.'

As Cotton was walking back to his office, someone fell into step beside him.

'Which do you prefer, Peter?' said Ed Lowell. *'The Odyssey* or *The Iliad*?'

'I haven't read either of them for a while,' said Cotton. He saw Ed Lowell was dressed in tweeds as if he had just been shooting pheasant or was intent on showing how mannered clothes maketh man.

'You do know we haven't the faintest idea who Homer was.'

'Yes. Wasn't it Samuel Butler who suggested he was a she?'

'Really?' said Ed Lowell. 'Homer means "witness", doesn't it? Or rather, since I always heard Homer was not a single author, "witnesses". *The Odyssey* and particularly *The Iliad* are a group effort.'

Cotton nodded. He wondered how long Ed Lowell would take to get to the point. 'Over time. A sort of chain. I've heard that.'

'Yes. It's really the oral becoming the written, I suppose.'

Cotton shrugged. 'Then there were different scribes, some making changes and additions.'

'In different places.' Ed Lowell smiled. 'We're moving ahead,' he said. 'By summer we should have a National Security Act. Three parts. A board to oversee intelligence from the White House. The military coordinated in one Department of Defense. And an entirely new agency.'

'Based on the CIG?'

'Yes. It'll have a slightly different name. Central Intelligence Agency is the front-runner. That'll deal with . . . abroad.'

'And the FBI?'

Ed Lowell shrugged. 'They can go back to being the FBI.'

Cotton did not believe the FBI would rush to collaborate with the new agency. Nor did he believe Ed Lowell thought they would. 'Thank you,' he said.

'No. I should thank you,' said Ed Lowell. 'We think you were right about Watson. Not that we'll say so, of course.'

'What? You're saying he had never begun his reading on Trotsky?'

'Nor Lenin either. Nor Marx.'

'Conclusion?'

'One of those mix-ups you get in this line of work. I blame the French.'

'Why?'

'They're too obliging. If they don't have Camembert they offer you Brie.'

Cotton laughed as politely as he could. 'We think we've traced the rumour to a Swiss arms dealer called Bodard,' he said.

Ed Lowell half smiled and nodded. 'Yes,' he said. 'Bodard is the kind of man the new agency is very keen on. Naturally he has had to come clean on a few details to show how cooperative he can be.'

Cotton nodded and glanced at Lowell. 'But like Homer, the original source for his accusation is obscure, possibly multiple,' he said.

Ed Lowell shrugged. 'Watson died without knowing he was suspected of being more than a fag.'

'And things have moved on.'

'Yes.'

The Horse Guards rattled past in the winter gloom. The horses' snorts mingled with the sound of their hooves on ice and grit. Cotton was struck that even their brightly polished breastplates looked dull. Mist, horses' breath – he frowned, unsure that he wasn't dreaming. Some of the patches that appeared looked momentarily oily like contour maps made into sodden rainbows.

'We're getting a new ambassador after the hiatus,' said Lowell.

The previous appointee had died in December 1946 before being able to take up the post.

'Has it been announced?'

'It will be shortly. Lewis Douglas.'

'A career diplomat?'

'Not in the least. Mining, academia, insurance, occasional politician.'

'Tough?'

'What do you say? As old boots? Yes, we're getting there, Peter. Have you heard Voice of America yet? No? Try listening and tell me what you think.'

Cotton wrote two separate messages to Ayrtoun – on Lowell and on Derek:

Conversation in the Mall with Ed Lowell. He mentioned the author of the Odyssey and the Iliad. It was too clumsy, overbearing and deliberate to be casual. He filled me in on the likely future organization of US Intelligence Services. He claimed at least to be unfussed by FBI. He agreed, off the record of course, that Watson was not a Trotskyite and went along with the suggestion that the rumour came from the arms dealer Bodard. Lowell says Bodard is doing something for the new American Agency.

Ayrtoun got back at once.

Essential you do not relay first or Greek part of conversation to anyone. Lowell fishing. Watch your back – your job may, from the American point of view, make your 'attitude' worth investigating.

Bodard is doing something for many people – he'd be a fool not to recognize the Americans have more money than anyone else. I suspect they are simply paying him to tell them where he is sending arms, in the hope they get more out of him later. I don't say the Americans have a monopoly on straight-shooting and innocence, but they are the leading players.

On Derek, Ayrtoun said: 'By all means see if the little bastard's information is correct. Your decision on what to do with him. If you do let him go, strongly suggest you get him to give you his replacement.'

Cotton was surprised by Ayrtoun giving Derek up, and dismayed by Ayrtoun's response to Lowell. If Bodard had supplied the story that Watson was a Trotskyite, it meant that the Americans had been involved even before Ayrtoun had been appointed to hunt spies in a British response to American pressure. Cotton took the warning about his own position. He thought Ayrtoun was even more exposed.

He had a conversation with Miss Kelly. Cotton really wanted a report on Ayrtoun's state of health and mind but Ayrtoun was of a superior rank, and a couple of minutes with Miss Kelly demonstrated clearly the extent to which the high-ranking were buttressed. Almost any enquiry would be construed as lack of deference enough to end a career.

He was left with simple social enquiry. Later, when he telephoned his father, James Cotton told him he had received 'a couple of Christmas cards'.

'In February?'

'They're both from America. Washington postmark.'

Cotton asked him to open them.

'The first is from a Dr Aforey. It has palm trees on it. It says "Seasons Greetings and sincere good wishes from an old friend".'

'The other?'

His father sighed. Cotton heard ripping paper. 'This one is from an Evelyn Duquesne. It says "I hope your trews still fit." I have no idea what that's about.'

Cotton smiled. That evening he wrote to Evelyn Duquesne, an elderly but spritely and very rich widow who lived in Dupont Circle, who had once introduced him to the very drunk Hon. Penelope Ayrtoun. He did not ask direct questions and doubted (a) that his letter would get to her very soon and (b) that she would volunteer very much anyway, but it was something to do.

CHAPTER 32

Dawkins got back to Cotton on Saturday, 22 February. They met up at the King's Arms in Buckingham Palace Road.

'Sorry to disturb your weekend.'

'That's fine.'

'The planning committee in Beddington is really run by a man called Cedric Hammond. He's, well . . . hoping to make good use of the damage caused by doodlebugs in that area.'

'Where exactly is this?'

'West of Croydon, across Purley Way. Hammond has been there for quite a while. That area got a lot of housing pre-war. Height restrictions, you see, because of Croydon airport. He's got quite a reputation with house builders from that time. There's an area now north of Mill Lane and Waddon ponds that got so badly hit it's looking good for postwar development.' Dawkins paused. 'Mr Hammond is an elder at his local chapel, you know. He lives quite near the gasworks.'

Cotton raised his eyebrows.

'The Lord has just given him a new Austin car,' said Dawkins. 'The garage owner also got a

372

hundred pounds to help the Lord move Hammond up the waiting list.'

'And these garages Bly built?'

'Yes. Well placed, apparently. They're screened a bit by trees and have a good view out towards the ponds.'

'Are there other decisions that might bring Hammond to the attention of the authorities?'

'We've got four so far. Is that enough?'

'Anything big?'

'There is something biggish in the pipeline. Permission for thirty-four semi-detached houses is going through.'

'All right. Would that be enough to screen Derek?'

'You should ask him.'

'I will.' Cotton sat back. 'Do you think this is enough to disturb Mr Bly into action? He's really got to believe these garages will have to come down. He could appeal, surely? It could take months.'

Dawkins squinted at Cotton. 'Colonel, he's a five-bob man!'

'What are you saying?'

Dawkins meant that Bly's standard loan was five shillings.

'Believe me,' said Dawkins. 'At five bob, he's hands on.'

'You mean he'll be there?'

'With Vernon he'll have used one other man. No more. Not in Croydon or Beddington.'

'Do you know who the other man would be?'

'Oh yes, big fellow, called Turner.'

'All right,' said Cotton. 'What are you going to do?'

'Tip off Croydon police, draw up the charges, break down Hammond's door, you know, make noise and watch what Bly does.'

Cotton nodded. 'This is yours,' he said.

Dawkins shook his head. 'It's the Chief Constable's,' he said.

Cotton saw Derek Jennings on Monday, 24 February. He brought him up to date on what was happening about Bly. Derek nodded but had other things on his mind.

'I'd like to get out of my present line of work,' he said.

'I'm afraid that's not up to me, Derek.'

'I know, Mr C. But I'm thinking ahead.'

'And what have you thought, Derek?'

'I told you about my brother-in-law, the greengrocer?'

'Yes. He has a stall in Croydon market, storage facilities in Wallington?'

'Very good, Mr C. We've been thinking about expanding.'

'You want to be a greengrocer?'

'No, no. Ha! My sister's thinking of china. I'm thinking of a gentleman's outfitters.'

'You want to open a shop?'

'No,' said Derek, 'a stall. It's a step up, Mr C,

and it makes sense. I'm not getting any younger and I've got some experience with clothes.'

'If we manage to get Mr Bly, Derek, do you think you'll be safe?'

'Yes,' said Derek. 'Maurice is a mean bastard. Not a lot of loyalty around him, if you know what I mean. Apart from Turner, that is. But he's stupid.'

'Who'll take over from him?'

'Greek Randall, you know, the bookie in West Croydon.'

Cotton nodded and changed subject. 'When is the next conga party in East Grinstead?'

'Are you thinking of coming, sir? They'd like a big chap like you.'

Cotton shook his head. 'Remember neck ties, Derek.'

Derek laughed.

'Don't laugh, Derek. When is this party?'

'March the 1st,' said Derek.

'Good,' said Cotton. 'You can take some photographs.'

Derek protested. 'I'm not a party pooper.'

'You're a party snapper,' said Cotton. 'You'll be given a small camera and you'll think. The only thing I want is a link between Sir Hear-Hear Johnson's house and the conga. Got it?'

Derek frowned. 'I don't get anything for this? Christ, I've given you Bly, Colonel.'

'I don't care about Bly. You do,' said Cotton. 'I care about this. Do it well and I'll do my best for you. Fair?'

Derek did not look as if he thought it at all fair. 'But where am I going to put a camera?'

'Who wears what?'

'Nobody wears much of anything,' said Derek. 'Some of the toffs wear masks.'

'Then be a toff for the night, Derek. I think we can do that for you.'

'Christ,' said Derek.

On Wednesday, 26 February Dawkins called Cotton.

'A man started digging up the floor of one of Bly's garages today.'

'All right. What's happening now?'

'We've put a watch on it. We're waiting for Maurice.'

'Good. Keep me informed.'

In Wardour Street Freddie Igloi said he had 'just the thing' for the East Grinstead conga party.

'It's actually German,' he said. 'Look at that.'

The camera was remarkably flat, about the area of a matchbox. The biggest part was the lens.

'We can dress this up as part of a mask. With a bit of glitter, you know.'

'Do you know who can do this?'

'I always go to the Chinese. They're very quick at sparkle. And they keep quiet.'

'How long?'

'Couple of hours. It'll probably be red, though. Is that a problem?'

'I don't know.'

'Focus will be a problem. But he can take the shot and look like he's adjusting the mask. The other problem is that he only has six exposures. Can he manage that?'

'We'll have to hope so.'

On the morning of February 27, Dawkins called Cotton again.

'They got Maurice at 2.15 this morning.'

'Vernon Carter?'

'Not looking too well. Well, he'd been under concrete since December 1945.'

'But they have to prove it was Maurice,' said Cotton.

'Well, there's the chair as well. Not Dopey's, you know.'

'No?'

'Guess,' said Dawkins.

'I've no idea.'

'Bashful's,' said Dawkins. 'They'll get him. Turner is too thick to stand questioning. He contradicts himself, you see. Doesn't understand the word "accessory" when applied to "after the fact". But he'll get there.'

In the afternoon Derek called to say he had received the mask.

'It's fucking red,' he said.

'Do you understand how it works?'

'I think so. I'm not happy about the red.'

'Why?' said Cotton.

'Most masks are black or deep blue.'

'Be notorious,' said Cotton. 'And tell me about Bly.'

'What about him?'

'Come on, Derek. He's been arrested for murder.'

Derek was determined to be unimpressed. 'Nah,' he said. 'He got what he deserved.'

'If you say so, Derek. You've got very few shots with this camera. Get used to wearing the mask.'

Anna Melville was back at work. On Saturday evening she appeared with two pound notes and offered to take him to lunch on Sunday. They went to a small place and ate something containing chicken and mushrooms. She talked a lot about her blacklight play – she had now settled on children talking to coloured ghosts in the Underground.

'But I don't want the ghosts to be sentimental, you see. I want them to be witty, even tough.'

Cotton smiled and encouraged her but he was really waiting to hear how Derek had managed on Saturday night.

On the morning of Monday, 3 March Cotton heard from Freddie Igloi. He had the camera back and was about to develop the film.

'Did you see Derek?'

'The little fellow who delivered the film? He said the party had been fucking great and that he was exhausted.'

378

Cotton grunted. 'Call me when you have something.'

Freddie Igloi called about two hours later. 'We have four usable pictures. Two are hopeless.'

'What have we got?'

'Do you want to see them?'

'Not particularly. What matters is that Sir Hear-Hear is in one.'

'He's the star,' said Freddie. 'He's in three.'

'Could an MP with a keen interest in security matters and prurience be able to use them?'

'Oh yes.'

'All right. Would you send copies to Alfred Perlman in Jermyn Street with my compliments. There's a message. Say: "Not to be seen by girls." Yes, add: "I hope your client approves."'

CHAPTER 33

At around five in the afternoon of Monday, 3 March Dickie Dawkins came in person to Cotton's office.

'We have a suicide attempt,' he said.

Cotton frowned. 'It's not Mair, is it?'

'No,' said Dawkins. 'It's a civil servant called Vine. You know him, apparently. Lives in Purley.'

'What did he do?'

'They say he cut his wrists.'

'He's still alive?'

'That's my information.'

Cotton stood up. He had forgotten again that going outside merely meant tightening up the clothes he already had on and adding a hat and gloves.

Dawkins and Cotton took a crowded commuter train from Victoria to Purley. Though the passengers thinned out, particularly at East Croydon, they did not speak until they were walking towards the Cottage Hospital.

'Why do you get this kind of thing?' Cotton asked.

'Special Branch gets flagged if someone who has

had access to sensitive information does anything silly.'

'Not MI5?'

'In the first instance, attempted suicide is still a crime.'

The Cottage Hospital, built to be homely, was all beige linoleum, pale green walls and the smell of bleach. After a short wait Cotton and Dawkins were seen by a youngish doctor.

'It's what they call a cry for help, apparently,' he said.

'Why do you say that?' said Dawkins.

The doctor was almost too bored to be impatient. 'If Mr Vine had been truly serious he would have cut here.' The doctor pushed out his hand and used the middle finger of his other hand to draw a line quite near the base of the thumb.

'Maybe he didn't know,' said Dawkins.

'But that's precisely my point,' the doctor said. 'If he had been really serious he would have taken the trouble to learn what cut would have caused him to bleed out. As it is . . . well, you've probably cut yourself worse shaving, certainly on the right wrist. The left cut opened three veins. Nothing too deep. There's tentative and there's fumbling with a razor-blade.'

'Where was he found?' said Cotton.

'In the bath,' said the doctor, as if he had never heard anything quite so feeble. 'Apparently his wife heard him sobbing. Quite loudly, I understand.'

Dawkins blinked. Whatever his respect for the

medical profession, it did not excuse a doctor who spoke so dismissively of a patient.

'The drawbacks to a classical education,' said Cotton. 'The Roman way out but poor at anatomy.'

The doctor frowned at him. 'You could say that, I suppose. He's under mild sedation but is perfectly able to talk. Mrs Vine insists it was an accident. We do treat flesh wounds. A real suicide attempt would have gone to another hospital. Nurse!'

The doctor turned and strode away.

'Busy man,' said Cotton.

Dawkins shook his head. 'I wouldn't want him,' he said, 'near my family.' He unbuttoned his coat. The Cottage Hospital had priority heating.

The nurse took them to Vine's room. There was a night-light, his wife may have been dozing but she came to and stood up very promptly. She was not as huddled as Cotton remembered her, was slim and had more neck. She lifted her chin.

'I know you,' she said to Cotton. 'Do you have anything to do with this?'

'It's possible. This is Mr Dawkins, Mrs Vine. He's from Special Branch.'

Mrs Vine let her arms drop. 'Oh God,' she said. 'Has my husband done something utterly stupid?'

Dawkins shook his head. 'We're here to make some enquiries, ma'am.'

Mrs Vine frowned, possibly at Dawkins's soft, careful, south London accent.

'Are you going to arrest him?'

'We haven't asked him any questions yet.'

Mrs Vine gave up on Dawkins and turned to Cotton.

'What is it you want to know?'

'How serious was this attempt? Was it planned? Did he make arrangements?'

Mrs Vine stared at him.

Cotton added a little snap to more volume. 'Did he leave a note, for example?'

Mrs Vine's head came up. 'Oh yes. Propped on the mantelpiece, like an invitation to a drinks party.'

'What did it say?'

'It said "sorry",' said Mrs Vine. She paused. 'That's all. "Sorry"!' If she was near tears, they were tears of rage. 'He was never a good father nor much of a husband, but this really is quite, quite despicable.'

Cotton looked at Andrew Vine. He had his eyes closed but Cotton had the impression this was more a try at self-protection than to rest.

'All right,' he said. 'Why don't you let us handle the next part now?'

'What do you mean?' said Mrs Vine.

'That we'd like to speak to him on his own. Would you mind stepping outside for a moment?'

Mrs Vine paused, then shook her head. 'Do you know something? The only advantage I can see to this entire wretched business is that we are all warm at last.'

Dawkins couldn't help himself. 'There are some draughts in the corridors,' he said.

Mrs Vine was not a woman who would ever really swear but her face expressed quite clearly that, had she not been a lady, she would have used a verbal spade on him.

'Lids up,' said Cotton when Mrs Vine had gone.

Vine obeyed, with a little theatrical flutter, rather badly done.

'How serious was this?' Cotton asked.

'I couldn't see a way out!' Vine's voice was extraordinary, all sloppy quaver and bleat, and Cotton instantly understood what had so irritated his wife and the doctor.

'Way out of what?' The rest – 'Don't lie or I'll tear off the bandages and work at the cuts myself. The doctor has told me what to do' – Cotton kept to himself.

Vine was still moaning. 'I got a letter. It said I was being moved to Work and Pensions.'

'So you got out your razor?'

'I can't hold my head up in Work and Pensions! Everybody would know I had been sidelined. It's humiliating! Utterly humiliating!'

Before Cotton could reply, Dawkins leant forward.

'Then you lump it – or you leave the Civil Service! You don't mess around with your family or get other people who have families to run after you when they'd rather be at home!'

Vine looked awfully aggrieved, as if baffled and put upon by the aggression in Dawkins's tone. Cotton had seen an army sergeant really break in Sicily. The horrible thing was that the poor man had no defences left. There had been no trace of self-concern, complaint or self-pity – the sergeant was incapacitated, besieged by nightmare images, what looked like waking blackouts and a disorientation so complete it had become physical. The man had been warding off bits of air.

'He means,' said Cotton, 'that you may want to consider another career. After all, there's business, any number of other possibilities. Though, on the other hand, if you want security, Work and Pensions wouldn't be so bad.'

'I felt my life was over,' said Vine. 'That woman despises me.'

Cotton nodded. 'Yes,' he said. 'Where are your children?'

'With her parents, I think.'

'What does your father-in-law do?'

'He's retired.'

Cotton suspected Mrs Vine's father was of sterner or more successful stuff than her husband.

'What did he do when he worked?'

Vine shook his head. When he did so his lips were loose enough to flop. 'I am not going to work for Imperial Tobacco. I'm not. I'm not—'

Cotton sighed. 'Has Mrs Gardener been in touch with you?'

'Oh no!' said Vine. 'I did absolutely everything you said.'

Cotton was taken aback. He had remembered

Vine being huffy and reluctant but not such a prompt and very bad liar.

'Anybody else get in touch with you?'

'No! I've told you. I felt my life was over.'

'You felt,' said Dawkins, 'that what you wanted your life to be was over.'

Vine blinked. He could see no difference. 'All right.'

'And now?' said Dawkins.

Andrew Vine combined tremor and sigh. 'I really don't know any more.'

Dawkins raised his eyes. Cotton took over.

'Does your wife know about Work and Pensions?'

'No!'

'We'll get her in soon,' said Cotton.

'But why?' wailed Vine.

'What the hell do you think this is?' said Dawkins. 'You're not choosing where to fucking go on holiday!'

'Shhh,' said Cotton. 'Did Mrs Gardener ever try to contact you?'

'No!' said Vine. He sounded put upon. 'I said that.'

Vine's skill in lying had not improved. Cotton nodded.

'I'm going to ask your wife to come in. You have a lot of talking to do. Start with Work and Pensions, all right? We'll take it from there.'

'But I need to think things out,' said Vine. 'And I can't.'

Cotton stared at him. 'Are you saying your

suicide attempt was your way of asking for a divorce?'

Vine's face crumpled again. 'I don't know,' he said. He frowned. He shook his head. 'I don't even know if I could afford a divorce.'

'Does your wife know about Mrs Gardener?'

'I haven't said anything.'

'And do you think that means a lot?' said Cotton.

'I don't know,' said Vine. 'I really don't.'

Cotton grunted. He thought Vine was overdoing ignorance as a mysterious condition. He nodded at Dawkins who opened the door. Mrs Vine came in.

'Well?' she said.

'Your husband has been appointed to a post in Work and Pensions,' said Cotton. 'He seems to think this is a dreadful come-down.'

'Is it?'

Cotton shrugged. 'He was worried you would feel let down.'

Mrs Vine frowned. 'But is it less money?'

Cotton turned round. 'It's the same,' said Vine.

'Will he have to travel?' asked Mrs Vine.

'No,' said Vine.

Mrs Vine looked at Cotton. 'Is that *it*?'

'More or less.'

'But it has something to do with you seeing him in the first place.'

Cotton nodded. 'That was a security check.'

Mrs Vine looked baffled. 'He can't handle security,' she said. 'Just look at him!'

Cotton took out one of his business cards. 'I'm giving this to you,' he said. 'I really don't think this episode is more than an unfortunate personal crisis, but should you have any reason to think differently, please contact me.'

Mrs Vine took the card. Cotton did not think she needed reading glasses or really had to hold the card that far away from her.

'Are you suggesting he needs help? Psychological perhaps? Even spiritual?'

'I don't know,' said Cotton. 'I have no training in psychology or the spiritual.'

Mrs Vine shook her head. 'I really don't like you people,' she said.

Cotton nodded. He in turn was not particularly fond of her but recognized she was trying to hold her family together and he was not going to make any observations on how she was going about it. She had, as yet anyway, not used any expression involving the phrase 'man enough'.

'He did say,' said Cotton, 'that he's not keen on business.'

Mrs Vine slowly raised one eyebrow but then spoke quite sharply. 'In business I understand the ability to make decisions and carry them out with resolution and dispatch is a plus,' she said.

She lifted her chin. She had better skin than Mrs Gardener. She was determined not to break down and Cotton was quite confident she would succeed.

'Thank you very much,' he said. 'If there's anything else, we'll get in touch.'

Cotton and Dawkins left the hospital room.

'I can't wish them well,' said Dawkins.

'Any particular reason?'

'She's a snob and he's a coward. I don't like this kind of area. It's snippy. And it's a lie.'

They paused to prepare themselves for the outdoors again.

'He had an affair she may not know about,' said Cotton. 'My guess is that Mrs Gardener is in London.'

'Right,' said Dawkins. 'He's a piss poor liar, that's for sure.'

'Mrs Gardener was introduced to Andrew Vine by Mair in Paris,' said Cotton. 'Vine raised the European alarm on Watson.'

Dawkins nodded. 'Right. I think there's a train in fifteen minutes,' he said.

CHAPTER 34

Thanks to Mr Shinwell's ruling on external lights, the night was as dark as the wartime blackout. Cloud shut off any light from the night sky. Cotton could just see something of Dawkins's breath issuing from the thicker dark where he was.

It was eye-wateringly cold, the ice underfoot sounded brittle. Cotton's feet throbbed briefly from the heat of the hospital, but the cold coming through the soles of his shoes finished that, even before they got across the car park.

Helped by the headlights of a van creeping towards them from Croydon, they crossed the Brighton Road and headed towards the High Street. On their right were the iron railings of a Church of England junior school called Christ Church and about forty yards ahead of them, to their left, there was a little light coming from a pub window. Beyond the school on their side, chinks in curtains from the people who lived in the flats above provided a little more, enough to make out the slight curve in the street.

More out of habit than need, Cotton glanced

behind him to check on any traffic before he started crossing the street towards the pub. As he did so, he heard Dawkins let out a short groan, and a scratching sound turned into a flaring match about four yards ahead. The match looped off in a low arc about head high towards Cotton's left.

Then Cotton glimpsed a ribbon moving like a sectioned snake towards his face. He jerked his head back and remembered to turn his body and push out his right thigh. Razor fighters use both hands, one coming in high, the other low.

Something, a button on his coat, clicked. There was a quick hissing noise. Cotton clenched his left fist. Using the natural recovery of his body, he added everything he could and delivered a short downwards punch towards an area about a foot in front of his right hip. Through the pain in his knuckles he knew he had hit skull. A couple of yards in front of him there was a dull spark and the sounds of metal breaking facial bones.

He resisted the desire to start kicking out and squatted. His right knee touched something human, somewhere about the lower ribs of someone's back. Cotton flattened his right hand and drove it downwards, to where he thought the head might be. He was over-generous in guessing the man's height. Only half his hand struck the very top of a cold, bald head. There was a crunch and a reflex gasp as the face hit paving stone and ice.

Frantic to get his bearings and frantic to stop

those razors, Cotton scrabbled round and got his right knee on his attacker's right upper arm. The man struggled. Cotton drove the head down again.

'Shit!' hissed Dawkins. He grunted. There were more bone-crunching noises. Then a police whistle sounded. Cotton had straddled the man's back and now banged the head against stone and ice several times. He gave it one more bang and sat back. He thought the man was an odd, short-limbed shape, but was not sure if that was not his own distorted impression.

'Are you all right?' said Dawkins.

Cotton thought he probably was. 'Yes. You?'

'Yes.'

'You blew the whistle?'

'Yes.'

There was a grunt and a number of wriggling, clothy sounds, then a crack and a shriek almost coincided.

'I'll do your other knee,' said Dawkins. 'Just you move.' He breathed out. 'Damn!' he said. 'I've got the shakes!'

Cotton did not feel he was doing much better. He felt weak, not quite as if he were melting, this was more as if he was about to faint and might be dribbling away. Two policemen on patrol arrived, handcuffed the men and called for a car.

'Sinclair and Boyle?' asked Cotton.

'Yes,' said Dawkins.

The razors were gathered up. By torchlight Cotton saw a length of blue ribbon about an inch wide and a yard long to which razors had been sewn. The other razors were more old-fashioned.

'Safety razors in one hand, old-fashioned cut-throat in the other,' said one of the patrolmen.

When the police car arrived, Dawkins spoke up.

'These men are under arrest. Take them to Croydon and lock them up.'

'Probably better to check them over first, sir,' the policeman holding the razors said. 'They may need treatment.'

The Cottage Hospital was displeased by the number of people and the quantity of blood.

'What's going on?' asked the doctor they had already seen. 'I am the duty doctor here and I can assure you cases like this are taken to Mayday Hospital.'

Dawkins stared at him. 'I don't care,' he said. 'I want you to check them over, make sure we can lock them up.'

'We have women in labour here.'

Dawkins was so angry he stepped forward until he was very close to the doctor. 'My wife has given birth twice. I remember blood and I remember shrieks,' he said. 'You check them over. If you need to call an ambulance for them, then you call one. We are deferring to your professional knowledge, Doctor. Will you accept that?'

The noise of a siren and the arrival of more police at the Cottage Hospital did not help, but the doctor did as he was asked.

Boyle had lost teeth and suffered a broken jaw,

cheekbone and nose. His left knee was very swollen.

Sinclair, the person Cotton thought of as his, had sustained a broken nose, heavy bruising, a swollen lip and several ice cuts to his face. He was short, about five foot two, with chunky legs and prominent buttocks, a large, top-heavy head that showed how close razors could shave, and very pale, almost milky skin. Neither man was saying a word, looked sealed in.

'These men have been assaulted,' said the doctor.

'You have that the wrong way round,' said Dawkins. 'These two delights are razor boys. They attacked us in the dark and without warning. Do you understand what I'm saying, Doctor? They are going to be charged with a serious crime. What I want to know from you is whether they can be taken from here to a cell now, or whether they need to be given treatment first. Is that clear?'

'Yes. That looks like a shattered kneecap,' the doctor said, pointing at Boyle. 'He also needs facio-maxillary work. The other needs his nose set but is mostly cuts and bruises.'

Dawkins cocked his head.

The doctor nodded. 'They would be better treated at Mayday Hospital but they don't need an ambulance to get there.'

Dawkins smiled. 'Good.' He turned. 'Read them their rights,' he said to a police sergeant. 'Then get them formally remanded at Croydon police station and call the Police Surgeon. We'll be along later.'

Cotton spoke into Dawkins's ear. 'Don't have them charged. Not yet.'

'Why the hell not?'

'We don't know enough. They may have been sent. They may have acted on their own.'

Dawkins nodded. 'Right.' He waited till the sergeant had finished reading the two men their rights.

'Just hold them for now,' he said. 'We have to make further investigations. The Police Surgeon should have enough to do till we get there.'

Cotton stepped aside to allow Boyle and Sinclair to be taken away. He was aware that his left hand was swollen. Now when he moved, he realized his right shoe squelched. He looked down. Blood was oozing out of his sock and over the rims of shoe.

He looked up. Dawkins was rewrapping a handkerchief round his hand. The razor had cut him above the knuckledusters, up to his wrist and across the veins of the back of the hand.

'That's razor work,' said Dawkins holding up his hand for the doctor. 'And that is too.' He pointed at Cotton. Cotton looked down again. His overcoat was cut through.

A nurse came up to him.

'Where will I start?'

Cotton held up his left hand.

She looked and made a face. 'I hope you've got more gloves.'

She cut the glove off in the same way he had had plaster cut off in the war. As the leather peeled away Cotton saw the left side of his hand was grotesquely puffed and tinged with blue.

'Two. Maybe three fingers broken,' said the nurse.

Cotton learnt that Mrs Vine had come out to see what the noise was when he heard Dawkins speaking to her.

'Next time, if your husband's really serious, he may want to ask a razor gang for assistance. More convincing, ma'am.'

Mrs Vine looked at Cotton's hand. 'What's going on? Are we at risk?' she said.

'I don't think so. But I think we may need to talk a little more.'

'Sorry,' said the nurse, 'but I need to take this gentleman to the treatment room.'

Mrs Vine nodded and turned away. She looked pale but, Cotton noticed, almost beautifully grim.

'Where do I go?' said Cotton.

'Stay where you are,' said the nurse. 'You're making enough mess as it is. Somebody has to clean the floor here, you know.'

She got him some crutches and he swung along behind her till they reached a tiled room. Quite large, it contained only a high birthing bed and a glass and enamel cabinet. To one side was an alcove with two large sinks.

Cotton leant against the bed. On the wall facing the end of the bed was a large drawing of three babies. One was white, one was blue and one was divided vertically into blue and white. Cotton did not ask. Was this to encourage the mothers in labour or to remind the staff to be on the lookout for blue or partially blue babies? He glanced down. His hand had blue patches not dissimilar to the blue of the drawing, but some were darker and other patches were red and bloodless white.

The nurse helped him with his overcoat and then his jacket. The cut-throat razor had sliced through both.

'Well, I hope you know a good tailor,' she said.

The razor had continued through his trousers, the trouser pocket and into his right thigh.

'Drop your trousers, please.'

Cotton did. He saw that the skin of his leg had been parted and the cut had gone into the muscle. The cut was on a mild curve with an abrupt sideways snick at the end nearest the knee. The wound had stopped bleeding and the coagulated blood was drying.

'You've been lucky,' said the nurse. 'Think if he'd got you a bit further this way.'

'That's a comfort,' said Cotton.

The doctor came in and pressed the wound together. The cut began to bleed again.

'You're lucky,' he said. 'More than half an inch causes problems. This will take stitches.'

It took twenty-three. While the stitches were going in, the nurse put a splint on each of the last two fingers of his left hand and bandaged them very tightly. It made his middle finger throb.

'That's only sprained,' she said. She bent down and took off his shoe and sock and went through to the alcove to clean the shoe out and wash the sock.

Cotton closed his eyes and concentrated on the smells. He smelt the powdery smell of cotton wool, the sharpness of surgical spirit and then something thinner and meaner like thin, acidic vomit. He grunted. The doctor was at about the thirteenth stitch.

'Doing my best, you know,' said the doctor.

'I know. I'm just taking breath.'

'Do you want me to stop?'

Cotton breathed in. 'No,' he said.

Cotton closed his eyes again. He had, of course, done army training in what had been called 'unarmed combat', but could not remember actually ever having been unarmed. There was also the business of creeping up behind a guard, the 'guard' being one of the other trainees and liable to be rather deafer than an enemy guard might be, or like a man called Abbott (subsequently removed from the course) who would keep saying 'Heard you! Heard you!' when nobody had yet moved.

'There you are,' said the doctor.

Cotton looked down. It took a moment for the liquid in his eyes to clear and for him to see that the stitches really did look as ragged and black as he had first thought. They covered, with what looked like soldier ants' legs and knots, a cut about eight inches long.

The nurse began smearing iodine round and on the wound. There was a second Cotton thought his teeth were seething. He breathed out. The sharpness gave way to heat and a smell that reminded him of the sharp stuff his mother had used to remove nail polish.

'Thank you,' he said. He looked down again. There was something particularly ugly about the black stitches and the yellow and brown iodine.

'The nurse will bind you up,' said the doctor. 'I'll get you some pills.'

'I've put your shoe under the radiator and your sock on it,' said the nurse. 'I really gave that sock a good wringing.'

'You're both very kind. Thank you.'

The doctor left, the nurse went to fetch bandages from the cabinet and Dawkins put his head round the door.

'I've been done,' he said. Dawkins's eyes had puffed up, looked almost closed. One of his hands was bandaged. The other, in which he held his bloodied handkerchief, he waggled at the nurse.

'Waste in here,' she said and got a metal bin.

The rolled handkerchief gave a decided clunk as it went in. The nurse started but Dawkins smiled at her.

'I have to speak to the Colonel,' he said. 'Can I do that without you listening?'

'I have to bandage his thigh.'

'Good,' said Dawkins to her. He grimaced at Cotton. 'Christ!' he said.

'Now, now,' said the nurse.

'Shhh,' said Dawkins. He turned to Cotton. 'Are you out of action?'

'I don't think so. It just looks messy.'

Dawkins was not really listening. The nurse indicated for Cotton to stand. She considered, then shook her head and got him to sit again at the very edge of the bed. She bent to put the first dressing on the cut.

'Fucking hell!' said Dawkins. 'This is a right fucking mess!'

The nurse looked up.

'Oh come on, love,' said Dawkins. 'You're a nurse not a nun.' He looked at Cotton. 'What are we going to do?'

'Right down the middle,' said Cotton.

The nurse began wrapping the dressing to his leg.

'We don't want to cause any embarrassment,' said Cotton. 'We have the very best interests of the agencies involved at heart.'

Dawkins frowned. Cotton insisted.

'Look, we can give certain colleagues pause, maybe even a little more. But we will have to show we are only too anxious to collaborate, for the sake of the agencies' reputations, you understand, if we are to get anywhere at all.'

Dawkins leant down. 'How are you doing?' he asked the nurse.

'I'm doing well,' she replied. 'But I'd do better without interruptions.'

Dawkins raised his face to the ceiling.

'We need the use of a car,' said Cotton. 'We'll go to Croydon police station. I'd really like a meeting with the Chief Constable when we're there. All right?'

Dawkins nodded. 'All right. I'll get a car.'

Dawkins left and Cotton closed his eyes. As a last bandage, the nurse was wrapping crêpe round the dressing and the first bandage on his thigh. The smell was faintly rubbery. He pulled up his trousers.

The doctor had several pills for him, divided into two paper-cum-cardboard receptacles, like tiny cupcake holders with ruched or pleated lids.

'These are painkillers, should you need them. Codeine really. These are penicillin. Possible side effects include nausea and diarrhoea. They are, however, absolutely marvellous against bacterial infections.'

Cotton nodded. 'Thank you,' he said. He saw the nurse turn his steaming sock over on the radiator. A trickle of sweat ran down his forehead. He wiped it away.

'You'll need to have that bandage changed. I take it you don't live locally.'

'No. I live off Sloane Street and I work in St James's.'

'Right,' said the doctor. 'I have a friend at Guy's. Where I studied. How would that be? They rather specialize in accidents.'

'All right,' said Cotton.

'And in due course, those stitches will have to be taken out. Unless you want to come back here, of course.'

'No.'

'Then I'll refer you. The other man calls you Colonel Cotton.'

Cotton got a card out of his jacket and gave it to the doctor. 'Thanks,' he said. 'I'd like to see Mr Vine again. Would that be all right with you, Doctor?'

The doctor raised his eyebrows. 'It's like that, is it?' he said. He shrugged. 'I have no objection. But let the nurse finish helping you first.'

The nurse was sticking the cuts in his overcoat and jacket from the inside with tape.

'This should hold till you get to a tailor,' she said.

'You're very kind,' said Cotton.

The nurse smiled. 'The sock is still a little damp,' she said.

'That's all right.'

The sock was damp but warm. It reeked of surgical soap. The nurse helped him with that and his shoe. Cotton put on his jacket and his coat.

'How's that bandage?' she asked.

'I can hardly feel my thigh.'

'That means it's tight enough.'

Cotton smiled. 'I'll take your word for it. Thanks for all you've done.'

Cotton walked back to the hospital entrance.

'I've got us a car,' said Dawkins, 'and the Chief Constable will be there in half an hour.'

Cotton and Dawkins went back to Vine's room. Cotton asked Vine's wife to leave again.

'Do you really think that's helpful or necessary? He's in a vulnerable condition.'

'Yes, I do think it's necessary,' said Cotton. 'And I do appreciate his condition.'

'This was done with a cut-throat razor,' said Dawkins, holding up his bandaged hand. He used it to point at Cotton. 'They got him in the thigh. I don't know about vulnerable but—'

Mrs Vine left the room. Cotton looked at Vine. He was sitting up in bed, looked pale, but his wife had certainly frightened some energy into him.

'It is essential we know whether or not you have been in contact with anyone,' said Cotton.

'I don't know what you mean. You simply can't be suggesting I've had anything to do with this. I didn't even know you were coming. I haven't been in touch with anyone. I mean, I didn't even know I'd be taken here.'

Cotton nodded. He thought this a pretty fair rundown and very likely true. 'Where is Mrs Gardener staying?'

Vine blinked.

'Look. Forget Work and Pensions,' said Cotton. 'You'll have no work and no fucking pension.'

'She's staying with a friend in Pont Street.'

'Number?' said Cotton.

Vine gave it up.

'What happened?'

Vine shook his head. 'Nothing,' he said. 'She told me it was over.'

'What did she want?'

'I don't know.'

Cotton frowned. 'Mr Vine—'

'She wanted me to pay for an abortion.'

'Did you?'

Vine groaned. 'I can't win,' he said. 'I just can't.'

'What are you talking about?' asked Cotton.

'If you pay you're not a gentleman. If you don't, you're a cad.'

'How much?' said Dawkins.

'Forty pounds,' said Vine.

Dawkins nodded. 'He paid. And that's more Harley Street than Wigmore Street.'

'Mr Vine,' said Cotton, 'I really hope we don't have to see you again. I'd prefer never even to hear of you. Is that clear?'

Vine looked unhappy.

'Mr Vine,' said Cotton, 'is there anything else you want to tell us?'

'No!'

Dawkins cleared his throat. 'Both of us have just learnt what an improvement safety razors are, sir. You might like to think about that, for the future, you know, if you're feeling a bit self-pitying or anything. Choose the cut-throat.'

Outside the room Mrs Vine was waiting for them.

'I do have contacts, you know,' she said.

'Good,' said Cotton. 'Use them. And I can use

mine. To start with I could ask my colleague here to arrest your husband. Now. To attempted suicide I am sure we could add some other charges.'

Mrs Vine narrowed her eyes. 'You're vile,' she said.

'Ma'am,' said Dawkins, 'the Colonel is a gentleman who understands a lady even when she's distressed. We wouldn't have stitches if your husband had been honest with you.'

They walked down the corridor.

'I'm thinking,' said Dawkins, 'the forty pounds for the abortion may not have been all abortion.'

'Mrs Gardener claimed a little cash as well?'

Dawkins grunted. 'Nothing grand. Is your sock quite dry?'

'Not quite,' said Cotton.

'Better to talk, then, before we go outside.'

They sat down on a bench.

'First question,' said Cotton. 'How did Boyle and Sinclair know we were here? You came to see me about five.'

'I got a telephonist's note about four thirty. It said Vine had attempted suicide and had been taken here.'

'Well,' said Cotton, 'we can't prove Radcliffe, and by extension Starmer-Smith, had anything to do with this. They'd certainly deny it. But it's clear Boyle and Sinclair also got the information about Vine's attempted suicide, his whereabouts, and where we would be going. It wouldn't have meant anything unless they had also known that a report on them had been submitted. I don't know whether or not Sir Percy Sillitoe has the report, is going to get the report, or whether it has been made to disappear. But our friends from Glasgow decided to act.'

Dawkins nodded. 'We were set up,' he said.

'Yes, it looks like it. But we don't know whether or not it was Boyle and Sinclair being stupid with razors. So now we're going to report what happened but we will draw no conclusions. We will be serious, we will be concerned and very careful about the reputations of our respective agencies. We will be respectful. And leading.'

'What do you mean – leading?'

'We'll lead our superiors towards certain conclusions. The main one is, whatever the association between Boyle and Sinclair and Starmer-Smith, that our superiors mark it at least as unwise. And if we're lucky, we'll get them to see that Starmer-Smith and Radcliffe lost control of the violent criminals they were using. It's going to be very difficult to prove that Boyle and Sinclair are being paid by MI5.'

Dawkins frowned.

'Well, I know my boss is paying people who don't figure on the payroll,' said Cotton. 'In a modest way I even do it myself. It's simply called expenses and gets tucked away.'

Dawkins sighed. 'Yes. All right.'

'The other thing is that we've been unable to

get a shred of usable evidence on what our cut-throats have been doing for seven years. That's seven. Mr Causley of the Scottish flags has been our best source for all that time and we can't use him.'

Dawkins shook his head and sighed. 'You don't understand. You don't work with Starmer-Smith,' he said. 'I'll have Radcliffe all over my back.'

'Don't accuse him of anything. Don't do more than describe the attack. In Purley of all places!'

'Shit,' said Dawkins. 'I should have kept the knuckledusters.'

'For the future? Or because they might be found?'

'What?' said Dawkins.

'Come on,' said Cotton. 'My sock's dry. Let's get started.'

They stood up, walked out of the hospital, got into a police car and headed for Croydon police station.

CHAPTER 35

Chief Constable Kitson was waiting for them in his office, buttons gleaming, uniform brushed. He stared at them, but continued with what he already had prepared.

'I am duty bound, Colonel,' he said, 'to thank you for your assistance in bringing down the Bly gang.'

Cotton briefly remembered Maurice Bly in his brown dustcoat, showing his gappy little teeth, and wondered whether or not Bly would be flattered to be elevated into a gang leader. Probably not.

'No, sir,' said Cotton. 'That was a police and Special Branch success. The help provided was very small.'

The Chief Constable frowned. 'I say, do sit down. Do you need any attention?'

'No, thank you sir,' said Dawkins. 'We were well looked after at the hospital.'

'Am I to understand you were attacked in the High Street?'

'Yes, sir,' said Dawkins.

'I'm familiar with the blight of brawling amongst soldiers, though that is properly a military matter.

But this kind of thing is quite unknown in Purley. Purley is not like that.'

'Well, properly speaking,' said Dawkins, 'Purley was incidental to the attack.'

'What are you talking about?'

Dawkins looked at Cotton. 'We were attacked by two men, originally from Glasgow and originally part of the gang called the Billy Boys,' said Cotton. 'It would appear that they have been employed, certainly in the recent past, by one, possibly two of our own Intelligence agencies.'

Had he been in less pain, Cotton would have felt like kicking himself. He had forgotten the Chief Constable treated bad news as an impertinence.

'It's a very delicate matter,' he said quickly. 'We'd be grateful for your advice.'

'What do you mean?' said Kitson.

'At one level it's simply that there was an element of shock in the attack. I don't have to tell you, sir, that shock does not give good advice.'

Cotton saw Dawkins glance at him. The glance did not show much approval of his playing the 'I was recently a soldier' card.

'More importantly,' said Cotton, 'though the injuries are clear enough, we don't know why we were attacked.' He paused. 'We have to assume that there was a catastrophic breakdown of communications. After all, it is hard to think that an agency would deliberately use two Billy Boys to carry out a razor attack on two officers from other agencies.'

Kitson looked at them. 'I'm not quite clear,' he said. 'What is it you want from me?'

'At this stage, sir, two things. First, that the men in your cells are not yet formally charged. The second thing, if you are agreeable, is a letter of protest. An attack like this in a public place, apparently involving a fight between Intelligence agencies, is intolerable.'

'You're expecting some kind of comeback or explanation for the confusion?'

'Yes, sir. But it is quite late at night and—'

'You want to give them time?'

Cotton nodded. 'I think that would be wisest all round, sir.'

'Yes. I see what you mean.' Kitson paused. 'You know, it *is* intolerable. Quite, I'll fire off a letter, then.'

'Thank you very much, Chief Constable.'

'Good. How about some tea, chaps? I'll do this letter.'

Dawkins and Cotton sat downstairs and drank a mug of tea.

'Why did you do that, ask for a letter of protest?'

Cotton blew out. 'We don't know what form the comeback or explanation the Chief Constable mentioned might take.'

'They know where we live,' said Dawkins quietly. 'Have you got a family?'

'No. But you've got—'

'A wife and two little girls. Yes.' Dawkins paused. He made a face. 'Look,' he said, 'Radcliffe is what he is, you know, talks about his "people" and things like that.'

'What people?'

'His family. Where he comes from, that sort of thing.'

'Are you really saying he's got more friends in Glasgow?'

'Shit,' said Dawkins. He shook his head. 'He's the kind of man who attacks to defend himself. I mean, he's loud. But this! This is . . .' Dawkins did not go on.

Cotton nodded. Dawkins evidently felt betrayed. 'I know it's hard but could you have another push to find someone who's had dealings with Boyle and Sinclair? Our kind of dealings.'

Dawkins nodded. It did not mean he agreed. 'I'm knackered,' he said.

They were taken home in a police car. First Dawkins to a terraced house in Vauxhall, then across the river to Cotton's flat in Wilbraham Place.

Cotton let himself in. It was a quarter past one in the morning. Between the throbbing of his hand and what felt like a toothed clamp on his thigh, the rest of him felt quite badly lacking. He had heard of the cilice, used by penitents to mortify the flesh and atone for Christ's suffering. This felt as if he was wearing not one but about three barbed metal belts, and not just for a couple of hours. He went to the kitchen and with his good hand got out two codeine tablets and swallowed them.

411

'Where the hell have you been?'

Cotton closed his eyes for a moment, then shuffled himself round. He was too weary and sore to do much else except shake his head.

Anna Melville put on her glasses. 'God, you've been in a car accident.' She moved towards him.

Cotton surprised himself with his own vehemence. 'No!' He tried to soften it. 'Not really.'

She had pulled up. She stared at him. 'What happened?'

Cotton sighed. 'Nothing terribly grand,' he said.

'Have you broken your arm?'

'Just a couple of fingers.'

'Anything else?'

Cotton nodded.

'You look like shit,' she said. It sounded like an accusation.

'Yes, I imagine I do. Anything else?'

She frowned and looked hurt. 'You don't want me here, do you?'

Cotton was weary enough to think he might as well be honest. He accepted this was not a kind decision. 'No,' he said.

'You're a bastard.'

'I'm battered,' he said.

She frowned. 'You're not going to do it, are you?'

Cotton breathed in. 'Do what?'

'Back me.'

Cotton squinted at her. Anna Melville was talking about her blacklight play. He paused, felt the various thumps and throbs in his body. 'I don't have that kind of money,' he said.

She said nothing.

'I can't help,' he said.

She shook her head. 'You wouldn't have helped anyway.'

Cotton thought this was probably true or, at least from her point of view, accurate enough. He nodded.

'You need someone with real money, spare money,' he said.

She looked at him and shook her head again. He was clear her head shake was at him.

'How serious are you?' he said. 'Five hundred pounds is half my salary before tax. And considerably less after it. You can buy a small house for that kind of money!'

'At least I thought you might know people, introduce me to them.'

'All right,' said Cotton. 'What kind of person are you looking for?'

She had decided to be wistful. 'I've liked it here,' she said.

'I'm serious,' said Cotton. 'I don't even know what kind of person invests in plays. Theatre enthusiasts? People who want to be around actors? Family and friends helping out? And aren't there people called angels? Get a few of them together. You need twenty-five people with twenty pounds. Isn't that right? And I think there are also businesses that are anxious not to make money. They get a little kudos and some tax relief. Have you thought of that?'

'I'm not in with that set,' she said.

Cotton had not heard the word 'set' for some time. It was a word he associated with his mother's generation and even she had used it with irony. 'I could put you in touch with someone. No guarantees but you could try.'

She squinted at him. 'You're playing straight with me?'

'Yes! It's a man called George Dyce. He has one of those surnames that is really part of a title. He lives in Cadogan Square. I'm not sure what he does any more amongst his family's interests, or what he is allowed to do, but he does know people.'

Anna Melville considered. 'How could I meet him?'

'I'll write you a letter of introduction. How about that?'

'You'd do this?'

'Yes, I've just said so. I have his card somewhere.'

'I'll find it.'

'All right. But don't use it until I have contacted him. Fair? I'll write to him tomorrow. I promise. What do you think?'

'Yes.'

'Good.'

'You've hurt me.'

'I'm sorry. I'm tired.'

'I'm sorry too. About your injuries.'

'Thanks. I really need to get some sleep.'

'All right.'

Cotton took penicillin and went to bed alone.

A while after he heard the front door bang. He closed his eyes. Was the door slamming a grand gesture on a freezing night? Or was she going downstairs to see Margot? Cotton did not have the energy to shrug. He fell asleep.

CHAPTER 36

Cotton woke around six in the morning. He felt very stiff and very sore. He struggled up and sat on the edge of his bed. He could see his breath in the air but he felt over-warm. The pain in his leg made him feel sick. He closed his eyes and breathed in. He went to the window and looked out. It was snowing heavily. He went back and sat on his bed.

Wondering how he could get a sock on his right foot, he could not remember how he had managed to get it off when he went to bed. The telephone rang.

He hobbled along the hall and picked it up. 'Yes?'

'Colonel Cotton, this is Olivia Marx here.'

'Good morning, Miss Marx.'

'Mr Perlman would like to see you at your earliest convenience.'

'Does he know I have some injuries?'

There was a pause.

'He does.'

'Then he'll understand that I find movement quite difficult.'

'I don't understand, sir.'

'I'm happy to see Mr Perlman but it will have to be here, at my home.'

There was a very brief pause. 'Mr Perlman is most extraordinarily busy,' said Miss Marx.

'And I am most extraordinarily limited as to movement. It's entirely up to him.'

'I really don't think he'll be very happy, Colonel.'

'I'm not in the slightest bit happy myself, Miss Marx. But I'm not going to get happier opening up stitches to save Mr Perlman a small trip.'

'Very well, sir. I'll pass that on. Will you be at home in the next couple of hours?'

'I'm not thinking of moving from home at all, Miss Marx.'

Cotton put down the telephone, then picked it up and rang Dickie Dawkins. Dawkins answered the telephone at once. He sounded hoarse.

'Have you managed to sleep?' asked Cotton.

'No,' said Dawkins. 'It's not the pain exactly, it's the worry. How's your leg?'

'Stiff enough to insist Alfred Perlman comes to my home address.'

There was a pause. Then a groan that turned into a hiss that included the word 'shit'.

'Do you think you can get here before Mr Perlman arrives? I can try to get a car to you, if you want.'

'No,' said Dawkins. 'I don't want that. I'll get there.'

'All right. Come on,' said Cotton, 'this is not so

417

bad. Perlman is a lot better than Boyle and Sinclair's friends.'

'It'll be horse-trading,' said Dawkins.

'Yes,' said Cotton. 'But we have something to trade.'

Dawkins's sigh did not sound very confident.

Cotton went through to the kitchen. He found a note on the table from Anna Melville weighed down by a set of keys.

'No hard feelings on my side – but no kind ones either.' She had written down what she called a contact telephone number – 'if you are really serious'.

Cotton made himself some porridge, mostly for the warmth. His jaw ached from having clamped his teeth so much during the night. He mashed a couple of codeine pills in with the oats. Then he wrote George Dyce a note:

Dear George,
Having been involved in a slight mishap on ice (couple of broken fingers, stitches in my right leg) I find myself, rather literally, in a bind. Could you help me out?

A talented young woman called Anna Melville is trying to put on a blacklight play and I had agreed to help with some contacts and pointers. She's originally from Czechoslovakia where blacklight theatre is well established. She has some intriguing

418

developments in the form and presently works at places like the Arts Theatre.

Could I give her your number and address? You'll find her pleasant and good fun.

Yours,
Peter

The telephone rang again.

'Colonel,' said Miss Kelly. 'Two telegrams.'

'Go ahead.'

'The Hon. Penelope Ayrtoun died at 10 a.m. – that's Washington time – yesterday.'

Cotton had no response. He did not even grunt.

'Sir? Are you there?'

'Yes. What's the other telegram?'

'It says Mr Ayrtoun has been granted indefinite leave with immediate effect.'

'All right, Miss Kelly. Thank you. I won't be coming in today. I'll be at this number.'

'Yes, sir.'

Cotton got out an envelope and addressed it to George Dyce. He put the note inside and a stamp on the envelope. As he did these things, slowly and deliberately, he kept calm. He had just lost his boss and Operation Sea-Snake. He went down to the porter's desk with the letter.

'A bit of an accident, sir?'

'Yes.'

'Is the letter urgent, sir?'

Cotton thought and nodded.

'I can have it delivered quickly, sir.'

'Thank you.'

As Cotton turned to take the lift upstairs again Margot Fenwick came out.

Cotton smiled. 'Good morning,' he said.

Miss Fenwick looked alarmed then flustered.

'Mummy's not well,' she said.

'I'm sorry to hear it,' said Cotton. 'I hope it's nothing serious.'

'I'm not sure,' said Miss Fenwick.

'Are you going to visit her?' asked Cotton.

'Perhaps.'

'Good,' said Cotton. He nodded, smiled again and got into the lift.

A few minutes later Dickie Dawkins arrived. He looked startled. He remained looking startled.

'Are you all right?' said Cotton.

Dawkins winced and blew out.

The telephone rang.

'Ten minutes,' said Alfred Perlman's other secretary.

'Thank you,' said Cotton. 'That's Marion, isn't it?'

'Yes, sir.'

Cotton put down the phone.

'Perlman and his other secretary will be here in about ten minutes. My news is bad. Ayrtoun's wife died yesterday. He's been given indefinite leave with immediate effect.'

'Oh God!' said Dawkins. 'Does that mean you're high and dry?'

Cotton shook his head. 'Right now we have to manage Perlman.'

'What did she die of?'

'She was an alcoholic. I'm guessing something related. He said she'd had a bad attack of jaundice last year.'

'Right.' Dawkins looked to be in pain.

'What is it?'

'I don't know how to say this without sounding as if I'm whining,' said Dawkins. 'But – well. You are better provided for in life, if you know what I mean.'

Cotton nodded. 'I think Mr Perlman will huff and he'll puff. He may then bluster and threaten,' he said. He shook his head. 'We are not going to be influenced by that.'

'How do you know what he'll do?'

'I don't,' admitted Cotton. 'But you'll be able to check whether or not I'm right. If I'm wrong, we'll pause and talk in private. All right?'

Alfred Perlman arrived with Miss Olivia Marx. She was carrying a rug, a briefcase and a small picnic basket. He was wearing a black homburg and an extraordinarily large black coat that hung like cape. He took neither cape nor hat off. He dispensed with greetings.

'We need a table,' he said. He still had that awful head cold.

'Then we're in the kitchen,' said Cotton. 'Mr Perlman, Miss Marx, this is Mr Dawkins, of Special Branch.'

If Alfred Perlman acknowledged the introduction it was very briefly. He walked to the far end of the table and plumped himself down, his back to the window, hard enough for his jowls to shake. Miss Marx put the briefcase in front of him and the small picnic basket to one side.

'Put the kettle on,' he told her.

'By all means, Miss Marx,' said Cotton.

'Mr Perlman has not had time for breakfast,' she said.

'Quite,' said Cotton. He turned to Dickie Dawkins. 'Did you hear the weather forecast for today?'

Dawkins looked doubtful. 'More snow,' he said. 'I think they said something about a blizzard coming.'

Cotton smiled. 'Oh dear. We'll just have to manage, then.'

Even if Miles Crichton's ortolan anecdote was not true, the preparations for Mr Perlman's breakfast indicated how it might have come about. When Miss Marx had put the kettle on she opened the hamper and began taking things out. These included a silver knife and salt shaker and what Cotton thought of as a Russian tea glass or *podstakannik*, the holder also in silver. There was a white, monogrammed plate and a monogrammed linen napkin. Alfred Perlman's breakfast consisted of three hard-boiled eggs, what looked to Cotton like madeleines or *magdalenas* but, he guessed, were not as sweet, and a jar of black roe, possibly caviar. 'When available', the egg allowance in Britain was one per ration book. Put another way, there was no fixed egg ration in the United Kingdom. Cotton took it that for a lawyer like Perlman this meant private or other egg arrangements were entirely legitimate.

Perlman had also brought along a silver thermos flask that looked like a sizeable cocktail shaker. Miss Marx unscrewed the top and sniffed the contents. She nodded.

Cotton saw that Dawkins, sitting to his left, was most taken by Alfred Perlman loosening his coat and fitting the napkin between his neck and his shirt collar. While Perlman was doing this, Miss Marx was shelling the hard-boiled eggs. Alfred Perlman picked up the first egg and shook a little salt on it.

'My firm,' he said, 'has been asked to represent Messrs Francis Sinclair and John Boyle.' He bit into the egg.

'Have you accepted?' said Cotton. 'Or are you still considering your response?'

Perlman ignored this. He indicated Miss Marx should put hot water into the thermos flask. She turned off the kettle and added a little hot water, no more than a couple of egg-cups' worth.

'My clients,' he said as he swallowed, 'have not been formally charged yet. Do you know what the charges might be?'

Perlman put the rest of the egg into his mouth. Cotton looked round at Dawkins, only to find he had seized up. 'I'm no lawyer or policeman,' said Cotton. 'But I'd imagine there would certainly be assault, perhaps grievous bodily harm—' He turned again to Dickie Dawkins.

'I can do you anything from attempted murder down,' said Dawkins. 'I can do you years and years of jail time – and then I can add some more. I can go down to loitering with intent and disturbance of the peace and I can go up to possession of a—'

Perlman held up his hand.

'My clients have to be charged or let go within twenty-four hours.'

'Yes,' said Cotton. 'We still have plenty of time.'

Perlman paused and indicated Miss Marx pour him some chamomile tea from the thermos flask.

'I've helped you,' he said.

'And I you,' said Cotton.

Perlman looked surprised. 'You equate them.'

'Yes!' said Cotton.

Cotton had meant to be polite but firm. It was only when he felt Dawkins's sudden start beside him and saw Miss Marx was in the act of knocking the glass cup off the table that he understood he had gone a long way past firm. The empty *podstakannik* tilted and fell towards the floor. Instantly Cotton shot out his hand and caught it. To do this he had to lurch forward and stamp his right foot. The pain that came up through his thigh made him grunt and bring his splinted left hand down on to the table: he just managed to hit the edge of the table with his wrist. With his right hand he put the Russian tea glass back on the table and looked up.

Alfred Perlman had flinched and was now, at the very least, wary of physical harm. Miss Marx was staring at him. Cotton smiled, partly to reassure them but then out of shock at understanding they considered him potentially violent. He had access to violence, could lay his hands on the stuff. He shook his head. He knew that shock and anger increased adrenalin. He breathed in very carefully. To help him in this Miss Marx trembled as she poured the chamomile tea into the glass he had saved.

Perlman cut his second egg in half, salted the first half and popped it into his mouth. He picked up a madeleine.

'So what is it you want?' he asked.

'In exchange for what?'

'My clients uncharged and let go.'

Cotton answered in a drawl. 'You simply cannot be serious, Mr Perlman. They committed a crime.' To emphasize this he held up his left hand but did remember his own part in breaking the splinted fingers. 'I don't employ people who use cut-throat razors.'

Mr Perlman sighed. 'You're being difficult,' he said. He made arrangements to the inside of his cheeks. 'Miss Marx, perhaps you'd be better in another room.'

Olivia Marx blinked at Cotton. He got up and pushed open the double doors.

Dawkins got up too. 'I'll join her,' he said.

Cotton was taken aback. 'Are you sure?'

'Yes.'

Cotton had not expected Dawkins to quit so soon. He decided to take it as a vote of confidence and leave any other considerations out of it.

He closed the glazed double doors after them. They had never been particularly well hung and Cotton thought it was entirely likely Miss Marx and Dawkins would be able to hear everything that was said.

For the third egg Alfred Perlman had put a smear of black roe on the top.

'Colonel, you really should think of me as a go-between,' said Alfred Perlman.

Cotton watched him bite.

'But you're not just a messenger, surely?' he said. 'You have a degree of autonomy, certainly; power of attorney, perhaps.'

'I advise my clients. Whether or not they take my advice, well—'

'Yes, of course. That must be tricky. The case against them is pretty strong.'

'I should tell you,' said Perlman, 'that I was not contacted by Messrs Boyle and Sinclair.'

'Of course not. I suppose that's also a problem.'

'Colonel, I don't have to tell you about lawyer–client confidentiality.'

'What are Starmer-Smith and Radcliffe offering?'

'You are making unnecessary assumptions.'

'Of course. If I don't, we're not going to make any progress at all. I'm perfectly happy to see Boyle and Sinclair charged and sentenced.'

'This conversation is off the record.'

'I'd prefer it to be pre-record, Mr Perlman.'

'I don't quite know what you mean,' said Alfred Perlman. 'Some things are better left undefined. At least at the beginning. Definition and resolution are the final stages. Your willingness to meet would suggest you agree with me on this approach.' Alfred Perlman spread more black roe on egg. 'I take it you share the view that public knowledge of this terrible attack would be damaging for the Intelligence Services and distressing to the public.'

'I see,' said Cotton. He nodded. 'Let me tell you my thinking, then, Mr Perlman. However I look at it, the attack was extraordinarily stupid. A couple of razor boys went for a pair of intelligence officers. What did they have in mind? Were they trying to frighten us off? Or were they just after revenge because my chief had drawn attention to the fact that a part of MI5 and possibly Special Branch were making use of criminals?'

'Criminals are for the courts to sentence,' said Alfred Perlman, 'and there has been no trial. As for your chief—'

'Exactly. I heard of Mr Ayrtoun's fate earlier this morning. I imagine others may have heard what was going to happen yesterday.' Cotton shrugged. 'But I'm still left with two considerations. If your clients' employers did know and set them on us, they'd be unfit for their jobs and better out of them. If they did not know, it means they had lost

427

control of them and are also better out of their jobs.'

'In your shoes, Colonel, I'd certainly consider my own future career.'

'But I have. That was the first thing I did. Although I went through the usual unarmed combat course in the army, I didn't think I'd need it in the Intelligence Service or that I'd get in the way of a department that employs razor-gang boys from Glasgow. But I do know that now. And that's where the lesson of unarmed combat comes in.'

Cotton paused. 'I don't mean beating a man's face against ice and flagstone as I did yesterday. In unarmed combat you are taught, if need be, to take an attacker's knife through your hand. The theory is that it parries, surprises, ties up the attacker's thrust and leaves you with your other hand to strike back. Now I'm not much of a nego-tiator but I decided to proceed from a position that my career was already over. My left hand, as it were.'

Cotton hoped Perlman would think this too passionate and too personal, but that it would persuade the lawyer that he was not going to be biddable.

Perlman grunted. 'I should make a telephone call,' he said.

Perlman went to the telephone in the hall. Cotton went through to Dickie Dawkins and Miss Marx. They had been talking about a film called *Hue and Cry* and were now on to the extraordinary number of expectant women about.

'What do you want?' said Perlman when he came back.

'In return for letting Boyle and Sinclair go? What are you offering?'

'I have consulted with my client and have additional powers.'

Cotton thought Perlman had had time to call one person. He thought that would have been Starmer-Smith.

'To settle this? Good. What would be the chances of having Radcliffe transferred from his present duties?'

Alfred Perlman did not have the kind of face that showed surprise but there was a small twitch.

'I don't know that I can do that.'

'An alternative would be that Sergeant Dawkins is promoted to Inspector. Immediately. One or the other – or our conversation can't make progress.'

Alfred Perlman considered. 'Miss Marx,' he called.

Miss Marx came through.

'Item 1,' said Perlman. 'Mr Dawkins is promoted.'

'By nine thirty this evening.'

'Nine thirty-six,' said Perlman.

'Item 2,' said Cotton, 'involves another client of yours. He will find that Sir Cyril Healey-Johnson is worth investigating.'

'Why?'

'Because that is the level he should be at and

stay at,' said Cotton firmly. 'This way he'll get a story rather than being the story. Something to do with kerbs, I understand.'

'Difficult to prove.'

'The kerfuffle would be enough.'

Alfred Perlman ate another madeleine. 'Very well.'

'Item 3 is a meeting for me with Robert Starmer-Smith.'

Alfred Perlman sighed quite loudly. 'Is there an Item 4?'

'Of course there is. Your client or clients will send one hundred pounds in cash to a Mr Paul Mair.'

'Who's he?'

'He lives in Totteridge. I'll give you the address.'

'I don't know who this person is.'

'He supplied the cyanide to a scientist called A. A. Watson. Watson, as you know, used it to commit suicide. Mair wants to leave the country and this money will enable him to do so. Item 5 is that Boyle and Sinclair are bound over and sent back to Glasgow. They can make that Edinburgh, if they want. I don't mind. But it is essential they leave the London area and take up other employment. I can't, of course, ask your clients to give a general assurance that they will eschew the employment of a person or persons with a criminal past in the pursuit of their aims but – and let me put this very clearly – they have to relinquish Boyle and Sinclair. I'd also suggest they reconsider their methods and tactics.'

'Do you understand all that you are asking?'

'A promotion, a tip-off, a chat, a hundred pounds and a one-way ticket for a couple of criminals. That's barely anything, Mr Perlman.'

'And yourself?'

'I imagine I'll be reassigned in due course. Or I can resign. Unless, of course, I'm told Operation Sea-Snake is ongoing and Mr Ayrtoun has handed it over to another intelligence officer.'

'Can we shake hands on that?' said Perlman.

'Yes.' Cotton stood up and got a look of surprise out of Alfred Perlman.

'Do you want the physical gesture?' said Perlman. He sounded almost aghast.

'Would you prefer I shook hands with Miss Marx?'

Perlman looked confused. Cotton smiled.

'No, no,' he said. 'Your word is sufficient.'

'I don't have to tell you,' said Alfred Perlman, 'that henceforward you will not speak of this matter to anyone under any circumstances.'

'I will only take such precautions as I think necessary.'

'What does that mean?'

'In the event of my sudden death by razor or similar.'

Alfred Perlman tutted at the thought of such a thing.

'Crichton wouldn't be able to publish, you know.'

'I have no intention of informing Miles Crichton of what's happened at any time.'

Perlman nodded. 'Miss Marx,' he said. 'The money.'

Miss Marx demonstrated that Alfred Perlman thought ahead. From an envelope she counted out one hundred pounds. From what Cotton could see that left another one hundred and fifty. He did not know whether or not that was the only envelope.

'I'm not accepting any money from you,' Cotton said. He gave Miss Marx a piece of paper with Paul Mair's address on it. He also gave her the note with Derek Jennings's information on Sir Hear-Hear's next conga party on it.

'This is for your distinguished client. The provider of this information has also offered to take photographs if supplied with a suitable camera. I'd prefer a note from you on your stationery about any meeting with Mr Robert Starmer-Smith.'

Perlman glanced at Miss Marx. She put the hundred pounds in a fresh envelope along with Paul Mair's address. She put the note about the conga party in another. She began clearing and packing Alfred Perlman's breakfast things.

'When will you remove the possibility of charges against Mr Sinclair and Mr Boyle?'

'When I know there is someone into whose custody I can deliver them.'

Mr Alfred Perlman may have smiled.

'Would Radcliffe do?' he said.

'I might even go to Croydon for that.'

'When would that be?'

'Two o'clock this afternoon. Although of course I'm not sure Mr Dawkins would go. I imagine he'd be waiting to hear about his promotion.'

'Three o'clock,' said Perlman.

'All right,' said Cotton. 'I'll arrange for that.'

Cotton was not sure if Perlman was thinking or simply waiting for Miss Marx to finish repacking the hamper. She rinsed the plate, the knife and the Russian tea glass. Alfred Perlman handed her his napkin and did up his coat.

'Miss Marx?'

Miss Marx looked at him. She moved forward and used the napkin to wipe at one side of his mouth. She stood back and checked his appearance.

'Perfect,' she said, folded the napkin and put it in the hamper. She checked that she had packed everything. She nodded.

'Three o'clock,' said Perlman again. He got up and moved towards the front door. Miss Marx was quick enough to gather up the briefcase, hamper and rug and get to the door before he did. She opened it for him. Alfred Perlman did not say goodbye.

The telephone rang again.

'I got your note,' said George Dyce. 'I'm always on for a show. Just one thing. What exactly is blacklight theatre?'

Cotton explained.

'So it's sort of disembodied lights moving in the dark?'

'Sort of. She'll be able to show you.'

George Dyce laughed. 'I hope she will. I say, would you yourself be on for a spot of supper next Saturday?'

'That bit about a mild mishap was a little on the underplayed side,' said Cotton.

'Did you cut yourself on paper or something?'

'No, George, it was more icy roads and surprisingly sharp metal.'

George Dyce laughed again. 'Well, if you have any more young women around, do send them along.'

'What are you doing just now, George?'

'I'm drinking, old man.'

Cotton called the contact number Anna Melville had left. Gus Mallory answered.

'She says you're pimping her, artistically, that is.'

'Is she there?'

'One moment . . . No. She definitely says she's not in.' He giggled. 'Sorry. She doesn't want to talk to you. A bit emotionally bruised, you see?'

'Right. She's hurt but prepared to use the contact?'

Gus Mallory laughed. 'I see your mincing is not quite like mine,' he said.

'Just tell her George Dyce will see her, will you, Gus?'

'Yes. I will. I say, old fruit, you wouldn't want to help me out too, would you?'

434

'No,' said Cotton. 'I wouldn't.'

Gus sniggered. 'So the curtain closes on your brief theatrical foray.'

'Goodbye, Gus.' Cotton put the telephone down.

'What's happened to your records?' called Dawkins.

'What do you mean?'

Cotton limped through. Dawkins pointed. Cotton looked. Nineteen of his twenty records had been broken. Judging by the heel mark on the cover of the one on the outside, by foot. Cotton flicked. She had broken the records by stamping on five at a time. For some reason, one had not broken. It was an Art Tatum version of *Tea for Two*.

Cotton nodded. 'How do you feel?'

Dawkins rubbed his eyes. 'A bit raw.'

'Yes,' said Cotton. 'That's about it. Some of these records are going to be difficult to replace.' He winced. 'What do you say to Pont Street? Julia Gardener?'

Dawkins looked at his wristwatch. 'No,' he said. He blinked. 'If we turn up at her door looking like this she'll probably laugh. Have I got that right?'

'Probably. I could write her a note and give her a rich man's address.'

'That would be a bit mean,' said Dawkins. 'Are you all right?'

'Just a bit tired,' said Cotton. He sighed. 'What have we got to do?'

'I've got to get back to the office.'

'Right. Call me before three. I'll phone Paul Mair.'

It took some time to get through.

'Mr Mair? This is Peter Cotton. You're going to get one hundred pounds. Please take it and leave.'

'I haven't managed to sell the Lagonda, you know.'

'Then you're rich,' said Cotton. 'Do you understand what I'm saying?'

There was a pause. 'Yes,' said Mair. 'I'm getting some money and pissing off.'

At two thirty Dawkins telephoned. 'I've been promoted to Inspector,' he said.

'Congratulations. Will you phone Perlman or will I?'

'You,' said Dawkins. 'I'll phone Croydon police station.'

'Well done,' said Cotton.

He called Alfred Perlman.

'Inspector Dawkins is about to give permission for Sinclair and Boyle to be released without charge. Do you have someone to take command of them?'

'I do,' said Perlman. 'He's there already. Mr Starmer-Smith is sending you an invitation to have tea with his family next Sunday.'

'Good. Is your distinguished client in Parliament pleased?'

'I believe he is,' said Perlman. 'He thinks it would be a good start.'

CHAPTER 37

On Sunday, 9 March, Hans Bieber drove Cotton to Worplesdon, near Guildford in Surrey to have tea with Robert Starmer-Smith and his family.

Beyond a drive flanked by Lombardy poplars, fronted by a formal rose garden, the very large house combined various styles popular around 1900 to 1910. These included Surrey hanging tiles, Tudor-style patterns in the exposed red brickwork, chimneys that were both enormously tall and quirkily placed – one was in an inner angle between a projecting black-and-white wing and the brick frontage – and stone coping round the mullioned windows and studded front door. The house sat in the middle of six acres, presently of new snow, old ice and mist and brittle-looking trees.

As requested, Cotton arrived punctually, at 3.30 in the afternoon. Hans jumped from the car and opened Cotton's door. Above the front door of the house was a carved stone scallop shell, something Cotton associated with the pilgrimage to Santiago de Compostela in Spain. He did not know what this one was for.

An elderly uniformed maid opened the door and welcomed him with formal respect but without enthusiasm.

'Colonel Cotton?' she said. 'I have been instructed to point out the stone around the door.'

Cotton nodded. 'I see it,' he said. 'Thank you.'

It was Bargate stone, what Charterhouse School was built of. It is a hard-wearing sandstone usually described as butter-coloured, though the stuff round the door looked pale and had acquired faint grey lines where the frost was clinging to the saw marks.

Cotton had no difficulty accepting that Starmer-Smith had seen his file, was a shrug's worth less happy to be reminded of four years of Sundays at school, the entire day a gloomy tithe on the week, two services at church, the sound of clocks ticking in the imposed periods of silence.

The maid showed him into a double-height, beamed reception hall, large enough to have a spectator gallery, and told him she would be back.

On an oak refectory table a guttering candle the size of two logs of wood was the only artificial light. Cotton had seen candles as big in Mexican and Spanish churches, usually used to illuminate ornate altarpieces. This candle had a peculiar scent, like burnt lavender, and there was no altar. Against the far wall, an oak chest was topped by a huge brass flagon containing dried bulrushes. Above that were three diamond-paned windows too high to look out of and too overshadowed to

438

let in much light. The baronial-style fireplace was not lit.

A door groaned. A white-haired man dressed in a green tweed three-piece suit, not that different from Paul Mair's, came into the hall.

'Is that Colonel Cotton?' he asked.

Starmer-Smith extended his hand, shook Cotton's but then, rare in England, put his other hand over the clasp and smiled. Starmer-Smith exuded a powerful if distracted delight. Cotton did not think the delight was directed at him, more that he was included in it. He smiled back while noticing that Starmer-Smith looked decidedly elderly for a man of fifty, had dry, fine-lined skin and eyes that had lost most of their colour and expression.

'Do come and meet my family.'

'Thank you.'

Cotton followed him into a small panelled ante-room, then into a large but low-ceilinged room, the floor of which was covered with overlapping rugs. On either side of a well-piled wood fire were two settees on which Mrs Starmer-Smith and her daughters sat. The settees, he thought, were named after Knole in Kent, having high sides attached to a high back by rope ties. These ropes were thicker than a hangman's, ended in tassels and were scarlet.

The female Starmer-Smiths were also dressed in tweed, Mrs Starmer-Smith in brown and white check, her daughters in identical suits and blouses but of differently coloured barleycorn tweed and embroidery. Mrs Starmer-Smith was rather regally short-sighted. Daughters Lily and Iris reminded Cotton of the royal princesses. They looked healthy, innocent and ruthless.

'Colonel Cotton is a war hero,' said Starmer-Smith.

Cotton was pleased when one of the girls spoke up. 'Ooh. Are they still having to operate, are they?'

Cotton laughed. 'No,' he said, 'this is only a couple of broken fingers. Much more recent.'

Cotton had thought of wearing his patched-up 'attacked' suit but had decided against it. He thought he had been right.

Behind him, two maids, the one he had already seen and another much younger, began bringing through tea things. There was a lot on the trays; clotted cream, various preserves including damson jam, greengage jam, crumpets and a home-baked cake.

'You sit down here, Colonel,' said Mrs Starmer-Smith patting the place beside her. 'Girls, you toast the crumpets.'

Starmer-Smith himself poked at the wood fire and gave each girl a toasting fork.

'To survive,' said Mrs Starmer-Smith, 'we've really had a go at the copse. We did have a small stand of willow but that's long gone.'

'You're doing very well,' said Cotton.

'Oh!' said Mrs Starmer-Smith. 'Of course! How do you poor people manage in town?'

'Well, I just stumble from the Connaught to a fish paste sandwich,' said Cotton.

There was a pause before she laughed. 'You're

making a joke,' she said. She did not sound disapproving.

Cotton duly ate a toasted crumpet. And then a slice of what turned out to be carrot cake. The sweetener used was honey. The combination quickly palled.

'I really don't know what we are going to do if this awful weather continues much longer,' said Mrs Starmer-Smith. 'The tea is from Ceylon, you know. My sister is married to a missionary there.'

Cotton drank his tea without milk or sugar. It not only cut the sweetness of the cake, it was the best tea he had tasted for a long time.

Starmer-Smith, with evident enjoyment, had started doing a crossword puzzle. His daughters groaned when he started reading out clues, but evidently this was part of a ritual. Cotton was given a clue – the answer was Cerberus – and later he was shown the family collection of old English games, including a miniature set of skittles, bagatelle and a board for shove-ha'penny.

'Are you married, Colonel?' said Mrs Starmer-Smith.

'No, I'm not,' said Cotton.

'You shouldn't leave it too long,' she advised. 'Demanding jobs are better met with a stable home life.'

'I'm sure you're right,' he said.

There was a pause for Cotton to take in once again the joys of family.

Starmer-Smith nodded. 'I regret the Colonel and

I have a little business now. But I'll be ready for Evensong, of course.'

Starmer-Smith led the way to his study. It was a large room and he had arranged it somewhere between a library and an ops room. There were three desks, one a metal thing with a green telephone, and two partner's desks. The walls were lined with bookshelves. Cotton saw Starmer-Smith's tastes ran from Dorothy L. Sayers and G. K. Chesterton to St Thomas Aquinas and St Augustine.

Starmer-Smith showed Cotton to a chair, sat down himself behind one of the partner's desks and lit a cigarette. He used an ivory holder. Somebody, his sister probably, had once explained to Cotton that cigarette holders were classed like ladies' gloves. He thought this one, about six inches long, was dinner length, considerably shorter than opera or theatre, a little longer than cocktail.

Cotton was not aware he had shown any reaction but Starmer-Smith explained.

'My wife doesn't like nicotine-stained fingers,' he said. 'You don't indulge?'

'No,' said Cotton. 'Somehow I never got started.'

Starmer-Smith inhaled. He blew the smoke down his nose. The cigarette holder was in his left hand rather than the usual right. He put his elbows on the desk and used his right hand for emphasis, though the left hand, ivory holder, cigarette and smoke trailed along, a little later and not quite as emphatically.

'In the thirties, MI5 found a most valuable

source of information in the German Embassy itself. High-ranking. Very useful.'

Cotton waited. He did not, of course, know who the man was, but took this as the beginning of Starmer-Smith's justification of his activities since then.

'I dislike the word intensely,' said Starmer-Smith, 'but the man was a sodomite. Do you know what I mean?'

Cotton nodded. Starmer-Smith's question and pronunciation took Cotton back to school again. It wasn't just the 'ite' words he remembered, from 'catamite' to 'Canaanite'. In his last year the older boys were invited into the housemaster's study on Sunday evenings to listen to him, usually on the Book of Job as a useful preparation for life. The housemaster, a Classics teacher, had also treated varieties of sin: 'Sodom, Gomorrah, Lot's wife, pillars of salt and so on. From Sodom we have the word "sodomite". It lends itself more to that kind of thing than Gomorrah. You might like to consider that. Gomorrah sounds like some absurd Irish exclamation. What were they going to say? Gomorrahist? No, sodomite has more drum and smite to it. Incidentally, I don't want to hear the expression "hoe-moe". Homo is nothing to do with the Latin for man but comes from the Greek for same. Short o's, everyone.'

Cotton looked at Starmer-Smith. 'Was he black-mailed into being valuable?' he said. 'Or did he volunteer for other reasons?'

Starmer-Smith shook his head. 'That's not my point. You see, even before the war, we were already beginning to think of turning agents. And the natural consideration then was that if we could turn agents, what was to stop our enemies turning our . . . let's call them "vulnerable" people? I work for MI5, after all. And our duty is to maintain security here at home.' He paused and sucked on his cigarette holder.

'When I was in Washington,' said Cotton, 'I learnt the Americans had the acronym MICE, each letter representing the reason a traitor becomes a traitor.'

Starmer-Smith blinked at him, before exhaling. Cotton smiled politely, as if he were contributing to a conversation rather than interrupting an exposition.

'M for Money, I for Ideology, C for Coercion, E for Excitement.'

'But that's so American!' said Starmer-Smith. 'Intent on what they call being snappy, they forget how things link up and lead on.'

'Oh, I think it allows for that,' said Cotton. 'Take Dr Alan Nunn May for example. He was ideologically motivated. We can say he was mistaken, our legal system has judged him to be a traitor, but his motivation was perfectly sincere. I don't know how much money, 200 or 700 dollars, was involved, but in any case he claims to have burnt it. And nobody appears to think the money was a motive. Again, he could hardly be described as having been coerced. Certainly not at the beginning. He volunteered his information to the Soviets – and he appears to have taken no joy in the experience. His drive was his conscience, apparently. In his own estimation he was highly principled. He certainly was not so much abashed as determined to plead guilty. It's really only possible to say that in practice, his view of humanity tended to help one great power get a type of bomb the other great power already has, and that's less humanitarian than tit-for-tat.'

'That's just one case.'

'Quite,' said Cotton. 'But it's the only one that's been to trial. It had considerable influence in persuading the Americans to bring in the McMahon Act and has rather established us as a weak ally, one with more traitors to find. Finding traitors is tricky, unless they're as cooperative as Alan Nunn May. Using people to find them who are them-selves coerced, who have found it convenient to aquire an ideology and rather like the money, can cause problems. I don't know about "excite-ment", but they certainly enjoy and sometimes abuse the power given them.'

Cotton hoped he had just given a description of Jackie Boyle and Frankie Sinclair fit for a Sunday afternoon in a large house in Worplesdon.

Starmer-Smith smiled. 'I had understood,' he said, 'from a lawyer we both have met, that you were susceptible to the arguments of leadership. Welfare also concerns peace of mind. To a degree, the public realm has to be protected, guided and reassured.'

'There was never any risk from me that any of that public peace of mind would be disturbed,' said Cotton. 'I made that perfectly clear only a few minutes after being attacked in a public place, and I repeated that later to the lawyer you mention.'

Starmer-Smith smiled. 'I know what it is,' he said. 'You don't see why a department should, as it were, specialize, concentrate on one group of potential traitors above others.'

Cotton decided to wait.

'Because a group is relatively easy to identify does not mean we should ignore them,' said Starmer-Smith. 'What? Do you think it's distasteful to pursue effeminate men, inverts and all the rest, and therefore it shouldn't be done?'

'No,' said Cotton. 'I think it's ill-advised. The notion that homosexuals are more likely to betray secrets than other groups you can classify has hardly been examined, let alone proven. But the main problem is that a department with such a limited aim starts manipulating the evidence. A. A. Watson was not compromised so that he could be blackmailed, so I suspect he was being made an example of – to reinforce the need to identify what you call "vulnerable" people. I'm not sure that the operation worked. It was a political rather than an intelligence operation. He had to acquire another characteristic – as a Trotskyite – to attract wider attention. And while he may have been a homosexual, he was not a Trotskyite. He was a sacrifice.'

'He killed himself, Colonel.'

'That was the only point left for him to make, apparently. If he had lived, he would have been more your point, a justification of your activities. And he chose the Snow White option.'

Starmer-Smith shook his head. 'Colonel Cotton, I'd hate to patronize you but you are, what, twenty-eight now? Your experience is necessarily limited. Your talent for analysis is undoubtedly consider-able, even striking, but do you mind if I suggest it is a little naïf.'

Cotton nodded. He added another word to Ayrtoun's list of French for unpleasant things along with Derek's 'etiquette'.

'No,' he said, 'you may call Dr Alan Nunn May and A. A. Watson that. One is in prison, the other dead. Both men are far cleverer than me and with clearer principles than I have ever managed to have. I'm too fearful for that.'

'What do you mean?'

'My worry is that I'm party to an illegal and secret arrangement that allowed two criminals to escape without charge. The illegality is troublesome but I'm also aware that secrets don't stay secret.'

'Oh, that's Ayrtoun's line. And Ayrtoun is out.' Starmer-Smith did not sound displeased. 'Come now, he signed the Official Secrets Act. Mm? What worries you? That you're on your own and that Operation Sea-Snake is over?'

'No, no. I had a conversation with the solicitor who represented my attackers and I'm wholly confident he will continue to honour all the agreements made. Nor is Operation Sea-Snake quite over. I have to write my report. And this now is in the nature of a consultation. On a personal level I'm rather keen not to have a cut-throat razor applied to my thigh again. And I wasn't the only one to be attacked, of course.'

'Are you referring to that Special Branch sergeant?'

'He's an inspector now. But no, not only him. I've had a conversation with someone "vulnerable". He had a saltire or Cross of St Andrew carved on each cheek. Of his face, that is, his face. He also lost a testicle, I understand, from being hit with knuckledusters. He was never a security risk.'

Robert Starmer-Smith made a very small hissing noise. He muttered something. It was probably the word 'contemptible' but Cotton did not mind at all. The cigarette holder in Starmer-Smith's hand moved quickly back and forward.

'Your operation should never have been allowed! It meant we had people working at cross-purposes. We were never even consulted,' he said.

'Nobody explained the larger operation to me, Mr Starmer-Smith. All I know is that both Sir Percy Sillitoe of MI5 and Sir Stewart Menzies of MI6 put their signatures on Operation Sea-Snake. I don't know their reasons. I don't know the scope of the operation. I do know I have to write a report.'

'I hope that is not some sort of threat, Colonel. That really would be ill-advised.'

Cotton shook his head. 'No threat,' he said. 'The reason I haven't written a report yet is because I want to know what *will* happen. That is why I accepted your very kind invitation to meet and have tea with your family.'

Starmer-Smith took a little time to consider this, during which he placed another cigarette in his holder and lit it.

'I'm not at all sure,' he said, 'you have begun to appreciate the grave risks our society faces. It is deeply unpleasant but I have spoken to several bishops and all agree that the spread of effeminacy is not only both marked and increasing, it is also highly pernicious to the fabric of society.'

Cotton thought of clothes moths and grunted. It also occurred to him to wonder whether or not Starmer-Smith viewed the effeminate as having somehow taken the easy way out, to avoid the demands made on men. Did he actually think male homosexuals wanted to be women? Or was it that he found what he thought of as their pretence particularly irksome, as if, like boys at boys' schools playing girls in plays, they had insisted on keeping girls' clothes and manners on. They were males determined to be weaker vessels.

'Anglican bishops?' asked Cotton.

'Certainly. And I have spoken to Catholic bishops as well and to those churches that do not have bishops. The agreement is complete.'

Cotton had read enough to doubt that. 'Isn't that enough?'

'Colonel Cotton, you're not married yet and perhaps are as yet too personally involved in finding a soulmate to have considered the true nature of the institution itself. But you must appreciate that marriage is the tie that binds our society together. The fundamental, natural loyalty is between a man and a woman. Homosexuals can't do this. They are not committed to an institution, have no concept of what it means in terms of restraint, discipline and the provision of security to future generations. Why? Because they are in thrall to their condition.'

Cotton usually liked to think he was a realist. He saw no point in getting into a wrangle with Starmer-Smith, discussing the Bible or defining differences between the concept of sin and the rule of law.

Starmer-Smith smiled. 'I take you for a pragmatist,' he said.

It did not sound much like a compliment to Cotton.

'No, no, that is not a criticism,' said Starmer-Smith. He smiled. 'Shall we get down to brass tacks?'

Cotton shrugged. He tended to be on guard when anyone mentioned 'brass tacks'.

'Certain errors have been made,' said Starmer-Smith. 'Certain problems to do with clear communication have cropped up.'

Cotton's stomach, unused to clotted cream, carrot cake and honey, was protesting slightly at what it had been given. He felt a little queasy.

'We need to be more precise,' said Starmer-Smith. 'Less blunt instrument.'

Mercifully, Cotton contrived to belch and let the gas down his nose in the guise of a sigh. Under the cut-throat circumstances he felt 'blunt instrument' did not meet the case.

'You said something to the lawyer we mentioned,' said Starmer-Smith. 'I don't mean the promotion for that man Dawkins.'

Cotton had asked Alfred Perlman if it was possible to get rid of Radcliffe. Perlman had suggested it was not.

'Yes. Mr Radcliffe lives close by, I understand,' said Cotton.

Starmer-Smith shook his head. 'Normandy,' he said.

Normandy village was a couple of miles south-west. Evidently Starmer-Smith no longer considered that close by.

'My proposal,' said Starmer-Smith, 'is that the police handle the law and we take charge of security.'

'MI5 is your "we"?'

'What? Oh yes. Special Branch are not included, unless in the case of arrest, of course.'

'Mr Radcliffe?'

'Something rather urgent has come up that will require his attention.'

Starmer-Smith handed Cotton a sheet of paper with a photograph attached.

'That's Sydney Stanley, born Solomon Wulkan,

sometimes Solomon Kosyski or Stanley Rechtand. It's being called Operation Greasy Palm. Last year he was invited to join a card game on a train from Manchester. The game included a governor from the Bank of England. Let's say there is a certain amount of anxiety about Mr Stanley's subsequent relations with some of the great and the good, including senior civil servants and some ministers of His Majesty's Government. He is of a giving disposition, apparently. Tricky when rationing is so ferocious.'

Cotton nodded. 'I can see that.'

'None of this leaves me defenceless, you know,' said Starmer-Smith.

'I'm sure,' said Cotton.

Starmer-Smith smiled. 'I have a principle to defend, Colonel, and a war of public opinion to win. Do you know who really started the Intelligence Services? The *Daily Mail*. They campaigned before the First World War, made the public aware of the dangers Germany presented. I'm not saying they got everything right, of course, but their campaign led to a climate of opinion. And that climate of opinion led to political action.'

Starmer-Smith looked up. 'You can't object to that. You've seen newspaper people yourself, haven't you?' He looked about his desk and found an envelope. He got up and handed it to Cotton. Cotton opened it.

On a single sheet of paper was the information

that Boyle, on the condition that the injuries to his knee did not hamper his mobility, would be joining the army and be posted abroad.

Sinclair was already serving six months for an offence committed in 1937. He had pleaded guilty and cooperated with the authorities.

'The problem with Sinclair,' said Starmer-Smith, 'is that he's so short. After his sentence however we've arranged something for him. Probably in anti-smuggling, very likely in Sierra Leone.'

Cotton nodded. 'I have one other person to see,' he said, 'before I agree.'

Starmer-Smith frowned. 'You don't need to see Radcliffe.'

'I want to see someone called Bosworth. His nickname is Bambi.'

'I doubt you are going to learn anything you don't know,' said Starmer-Smith. 'And, as I have said, our tactic is now other. Not, of course, that we can give up entirely on entrapment. It would be highly irresponsible of me to say that or to give that assurance.'

'I understand.'

'Well,' said Starmer-Smith, 'I should be getting along to Evensong. Will you join us, Colonel?'

'No, thank you,' said Cotton.

During his thinking on what to do about Starmer-Smith, Cotton had wondered, briefly, about letting Paul Mair loose on Iris and Lily. He grunted.

'I'll let you have a copy of my report, shall I?'

'No need,' said Starmer-Smith. 'I trust you.'

Cotton said goodbye to the Starmer-Smith family, thanked Mrs Starmer-Smith for tea, wished the girls well and thanked Starmer-Smith himself 'for all you have done, sir'.

He got into the Triumph.

'Successful visit, sir?' said Hans.

Cotton grunted. Hans Bieber drove down the drive and turned towards London. Cotton found it hard not to look back. This was intelligence work, strained if polite conversation about mistakes, some hapless, some violent, reluctant post-mortems on stratagems that had misfired, sometimes fatally, and the subsequent attribution of error or at least the rearrangement of responsibilities that would allow career survival and an official version. It occurred to Cotton that historians might study his reports and all the others intelligence officers sent in. He grunted again. It was unlikely historians would get an accurate version of what happened. They'd have to work out something plausible.

'We have to talk,' he said to Hans.

'You don't have to worry about me, sir.'

'I have no idea of your arrangement with Mr Ayrtoun.'

'For some time I haven't known what Mr Ayrtoun would be able to do for me,' said Hans, 'so I sought additional help. Robert has been able to assist with my residence permit. I have applied for citizenship and I have changed my name.'

Cotton was not sure why but he was suddenly suspicious. 'Where is Robert?' he asked.

'He's gone back to his family for now, sir. I'm about to move into a flat in Earls Court.'

'I have no idea of how you've been paid, nor of the conditions of your employment.'

'I wasn't paid, sir.'

'I have no idea what Mr Ayrtoun had on you.'

'No, sir. Neither I nor the car will be available after this, sir. Without Mr Ayrtoun, I have to give it back.'

'That's fine, Hans.'

'John, sir.'

'Of course. Did you work for anyone else?'

'No, sir.'

'Have you found a job?'

'It involves motor vehicles, sir. Robert has a share in a distributing company. I will be ensuring delivery standards and checks.'

'Are you happy with that?'

'Yes, sir,' said John Driver. 'I'll be pleased to leave this world, if that's possible.'

'Perhaps you'll leave me your new address, John.'

John Driver sighed. 'Yes, sir.'

Back in Wilbraham Place Cotton shook John Driver's hand and wished him well.

'Goodbye, Hans.'

'You know where I am,' he said.

CHAPTER 38

Cotton went upstairs to his flat and called the contact number for Derek Jennings. About half an hour later Derek called him.

'I'd like to see you. And Bambi Bosworth,' Cotton said.

'I don't know if he'll like that.'

'I don't imagine he'll refuse. Can you come up to Victoria station?'

'All right. There's that little news cinema to one side. Do you know it?'

'I know where it is. What time?'

'Can we say noon tomorrow?'

'All right.'

At noon on Monday, Cotton was outside the cinema. Derek and a tiny person with a very round face were waiting.

'Mr Bosworth?'

'That's my father,' said Bambi. He looked like a slightly wrinkled schoolboy, had no need to shave and spoke at deepest as a contralto.

'Derek, could you stay here, while we have a little stroll?'

456

Derek nodded first to Cotton, then to Bambi. 'It's all right,' he said.

Cotton and Bambi turned and began walking towards the main concourse.

'They cut your leg,' said Bambi.

'That's right. I'm going to speak. Interrupt if I get something wrong. All right?'

'I don't want trouble.'

'There will be none. About last October you were approached—'

'No. I was picked up by the police after I had met Mr Watson. Not the usual kind of thing. A man told me I should become Mr Watson's regular, if you know what I mean. I said I didn't know. I didn't know what kind of man Mr Watson was.'

'Were you paid?'

'Not then. But I got paid in January. A fiver.'

'That was for Watson?'

'No. Watson was extra. And that was after, when he was going to top himself. I got paid after the whistles blew and Watson was arrested. I had a little holiday in Brighton.'

'Was that it?'

'What do you mean?'

'Did you do more work for the people who paid you?'

'No. It was a one-off.'

'Who gave you the money?'

Bambi Bosworth pointed at Cotton's thigh. 'Two Scottish gents,' he said.

Cotton nodded. He turned back and they walked slowly towards Derek.

'Why are you called Bambi?'

'About 1943 a sailor knocked me down.'

Cotton glanced at him.

'Then he told me to get up. You know. "Get up, Bambi. Get up." Everyone laughed. So it stuck.'

'A client?'

'Yes. Some of them get uncomfortable afterwards.' He shrugged. 'I can buy children's clothes, though. That's cheaper.'

Derek was walking towards them looking anxious.

'Two coppers told me I should move on,' he said.

'Apparently you're going to have to get used to that,' said Cotton. 'They're about to change tactic, I'm told. A different emphasis.'

Derek shook his head. 'I'm not a cottager,' he said.

'You're going to have to take more care, that's what I am saying,' said Cotton.

'He means the police will be getting back to normal and charging us. Rather than the other way round,' said Bambi Bosworth. 'I've got to get back.'

'Yes,' said Derek. 'Anything else, Colonel?'

'No. You're free to go, Derek.'

Derek squinted at him. 'Your department?'

'Doesn't need you.' Cotton took a pound from his wallet. 'Your fares, gentlemen. Thank you very much.'

Cotton saw the policemen.

'I'll say goodbye,' he said. He walked directly at the policemen and took out his identification as he did so.

'Don't,' he said to them. 'You almost spoilt something. If you wish you may contact Inspector Dawkins of Special Branch. My name is Cotton. It's up to you, officers.'

'No, sir. That's satisfactory.'

Cotton shook his head. 'I'll bet,' he said.

He walked back across the Park to his office in St James's Street.

'Sir Desmond wants to see you,' said Miss Kelly. Miss Kelly had perfected a peculiarly impassive look that meant something was, at least potentially, going badly – in this case she meant Sir Desmond was displeased.

'When?'

'He asked to see you when you got in.'

Cotton prepared himself and went upstairs. Sir Desmond Brown made him wait for ten minutes, before calling him in and frowning at him.

'Your name is cropping up far too much!' Sir Desmond sounded exasperated.

'Sir?'

'Operation Sea-Snake has been terminated.'

'Yes, indeed, sir.'

'It's a damn pity about Ayrtoun. Dreadful shame about his wife.' Sir Desmond shook his head and looked up.

'Yes,' said Cotton. 'I was very sorry to hear it.'

'Ayrtoun was effective, I understand.' He shook

459

his head. 'Unbearable pressure. That's what the committee decided. Given his wife, it just wasn't fair to have him on the front line, as it were. Best thing for everyone.'

Cotton said nothing. He wondered if one or two of the people Ayrtoun had been hunting were on the committee.

'Awful business,' said Sir Desmond. He looked down at his desk. 'You've been recommended for something,' he said.

'Sir.'

'This United Nations thing. You'll be in New York. All very high sounding, of course. J. D. Rockefeller has given 8.5 million dollars to purchase some land by the East River. But I understand it is all getting rather grubby.'

'When would that be, sir?'

'In May, I think. The end of May. I understand you have some experience of the US.'

'I was in Washington in late '45, sir. With Mr Ayrtoun.'

'Good. It says here you were involved in the economic aspects of postwar decolonialization.'

'Only rather briefly,' said Cotton.

'Keynes got the money, didn't he?'

Sir Desmond was not listening. He turned a page on his desk and read a little more.

'Behind the scenes,' he said. 'You'll be behind the scenes. The Americans are awfully keen on decolonialization but rather remiss on what it actually means. What do you think?'

460

Cotton thought for a moment. 'Yes,' he said.

'Good man,' said Sir Desmond. 'I'll get the paperwork started.' But then he frowned. 'I wasn't entirely sure, you know, quite whether to give this the go-ahead.'

'Are you saying this is a promotion, sir?'

'I was referring more to this man Mair,' he said. 'Some snippy little estate agent has been on to us and given your name.'

'That's MI6 business, sir. MI6 let Mair go last September, then they or possibly MI5 employed him again unofficially. Do you remember the plutonium scientist A. A. Watson, sir? He committed suicide in Croydon. We have reason to believe Mair may have provided him the wherewithal.'

'Dear God!' said Sir Desmond. 'This is serious stuff!'

'But it's not our stuff, sir, under any circumstances. Mair mentioned two men he called Crouch and Cunningham. I doubt if those are the real names. I saw Mair about Watson and an interview he had had with Oleg Cherkesov of the Soviet Embassy.'

'Cherkesov has gone.'

'Yes, sir. Mair's house was rented and paid for either by MI6 or MI5 – or at least paid out from one of their funds.'

'This estate agent claims there's no furniture in the house.'

'I don't know anything about that, sir. The place

may have been robbed, of course. I believe Mr Mair is no longer in this country. But I repeat, under no circumstances is our agency liable for anything to do with Mair.'

'Have you a report?'

Cotton gave him the report Mair had given him.

Major Albert Briggs MP was pleased to invite P. J. B. Cotton for a drink at the Houses of Parliament. It was the first time Cotton had been there. Because of the bomb damage, the House of Commons was still meeting in the Lords Chamber while the Lords were meeting in the Robing Room. There was internal scaffolding. A couple of stone-masons were working on blocks of stone before the parliamentary session began.

'Hello, lad. You've heard, have you?'

'Heard what, Major?'

Major Bertie leant quite close. 'Sir Hear-Hear Johnson is leaving the country.'

'Did he say where he was going?'

Briggs laughed. 'Yes,' he said. 'The old goat has a place in Jamaica.' He laughed. 'I almost feel sorry for the Jamaicans!'

'And Lady Madeleine?'

Briggs made a face. 'Who cares? They haven't lived together for years.' Briggs beamed. 'Good riddance, I say. And if he could only take some more toffee-nosed cunts with him!'

Cotton glanced at him, but Major Bertie was not drunk.

462

'Good job,' said Major Bertie. 'I hear you're off soon.'

'Quite soon, yes.'

'I'll remember, lad,' said Major Bertie. 'I always do. I've got a memory like a fucking elephant.'

'Major Briggs, thank you.'

Cotton took a cab to the Garrick Club.

'Long time no see,' said Miles Crichton. 'It's all over, I take it.'

Cotton nodded. 'Yes.'

'Success?' Crichton summoned champagne.

Cotton smiled. 'I'd hardly say that. We've probably put a lid on Briggs. Not that you would know it. He's ecstatic that Sir Hear-Hear Johnson is off to Jamaica, all due to the photographs he now has in his possession. But I suspect Mr Perlman will have him concentrate purely on prurient things.'

Miles Crichton laughed. 'Quite! The purely prurient, eh!' He downed a glass of champagne. Cotton pushed his own glass towards him as he leant forward.

'We may have got MI5 to adopt a more roundabout, perhaps less violent, approach to homosexuals. And I think we may have got two razor boys removed from circulation, in this country at least.'

Cotton sat back. Miles Crichton smiled and took a sip from the second glass. 'That's bloody good,' he said. 'You've achieved something. Yes, I'd say you've probably done rather well.' He looked up.

'And you yourself? What's next? No, no. Don't answer.' He considered. 'You've probably caused some alarm, even consternation in the constipated corridors of Whitehall. That would suggest . . . let's see. They won't quite punish you for being a laxative, I don't think. Ah! Wait a minute. I always think of Dickens in these cases.'

Cotton laughed. 'We were told not to use the name when describing our conditions of work.'

'No, no, dear boy, I'm talking about movement. What happened when sales flagged?'

'Are you talking of *Martin Chuzzlewit*?'

'Yes. He was sent to America, wasn't he?'

Cotton laughed. 'You've been talking to somebody?'

Miles Crichton was delighted. 'I have not! Oh, all right. A member here told me Alfred Perlman had said you were international level.'

Cotton shook his head. 'I believe the Americans call that failing up. I hadn't appreciated that Mr Perlman was quite so generous.'

'Balls,' said Crichton. 'The British Empire looks not for Judas but for Pontius Pilate, a pretty decent colonial governor if you think about it. He upheld a version of the law, kept his subjects happy and gave Christians the Resurrection.'

Cotton smiled dutifully. He summoned another couple of glasses of champagne.

'Oh, I really am going to miss you,' said Miles Crichton. 'Am I out now?'

'I'll recommend they keep you on,' said Cotton.

'I understand Inspector Radcliffe of Special Branch has been put to investigating a certain Sydney Stanley. Apparently Mr Stanley is decidedly generous towards certain civil servants and government ministers.'

'Ah,' said Crichton, 'the British Establishment may be an unholy mix of stodge and privilege but, by God, it survives. A little whiff of bribery? The Government will be in a panic.'

With difficulty, some of it apparently emotional, Miles turned his head towards the large, shabby eighteenth-century window of the Garrick Club and the grey view from it.

'God, it's fucking dreary,' he said. 'Thanks, old man.'

It was time to leave. Cotton shook Crichton's hand and walked downstairs. The light showed up the heads on the portraits on the stairwell as blank ovals, where the original space on the canvases left for the faces and the later varnish combined to make the features vanish and reappear.

Cotton stepped outside on to Garrick Street. In a grey, overcast sort of way he felt relieved and free.

CHAPTER 39

On Friday, 14 March, Cotton went to Guy's Hospital and had the stitches in his thigh taken out. The doctor was pleased but the skin around the scar looked puffy to Cotton and the stitch marks looked a long way from neat invisible mending. They resembled more the scars on Frankenstein's movie monster. He was told to apply an ointment and to avoid violent exercise.

On 16 March 1947 the cold ended, the grey skies darkened and it started to rain. The rain was abundant, the snow melted, but since the ground was still frozen to some depth, the water ran off the surface and caused widespread flooding. Gales and even more rain followed and though limited to a fortnight, made that March one of the wettest on record. The soldiers, German POWs and Poles were moved from snow clearance to stacking sandbags and rescuing stranded people, sometimes in rowing boats.

On March 17th the Prime Minister suggested that the British people were now engaged in a Battle of Britain 1947. There was some coal in fireplaces by the end of the month. The stuff was wet, difficult to light, and when alight smoked and spat. The smoke from millions of chimneys rose into the rain. On his way home on the Tube, Cotton saw a girl wipe her face and leave a sooty streak. On the tip of his umbrella was a drop with tiny specks of black suspended in it. London smelt of dampened sulphur and acrid tar.

On Friday, 28 March, Charles Portman came to see Cotton. He told him that 'the selection process was over' and that a new person had been appointed to the Malayan desk. Cotton could now remit all papers. Cotton stared at him.

'I don't have any,' he said.

Portman was only momentarily discomforted. 'Ah, yes. Of course.'

On Saturday, 29 March, Cotton went down to see his father in Peaslake.

'You're looking better,' his father said. 'You've found your feet with the great and the good, have you?'

Cotton laughed. His father wasn't usually so pointed. 'No great, no good,' he said. 'Just the usual Horlicks.'

His father blinked. 'I never understood that,' he said.

'Understood what?'

'Well Horlicks is a bedtime drink, isn't it? It avoids something called "night starvation", something else I never understood. So how did it come to mean a mess?'

Cotton shrugged. 'I'm not sure. I always thought it was a euphemism. Rhyming slang? It's a sort of milky gruel, isn't it?'

James Cotton made a face. 'These Cockneys are awfully roundabout, you know.' He looked up. 'I'm not going to America. I'll stay here and do up the house. Then they can come and see me.'

'They being Joan and family?'

'Of course.'

'Pity,' said Cotton. He looked around and saw Joan's letter paper on the kitchen dresser.

'Why do you say that?'

'Because I'm off to the States at the end of May. United Nations.'

'I see,' said James Cotton. 'Well, at least one member of the family will be on this side of the Atlantic. Ah! That girl who used to come here. Caught shoplifting in Woolworths, you know.'

'What did she steal?'

'I really don't know. Something trivial. Nail varnish, I think. It wasn't lipstick, I know that. I'm afraid I felt unable to provide a written character reference, you know, to present at the hearing.' He shrugged. 'I don't think even the Australians are that keen on criminality now.'

'Are you saying they won't be able to emigrate?'

'I really don't know,' said Cotton's father. He looked up and sighed. 'It's going to have to be patch and repair for this old place, you know, rather than new. But not to worry. I'm pretty sure we are getting back to normal.'

'What do you mean?'

'We'll get back, old boy, to a certain decency. At least in public.'

Cotton looked at his father. He decided not to say 'Have you no desire at all to see your grand-children?'

'Oh, there are a couple of letters for you, one foreign,' said James Cotton. 'On the mantelpiece. In the drawing room.'

The drawing room smelt dank and was still cold enough for Cotton's breath to show. His father had put the letters behind the clock. Either his father had stopped winding the clock or it had not survived the winter.

One was from Washington DC from Evelyn Duquesne. The letter was typewritten, dated March 17th. Her signature had taken on a slight tremor.

So sad about Penny Ayrtoun – not, of course that it was a complete surprise. What was a surprise was that he, as we say, just folded. It's strange how dependent we can be, however unlikely the dependence can look. At least that is the story I hear. Nobody got a chance to say goodbye to him. I understand he's now in Canada, Ottawa I think. Somebody told me that there's a doctor there who uses electric shock therapy with some success on the dispirited and depressed. This being Washington, I can't be sure that is true, of course.

Cotton folded the letter and put it in his inside pocket. He noted he felt next to nothing. Was that resentment? He did not know. His ignorance did not bother him.

The other letter was from Dr Powell in the village. It acknowledged payment for treating Mrs Douglas. The doctor had added a note:

> I don't, of course, know how far you want to take this, but I'd say Mrs Douglas needs to have her varicose veins stripped. It is a fairly simple, certainly well-tried procedure – I have done some myself – and the results can be the nearest we humans ever get to magical. I'm not entirely sure how much the procedure costs these days, but I imagine somewhere in the region of forty pounds at a good clinic. Should you wish to pursue this course of action, I will, of course, be happy to provide further assistance.

Cotton shrugged and refolded the letter. The rain was dripping from the eaves. He grunted. He was aware that, pre-winter, he would have smiled at the doctor's letter. What was it the old fraud had said? The nearest we humans ever get to magical.

He was interrupted by his father. 'Do you know what? The bloody roof is leaking.'

AFTERWORD

Historians sometimes complain of historical fiction that accuracy takes second place to drama or market.

As usual, however, I have tried to fit the fiction into the historical background and be accurate in that.

For example, Miss Ellen Wilkinson was indeed Minister of Education. Responsible for introducing free milk to schoolchildren, she was reportedly depressed at the time of her death, possibly, according to some sources, because of her failure to get the increase in the school-leaving age to 16 through Cabinet. She did indeed have an affair with Herbert Morrison. Incidentally, I see that in 1932 she also published a crime novel, *The Division Bell Mystery*.

Likewise, Sir Percy Sillitoe was head of MI5 and Sir Stewart Menzies head of MI6, and the details, particularly of the first, stick pretty much to the records.

The organization Common Wealth existed and survived until 1993 as a political pressure group. Sir Richard Acland himself, however, won the

Gravesend seat for Labour in November 1947 in a by-election caused by the expulsion of the also Labour MP Garry Allighan for making allegations of corruption.

Christopher Mayhew MP (1915–97) is the source for the conversation between Foreign Secretary Ernest Bevin and the US Ambassador Lewis W. Douglas on aid, Palestine and Jewish immigration. He was Bevin's PPS at the time.

In A. A. Watson's case, the method of suicide, but not the character nor the place, is very much Alan Turing's in 1954.

Of course, Cotton works without the benefit of hindsight or information that would later become available. The man in Istanbul Ayrtoun mentions is Kim Philby. Likewise, 'Homer' would turn out to be Donald Maclean. The 'valuable source of information in the German Embassy' mentioned by Robert Starmer-Smith was Wolfgang zu Potlitz.

Those interested in Sydney Stanley should look up the Lynskey tribunal.

The biggest difference with my previous novels is this. Alfred Perlman and Major Albert Briggs MP should not be confused with or thought of as referring to Arnold (later Lord) Goodman or Colonel George (later Lord) Wigg MP, the latter being Manny Shinwell's PPS during the coal crisis.

Finally, the winter in early 1947 was every bit as bad as is described. Most reports mention the stoicism of those who suffered through it. Some mention the lack of an enemy to fight against.

Almost everyone remarks on the depressing shabbiness and threadbare quality of life available postwar. The winter is also credited with a loss of popularity for the Labour government and a very steep rise in emigration.